FORGOTTEN VALOR

A NOVEL OF THE KOREAN WAR

BY

RICHARD THOMAS LANE

Book 1 of the Jonas Stuyvesant Saga

Learn More about Richard Thomas Lane

&

The Jonas Stuyvesant Saga

at

www.richardthomaslane.com

1

"The inexorable law of combat is the disintegration and
replacement of rifle companies…"

This Kind of War: A Study in Unpreparedness
The Classic Korean War History
T. R. Fehrenbach

JUNE 24, 1950

EVERYONE KNEW YOU had to wait to launch a military attack until after monsoon season was over. It was the way armies in Asia had always operated. For centuries generals and military planners had known this. During the rainy season, armies huddled inside their barracks and waited out the never-ending downpour. This was how it had always been done. Until today. Until tonight.

Thick clouds blackened the sky and torrents of rain muffled the rumble of the North Korean army vehicles headed south. Men in drab mustard-colored uniforms sat crammed into the backs of tarpaulin-covered trucks. Between their knees they clutched their rifles and burp guns. Other trucks carried crews with machine guns and mortars. Columns of jeeps, trucks and tanks hauled ninety thousand troops over the muddy roads. All were headed for jump-off points along the 38th Parallel that divided North Korea from South Korea.

Peasants, they had trained hard for just this day, the liberation of South Korea. But as important as it was to free the South and unite their homeland, these soldiers knew they were part of something larger. A new movement was sweeping the globe: International Communism. The Soviet Union had led the way. China was even now remaking itself into a Workers Paradise. Each man in each truck could look to a comrade on either side and know that they were all part of the vanguard of history.

Tomorrow morning the world would awaken to shocking news: the invasion no one saw coming.

Four hundred miles to the southeast, across the Sea of Japan, the stars still shone brightly in cloudless skies. On the American military base at Kokura, Japan, a costume party was just getting underway. The band was tuning up their instruments for the first waltz of the evening. Officers and ladies attached to the headquarters of the 24th Division mingled, chatted and joked with one another. The ballroom was adorned with the reds, blues and greens of their costumes.

Lt. Jonas Stuyvesant came dressed as a pirate. Having just arrived at the base, he might have skipped the affair, but when he learned General Dean, the commanding officer, would certainly attend, he'd gotten creative and thrown together a costume. He donned a white shirt, open at the front, stuffed the legs of a pair of black pants into his military boots, covered his hair with a red bandana and affixed a black patch over one eye.

That accomplished, he still had a problem. He had no idea what the general looked like – or how to get to talk to him. And talk to him he must, even though it was brash for a 2nd lieutenant to jump the chain of command with a personal request.

He scanned the crowd. Although this was his first officers' dance, he knew how to read a social gathering. There was always a group clustered around the most powerful personage, but he spotted no such knot of people here. The general hadn't arrived.

He glanced toward the doorway and found himself staring at the newest arrival, a graceful young woman in a green, ankle-length dress. Glistening black ringlets flowed out from beneath her bonnet. He was pretty certain he was looking at Scarlett O'Hara.

Escorting her was a gentleman wearing a black frock coat over a white shirt, a black bow tie, and a wide brim black hat. The man had to be Rhett Butler. Behind them came Cinderella. She was on the arm of a young man wearing a fake handle-bar mustache, monocle, cowboy hat and khakis: Teddy Roosevelt.

None of the men looked old enough to be the general.

From behind him came a woman's silvery voice. "Boarded any prize vessels lately?"

He turned, and although he was only five-foot-eight, found himself staring down into the sparkling blue eyes of Shirley Temple. The little-girl costume emphasized the grown woman's curves. He guessed her to be closer to thirty than to his twenty-three years of age. Her tone and meaning were clearly flirtatious; and while he was not averse to a little innocent flirtation, he felt himself involuntarily tense up.

She said, "I don't believe we've met."

Her voice was husky, and her lipstick, moist from the drink she'd been sipping, glistened. The sweet odor of bourbon mixed with the musky scent of her perfume played about his nose.

"No," he said, smiling crookedly, "I'm new on the base. Lt. Jonas Stuyvesant." He would have reached out to shake her hand, but both were clasped firmly around her drink. He nodded instead.

"Cecilia Gibson," she purred. So this was the Cecilia Gibson he'd been warned about, warned about with a wink.

"Where is Capt. Gibson?" He glanced around the room, expecting to see somewhere a man nervously eyeing his wife. He didn't find anyone looking like the jealous husband.

"Oh he's been sent off for a few days on some job in Korea." She pursed her lips in a pout. "Just like the Army to spoil a good dance. I've been looking forward to this night for oh-so-many weeks."

In the background he heard the strings and horns of the orchestra trying out different measures, making runs of several bars at a stretch.

"I guess Army life can be hard on the family," he said, adjusting his patch with his left hand so she could see his wedding band. Maybe she would suddenly lose interest in him and wander off to find more eligible prey.

"My husband's West Point, fourth generation. Are you West Point, Lieutenant?"

He cast a quick glance at the entrance again. No sign of the general. "No. I'm a reserve officer. Just here doing my tour." The first strains of a waltz began to float above the hum of conversation.

"At West Point all the cadets have to learn to dance, part of being an officer and a gentleman. But so many of you R.O.T.C. boys haven't. Do you know how to dance, Lieutenant?"

Jonas forced a smile. Her question suggested a way he might get to the general.

"In fact, I do." He bowed. "May I have this dance?"

Cecilia made a slight curtsey, her dress rustling. "I'd be delighted."

He took her drink, parked it on a nearby table and led her out onto the center of the polished floor. Soon they were swirling gracefully among other pairs: George and Martha Washington, Abe and Mary Lincoln, Daniel Boone and Marie Antoinette, Frankenstein and Little Bo Peep.

Mrs. Gibson proved to be a graceful dancer, even though a little tipsy.

"I'm surprised," he said, grasping for any topic of conversation, "that none of the women here have opted to wear a kimono."

"You *are* new," she laughed, her cheeks flushing and her golden curls bouncing. "All the wives hate Japanese girls."

He frowned. "Oh, why is that?"

"Because so many of the men are shacking up off base with some little Japanese thing." She looked at him intently. "Does my language shock you?"

He shook his head. "Not at all, Miss Temple," and executed a promenade, hesitating the required beat on the first step, completing it, and moving expertly into a box-step.

As he led her, curving around the floor, he noticed Martha Washington and Mary Lincoln eyeing him. And not, he guessed, because they were admiring his dancing skills. But for how closely he was holding Mrs. Gibson. He gently re-established a more discrete distance than the one she'd slipped into. Alienating any of these army wives would derail his plan to get to the general.

With the next underarm turn, he glanced again at the entrance. At the same time, he thought he caught his partner trying to make coy eye contact with someone else. His suspicions were confirmed when Rhett Butler and Scarlett O'Hara swirled past. Rhett and Cecilia were doing a poor job pretending not to notice each other.

While it irritated him that he'd been set up as a decoy, he decided to use their little game to advance his own purposes. He maneuvered until Scarlett and Rhett were nearby. His timing was so good that as the last strains of the waltz died out, the two couples were standing as a natural foursome.

Rhett grinned at his seeming good fortune. He held out his hand. "You must be new on the base. I'm Lt. Matt Grayson."

"Lt. Jonas Stuyvesant." He matched Grayson's firm grip and cocked his head slightly as he looked at Scarlett. He noticed she had green eyes, beautiful green eyes flecked with hazel.

Scarlett felt the heat rise up her neck and spread across her cheeks. Her date's strutting posture, as Mrs. Gibson batted her eyes at him, made it all too obvious what was going on. She looked away momentarily to hide her pain.

Trying to recover her poise, and since her partner was making no move to introduce her, she took it upon herself. "Lt. Donna Campbell," she said in her Georgian accent and curtsied in the old Southern manner.

Stuyvesant, she noted, was quick on the uptake. He bowed, as would a gentleman from the Civil War era, and said, "Charmed, I'm sure."

Mrs. Gibson's tone was patronizing, and her eyes glittered in triumph as she put in, "Ms. Campbell is one of the nurses on base." She turned to Donna. "Perhaps you'd like to introduce the lieutenant around."

Donna glanced at the newcomer and saw a hint of disdain flit across his face as he looked back and forth from Mrs. Gibson to her date.

The orchestra struck up the first bars of the next waltz. Matt Grayson said, "While she's doing that, may I have this dance?" and quickly swept the smiling Mrs. Gibson away.

Donna stared after them. She'd looked forward for weeks to this night, this date with Matt Grayson. When she'd told him she planned to go as Scarlett O'Hara, and his response was, "Then I'll go as Rhett," she'd been overjoyed.

Now whatever hopes she'd had for the evening were shattered. Along with her desire that something more would come from this date.

"Would you care to dance?"

She heard the voice as though it were from far away. Forcing herself to pull her eyes away from her disappearing date, she couldn't bring herself to meet Stuyvesant's. "Oh, yes." She swallowed hard. "Thank you."

As she allowed him to take her into his arms, he said, "I gather you're a fan of Scarlett O'Hara?"

She turned her face up to him, and cocked her head questioningly, but didn't answer.

He said, "I've never met a woman who wasn't."

He was trying to make conversation. She gave him that. He was being a gentleman. Well, she couldn't spend the whole night moping because she'd been stood up. She took a deep breath, sighed and resolutely turned her attention to this newcomer to the base.

"Yes," she said, "I was practically raised on *Gone With The Wind*." She found herself unexpectedly smiling as she remembered those days. "My mother read it to my sister and me when I was nine."

"Quite a tome to listen to."

"I couldn't wait for evening to come and dishes to be done, so we could settle in to hear more. When I was ten, the movie came out. I snuck in three times to see it. And read the book another two times on my own."

Stuyvesant led her in an underarm turn, and when they came together again, he said, "My, weren't you the precocious one."

She pulled her head back and searched his face, wondering whether that was a jab. His tone didn't sound malicious. She could see only one eye because the other had a patch over it, but the one she could see seemed to have a twinkle in it.

When in doubt, flirt. "Why sir," she said, batting her eyelashes and exaggerating her drawl, "I'm not sure I've ever been complimented that way before – if that was a compliment."

"It was."

She raised a skeptical brow.

"I would never lie to you, Miss Scarlett."

"Hmm, a pirate who claims to be a Boy Scout. Whatever is a girl to believe?" And she really didn't know how to take what he was saying. She looked into his face and saw a caring look there. Unexpectedly she felt herself relax. Yes, she read gentleness in his face, but also strength. At once she began to feel safe.

The atmosphere in the room shifted and the band abruptly stopped playing. A hush settled over the partygoers. As she turned to look, her partner turned with her.

At the entrance stood two figures, a man and a woman. The woman, a minute figure with her hands folded modestly in front of her, wore a richly embroidered blue silk dress. An Oriental dress with billowing skirts. She seemed to disappear next to the man towering beside her.

He stood preening in a white robe, its sleeves large and flowing, a tasseled sash wound about his waist. On his head he wore what might have been a black stove pipe hat, except it was much shorter and was fastened to his head by a black ribbon tied under his chin.

Donna looked up at Lt. Stuyvesant who was clearly taken aback by the strange, even bizarre spectacle. Her hand flew to her mouth to suppress a giggle. When he glanced at her questioningly, she leaned toward him and whispered into his ear, "Gen. Dean and his wife Mildred."

"Ah," he nodded, but still seemed confused.

The most senior officers began to chuckle as the general stood haughtily surveying the room. He was far too tall for the robes, which had been tailored for a Korean of average height. They didn't even reach his hairy calves, left bare down to his black military socks and spit-shined shoes.

The whole room broke into laughter. Gen. Dean blinked. The skin around his eyes began to crinkle, and he broke into a loud guffaw. Giving his arm to his wife, he escorted her into the party.

Stuyvesant said, "I don't recognize the costumes."

"Definitely not what you'd see stateside. They're dressed as Korean nobility. The general, you know, was military governor of South Korea for almost a year, before the country became independent in 1948."

She sensed his attention withdraw from her and become fixed on the general. The room felt a little cooler. That's when she also noticed the yellow band on his finger – and felt a pang of disappointment. She hadn't realized she'd begun to feel attracted to him.

She said, "Your wife's not with you?"

Her question brought his attention back to her. The orchestra had not yet resumed playing. "No... uh, would you like a drink?"

"...Jack mixes a wicked cocktail."

"Jack?"

"The bartender." She pointed.

The bar was in an adjoining room, separated from the ballroom by a wide doorway. Behind the bar stood a young man with a military haircut, wearing a white shirt and black tie. He was topping off a tall glass with a twist of lime.

Stuyvesant gave her his arm and headed that way.

"So, your wife…"

"Is back in New York. Finishing up some business before she joins me."

Getting her the cocktail she wanted and a scotch for himself, he found seats for them with a view of the dance floor. Simultaneously each took a sip. The music started again. Gen. Dean and his wife were dancing.

He broke off staring at them and turned to her. The flirtatiousness, mild as it had been, was gone. "Let me ask you a professional question?"

She suppressed a sigh of resignation. "A nurse is always on call."

"My wife and I have been talking about having a baby, but she's — we're a little worried about having a baby in a foreign country like this one. You know, when the war ended, right afterward, the magazines reported epidemics here in the islands."

She stirred her drink. "It's safe now. You can tell her for me that a military base is a great place to have a baby. In the year I've been here, I've helped deliver four, and they are all healthy and doing well. We've got a great medical staff. And the wives on the base, they make such a fuss over the mothers. Are you going to be stationed here at Kokura?"

He glanced in the direction of the general. "I don't know yet."

She settled in to asking him about himself. He reciprocated but seemed preoccupied all the while.

He was in the middle of a sentence when his attention shifted to a couple on the floor, Abe Lincoln and Mary Todd.

She followed his gaze. "What?"

"That Abe Lincoln, the one talking to the general, is that Col. Crawford?"

"Yes."

"My older brother knows the Crawfords. He asked me to pay his respects when I arrived." He hesitated. "I'd hate to miss this chance to introduce myself."

She gave him a little mock pout. "I guess I'm the girl who's always left behind."

"Please, I don't…"

"I'm teasing. Of course, go pay your respects. And good luck with your assignment."

He stood. "Thank you. Maybe we can dance again later."

"That would be nice."

She stared after him as he crossed the floor, and then looked down into her drink. It was strange, she thought, how her feelings about Matt Grayson had changed. It wasn't even that he'd deserted her and gone off with another woman. That might have left her heart-broken but still wanting to see him again. No, it was comparing him to this newcomer that had changed everything for her. There was a solidity about this Jonas Stuyvesant that she'd never realized was missing from Matt Grayson. Something solid a girl could count on. That some other girl could count on. She smiled wistfully.

Within moments Jonas had introduced himself to Col. Crawford and was chatting pleasantly with both his wife and him. With the colonel's permission, he took Mrs. Crawford onto the floor for a foxtrot, and afterward asked her to introduce him to Mildred Dean.

Leading her about the dance floor, he watched as the senior officers finally began to drift away from the general. Only the younger officers remained. The general had started to detach himself from them. Seizing the moment, he asked Mrs. Dean to present him to her husband.

But as soon as she'd made the introduction, Jonas realized his timing might be bad. The general seemed more preoccupied with his headgear than in conversing with another young officer. He pulled at the black ribbon under his chin as though it was rubbing him uncomfortably. Jonas waited for a long moment, expecting the general to politely brush him off. He didn't, and instead led Jonas away to the end of the bar where it was a bit quieter.

"Name your poison," Gen. Dean said.

"Uh, scotch would be fine."

"Jack, give us two scotches," he said holding up two fingers. And then said nothing until the drinks arrived and both had taken a first sip. He turned to Jonas, one hand resting on the bar, the other clasped around his drink.

"I knew your brother in Europe. A fine officer," he said, locking his gaze on Jonas. "He wrote me that he thinks you have the makings of a good intelligence or operations officer."

Jonas grimaced. "It might have been my brother writing, but that's my mother speaking, sir. She wants me in a desk job. Sir, I don't want to be presumptuous…"

Gen. Dean glanced away, his gaze sweeping the room. "Speak your mind, Lieutenant."

"I want to be a line officer, a platoon leader."

The general said nothing. In the silence that settled over them, Jonas feared he'd made an irreparable mistake. He'd taken the wrong tack. He'd breached military etiquette. His mother wasn't going to get her way, but neither was he. Now Gen. Dean was going to assign him the lowliest, least desirable job a second lieutenant could be handed.

Gradually the older man's tanned and lined face relaxed into a smile. He nodded. "That's where I started. Best job in the Army for a second lieutenant." His face took on a faraway look for a moment. "Get right down there with your men and live in the field with them." He focused again on Jonas. "Brad Smith at Camp Wood needs a platoon leader. That's the 1st Battalion, 21st Regiment. Report to personnel Monday morning, son. I'll see to it that your orders are cut."

Jonas let out the breath he hadn't realized he'd been holding in. "Thank you, sir."

The general raised his glass and glanced over the dance floor, a quiet dismissal, his attention turning to his wife.

Jonas stepped away and scanned the crowd several times, trying to spot Donna Campbell, but Scarlett had disappeared from the party. So had Shirley Temple and Rhett Butler.

Jonas fell into his bed in the base's Bachelor Officers Quarters. He'd written Ellen a quick letter describing his first two days in Japan, ending with a description of the costume party. That would give her an inkling that there was a social life to be had on an Army base.

He thought about writing his mother as well but decided to wait until he was settled in as a platoon leader. He could understand her worry. His older brother had been in combat and was lucky to have come out alive. But World War II was over, and all the top military planners were saying that, with the advent of atomic warfare, the infantry was obsolete. A platoon leader's job in occupied Japan didn't exactly qualify as hazardous duty. When he did write his mother, he could assure her of that. The next war, when and if it came, would be fought with bombers carrying A-bombs. And it would start in Europe, not Asia.

He turned out his light.

2

S EVEN DIVISIONS OF North Korean infantry huddled, waiting in the pouring rain along the hundred-mile front. At 4 a.m. artillery began to hurtle thousands of shells south onto their targets. Orange flames spat from their mouths. After an hour, the bombardment subsided. Moments later, green signal flares shot into the skies and a hundred and fifty tanks lurched forward. Soldiers with red stars sewn to their caps forged through gaps in the hills and surged into South Korea.

Seeing the signal flares, Comrade Chen Jinquan, rifle at port, scrambled to his feet and charged. The rain had soaked his uniform. Cold rivulets streamed down his face. He could hear the crack-crack-crack of rifle fire from an enemy position up the hill. Single shots from a handful of defenders. No automatic fire. That was good. None of the men in his squad had been hit – yet.

When Chen reached the bottom of the hill, a machine gun opened up, catching three of his comrades in the first burst, ripping their bodies and tossing them on the ground in sprawling heaps. Chen dove into a waist-deep gully. On hands and knees, he scanned right and left and saw that six members of the squad were safe. They looked at him, waiting for a signal. There was no officer this far forward. Chen grinned and shrugged his shoulders. He shifted from kneeling to sitting and squeezed his back into a faint hollow in the wall of the gully. He laid his rifle across his lap. There was nothing to do for the moment. They were pinned down. Hunching forward, he wiped the mud from his fingers on his shirt and dried his hands as best he could. He pulled out his bag of cigarette makings, took out paper and tobacco, and rolled a cigarette, lighting it behind cupped hands with practiced ease. The tip glowed red.

His comrades had looked to him for direction because, in another war, he'd been an officer and commanded these troops. But here, in their country, he was just another foot soldier. He took a long drag, the warm smoke soothing his throat and filling his lungs, tempering his keyed-up nerves. He expelled the stream through his nose, the grey smoke disappearing in the rain.

Chen was probably the only soldier in the North Korean People's Army who was Chinese. Despite having been in dozens of battles in China during the last thirteen years, Chen just wanted to keep on fighting. He'd been wounded eight times, one of them leaving him with a blind, milky-white orb for an eye. As long as he still had one good eye, he reasoned, he could see well enough to shoot.

The other soldiers in his squad had been among those hundred thousand Koreans who had fled a Korea occupied by Japan, choosing instead to fight the Japanese imperialists alongside the better organized Chinese Communists. After WWII, many Koreans stayed in China to fight the imperialist lackey Chiang Kai-shek in the Chinese civil war. Forty thousand survived. After the war ended, the North Korean Premier, Kim Il-Sung, requested the Korean veterans be returned home. Mao released them to Kim.

Major Chen petitioned his superiors, Chou En-lai and Chairman Mao, to allow him to go with the Korean veterans to help further worldwide Revolution. Chou honored Chen with an audience and then personally interceded with Kim Il-Sung, who was pleased by this gesture from China. However, Kim's Russian military advisors were not eager to have a Chinese officer commanding Koreans. But they agreed to have him if he came as a common foot soldier. It did not matter to Chen whether he was a private or a major as long as he could kill imperialists.

The machine gun fire had shifted far to the right, taking aim at one of the other squads leapfrogging up the hill. Chen grabbed a quick peek over the edge of the gully, using his one good eye to peer around a clump of dirt.

He brought out a pocket telescope, left over from his days as an officer, and scrutinized the enemy position. They were dug in along the ridge of a hill. It looked to him like a single squad and a machine gun team, fourteen or fifteen men, and little cover between them and him, only scrub brush and a few scattered boulders. There'd probably been more troops up there, but the tanks that'd rolled through earlier must've routed most of them, leaving the mop-up to the infantry.

But right about now, a little help from artillery would be appreciated. And as though some officer in the rear had read his thoughts and radioed in the coordinates, a shell whistled overhead, exploding just below the peak.

Chen shouted, "Get ready." He kept his telescope fixed on the South Korean position. Through grey sheets of water, he could see helmeted heads turned to see where the shell had hit. If the forward observer calling in the strike knew his business, the next shell would be almost right on top of the enemy.

It was.

"Move out," Chen yelled and sprang over the embankment, sprinting up the hill. He didn't look back to see whether the men were following. His entire focus was on covering as much ground as he could. If artillery kept firing, he might make it all the way to the top before the machine gun opened up again. If. Who knew how well the Russians had trained the North Koreans to use artillery? And even if they did their job, the firing had to be lifted just before he and his men reached the enemy emplacement. That still left the riflemen and machine gunners time to pop up and mow down these men and him.

The running got harder. Under his rain-soaked uniform he was sweating. He was thirty years old. Two younger men sprinted pass him on the right. His heart pounded.

Then, at precisely the right moment, the artillery barrage lifted. Any later and he and his men risked being victims of "friendly fire." He hoped these enemy troops were green enough that they kept their heads down for another few seconds. He only had a few dozen feet to go. Was that too much to hope for?

He saw their helmets pop up, and he dove down. From above, five riflemen and the machine gun crew opened fire. He hit the rocky ground hard as the first bursts swept over his head. Feeling a little dazed, he shook it off and scrambled on all fours for a rock, squeezing himself behind a hunk of granite not really wide or high enough to protect him. He willed himself to shrink, pulled in his whole body. He heard groans from other squad members, those cut down. How many? He couldn't look without exposing himself. The sucking noises of a chest wound reached him from nearby.

He backed away from his sheltering rock just far enough to pull out three grenades. He heaved them one after the other. Three quick explosions and Chen was on his feet, rifle in hand with bayonet fixed, covering the intervening ground. He leapt into the emplacement, a trench four feet across, reinforced with sandbags, and landed right on top of a rifleman. He stomped down on the man's face and drove his bayonet through his throat.

Shouts and a shuffling of bodies behind him. He whirled. A South Korean lieutenant cocked his pistol. Chen shot him in the chest – three bullets. The officer spun around and slammed into two soldiers behind him. They all went down together. Chen put a bullet in each man's face. Behind them, taking aim at him, was another rifleman. Chen dove down in the narrow trench, landing on top of the pile of men he'd just killed. He fired up from his prone position and caught the rifleman in the hip. The man twisted and slammed against the dirt wall, trying to regain his balance but sinking to one knee, looking confused as he struggled to lift his rifle.

Chen fired another round into him, his last, scrambling, trying to get to his feet as that man dropped. Fifteen feet away, another South Korean soldier, a mere boy, his face taut with fear, hefted his rifle to his shoulder.

Comrade Chen, of late Major Chen of the Chinese People's Liberation Army, prepared to die. The shot reverberated against the wet mud walls of the trench, and Chen flinched, releasing his breath in an "Achhh!" He felt no pain, but that was often true. He'd seen it many times. A man was shot but wouldn't feel any pain for a couple of minutes. Even so, it was strange that he hadn't even felt the impact. Maybe he hadn't been shot.

Ahead of him the boy's face exploded, and then the faceless corpse fell forward. Chen turned around. Behind him was a North Korean soldier from the squad that had advanced on Chen's right, an old comrade who had served with Chen in China. They grinned at one another.

The firing sputtered and died out. The enemy soldiers were either all dead or too wounded to move. Chen climbed out of the rain and blood-soaked trench and walked back down the hill, checking the strewn bodies from his squad. Most were dead. Hwang and Kim were badly wounded but might survive if the medical team got to them quickly enough.

Hwang was unconscious. Chen pulled the man's battle dressing from his kit and pressed it against the bleeding abdomen – a bad wound, but the artery hadn't been hit. Pressure would have to be kept up if the bleeding was to be stopped, but if he stayed with Hwang, he couldn't get to Kim. He found a large flat rock nearby and put it atop the bandage.

Kim's face contorted as he gritted his teeth against the pain. Chen checked him quickly. The man had three wounds, the worst being his shattered knee. There being nothing he could do for the pain, Chen pulled out a cigarette and lit it for him. Kim gave him a weak smile of gratitude, and Chen nodded and gave his hand a quick squeeze.

Capt. Hyon and another officer, his second in command, trudged together up the hill, conferring with one another, shaking their heads over this or that body. The medical and burial teams followed behind them. Below on the road, half a dozen trucks rolled to a stop and sat, their motors idling.

"Magnificent assault, Chen."

"Thank you, Comrade Captain."

The captain squatted and peered into the wounded soldier's face. He glanced at the white protruding bone of the splintered kneecap and looked back to Chen. "We have to keep moving. Collect everyone who can walk and get them into the trucks."

It was an understatement, Chen thought, that we have to keep moving. From now on, there would be pressure every day to keep advancing. Just over two weeks ago, Kim Il-Sung had announced that a parliament would be elected in early August from both North and South Korea. They were to meet in Seoul on August 15th, the fifth anniversary of the liberation of Korea from Japanese occupation. It took no great leap of imagination for Chen to conclude Kim meant to have himself elected Premier of a united Korea.

Destroy the South Korean army in only fifty days? Difficult, but not an impossible task. Kim's Russian advisors must have studied Hitler's strategies. This would be like a German Blitzkrieg, a steady drive from the border all the way down to the farthest tip of the Korean Peninsula, rolling over and crushing the ill-prepared South Koreans all the way.

Chen reluctantly conceded that the Russian plan was brilliant. A fast-moving attack would neutralize the one hope the South Koreans had of defending themselves: help from the Americans. The Russians had obviously studied not just Hitler's tactics but the Americans'. It had taken the United States nine long months after Pearl Harbor to put their first troops on Guadalcanal. Rapid responses were not their forte. It was obvious to Chen that Kim's Russian advisors were counting on this.

He moved to a spot where he could be seen easily from all points of the battlefield. He raised his hand and made a circling motion. Soldiers converged on him from all directions and followed him to the trucks – even though he was only a private and not Korean.

3

THREE DAYS LATER, 2nd Lt. Jonas Stuyvesant reported for duty. A Japanese cab took him from the train station at Kumamoto through the city and outlying rice fields to the entrance to Camp Wood. An American MP passed the car through the double-arched gate. He got out at the door of regimental head-quarters just in time to have to come to attention as the flag was being lowered for the day. He held his salute until the bugle call ended.

As the four-man squad folded the stars and stripes, he turned back to the two-story rectangular building. Shouldering his duffle bag, he squared his shoulders and opened the door.

Inside, immediately to his left was a large open office with six desks, each with a black typewriter and phone. Behind them, lining the wall, was a row of gunmetal grey file cabinets. In the middle of the far wall stood the regimental trophy case, stuffed with silver and gold statuettes of baseball and football players and boxers. A Japanese janitor, dressed in grey shirt and slacks, was emptying wastebaskets.

The only other occupant was an American soldier in khakis. Tilted back in his chair, the heel of one foot anchored to the desk's edge, the sandy-haired man in his early 20s was engrossed in reading a comic book. A half-empty green Coke bottle sat within easy reach, while a large black fly buzzed around his head. Absentmindedly, he waved it off as he glanced over, caught sight of Jonas and looked him up and down. His eyes rested momentarily on the officer's signal of rank, his gold bars, but didn't stir himself.

Jonas dropped his bag and barked, "Corporal, come to attention."

The soldier eyed Jonas for a moment and slowly climbed to his feet, gathering himself into a posture resembling that of standing at attention. He saluted in an offhanded way.

Jonas snapped a return salute. "At ease," he said.

The corporal turned his head toward a door behind him and shouted, "Lieu, we've gotta officer reportin' in." Turning back he said, "The duty officer'll be right with you,… sir."

The door burst open and a first lieutenant, cigar in mouth, strode out and crossed the space. He had intense blue eyes and looked like he got up every morning before dawn to run five miles. "Paul Girard," he said without removing his cigar. He shook the new arrival's hand vigorously. Standing six feet tall, he seemed to tower over the newcomer.

"Jonas Stuyvesant."

"Welcome to Camp Wood and the 21st Regiment, Lt. Stuyvesant," he said. "Those your orders?"

Jonas handed over the envelope. Girard dropped his cigar to an ashtray and flipped through the documents. He looked up. "Hmmm, reserve officer, your first duty assignment." He glanced at his watch. "I've got time to drive you over to the BOQ and get you settled in." Then noticing the gold wedding band on Jonas' hand, he said in a half-joking tone accompanied by a little smile, "Unless you're trailing a missus that I haven't seen?"

Jonas smiled back and shook his head. "My wife is back in New York. She might follow. I wanted to check out the base first."

"Not every wife is cut out for overseas duty, that's the truth." Girard handed the paperwork to the corporal and grabbed up his cigar again. "Turco, make sure the Top knows we've got ourselves a new man. The colonel will want to see him first thing tomorrow."

Girard put his hand on Jonas' shoulder and ushered him out to the street.

Nodding back toward the office, Jonas said, "The corporal seems a little lax on discipline."

Girard rolled his eyes. "You'll find that's a problem here. These kids, a lot of them didn't finish high school. Some recruiter sold them on how easy occupation duty is. American money goes a long way here. Booze and pussy are cheap. And if a soldier decides he's got a squawk, next thing you know you're hearing from his congressman. But Turco, he's a whole other kettle of fish."

"He's not right out of high school, that's for sure. So what's his problem?"

"He's a veteran, three purple hearts, a bronze star and two silvers. Finds this peacetime Army boring."

"Why doesn't he get out?"

Girard climbed into one of the jeeps parked outside. "A kid like him, the Army's the only home he's got." He waved to the passenger seat. "Once we get you a room in the BOQ, let's grab a bite at the officers' mess, and then how about I take you on the town for a drink? After tonight, there's no liberty," he said, twisting his mouth. "We're going on standby. The Korean thing, you know."

Jonas got himself quickly settled in. He found it strange that although he was now married, he was back in quarters much like he'd had at boarding school and college. Hanging his uniforms in his closet, he remembered his room at Exeter, the green playing fields outside and a certain day in 1944 when all the newspapers and radio programs were filled with speculation about the impending Allied invasion of Europe.

Jonas' parents, his older sister Katherine and his big brother David in his officer's uniform had all traveled up to the prep school. Still in cap and gown, diploma in hand, the first thing out of Jonas' mouth after hugs and handshakes was "I'm going to enlist."

His mother's face crumpled beneath her pale blue hat as she crushed a lace handkerchief to her mouth. He was stunned. He'd never known his mother to be anything other than the domineering matriarch.

His sister Katherine looked at him with pride momentarily; but seeing her mother's reaction, she gasped as though shocked. His father, who'd served in World War I, shifted uneasily from foot to foot while glancing back and forth from Jonas to his mother and finally to Jonas' brother.

David put his arm around Jonas' shoulder. "Let's go for a walk, buddy." He led the boy away from the little knot of family, along the cobblestone walkways, past huge, ivy-covered brick dormitories and the Colonial- and Georgian-styled academic buildings to a bench in the shade of an old elm tree. The bell atop the Academy Building began to toll as they sat down.

Jonas found himself envying the gold oak leaves on his brother's collar and the three rows of ribbons on his army jacket. David took off his army cap with its brightly polished bill and set it beside him. He ran his fingers through his dark red hair as he looked out in the direction of the vast playing fields of the campus and to the woods beyond. The scent of freshly cut grass permeated the air.

David took a deep breath. "I spent a lot of time playing ball on the fields here. Seems like a lifetime ago." He looked at Jonas. "They're running me ragged at the Pentagon these days. I'm sorry I haven't stayed more in touch."

Jonas nodded. "There's a war on."

"Yeah. You make any varsity team?"

"Boxing."

He looked back out toward the playing fields. Reaching inside his jacket, he pulled out a pack of cigarettes and tapped several loose, offering Jonas one. Trying to look nonchalant, Jonas took one and, as David flicked his lighter, leaned toward the flame.

David took a deep drag. "You know, we Stuyvesant men have always served our country all the way back to the French and Indian War."

Jonas beamed, grateful that David understood how he felt. A lot of his classmates were enlisting, and he wanted to do his part. Just as his brother had done.

David tilted his head down at him, fixing him with serious eyes. "We've always served… but as *officers*, not enlisted men."

Jonas' stomach dropped. "There isn't time. The war will be over before I earn a commission."

"That's true." David took another drag, expelling the smoke slowly. When he turned back, his face had a dark troubled look. "I'm going to tell you something, but I don't want you talking about this to anyone else."

"Okay."

"When this war is over, and we've beaten the Japs and the Krauts, and Europe is in shambles, it's going to be America against Russia."

Jonas had a newspaper picture in his head of FDR, Churchill and Stalin meeting, smiling, sitting side by side. "But Russia's our ally."

David dropped his cigarette and ground it out. "Our enemy's enemy is our friend. For today. I'm telling you what some of our finest military and political minds in Washington believe. When the time comes a few years from now, and the Russian bear turns on us, we're going to need a whole new crop of young officers on the front line."

"So I'm just supposed to go on to college?"

"And ROTC. Get your commission. Study. Study history and economics and get some perspective." A breeze stirred the branches and leaves above them. David sighed. "Look, when mother learned I'd parachuted into occupied France and gotten wounded, she was torn up. Even though I was home before she found out. Let's give her a break."

Jonas met Girard for dinner at the officer's mess. They were both dressed in civvies, prepared to go off-base for a drink. They passed through the camp's gate, where MP's checked the IDs of everyone coming and going. Strolling the sidewalk outside were Japanese prostitutes. Most wore western skirts and makeup, while others dressed like bobbysoxers. But there were a few in traditional kimonos wearing white tabi socks and white cork sandals.

Girard turned into a crowded, twisting lane, too narrow for a car, lined with dozens of tiny shops. Midway down a street, Girard again turned suddenly, ducking to get through the door, red and white streamers brushing Jonas' face as he followed.

As Jonas' eyes adjusted to the darker interior, he heard "Hey, Girard, over here." Down a row of booths, he saw a rangy looking man with a thin blond mustache and naturally curly hair. He was sitting in a booth next to an exceptionally pretty Japanese girl. Getting up to greet them, he looked to be all of six-foot-three in his cowboy boots.

Girard led the way. "Jonas Stuyvesant, meet my fellow platoon leader, Lt. Buzz Parker. Jonas here is new on base, his first assignment."

"Welcome to Jap-land," Parker said, and grabbed Jonas' hand. "Maybe we should get a bigger table and a couple more girls."

Jonas eyed the bar where several unattached young women were watching. One smiled coyly at him.

"No," Stuyvesant said, flashing his ring. "I'm married."

Buzz Parker raised an eyebrow. "So? That don't mean much here in Jap-land."

Girard squeezed into the booth and motioned for Jonas to join him. Buzz sat down again next to his girl.

"Don't rush the man, Buzz. He's not out of the States more than a couple of days, let him get acclimated."

An older woman padded pin-toed across the room, bowing as she approached.

"Mama-san," Buzz said, "beers all around." He turned to Jonas. "Japanese beer okay?"

Jonas shrugged. "Never had it."

Buzz laughed. "The beer here, it's like the Slopes boil smoked wood chips, drain off the water and serve that. But you get used to it."

Jonas glanced around the bar. In some ways, it seemed very American. Against the back wall stood a jukebox. When they'd come in, Perry Como was crooning "Some Enchanted Evening," and now the Andrew Sisters were singing "Rum and Coca-Cola." Off-duty G.I.s in civilian clothes lounged, spread out in booths and at tables, blue smoke rising over each cluster of men and their women, the sounds of joking and arguing rising and falling in waves. The only differences Stuyvesant noticed between this and a bar back home were the Japanese prints on the walls, no American girls, and a wood floor so clean it looked like someone got down and sanded it every single day.

"So what's the story on you?" Buzz tipped his beer to his mouth.

"What do you mean?"

Girard interjected. "He's R.O.T.C. out of Yale."

"How do you know that?" said Jonas.

"I scanned your file, remember?"

"So where do you hale from?" said Buzz.

"New York City."

"You don't sound like a 'New Yawker,'" Buzz said, doing his best to drop his western twang.

"Didn't you hear the man?" said Girard, "He said 'City,' not Brooklyn or the Bronx. I think what we've got here is a product of Eastern prep schools."

Buzz turned to his girl. "You hear that, Mariko? We've got ourselves a bit of high society joining the outfit."

The girl smiled nervously. "Prease, I no understand what you say. I try hard, practice my Engrish."

Buzz smiled and squeezed her. "That's okay, darlin'. You speak the most important kind of language just fine, all night long. We go make goochy-goochy soon, okay?"

She nodded repeatedly. "Okay, Buzz, we go soon."

Jonas had to strain to hear because a party of soldiers behind him was getting a little rowdy. He tried to ignore them.

Buzz shook his head, still smiling. He took a drag and said to Jonas. "So what are we going to call you? What's your moniker going to be?"

Jonas cringed. All through school he'd been dubbed "Red" for his auburn-colored hair. "My name's Jonas. That works pretty good."

"I like 'Sty,'" he said, stubbing out the cigarette, a hint of a malicious smile playing around his mouth.

"I prefer Jonas." He smiled, but he spoke firmly and evenly, with a little edge in his voice. He'd gone through freshman initiations in both high school and college, and he wasn't leaving himself open to some sophomoric wannabe out here in the no-man's land of the Pacific.

Not wanting to give Buzz another opening, he turned to Girard and said, "So what's your story?"

Girard laughed and toasted himself. "My Dad's a full bird colonel from a long line of career officers. I intend to be the first in my family to get on the Joint Chiefs of Staff. Maybe this Korean thing will blow up, and I can at least get my combat infantry badge."

Jonas shook his head. "Oh, I doubt you or I will be seeing Korea, let alone combat."

"Why's that?"

This time a bellow erupted from the booth in the back. Jonas turned his head and saw that the G.I. making the most noise was a big man with close-cropped hair and wearing a loud shirt.

The soldier lurched to his feet. "You doan know nuthin' bout it, you punk-ass turd." He grabbed the pitcher of beer from the table and poured it over the younger G.I.'s head.

"Hey," the boy protested, "watcha do that for?"

"'Cause you're ignorant."

Mama-san rushed to the scene waving her arms. "No trouble, no trouble, I get MPs."

The big man scowled at the little woman. "Don't fuck with me, mama-san." He had a lined, darkly tanned face, with bushy eyebrows and beetle-like eyes. His nose was squashed. "I ain't in the mood." He spat a stream of tobacco juice on to the white pine floorboards.

Jonas flushed with anger. "I'll be right back."

In a few quick strides, he reached the side of the old woman who now stood whimpering, her whole attention on the tobacco juice staining her floor.

Jonas automatically employed a tone he'd used with drunks at frat parties, friendly but firm, not overly confrontational.

He smiled. "Okay, soldier, time to put a lid on it."

He wasn't afraid of the G.I., despite the older man's extra pounds and several inches of height. After all, at Yale he'd been on both the rowing and boxing teams. He rested easily on the balls of his feet, knowing he was in peak physical shape, his reflexes honed.

"Who asked you to butt your ugly face into my business?"

"Look," Jonas started to say, but just then a brown stream of juice shot out of the man's mouth and splattered all over his face. As he instinctively reached for his stinging eyes, a heavy fist smashed into his jaw with the power of a sledgehammer. Everything went black.

When he came to, Girard was kneeling over him. Two MPs towered above. Buzz Parker and his date hovered in the background. One of the MPs asked. "Anyone know those guys?"

Girard shook his head without looking up at them. "They all ran out the back way." To Jonas he said, "You okay? Can you get up?"

Jonas stretched his face one way and then another, working the muscles. He rubbed his jaw. "No, I'm all right. Just let me get up."

Girard reached out and gave him a hand to steady him. Jonas staggered a bit as he climbed awkwardly to his feet.

He smiled sheepishly. "As Buzz said, welcome to Jap-land."

Girard and Buzz both laughed. Girard said, "Maybe we've had enough for a first night off base."

"Yeah, I hope my meeting with the colonel tomorrow goes better than this." He felt his jaw again.

The next morning, the sergeant at the desk said, "The C.O. will see you now."

As Jonas entered, the two officers inside were standing and talking to one another. When they looked his way, he saluted the senior officer, a lieutenant colonel.

"Lt. Stuyvesant reporting for duty, sir."

Lt. Col. Brad Smith, a compact man of medium height with combat decorations spread across his chest, returned Jonas' salute. "At ease, Lieutenant."

He dropped his hand.

"Lt. Stuyvesant, this is Capt. Richard Dasher, C.O. of Charlie Company."

Capt. Dasher reached out his hand and shook Jonas'. "Welcome to the 1st Battalion, Lieutenant." Jonas noted that Dasher was perhaps a half-inch taller than Smith, with a stockier build and darker, coarser hair. But where Dasher smiled warmly at him, Smith's gaze was more one of cool appraisal.

Smith motioned both the captain and Jonas to seats in front of his desk as he skimmed Jonas' personnel file. His oak swivel-chair creaked as he flipped through the pages.

President Truman's photo stared down at Jonas from the wall. Smith read. Jonas and Dasher sat in silence and waited. When Smith finished, he set the paperwork aside and said, "You've heard the latest on Korea?"

"Not much. Just what's been on the Armed Forces Radio, that the UN has condemned the North's invasion." Jonas, who was used to reading at least three New York papers with his morning coffee, was already finding himself news deprived.

"Yesterday the North Koreans captured Seoul, the capital," Smith said. "There is the chance that Truman will order in American troops to back up the South Koreans."

"I hardly think that's likely,…" Jonas brought himself to an abrupt halt. "…sir."

Smith rocked back in his chair, his lips compressed into the thinnest of smiles, a glint in his eyes. He glanced briefly at Capt. Dasher and then said, "What makes you say that, Lieutenant?"

Jonas could feel both men taking his measure. "Sorry, sir. I spoke out of turn."

"No, no, I'm really interested in what you think of this situation. 'Opine' away," he said, with a little wave of his hand.

The last thing Jonas wanted to do was say that from his earliest years he had been accustomed to listening to mayors, congressmen and Wall Street tycoons discussing issues at his father's dinner table. His brother David flew to Washington frequently to confer with State Department officials. While it was true Jonas hadn't really studied the political situation in the Far East, he did have a sense of the drift of Congressional and State Department sentiment in these matters, almost an insider's view. But he also knew better than to present himself this way.

"Only what I've read, in passing, in the papers, sir."

"I'm listening."

Jonas took a breath. "Korea is of no real strategic interest to us. As long as we maintain a defensive perimeter from Japan down through Okinawa and the Philippines, it doesn't matter much what happens on mainland Asia."

When neither of the senior officers replied, or even nodded, he said, "Additionally, the Army's had a long-standing doctrine against getting involved in a land war in Asia. Even if Russia is making a grab for the whole of Korea – and we have to assume that Kim Il-Sung isn't going to lift a hand without Stalin's leave – we can't afford to be distracted from Europe, where our real strategic interests lie."

"You make a good argument, Lieutenant. It could play that way." Smith rocked forward in his chair and sat up ramrod straight. "But just in case Truman has a different take on this invasion, it's our job to be prepared. I'm assigning you to Capt. Dasher's Company as a platoon leader. Think you can handle that, getting your platoon shaped up?"

Jonas felt the hint of a blush creep up his neck and cheeks. Was that a subtle reprimand? He couldn't tell. Dasher was regarding him closely.

"Yes, sir." He said the words forcefully, hitting the 'sir.' It was always important in the Army to demonstrate a can-do attitude. He'd learned that from David.

He suppressed a smile. He'd done it. He'd outmaneuvered his family, who he knew had worked behind the scenes to get him a cushy desk job at division headquarters. Instead he was getting the chance to command a rifle platoon: forty men and a platoon guide, a sergeant.

"The Secretary of Defense," Smith said, his eyes narrowing, "has cut our manpower. We're running at two-thirds authorized strength. You'll be assigned—" The colonel turned his head toward Capt. Dasher.

"—the 3rd platoon," Dasher put in. "Twenty-one men. The squad leaders are experienced, but the rest are pretty green."

"Fortunately," said Col. Smith, "you're being assigned a first-rate sergeant, a combat veteran, just transferred in here from the First Cavalry Division to help us beef up. I know he's good because he served with me on Guadalcanal." With that, he got out of his chair and marched around to the door. "Strosahl, come in here."

In walked a big man with three chevrons on his arm. He had black hair and deep-set, beetle-like eyes, and a squashed, fat nose – the spitting image of the man who had knocked him out in the bar.

"Lt. Stuyvesant, meet your new platoon guide, Sgt. Strosahl."

Jonas stood up. His voice had an edge to it as he said, "I think the sergeant and I have already met." He clenched his fists at his side.

Col. Smith cocked his head and looked impatiently from one to the other. Dasher, too, looked puzzled.

"Beggin' the Lieutenant's pardon," Sgt. Strosahl said in a raspy voice, "I don't recall ever havin' made his 'quaintance."

Jonas stared into the man's eyes. Strosahl didn't flinch from his gaze but looked innocent and mystified. Jonas started to doubt his own memory but shook that off. This was the man who'd knocked him out, and he should be brought up on charges. Then he took another look at the sergeant's face and noticed the red nose with its broken blood vessels and his ruddy cheeks, signs of a drinker. Maybe Strosahl had blackouts. Maybe he really didn't remember. Or was he pretending he didn't?

Jonas had to make a snap decision. He needed a good platoon sergeant and the colonel was personally recommending this man. Challenging his C.O.'s judgment his first day on the job would not be a politic move.

"I guess I mistook you for someone I once ran into," he said, testing Strosahl's reaction. He got only a blank stare in response.

"That's most likely it, sir," Strosahl said.

Jonas, keeping his face devoid of emotion, attempted to match the sergeant's poker face.

The colonel finally broke the silence. "I'll leave you to get acquainted on your own," he said. "The captain and I have business to attend to. The two of you can meet with Capt. Dasher at…" Smith turned to the captain.

"Thirteen hundred in my office."

Smith nodded. "You're dismissed."

Jonas and his new platoon guide saluted the senior officers, did their about faces – with Jonas' the snappier of the two – and left.

By Saturday night, the end of his third day as platoon leader, Jonas was bone-weary but exhilarated. Tired as he was, before he climbed into bed he wanted to pen an overdue note to his wife. The incandescent lamp on the desk cast a yellow light on the page of white stationery. He dipped his fountain pen in the inkwell and began:

June 31, 1950

Dearest Ellen,

I know it's been a whole week since my first letter. I'm sorry. I thought I would be writing sooner, but instead of getting a billet with the 24th Division's headquarters staff, I've been assigned as a platoon leader with the division's 21st Regiment.

What with all the bureaucratic processing that's involved in getting orders cut, and the travel, and now getting settled into Camp Wood, I have been caught up non-stop in a whirlwind of activities.

Today I was with my men on the rifle range, overseeing them "zeroing in" their weapons, i.e., adjusting their sights. Although officers don't normally shoot with enlisted men, I couldn't resist showing off a bit. It didn't hurt my standing with the troops that I easily qualified as expert. Thank God we weren't on the pistol range, since I've never been good with handguns. When we finished up, I led the platoon on a run back to the barracks. David always told me, the first rule of being a line officer is that you don't ask your men to do anything you wouldn't. That's one of the ways you earn their respect. I think I'm doing that.

I know neither you nor my parents envisioned me being a lowly platoon leader instead of having a cushy desk job at head-quarters. Certainly Mother had David pulling strings at the Pentagon to get me on Gen. Dean's staff. But that's not what I want. Dad was a line officer in WWI. David was a line officer in WWII. This isn't exactly the same, since we are not at war. I hope you can appreciate that I still feel I have to do this.

I've been kept busy these last few days. When the day is done for my men, I'm in staff meetings that often run till midnight. But I've had a chance to talk to a number of my fellow married officers and have found out the following: They are very satisfied with the Army's medical facilities here. Army wives have babies here all the time, and the deliveries go well. No one is coming down with exotic diseases. It's just a matter of getting the proper vaccination shots before leaving the U.S. And, while the housing on the base is pretty drab, we can easily obtain almost lavish quarters off-base for prices you can't find anywhere in New York – or even the whole of the U.S. Lots of officers and their wives live off-base.

For myself, I have resolved whatever concerns I had about having a baby here. I think you should start packing your bags and figure on joining me as soon as this flare-up in Korea dies down and life on the base here returns to normal. I can hardly wait to hold you in my arms again, to gaze into your beautiful eyes, to...

As he reached toward the ink well again, he heard a ruckus outside his door. The duty officer was running through the hallway shouting, "We're moving out. Everyone up. All officers grab your gear and report to your company office. Let's go! Let's go!"

Moving out? He couldn't have heard that right. Maybe it was just a drill, but even so, he couldn't afford to dawdle. He jumped up from his seat, strapped on his .45, and pulled his wet poncho on over his dungarees. Grabbing both his duffel bag and carbine, he headed through the door, hesitating a second as he cast a backward glance at the unfinished letter – and rushed on.

4

THE TWENTY-ONE MEMBERS of 3rd platoon stood in the rain facing Sgt. Strosahl as he finished roll call. Cold rainwater streamed down their taut faces. Each man stood at attention, draped in an olive drab poncho, a duffel bag hanging from one shoulder and a rifle from the other.

"Briody!" Sgt. Strosahl barked.

"Here."

When the sergeant called out a name in his raspy voice, he took great pleasure in hearing it bounce back to him off the barracks walls which loomed behind his men.

"Fleming!"

"Here."

"Waskow!"

"Here."

He did a snappy about-face. Lt. Stuyvesant stood several paces behind him. "Sir, 3rd platoon all present and accounted for." He called this out in sharp, clipped tones, clamped his mouth shut and stood staring impassively at the lieutenant.

Stuyvesant nodded, his face just as impassive. "Thank you, Sergeant. Have the men stand at rest."

Without further word Stuyvesant walked away and joined his fellow platoon leaders.

Strosahl was still taking his measure of the lieutenant. Three of his four corporals had combat experience. They could be counted on. But could Stuyvesant?

He'd served under five green 2nd lieutenants in campaigns from Guadalcanal to Luzon in the Philippines and watched three get themselves killed. Two of them had also unnecessarily gotten a lot of other good men killed.

True, Stuyvesant knew his military protocols. He had excellent physical stamina, able to run any of the men in the platoon into the ground. And he could shoot well on a range. But that first meeting seemed to tell the real story, how Stuyvesant had acted in the bar, butting into what didn't concern him. Strosahl had seen his type before. A fucking Boy Scout, the kind that wanted to do the right thing, but couldn't always do the hard thing. That worried him.

He heard the hum of motors in the distance and saw yellow headlights, blurred and bouncing. The column braked to a halt in front of the barracks.

Nothing. The troops waited in the rain. That was always the Army way: hurry up and wait.

It took two hours before the "Mount up," order came down. Drivers jumped from canvas covered trucks and rushed to the rear to drop their tailgates.

He shouted, "3rd platoon, get your fucking asses into those trucks. Move, move, move."

When all his men were loaded in the truck, Strosahl nodded to Stuyvesant and the two of them climbed in with the drivers. The convoy bounced for more than five hours over dark, narrow roads in the rain, arriving at Itazuke Air Base at eight in the morning. As he climbed down to the ground, he saw a military sedan with two stars on the door parked by a hangar. Gen. Dean in a raincoat and soft cap stood talking to Col. Smith in his poncho and helmet. It was a quick exchange. Col. Smith saluted. The general returned it. As an aide held the back door of the car open, the general paused, swept his eyes over the assemblage and got in.

More trucks arrived with recoilless-rifle and mortar teams. Half of the battalion's Headquarters Company, a communications platoon and a medical platoon brought up the rear. All told, Strosahl estimated, about four hundred men stood on the tarmac.

Almost immediately, fifty men from Baker Company were herded into a C-54 transport. It took off. A few minutes later another fat transport lumbered down the runway and lifted off with the battalion commander, Lt. Col. Brad Smith, and his headquarters staff.

When three hours later those planes returned carrying the same troops, unable to land due to foul weather in Korea, the men grumbled over the delays. Strosahl didn't waste his breath. This was the way it went most of the time in the Army. Besides, if any of these soldiers had ever done a tour in Korea, they wouldn't be so eager to get there.

It wasn't until the next day that the weather broke enough that 3rd platoon took the one-hour ride across the Sea of Japan and was deposited on the airstrip outside the port of Pusan, at the southern tip of the Peninsula.

Upon landing, he climbed out of the plane and wrinkled his nose. The air smelled just like he remembered.

Cpl. Holzer, following on his heels, screwed up his face. "Whew! What is that?"

Cpl. Turco was next. He pulled his head up and back. "Smells like rotting fish and shit."

Soldier after soldier exclaimed "Whew!" and tried to wave away the stench. Strosahl laughed and said, "Better get used to it. This is how all of fuckin' Korea smells."

It took mere moments for every man, except the sergeant, to reach for cigarettes. Even the lieutenant, whom he'd never seen smoke, lit up. The cloud of smoke that gathered over the platoon helped to mask the stench a bit.

Expelling a lungful of smoke, Stuyvesant said, "You've pulled duty here?"

Strosahl pulled out his bag of chewing tobacco. "'46 to '47."

He packed a chaw into his cheek. The lieutenant looked like he was waiting to hear more. Strosahl smiled to himself and let him dangle.

An odd assortment of trucks, jeeps and cars, all with Korean drivers at the wheels, sat waiting off the tarmac. He spotted a fellow sergeant who'd returned to Korea after the military draw-down in '49 to become part of KMAG, the 500-man U.S. military advisory group to the South Korean Army.

He left his men and strolled over. "Hey Collins, can't you do anything right? The Army gives you a simple assignment, and next thing we've got a fuckin' invasion to deal with."

"Ha! Who'd ya think's been holdin' those assholes in the North at bay all this time?"

The two sergeants shook hands.

"So give me the skinny," he said. "How bad's this dustup?" He took a few steps around Collins so he could keep an eye on his men.

"Hard to tell. The Reds seem to have halted their main advance in Seoul. The South Koreans blew the bridges across the Han River and are trying to rush enough reinforcements up there to keep the North Koreans from crossing. Your boys are being sent north to backstop the South Korean Army."

Strosahl saw some captain talking to Stuyvesant and gesturing toward the mini-convoy. "Who's that?"

"Gibson. Transportation officer, been here since just before all the action started. He'll be riding north a ways with you. Seems to know his job."

Lt. Stuyvesant was waving to him, so he clapped Collins on the shoulder. "Gotta go. But listen, I wasn't expecting us to pull out of Japan so quick."

Collins grinned. "And you didn't have time to scrounge up all the necessities."

"So you think…"

"I got a man who can get a flask to you on the train."

"Tell him to slip it to me, discrete like."

"Problems with the shavetail?"

"Don't know yet," he said, breaking off.

"Remember to keep your head down."

"Always," Strosahl called back over his shoulder and joined his men being loaded into the odd assortment of trucks, jeeps and cars. All along the road, knots of Korean civilians in greyish white pajamas and straw hats smiled and shouted. At the station crowds lined the tracks and waved little Korean and American flags. Banners and streamers fluttered overhead. A band played what passed for marching tunes. Strosahl shook his head as his men, those who were still green, grinned and waved back.

KMAG officers loaded the platoon into a railroad car of the most battered looking train he had ever seen, even in Korea. The engine had steel patches riveted over its boiler.

As his men found places on the hard, wooden seats, a burly sergeant with the KMAG group made his way to him. "Strosahl?"

When he said, "Yeah," the man slipped him a flask and moved on without a backward glance. He scanned the car quickly to make sure the lieutenant wasn't watching and tucked it into a side pocket.

Stuyvesant was halfway down the car staring out a soot-blackened window. He had a pained look on his face. Strosahl peered through the nearest window. Across the tracks another train of nine boxcars stood parked on a siding, looking forgotten. It was filled with wounded South Korean soldiers swathed in white bandages caked with dried blood. No medics were in sight.

Stuyvesant turned and looked at him as if to ask, "What the hell is going on?"

Strosahl shrugged. What was he supposed to say? War is chaos. What can go wrong does, and it gets worse from there.

They waited in the car as more of the troops and supplies of the task force arrived. The men ate C-rations, trading meat balls and spaghetti for beans and franks. Or cigarettes for the ever popular fruit cocktail. They struck up games of blackjack and poker, playfully hit each other on the shoulder and told raunchy jokes. All except the veterans. Cpl.'s Turco, Holzer, and Brill checked gear and cleaned weapons – and then did it again.

As did Strosahl. He pulled a large knife out of his pack and began sharpening it on a whetstone. It had a seven-inch serrated blade with leather bands wrapped around the handle. He didn't look up when the lieutenant returned from a meeting of the officers in another car, but Strosahl was aware he was headed his way.

"That's quite a knife, Sergeant."

Quite a knife? Strosahl smiled a taut smile and held it up before his face, turning the blade and inspecting the edge he was putting on it. "It's called a Ka-Bar."

"Not standard Army issue, is it?"

Was that a hint of disapproval in the lieutenant's voice? "No, sir, but this here blade's been with me since Guadalcanal. Marine Corps issue." He felt the edge carefully. "My unit was being overrun by Japs when the Marines arrived, as they say, in the nick of time. A Marine died saving my ass. This was his knife. I've carried it with me on every combat mission since. I even got this here S etched into the blade." He pointed to the engraved letter right below the guard. "Wouldn't want anyone thinking they could just walk off with it."

The lieutenant nodded and pursed his lips. "What about your bayonet?"

"It's good for what it is, but this..." he hefted the knife, "...is better for the kind of close in work you don't ever want to have to do."

He leaned back and fixed the lieutenant with a stare that was just short of challenging. He wanted to see if the lieutenant would blanch.

He didn't, but he did blink, the intense blue eyes disappearing just for an instant. "Carry on," he said and walked away.

It wasn't until eight in the evening that the train, belching black soot, finally pulled out. It slowly plowed its way into the oncoming tide of refugees fleeing the front toward which the G.I.s were headed. As the train crawled northward, other battered transports lumbered south on parallel tracks, soldiers packed into every inch of the cars, and peasants in white pajamas riding the roofs. Alongside the tracks ran the main highway connecting south and north, a dirt road peppered with military trucks and jeeps, some moving north, but more streaming south. Crammed in between, slowing the progress of the vehicular traffic, were hordes of peasants on foot, women clutching infants, and men bent beneath A-frames piled high with their families' meager possessions.

Two hours later, the train rumbled through Taegu. The city had a substantial railroad station built of stone, and there were lots of electrical and telephone poles running off in various directions. Refugees packed the streets, huddled in any door space they could find. Shortly after passing through the city, the train crossed the wide Naktong River.

Strosahl was back in fucking Korea with its never-ending rice paddies and hills. He shifted in his seat and wished he could get at his flask, but the lieutenant would certainly notice.

Duty in Japan was so much more pleasant. It wasn't just that there was no shooting going on back in the Land of the Rising Sun. It was that Japanese and Koreans were so different.

While the Japanese had been tough fighters who gave no quarter and expected none, when Japan surrendered, the whole people surrendered. They bowed politely to Americans. They worked cooperatively, respectfully side-by-side with their conquerors to rebuild the country. The Koreans, on the other hand, were a constant quarreling headache. You'd think that they would have been grateful to the Americans for liberating them from forty years of Japanese occupation. But five years after the war's end, there were guerrillas in the mountains, demonstrators in the streets, assassins killing politicians, and a Communist government in the North that wanted to overrun the South, while the U.S. backed government in the South wanted to overrun the North. These people were just itching for a civil war.

Strosahl stared into the black landscape of rugged hills nearly barren of trees. The train rumbled past villages, just clusters of huts, and an occasional larger town. In between, the land was all hills and rice paddies and more hills and rice paddies, punctuated by an occasional apple orchard. He'd seen it all before. He tried to sleep.

Dawn was breaking. Most of his men dozed as best they could on the hard seats. Strosahl, always awake at the slightest sound, heard someone get up and make his way to the middle of the car. He watched through half-closed eyes as Pvt. Whitaker from Alabama approached the wide-awake Lt. Stuyvesant.

The boy smiled broadly as he walked, accommodating the lurching of the car. "Hey, Lieu, look at that field."

The lieutenant turned and looked, turned back to the soldier, and shrugged his shoulders.

"Cotton. I know you Yanks – I mean you coming from the North like you do, sir – you don't know much about cotton. But that's a real cotton field out there. Fancy that, gooks growing cotton."

"Fancy that, Private."

Strosahl heard nothing condescending in the lieutenant's tone. It was inviting, waiting for something more.

"Lieu?" Whitaker said.

"Yes?"

"What's it mean, President Truman callin' what we're doin' a 'police action'?"

Strosahl stirred a bit, glancing around the rest of the car. No one else seemed to be awake. It was just the lieutenant and one of his men talking.

The lieutenant scratched his head. Finally he said, "It's like the MPs being called in to break up a barroom brawl. When you've got a couple of drunk guys acting like jerks, you have to call in someone legally empowered to use nightsticks and crack a few skulls, restore order. In this case, the United Nations is sending us in as MPs, along with some of our allies, like the Brits and Australians."

Whitaker seemed to chew that one over. "There really gonna to be shootin'?"

"Might be. But I don't think the North Koreans are going to want to tangle much with the United States Army. We might have a small scrap with them, and then everyone will back off while negotiators from the United Nations convince them to go back to their side of the border."

Whitaker stared out the window. "I know how to shoot well enough, but I never shot at no man before."

The lieutenant nodded. "If everything goes right, you might only have to point your rifle in their direction."

Pvt. Whitaker continued to stare out the window. The cotton field was gone, and the rice paddies had reappeared. "Never thought I'd see a cotton field out here," he said and made his way back to his seat, shaking his head over his discovery.

Through half-open eyes, Strosahl watched the lieutenant follow Whitaker's progress. Then Stuyvesant turned his head to the window and stared at the landscape, his body seemingly relaxed, not betraying the concerns he must have. At least, thought Strosahl, he seems to care for the men. And they seem to trust him. But what do they know?

Mid-morning the train screeched, groaned, and rattled to a stop. Jonas disembarked with the rest of the troops, as glad as any to be able to stretch his limbs and get some blood moving into his numb buttocks.

The town was ringed by hills, and all the hills were terraced with green rice paddies. Both the railroad station and the surrounding area were packed with refugees waiting for trains headed south. There was a large stone trough in front of the station with hundreds of Koreans, young and old, pressing forward to draw water.

The town stretched out south, west and north of the station with streets laid out on a grid, something he hadn't seen in any other town they'd passed through.

When he eventually caught sight of Strosahl, he asked, "Do you know where we are?"

"Taejon," he said. "It's a hub, a market town." He turned his head and spat out a stream of tobacco juice.

Jonas was amused. "Fond memories?"

"I was stationed here six months. It's a shit hole town in a shit hole country."

"Maybe in a few weeks we'll be back in Japan."

"And maybe my mother had three tits," he said, his gaze sweeping over the desperate crowd of refugees.

Jonas was surprised. The sergeant's tone wasn't so much sarcastic as mournful. When he didn't say any more, but seemed to suddenly withdraw into himself, Jonas detached himself and wandered off again on his own.

A few hours later, everyone climbed into another train, which then rumbled north another couple of hours to a much smaller town, Pyongtaek, a train depot bustling with activity.

Capt. Dasher gave for C Company to dig in on a rise north of town overlooking both the highway and the railroad. South Korean police and military were down on the road, checking and directing the civilians fleeing south.

Jonas' 3rd platoon was assigned the left flank, while Lt. Buzz Parker's 2nd took the right, and Lt. Girard put his men in reserve behind them. Jonas gave Strosahl the order to have the men dig in.

Strosahl examined the ground and began deploying the men along the ridge, one six-man squad and three five-man squads. Each squad was built around the automatic rifleman. Jonas watched approvingly, but when Strosahl put Turco on the Browning Automatic Rifle, the B.A.R., he took the sergeant aside.

"Cpl. Turco is squad leader," he said. "Shouldn't he be free to direct his men, not pinned down with that job?"

"Turco and I spent time together in the First Cav," he said, with a touch of irritation in his voice. "He's the best automatic rifleman I've ever seen. And he'll run the squad just fine while doing that."

Strosahl waited.

Jonas nodded. The sergeant, although he was a bit testy, seemed sure of what he was doing; and, after all, he had the experience. Jonas wasn't about to get into a pissing contest over something like this. "Makes sense, Sergeant. Carry on."

His platoon had just about finished digging in when he heard the sound of planes coming up from the south. He cocked his head.

Strosahl looked skyward and squinted. "Looks like Aussies, Royal Australian Air Force fighters."

To Jonas they were still specks on a grey sky, but as the word spread, some of the guys began to wave and cheer, glad to have some friendly air support, waving even though the pilots couldn't see them.

The fighters were several miles off, flying in diamond formation. Two of them peeled off and swooped down to check out all the activity on the ground, down in the town, three quarters of a mile south of Jonas' position. A locomotive with nine boxcars, having just arrived with a load of ammunition, stood in the station. Korean soldiers and civilians scurried about unloading supplies. The fighters climbed back up.

Jonas turned his attention to a round of horseplay breaking out among three of his men, only to hear Whitaker say, "Hey, they're coming back." Jonas looked over his shoulder. All four were flying single file low above the tracks. They looked just like the movie newsreels of dive bombers, only instead of being bombers these were fighters armed with machine guns and rockets.

He tensed up. Something wasn't right. As he stared at the planes, the missiles under their wings shot forward, leaving long streams of grey cloud in their wake. The rockets sped toward the train. Behind the rockets, machine guns cut in with staccato firing.

Jonas jumped into the nearest foxhole just as the string of explosions began erupting. Although the blasts were far off, the walls of his hole shook with little tremors. He shook, and he couldn't tell whether he was just feeling the vibrations of the ground or he was afraid.

In the pause between the first and the second strafing run, Jonas poked his head up. Down in the town, blasts continued as crates of ammo, catching on fire, exploded. Violent bursts ripped the air, each setting off a shock wave. Jonas scanned his position. Most of his men, like him, were in their foxholes. But Strosahl and Turco and his two other combat-experienced squad leaders, Holzer and Brill, stood above ground, watching the mayhem, calm, dispassionate professionals who obviously knew from long experience they were well out of the danger zone.

Embarrassed, Jonas too climbed above ground. He ducked his head, taking a quick peek around to see if Strosahl was eyeing him contemptuously. But the sergeant, standing on a mound of freshly dug dirt, was watching the action, seeming oblivious to, or unconcerned about, the reactions of the greener troops.

Jonas counted six separate strafing runs punctuated by the rattling of guns. It was twenty minutes before the last fighter plane snarled off.

The rest of his platoon climbed out of their foxholes one by one and looked wide-eyed over the carnage down in the town. The station house was a flattened mass of burning lumber, the engine a twisted heap of metal. Some boxcars were blown completely apart, others were on fire. Nearby stood empty scorched trucks, their tires burning.

The circle of destruction extended far beyond the station. The force of the explosions had flattened dozens of mud and wattle houses. Fires leaped from thatched roof to thatched roof across the rest of the town. Screams and cries rose up from all quarters.

"Why'd they do that, Lieu?" It was Pvt. Whitaker, dragging his rifle at his side, his helmet askew on his head. Damasio, Briody, and Fleming crowded behind him.

Jonas was totally at a loss. He turned to Strosahl – who spat out another stream of tobacco juice and turned away.

But his men were asking him, not Sgt. Strosahl, to explain. "I don't know," Jonas said, the words coming out slowly. "Mistakes happen."

Nothing he'd ever said before had felt so inadequate.

Damasio turned and stood gazing slack mouthed down at the town.

Fleming said, "Those are the South Koreans down there, right? We're supposed to be here to help them?"

"I don't know what to tell you. I don't know what orders those pilots had. I don't know how you even tell North Koreans from South from that high up."

Briody said, "What if we'd been down there, just getting off the train?"

No one said anything to that. A somber mood settled over the troops. There was no more horseplay. The men sat, squatted, or walked about in twos and threes, sometimes staring numbly at the town, and sometimes mumbling to one another in subdued tones.

A little before dawn the next morning, the Fourth of July, a rumbling of motors brought Jonas wide awake. The noise came from the south. As he climbed a little knoll to see, his men also began to stir. He watched as the first trucks came into view. Then slowly a long line of more than seventy vehicles rolled through the smoking ruins of the town. A hundred and eight men from the 52nd Field Artillery Battalion, with six howitzers in tow, halted short of the Americans' defensive position.

Word spread that reinforcements had arrived with cannons and stores of ammo, fuel, and medical supplies. All around him, his men's spirits were buoyed up, and Jonas felt his own lift as well.

B Company, which had been sent off to another town, Ansong, for the night, rejoined them mid-morning. Cooks from Headquarters and Service Company put together hot meals. Although the town was still smoldering, and civilian refugees continued to throng through their lines heading south, neither of these facts seemed so important in this new atmosphere. It didn't even matter that so many of those fleeing were South Korean troops. As Paul Girard said when he joined Jonas watching the weary, defeated-looking men pass by, "They aren't real soldiers anyway, not like us. What do you expect?"

That remark, given that it came from a West Point man, also boosted his confidence.

Late in the afternoon, he watched as Col. Smith and his senior staff drove north to reconnoiter. And then waited for their return with a sense of anticipation. Something was on the brink of happening.

The reconnaissance party returned. It got dark. Capt. Gibson, the transportation officer, had scrounged up Korean military jeeps and trucks. But there were no Korean drivers willing to take the Americans north. So G.I.s got behind the wheel and started out, driving at a crawl over twisted, bumpy roads, in the rain under blackout conditions, with no headlights. Col. Smith was in the lead jeep; the artillery brought up the rear.

Hours later the trucks pulled into a clearing three miles north of the village of Osan. Jonas climbed out of the cab of a truck as his platoon and the other platoons of Companies B and C disembarked. The rain made it hard to see anything except they had pulled up behind a line of hills. A saddle separated the two hills immediately before him.

Capt. Dasher led C Company along the road through the saddle to the north side, where Jonas and the men trudged up the hill along a line, a kind of shelf, fifty to seventy-five feet below the hilltop.

"3rd Platoon dig in along here," the captain said. "1st and 2nd Platoons follow me." He left Jonas and his men in the dark.

It wasn't until dawn was beginning to break that Jonas got an overall picture of their situation. The colonel had established a blocking position to stop the North Koreans from moving any farther south. The enemy could be coming either by the highway or by rail.

The road ran right through the saddle, but the railroad circled east of them. A couple thousand yards to the east.

B Company sat astride both sides of the saddle guarding the road, while C Company's 1st and 2nd Platoons covered the eastern flank overlooking the railroad. Jonas' 3rd Platoon was dug in right in the middle of both companies and could fire upon either the road or the railroad.

Of the over four hundred men in the task force, about three hundred were dug in on the north side of the hills, and a hundred more provided support in the rear.

Col. Smith and his command staff were positioned up the hill behind Jonas, at the highest point, about three hundred feet, where he could oversee everything. Below him, stretched out for a mile along the hills, were his two rifle companies, reinforced by four .50 caliber machine gun crews. Below them, in front of the hills, were the recoilless rifle and bazooka teams. They were concealed behind knolls on both sides of the road as well as farther east covering the railroad tracks.

When his men were pretty well dug in, Jonas went to the rear to supervise troops hauling ammo up to the line. There, on the reverse side of the slope, mortar teams had dug pits, anchored base plates in the rocky ground, and were busy adjusting the angles of their mortar tubes. The headquarters staff, a switchboard, and the medical platoon had also dug in east of the road. All the trucks were parked west of it.

The medics had carved out a large square, rigged a roof of ponchos for protection against the rain, and set up cots underneath. They'd stacked litters and laid out fresh bandages. He did hear a couple of noncoms cursing that they couldn't get the radios working because of the rain. But other soldiers from the communications platoon were running wire for field telephones from the switchboard to the platoons on the front line and back along the road to the artillery in the rear.

Looking back toward Osan, Jonas had a clear line of sight along the road for a mile and a half, at which point it curved around a hill. A single howitzer stood guard there, a precaution in case any enemy vehicles managed to break through the American line. Jonas was told the rest of the howitzers were stationed another mile and a half to the rear. Col. Smith could call upon the artillery to shell either the road or the railroad or both depending upon the situation.

Jonas was cold, wet, and tired. Rain trickled down his face. He hadn't slept much since arriving in Korea, and none at all last night. But he was exhilarated. Col. Smith was fighting from high ground of his own choosing. His troops were well dug in on the north side of the slope, with his mortars and supporting elements on the reverse slope, and with his artillery stationed three miles to the rear.

Except for the radios not working, it was textbook perfect.

5

THE FIRST LIGHT had worked its way through the cloud cover and drizzle. It cast a dim pall over the landscape as Sgt. Strosahl put the finishing touches to the two-man foxhole he'd be sharing with his platoon leader.

Lt. Stuyvesant, poncho clad, suddenly appeared and hovered above him, returning from walking the line. Again. Talking to the men, reassuring the nervous ones and joking with others to keep up their morale. He gave the appearance of being relaxed and calm, but Strosahl didn't believe his act. The man's eyes gave him away. By turns they darted or drilled or blazed, but they were never relaxed.

He was good with the men. The sergeant gave him that, even as he himself stayed focused on the task at hand. He used his Ka-Bar to finish smoothing the muddy surface of a shelf he'd carved out below the forward lip.

Stuyvesant squatted down. "What's that for?"

"The field phone, when it gets here." Strosahl looked up. "And hand grenades, so we aren't wondering where the fuck they are when we need 'em."

"And those?"

Strosahl had cut additional shelves a little below waist high out of the side walls. "Seats. It gets hard on the legs standing for long stretches. Easier to sleep at night, too. One man sleeping, the other watching."

He lowered the point of his Ka-Bar and rammed it into the front wall. It was level with his waist, easily grasped. "We get overrun, and some gook jumps in your hole, you don't want to be fumbling trying to get your bayonet out of its scabbard. You want your blade in your hand quick."

He grabbed it from the wall and held it up, twisting the blade slowly a few inches from the platoon leader's face.

The lieutenant blinked – and nodded. Strosahl dropped his gaze and shoved the Ka-Bar back into the wall.

"Lieu, just one recommendation."

"Yes?"

He spat a stream of tobacco juice over the front edge of the fox-hole and watched it splatter in the dirt. "If we get hit, and you have to puke, try to get it outside our hole."

Out of the corner of his eye, he watched Stuyvesant stiffen – and felt a glint of pleasure.

The lieutenant's eyes narrowed. "You think I'm going to puke?"

"Of course not, sir, but if it comes to that, just direct it outside. That's all I'm saying."

"You don't have to worry I'll puke all over your nice clean foxhole."

"Lots of good men puke in combat, sir. It don't mean nuthin'. I've heard tell great actors sometimes get the shakes and have to puke before going on stage, no matter how good they know their parts. Just the body getting rid of everything extra so it can move faster." He pressed his lips together to keep from smiling. "Like shitting in your pants."

He turned his head and spat another stream of tobacco juice over the lip of the hole. It mixed with the rain running down the hill and soaked into the mud.

A hint of a smile played around the corners of Stuyvesant's mouth. "Of course, that don't mean nothing either, right?"

"Right."

"Thanks for the education, Sergeant."

"Least I could do for a Harvard grad like you."

Stuyvesant's eyes flashed. "Yale. I went to Yale." Just as quickly he regained his composure, looking a little sheepish.

"Oh yeah," Strosahl said, looking directly into his eyes. "Yale. I forgot."

The lieutenant grinned. "Yeah, like hell you did."

Strosahl shrugged and looked away. It was good Stuyvesant could take a ribbing, but he wasn't about to get chummy with a 2nd lieutenant who hadn't proven himself yet. He'd seen green shavetails like Stuyvesant doing dumb things that got too many good men killed.

Cold rain ran down his poncho. Word was passed down from the hill for the troops to break out their C-rations for breakfast. Strosahl sat down on the seat he'd carved out and pulled two cans from under his poncho. One was ham and eggs, the other a tin of peaches.

Stuyvesant seemed to think about it for a second, then pulled out two tins himself. Pork and beans. Fruit cocktail.

Strosahl took out his bayonet and braced the can of ham and eggs on his knee. He jammed the point of the blade into the lid next to the rim and sawed around the rim until he could pry it up.

Looking up he saw the lieutenant eyeing his technique, paused and handed over his bayonet without a word. Stuyvesant accepted it and set about opening his tin. Strosahl pulled a wooden spoon out from under his poncho and dug in.

They ate in silence.

As they finished up, Strosahl said, "Not exactly the officer's mess hall out here, is it?"

Stuyvesant grunted and said, "I'm still waiting for a waiter to show up and give me a refill on my coffee."

"Yep, you spend a lot of time waiting when you're in the field."

A soldier from the communications platoon came slogging along with a field phone and wired it up. Ten minutes later the captain called them for a sound check.

Strosahl focused on everything in front of him. He didn't have
to keep looking back up the hill to know that the colonel stood
watch there, a figure in a dark poncho, scanning the road with field
glasses. The only good thing about this whole fucked up situation
was that Col. Smith was in command. Strosahl had served with him
on Guadalcanal. The man was the savviest C.O. he'd ever had. Of
course, as soon as the Army figured they had a good field officer in
the colonel, they pulled him out of the Pacific and put him behind
a desk in the Pentagon.

That meant the colonel didn't go with the unit when they landed
on Vella Lavella. Losing him as their C.O. probably made no difference
in Strosahl getting wounded there, and "missing out" on the rest of the
battles in the Solomons. But he was out of the hospital and back for
the 25th Division's final campaign on Luzon in the Philippines. One
hundred and sixty-five days of continuous combat in the rice paddies
and mountains, taking town after town. More than his fair share of
fighting. And here he was back in another fucking shooting war.

At 7:30 Strosahl heard excited voices and a rustle of activity
above in the command post. Col. Smith had his field glasses trained
on the highway. Other officers did too. Some were pointing. The
hairs on the back of Strosahl's neck began to tingle. He pulled out
his own pair of binoculars and scanned the road. As he adjusted the
lenses, what had been mere dots took the form of tanks – huge low-
slung green monsters armed with long cannons and machine guns.
He counted them as they came into view, one through fuckin' eight.
About three miles away.

"Uh-oh." Seeing the lieutenant didn't have field glasses, Strosahl
handed his to him. "Take a look, Lieu." When Stuyvesant looked
curious, he said, "I bought these myself. You wait for the Army to
issue you a pair, you'll be a captain."

"Right. I'm learning that."

Down below, his men stood up in their holes trying to get a
better view. They jabbered and pointed.

"Tanks?" the lieutenant said. "Where the hell did they get tanks? The North Koreans can't make tanks. They don't have the factories."

Strosahl shook his head. "You got me, but those suckers are a lot bigger than any of the tin cans the Japs had." He yelled down the hill, "Turco?"

"Yeah?"

"You ever see tanks like those?"

"Yeah, Russian T-34s. Outside Berlin. They're badass mutherfuckers."

Stuyvesant shouted, "But our bazookas can stop them, can't they?"

"Don't know, Lieu. Never had to try." Turco grinned up at him. "The Russkies were on our side."

The lieutenant shook his head. "We could sure use some air cover right now. Like those Aussie fighters with their rockets."

Strosahl looked at the sky. "Not in this weather. We're on our own." And of course, Strosahl thought, we didn't bring any land-mines. Didn't anybody back in Japan know these gooks had tanks, Russian tanks?

The field phone buzzed, and the lieutenant grabbed the handset, listened, and said, "Yessir, right away, sir."

"The captain wants me to make sure the men don't fire until ordered to." He jumped out of the foxhole and scurried down to the line.

Strosahl shook his head. The lieutenant could have called down to the squad below and had them pass the word, or he could have ordered Strosahl to run up and down the line. No, he had to do it himself. Well, he'd learn to delegate these things. Presuming he lived long enough. Which, if he survived this first contact, was probably somewhere between two weeks and six months. That's about how long platoon leaders lived on average. Another reason not to get too chummy with the man.

Strosahl reached under his poncho and felt the outline of the string of beads beneath his fatigue jacket, Buddhist prayer beads resting atop his dog tags. They had been given to him by Mika along with a parting kiss. His fingers lingered a second, and then he shifted his hand to his hip pocket. He pulled out his flask, took a swig, swirled it around his mouth and let it flow down his throat. Rye wasn't his favorite drink, but it served in a pinch. Certainly more soothing than prayer beads. He took another pull, capped the flask and put it away. A few minutes later the lieutenant returned, looking satisfied with himself.

"The men know to hold their fire," he said, as he climbed back into their hole.

Strosahl would've offered the lieutenant a drink, but he suspected the shavetail would get all huffy on him, so he kept his face forward, not wanting Stuyvesant to smell his breath.

"First man breaks fire discipline," Strosahl said, "I'll kick his ass. They know that." He waited for the lieutenant to respond – but got nothing.

Finally, when the tanks reached a point that Strosahl estimated to be a mile away, the American artillery fired one round. It flew whistling over them. A plume of white smoke rose from the rice paddies. Near the tanks. But not near enough.

"White phosphorous – Willie Peter," Strosahl said. "The colonel's just getting their range."

The lieutenant let out his breath.

A moment later, the U.S. battery began firing rounds in quick succession. Shells dropped all around the tank. But the column continued to roll forward. The lieutenant looked at him.

"High explosive rounds," Strosahl said, shaking his head. "Good for taking out troops and small vehicles; but for a tank, you need to get a direct hit."

The artillery shells kept missing.

At 700 yards, the American 75-mm recoilless rifle teams concealed at the bottom of the hills opened fire. One round, two, three.

The lieutenant's mouth dropped. "Nothing, they're having no effect!"

"Duds," Strosahl said, his tone flat. "Must be old ordinance....
No, that one was a direct hit. Fuck."

The lieutenant grabbed the field glasses. "I see a dent in the tank's
armor." He lowered the field glasses. "Damn it, that round didn't even
penetrate the skin." He stared at Strosahl in disbelief.

More shells struck. Some were duds and some exploded without causing much damage. The tanks continued to roll on. Strosahl
watched helplessly as the scene played out below.

The bazooka teams crept to within fifteen yards of the armored
vehicles. A lieutenant ran out almost onto the road with a bazooka on
his shoulder. He fired rocket after rocket, over a dozen, at one tank.
All of them just bounced off the heavy plate armor.

Finally the tanks seemed to take it seriously that they were under
attack. Their 85-mm cannons and machine guns began to search out
targets, training first on the recoilless rifle and bazooka teams. One
team dove for cover just before the tank's cannon blasted their position. The tanks then started to search the hills, the cannons sweeping
back and forth. One barrel halted, pointed directly at their foxhole.

Strosahl pulled the lieutenant down as the cannon spouted fire.
The shell roared overhead and a section of the hill directly behind
them exploded. Clumps of mud rained down and the smell of burnt
gunpowder settled over them.

He felt the familiar feel of warm piss trickling down his leg and
was glad to have that over with. He'd been in too much combat to
be embarrassed about it.

He poked his head out of the hole. Stuyvesant followed suit.
Together they watched as the tanks proceeded to roll along the highway through the saddle, through their lines, as though they had
wasted enough time with this minor nuisance.

Once out of sight behind the ridgeline, Strosahl heard more
cannon fire. He clamped his jaw tight. From the sound of the ruckus,
the tanks were shooting up their trucks. How the hell were they going
to get out of here without trucks?

A few minutes later he heard a single artillery piece fire off six rounds, and a little later there was a brief coughing of more artillery from farther away. He heard the distant staccato of small arms fire. It was impossible to make much sense of what was going on back there, but it didn't sound like their artillery had stopped any of the enemy tanks.

Another tank rolled down the road toward their line, ignored them and passed through. The rain drummed on steadily. A string of three more tanks made their way forward and clanked through the saddle.

"We can't just sit here, Sarge. We've got to do something."

"Like what? We've got nothing to stop them with. Pea shooters – that's all we've got."

"I don't understand. They shouldn't even be able to use tanks in a country like Korea. Tanks are for wide-open fields, like Europe and Russia. Korea is all hills and rice paddies."

"I guess no one gave the Korean command the U.S. Army field manuals to read, or they'd know that." Strosahl wanted to take a swig from his flask, but he wasn't going to risk it with the lieutenant right next to him. He put a new chaw in his mouth instead.

"And who sends tanks out front? I thought we'd get an advance party of infantry, maybe a company, coming down the road. We'd fire some warning shots. They'd realize they were up against a superior force and report back up the line. Their commander would send up a scouting party to find out what was up. They'd see we're U. N. troops. There'd be a little parley, and they'd back off."

The sergeant spat out a long stream and looked up the road. A total of twenty-two tanks had passed through their lines. There were no more to be seen. "We should check on the men."

No matter how Strosahl felt, he knew they had to keep up a front for the troops. He climbed out behind the lieutenant, and the two of them walked the line, checking on the men, working to keep morale up. The new men were shaken, their bluster gone, but no one was hurt.

About an hour later the command post began buzzing with excitement again. Strosahl peered through his field glasses. "I make out more tanks."

"Damn," Stuyvesant groaned.

"Slow moving." He lowered the glasses and handed them over. "Leading a column."

Three tanks, and behind them were trucks, then a long column of troops on foot. The convoy seemed to inch forward. It couldn't be traveling more than three miles an hour, the standard rate for troops marching long distances. The closer it came the longer it appeared. By the time it was within 1,000 yards, he could see the thin brown line stretching back for miles. A few thousand enemy troops were marching down the road.

"Doesn't look like a scouting party," Strosahl said.

Stuyvesant pressed his lips together and didn't reply.

They settled into a silence.

At the 1,000-yard mark the American mortar teams let loose with a barrage, shelling the trucks. Several burst into flames. Troops from the nearby trucks piled out and headed for cover.

The lieutenant turned to him. "Why are we just using mortars? Where are our damn howitzers? They're more effective."

Strosahl shook his head, his eyes glued to the road. "My guess? We've lost communications with the battery. We don't have radio contact, just wire. The tanks going through earlier probably ran over our comm wire. Chopped it the hell up."

As he scanned the field below him, he was surprised to see that the North Koreans seemed disorganized. In near panic even. At least that was something.

The field phone buzzed again, and the lieutenant answered it. When he hung up, he said, "Capt. Dasher, reminding us to hold our fire until ordered to."

Strosahl nodded. The men knew that.

The three tanks leading the column rumbled forward to within a couple hundred yards and opened fire.

When the first mortar rounds hit the North Korean convoy, Lt. Chen (formerly Private and now Lieutenant, promoted for heroism on the line) was riding in the cab of the fifth truck from the front. The truck ahead of him exploded in flames, as did a truck three vehicles back. Calmly he climbed out of the cab and began scanning the terrain ahead. He watched as troops up and down the line took cover. The troops on foot scrambled to get off the road, seeking cover in ditches and behind rice paddy walls. Those in transports jumped to the ground and followed.

The tanks rolling through earlier hadn't radioed back that there were enemy troops dug in here. Chen shook his head. The Russians could build tanks with heavy armor plates but couldn't design a good radio.

He pulled his telescope out. The enemy's mortar teams had to be taken out. Where was their spotter? Locating the spotter was a priority, because a mortar team, usually located on the reverse side of the slope, couldn't find its target without a spotter. To stop the mortars, take out the spotter.

Chen pulled out his telescope and started with the highest peak, scanning slowly. He jerked the telescope from his eye. No, he must be mistaken. He rubbed his good eye just to make sure there was nothing distorting his vision and tried again.

Yes, it was a command post. Several soldiers had binoculars trained his way. Something about them puzzled him. First, they seemed unusually tall. He scanned the line below them. It was hard to tell. Many of the soldiers had mud on their faces, but their eyes weren't Oriental. Were they Caucasian? Maybe American advisors? But advisors wouldn't be riflemen manning the ridge. He estimated two or three companies faced his men. And what were they wearing?

Some sort of slick covering to protect them against the rain? For soldiers, they certainly were a pampered lot.

He lowered his telescope and smiled. Capt. Hyon ran up alongside him.

Chen said, "I believe the Americans have decided to join the war." He pointed to the hills. The captain scanned the hills methodically with his binoculars. Then he called for a runner who came crouching along the line of trucks. The captain wrote out a quick dispatch outlining the situation and saying artillery would be needed. In the meantime, he would begin deploying mortar teams and an assault line.

Though Chen was pretty sure the North Korean strategists would not be happy about the U.S. involvement, he burned with excitement. He'd long dreamed of fighting Americans. Many an evening he'd argued with fellow officers about how such a conflict would go. Yes, the Americans had beaten the Japanese whom the Communists, even with Mao's brilliant leadership, had not been able to drive out of China. But he was convinced that the Asian soldier, grounded in Marxist-Leninism, properly armed and fighting on his home turf, was more than a match for the Americans. Now they were here. Let the test begin.

6

THE THREE TANKS moved up and began firing on the American positions. This time Jonas did not need Strosahl to
pull him out of harm's way. Even from below ground, he
could see red blasts flashing against the grey sky. Shrapnel whirled
overhead as mortar and artillery shells poured down on the hillside.
The walls of the foxhole shook, raining mud on them. His nose and
throat stung with the acrid smell of burnt powder.

He scrunched down across from Strosahl, knee-to-knee. The bee-
tle-eyed veteran chewed his tobacco and occasionally aimed a squirt
over the edge of their hole. "Want a chaw?" he yelled over the din.
Jonas shook his head and the sergeant shrugged.

Jonas' guts were roiling, and the offer of a 'chaw' was nearly
enough to make him puke. He had a sneaking suspicion that's what
the sergeant wanted.

"Just make sure, Sergeant—" he shouted back.

"Yeah?"

"—you don't get any of that spit in my face."

Strosahl hesitated and nodded. "I only hit what I aim at, Lieu."

"Me too, Sergeant." He narrowed his eyes. "Me too."

A deafening blast sent them ducking reflexively. Jonas cocked
his head as he began to sort out by their sound alone the differences

in the sizes of incoming shells. Soon he found he could distinguish between rounds that were coming his way and those headed elsewhere along the line. Taking advantage of a moment when there was no danger, he ventured a peek over the edge of the foxhole and saw, several hundred yards away, enemy officers driving men out of ditches and from behind rice paddy walls.

He pulled his head back beneath ground. "They're coming."

"Yep." The sergeant pressed his lips together and seemed to withdraw into his own world. Jonas poked his head up when he could and made quick surveys of the field.

Hundreds of scrawny men in baggy, mustard colored uniforms scurried about in the rain. In quick order, under cover of the barrage, the first wave of troops charged. For the first two hundred yards, most slogged through the water and mud of the paddies, as others ran across paddy walls. As they got closer to the American lines, there was more firm land. They forged forward, more sure-footed now. Two more waves followed, still navigating the wetter terrain.

The field phone buzzed. He snatched up the headset.

"Hold your fire." Capt. Dasher's voice was reassuring in its firmness.

"Yessir. Holding fire."

Jonas watched expectantly, hopefully, as American mortar shells dropped in front of, behind, and among the charging enemy soldiers.

"Hold your fire," he shouted down at his own men. "Pass it along."

He glanced at Strosahl who, with rain dripping from his helmet, gave him a quick nod.

The first assault wave was less than a hundred yards away. The enemy barrage lifted, and as the din died away, it was replaced by the bloodcurdling yells of the charging enemy soldiers.

He swallowed hard and found that he was shaking. He knew he was afraid, maybe more afraid than he'd ever been. But if he'd learned anything from his years in the ring, it was that fear was his friend. He tried to remember that, that fear could focus the mind.

Over the headset came, "Fire! Fire!"

Jonas sprang up and yelled "Fire! Fire!"

Simultaneously cries of "Fire" broke out up and down the line. Fifty-caliber machine guns cut loose along with the rifle and automatic rifle fire. To his left and right the whole mile long American line fired – and kept firing.

The front line of the mustard clad troops went down. Here and there he saw a body writhing. Most of the bodies lay still, face down in the mud. He felt a moment of exultation, watching them lay motionless as the grey rain beat down on them.

His body went numb as he took in the extent of the senseless carnage. He breathed out. It had to be over now. The charge was clearly a suicidal tactic – but here and there a Korean soldier climbed back to his feet. Teams of four and five jumped back up, one team running forward and hitting the ground, and another following, leapfrogging all across the front.

He stared wide-eyed. How could so many have survived? He grasped his carbine tighter, wanting to start firing himself. A large hand closed over his and he looked toward Strosahl.

The sergeant just shook his head and returned to scanning the line of men below him.

Jonas got hold of himself. His job was to be alert to the larger picture and direct his men. He wasn't there to shoot. He only had the carbine in case they were in danger of being overrun.

An enemy soldier, hit in the head, threw up his arms, his rifle flung back over his body as he was thrown backward. The man beside him kept charging forward, the red star on his cap clearly visible. And behind him two more assault lines charged on.

American mortar shells flew overhead, the explosions dotting the field of Korean troops, tossing men around like rag dolls. The American infantry line fired and fired. Enemy fighters went down.

Inexplicably, many rose, and more, coming up from behind, filled in for the fallen.

Then, far off in the distance, Jonas heard the thin piercing notes of bugles. North Korean soldiers slowed and pulled up. They cast looks to the rear and began to withdraw, carrying off as many of their dead and wounded as they could, while leaving dozens behind in the rice paddies. The three tanks withdrew. Whiffs of smoke and the rain-diluted smell of cordite hung over the quiet of the battlefield. The rain droned on.

He climbed up out of his hole, Strosahl following closely behind. Able to move again, he felt the pent-up tension drained away.

From up and down the line, calls of "Medic!" rang out, most of the cries coming from farther east where B Company defended the saddle. Litter bearers ran along the line, slipping in the mud. Carrying the wounded, they worked their way down the hill to the road and around to the medical station, and then raced back for the next load.

Jonas and Strosahl walked up and down the line checking for casualties, relieved to find no one killed, and only two wounded badly enough to be carried off the hill. The rest of the platoon had nicks, scratches and a couple of dented helmets. The men were shaken but holding steady.

They returned to their foxhole. Jonas lifted the phone to report in. It was dead.

A few minutes later Capt. Dasher, walking the company line, joined them. His face was hard-set, and his tone clipped. "Most of the phone lines are out. Shelling cut 'em up pretty bad. We've got men on repairs."

Jonas shook his head. There hadn't been time to dig trenches and bury the lines, and no one had expected enemy artillery fire. So now, not only was the colonel without contact with his own artillery, he had no phone lines to his platoons.

"I've sent for more ammo," the captain said, with a glance down the hill.

Jonas too cast a look over the field where the bodies of North Korean soldiers lay strewn. He felt grim pride that no enemy soldier had gotten within fifty feet of the bottom of the hill. "Do you think we're going to need more, sir? We hit them pretty hard."

Dasher smiled. "We did set them back on their heels, didn't we? What do you think, Sergeant?"

"They fight like seasoned troops. They outnumber us by a lot. We're in for more."

Dasher nodded. "Probably right. Lieutenant, you and the sergeant better get the men ready for another round."

For an hour both sides tended their wounded and reorganized. Jonas and Strosahl were just barely settled back in their foxhole when the shelling began, but this time the tanks stayed parked a mile back up the road, out of the battle.

The surviving North Koreans formed an assault line. More troops arrived by truck. Their officers hustled them into a second and third line. Bugles sounded. Again, they advanced under cover of their mortars and artillery.

Jonas knew from textbooks that once the mortar and artillery fire began, it was usually impossible for one side to even see the other side's line. The smoke from exploding shells quickly enveloped everyone in dark clouds. But that wasn't happening here. The constant drizzle dampened the smoke. Mortar shells exploded in rice paddies, part of the explosion buried in the mud. Jonas could see their lines clearly as they advanced.

There were many more enemy soldiers now, stretched out across the front, a much thicker mass confronting his own platoon this time. They were going to push line after line of troops up the hill until they overran the Americans.

The North Koreans began to advance. As they again reached the hundred-yard mark, the American line let loose almost in unison without anyone calling out "Fire!" Machine guns and automatic rifles rattled as they swept back and forth. Enemy soldiers dropped to the ground wounded, dead or taking cover, crawling, getting up and charging forward in short bursts, soldiers coming up from behind and running over the bodies of fallen comrades, yelling, bugles blowing, shells exploding, an acrid cloud rising and spreading over the whole field. The North Koreans fell back, regrouped, charged again, were repulsed, and charged again.

Shells exploded above, below and around his foxhole. Shrapnel whirled and bullets cracked overhead. More than once he felt something whip by his cheek and felt that strange quiver knowing he could be stretched out, wide-eyed in death, a piece of steel embedded in his brain.

When the firing finally stopped, he heard cries of pain and the shouts of "Medic!" up and down the line.

Below him Cpl. Holzer rolled on the ground clutching his eyes. Jonas clambered out of his foxhole and sprinted down to him. Strosahl was a step behind.

"My eyes, my eyes!" the corporal shouted.

Pvt. Damasio knelt next to him whimpering.

Jonas saw litter bearers to his left pulling another man out of his foxhole and fastening a compression bandage to his shoulder.

"Medic!" Jonas shouted.

"Damasio," Strosahl yelled, "pull it together. What happened to him?" He dropped down and took hold of Holzer's shoulders, stopping him from thrashing around.

The medic reached them. He knelt on one knee. As Strosahl continued to pin Holzer, the medic pulled the Holzer's hands from his eyes. His face was red and black, all blisters, his eyebrows singed.

"I'm blind! Ohmygod, I'm blind!"

The medic quickly injected him with a shot of morphine and taped a bandage over his face. "Get him to the aid station now," he ordered the litter bearers and was up and running to the next case. The morphine began to take effect. Holzer quieted down. The litter bearers lifted him onto the stretcher and moved off over the slippery, uneven terrain.

Damasio sat back on his haunches, no longer whimpering, but looking stunned. "It was a shell burst. Right in front of the foxhole. Burned everything."

Strosahl dropped down on his knee and grabbed a rifle out of the mud. He thrust it at Damasio. "Clean your weapon. You're gonna need it."

Jonas scanned the faces of the squad. They looked pale and taut, but no one else was wounded. Damasio was senior in rank, but he was in no shape to lead. He held his rifle in front of him, staring at it as though he'd never seen it before.

"Fleming, you're squad leader. Take charge."

"Yessir."

He moved west along the line and Strosahl east. He found Turco attending his men, checking bandages, joking with them. They were clapping one another on the shoulder, but their laughter was strained. One soldier even sounded like he was verging on hysteria. All their faces were stretched tight, but they were laughing.

Turco looked up. "I was just telling the guys, you want to take these bastards down, you got to aim for their nuts." He grabbed his crotch, giving it a quick lift. And grinned.

"Yeah?"

"Shooting downhill, you aim at some fucker's chest, and your bullets go over his head."

Jonas noted the mounds of spent brass lining the edge of the fox-hole. He looked down the hill. Aiming low, Turco had brought down a lot of North Koreans. Maybe the reason so many of the enemy had survived elsewhere was that his men were aiming too high.

"How're you men doing?"

"We're fine here, sir. Could you get us some more ammo? We're running low."

"It's on the way." Jonas took in again all the bodies sprawled out in front of Turco's squad. "Aim for the nuts. I'll pass that along. Carry on, Corporal."

A stream of G.I.s humped resupply boxes of ammo up and down the line while others lugged five-gallon water cans to infantrymen who'd already emptied their canteens. Machine gunners arranged belts and riflemen refilled clip after clip, as many as they could.

Phone contact hadn't been re-established with the artillery, and the radios still wouldn't work in the rain. The 1st Platoon of B Company, which had occupied the western side of the saddle, pulled back across the road and took up stations on the east side because, as they lost men, their flank had become too exposed.

Jonas borrowed Strosahl's binoculars and scanned the enemy lines. Truckloads of replacements kept arriving from the north, hundreds of fresh soldiers. Officers directed them east and west of the road in longer and longer lines. At least a thousand men were arrayed in front of the American position.

Clusters of enemy officers stood looking at maps, maps folded into the smallest squares possible and shielded from the rain. They jabbered all at once and pointed this way and that. What looked like a senior officer, senior because he was older and portly, silenced them with a raised hand. He tucked his map back into its pouch and, with a few pointed gestures, waved them off. The junior officers saluted and scattered, running back to separate units.

Jonas' stomach clenched up as he watched porters with stacks of mortar shells strapped to their backs disappear behind embankments and reappear with empty A-frames.

They were clearly massing their men for an all-out attack.

He lowered the field glasses. "I count *five* lines." He turned to the sergeant. "They really mean to overrun us this time."

The sergeant reached under his poncho and pulled out his flask. He handed it to Jonas, who looked at it for a second, uncapped it and took a swig. The rye burned his throat. He stared down at the field and took another swig, handing back the flask without looking at Strosahl. The sergeant took a long pull, recapped the flask and put it back beneath his poncho. He fiddled with the grenades on the shelf in front of him.

The battle had been going on for four hours. The three tanks hadn't participated in the second assault. They'd withdrawn. Now they rolled forward again, creaking and rattling, presumably resupplied with ammo. They maneuvered into positions to the right and left of the road and rested, their motors idling.

Quiet settled over the whole field. Nothing stirred. The rain stopped. Far back north along the road, a dozen artillery pieces barked. A dozen shells whistled on their way toward the American lines, and before those shells even hit, more batteries opened fire. The three tanks again raked the American lines with cannon and machine gun fire.

Jonas felt his body go cold as he hunkered down in his hole. He was knee-to-knee again with Strosahl, both leaning forward, jaws clenched, waiting it out as explosions rocked the hill. He felt the warm pee run down his leg as his bladder emptied and was grateful that, even though the rain had let up, he was covered with a poncho so Strosahl couldn't see the stain.

The pounding went on and on, the explosions so loud that Jonas almost didn't hear the distant soundings of the bugles. The faint strains wove in and out of the crashes. He ticked off the landmarks they must be passing: the long stretches of rice paddies, the last embankment, stepping onto solid ground. He waited. The charging enemy must have passed the hundred-yard mark. Still the enemy artillery and mortar barrage wasn't lifting.

When the cannons finally went silent, and Jonas thrust his head above ground, the whole side of the hill was covered with a thin layer of white smoke. He couldn't even see much of his platoon beyond the squad below. The few North Koreans he could make out at the foot of the hill were wisps of forms emerging from a mist. Although he couldn't see them, he could hear the American line left and right cut loose with automatic weapons. Below him, his men were pulling pins from grenades and throwing them downhill.

Jonas got no restraining hand or cautioning look from Strosahl this time. Shoulder to shoulder, he and the sergeant fired their carbines at the growing mass of North Koreans, shooting rapid bursts at them. Jonas aimed and fired. His man did not go down. He remembered Turco saying, "Aim for their nuts." He aimed lower and fired again. Thirty yards below him a thin wiry soldier caught two bullets midstride, spun around, and fell backwards. Another soldier jumped over him as he rolled down the hill. Jonas brought the leaper down with one shot. Strosahl pulled a pin from a grenade and heaved it. He pulled another pin, heaved, pulled another pin and heaved that grenade.

Jonas heard the continuous barrage of American mortar shells, but still no artillery rounds, whistling overhead from behind. The field below was covered in a cloud of grey smoke.

He prayed the mortar shells were doing their job on the second and third lines. If they could be broken up, this assault might fail. He tried to push any thought of it succeeding out of his head. Strosahl's Ka-Bar stuck in the wall of their foxhole was no comfort.

The first line of attackers, the immediate threat, slowed as the ground got steeper. More and more fell. The mass of sodden, yellow brown uniforms began dissolving in front of him, and they finally turned their backs and ran. As they retreated into the cloud, he heard shouts, strong voices that were probably urging them to regroup and press on. But the shouts dwindled, and the attackers failed to reappear.

Screams of wounded men and yells for medics and ammo sounded up and down the line. Litter bearers raced from foxhole to foxhole.

A breeze began to break up the cloud that had covered the field below. The three tanks had not withdrawn. With the American targets clearly visible, they shot at anyone above ground, the medics and litter bearers.

There, a hundred yards away, the North Koreans, with bugles blowing, were hastily reforming, troops coming up from the second and third assault lines to fill holes in the first, and men from the fourth and fifth ranks moving into the third. More American mortar shells, well placed, began to fall along this line, almost breaking it up, but the North Korean officers rallied the troops and drove them forward.

Jonas and Strosahl shoved new clips into their carbines and waited as the fifty-caliber machine guns began their systematic sweeps. The mortar fire continued, although it was falling at a slower rate. He hoped they weren't running out of shells.

The North Korean artillery launched a new barrage, and Jonas and Strosahl went underground. The enemy infantry advanced rapidly across the field. And again the shelling was lifted as the North Koreans reached the bottom of the hill and began scrambling up, clambering over bodies mangled and left from the previous assault.

Grenade after grenade flew at the charging troops. Automatic fire swept their ranks. Jonas fired and fired. The white smoke churned up, obscuring all visibility. The yelling began to recede. The bugles stopped blowing, at least the ones near at hand. No North Koreans were breaking through the line. And there were fewer shots coming from them.

The firing along the American line sputtered out. The air was saturated with the smell of gunpowder. The white smoke began to dissipate, and as it did, Jonas saw that the North Koreans had withdrawn again back over a hundred yards, and that farther back officers were trying to reorganize the ranks.

In a lull, while the North Koreans were regrouping, medics and litter bearers worked their way along the American line. He heard the cry for a medic come from his right. One of his men was hit. He ran down the line.

Pfc. Webb lay back in his hole trembling violently, eyes fixed skyward as blood poured from his neck wound. His foxhole buddy, Pvt. Turner, blubbered as he fumbled to find his field bandage. Jonas dropped to one knee just as Webb gurgled and choked and, with a last spasm, went limp. Turner had finally gotten the bandage out. He pressed it to Webb's neck.

Jonas reached over and put a restraining hand over Turner's. When the soldier looked up at him confused, Jonas shook his head. Beneath the black streaks of gunpowder, Turner went ashen.

Out of the corner of his eyes, Jonas saw two G.I.s carrying a litter. They struggled to maintain their footing on the uneven ground. As Jonas got up and stepped back, he saw they were carrying Lt. Buzz Parker. He was conscious but gritting his teeth against the pain. His shoulder was bound with a white pressure bandage already soaked red.

Jonas grabbed Parker's hand as the litter was passing by. He ran with them a few steps. "Hang in there, cowboy." Parker made a weak attempt to smile but gave up.

The litter bearers fought to keep the stretcher level enough that their load didn't fall over the side. They had to halt and wait as another team pulled one of Jonas' men out of his foxhole. Jonas could barely make out who it was – Pvt. Russo, a corpse missing its jaw.

Capt. Dasher came slipping and sliding down the hill from the command post. He stooped over, catching his breath. "The North Koreans are making moves to envelope both our flanks. We start withdrawing in ten minutes. Baker Company will hold the line while Charlie Company disengages."

Jonas stared uncomprehendingly at the captain. Withdraw? He shook off his moment of shock. Of course, they had to. If they didn't, the North Koreans would surround them.

The captain didn't seem to register his confusion. "The colonel wants Charlie Company to take up positions on that hill a mile and a half directly behind us."

"Where the howitzer was parked?" said Jonas. It was the only thing he could think to say.

"That's the one. Most of our trucks are shot up. We'll be hitching rides with the artillery, and that means holding that hill until they're organized. The first thing is we've got to get our wounded out. 2nd Platoon will provide initial cover while you and Girard lead your men to a rallying point by the medical station and help with the evacuation. I'll stay with 2nd Platoon and bring them back when you're clear."

"Sir." Jonas saluted unnecessarily just to make it clear he had gotten the order. Capt. Dasher ran off at a low crouch toward Parker's platoon.

Just then Jonas heard the cry from somewhere up the hill, "Every man for himself!" A ruckus broke out off to his left. He saw Lt. Girard's men scrambling out of foxholes. Girard was running up and down, waving his arms, shouting at them to stop, but his men were scrambling toward the path that led off the ridge, some without their rifles and packs.

Jonas' own men were now shouting. He and Strosahl yelled at them to get back into position. Jonas grabbed Damasio by his poncho as he ran by. "Stop right there, soldier," Jonas yelled. Damasio stared at him wide-eyed, like he didn't recognize him. Two more men ran past, and as he turned to shout at them, his grip loosened and Damasio jerked free.

Most of his men were already up and running now. Strosahl grabbed one soldier and threw him into an empty hole. There were a few soldiers in holes trying to keep a partner from climbing out. Jonas remembered an officer in a movie standing behind his troops with his .45 pointed skyward and threatening to shoot anyone who ran. He reached for his own pistol, but knew it was too late. The rout was beyond stopping. Over half his men were cutting out. He looked down the line to the west and saw the panic had spread to Parker's platoon. Capt. Dasher was having no better luck trying to control the men.

In the rice paddies, North Korean officers pointed up at the Americans and yelled at their men. Several squads charged. The last of Jonas' men bolted from their holes, running past him. Jonas shot Strosahl a look. Strosahl shook his head and spat out a stream of brown juice. "Let's go, Lieu. There's nothing more we can do here 'cept get our asses shot off."

Coming down and around the hill, Jonas saw the rear area in complete chaos. The trucks parked to the west of the road had been blasted into twisted hulks. East of the road was the improvised shelter for the wounded, cots under tarps. Mortar men had left their tubes standing deserted. A handful of terrified soldiers milled around with no direction. Most of the rest were already in full flight, bareheaded, with weapons and packs discarded. Some were sprinting down the road, while others were running full out for the rice paddies. A handful of medics stayed, clustered with the wounded, looking for stretchers. Jonas and Strosahl headed that way.

Strosahl ran from cot to cot getting the wounded up, those who could readily stand, and began herding them south.

Jonas scanned the more severely wounded men lying on cots and pallets. Some were oblivious while others looked terror-stricken. One grabbed his hand. "Jesus, don't leave me, Lieutenant."

"Can you get on your feet?"

Taut-faced, the soldier did, holding his bandaged side. He was shaky.

Jonas grabbed an ashen faced medic and said, "Help him down the road."

The medic braced him up and half dragged him away.

Two hundred yards to the east, a detachment of North Koreans rounded the flank of the hill and set up a machine gun. They fired. Screams punctuated the firing. G.I.s fleeing the aid station fell.

At the end of a line of cots, Buzz Parker tried to get to his feet as he clutched his left shoulder. He fell back exhausted. Jonas ran over to him.

Parker's face was white and drawn, his voice thin. "Help me."

Jonas frantically looked for litter bearers. There were none. Bullets snapped as they flew by him. He ducked his head and hunched his shoulders involuntarily.

Everyone was gone except a grim-faced medical sergeant gliding among the wounded, tending them, looking like he intended to stay put. The North Koreans were closing in. It was clear to Jonas that if he delayed any longer, he'd be killed or captured. He pulled a grenade from his pocket and closed Parker's hand around it. "The best I can do."

Parker's eyes widened. He bit his lip, and Jonas turned away.

His heart pounded madly as he sprinted down the road, carbine in hand. His mind churned. Capt. Dasher said the plan was to take up positions on the hill a mile and a half to the rear. That was where he had to get to. They could make a stand on that hill, buy some time.

He passed men who were limping, moving slowly because of wounds, or those helping the wounded. Beneath his poncho, his .45 flapped against his side and his canteen bounced on his hip.

Five hundred yards to the rear he found Capt. Dasher organizing thirty or so men. Lt. Girard was at his side.

"Stuyvesant," Dasher called out, waving him on. As Jonas ran up, the captain told the lieutenants and noncoms clustered around, "Col. Smith is in the rear trying to get the artillery out. We were supposed to make a stand on the hill behind us, but the North Koreans are already there."

Jonas was stunned.

"We have to try to make an escape east through the paddies and across the railroad tracks. Start organizing the men to move out. And don't let any more of them throw their weapons away."

Jonas started to turn away.

"Stuyvesant!"

"Sir?"

"We need a rear guard. I want you to organize it, and then join me."

"I'll stay with them, sir."

"No, I want you and Girard with me."

"Yessir."

As he wheeled around and began trotting back up the road, the weight of the order chilled him. He'd been ordered to choose the men who would not make it out alive.

He'd automatically volunteered to stay with the men to be sacrificed. He should be grateful that the captain had forbidden that, but he wasn't. He felt guilty. How could he look these men in the eye and give the order?

He saw Strosahl on the road, waving men forward like an MP. "Keep moving, keep moving." Turco was with him, as was Connors, still carrying his machine gun.

"Capt. Dasher ordered me to assign a rear guard."

"Yessir," said Strosahl. He stared at him with that flat stare of a man awaiting hard orders.

Jonas looked over the men available, some from his platoon, others he didn't know. He hesitated. He looked back to Strosahl and couldn't open his mouth. He couldn't give the order.

He watched as the sergeant's eyes narrowed, and then his lips curled in contempt. Jonas felt his insides wither. He flushed.

"Turco," Strosahl barked, "Connors, form up on me. We got any B.A.R. men here? You, you, and you – you're with me." Quickly he had a dozen men, four of them with automatic weapons. "The rest of you, follow the lieutenant."

He turned to Jonas, disdainful and impatient.

Jonas stumbled over his words. "Capt. Dasher is taking us… east across the railroad." He averted his eyes. "Then south."

Strosahl turned his head and spat out a stream of brown juice. "You better get going,… sir."

Jonas looked over the squad helplessly. "Right," he said, and turned. He took a few steps and then began to double-time it, joining others of the rag-tag band of fleeing soldiers.

A dozen steps down the road, he looked back over his shoulder. Beyond the handful of men struggling to keep up with him, he saw the tiny rear guard. It was divided between those lying in a depression and the others behind a small knoll. Fifty yards beyond them, a dozen screaming North Korean troops had begun their charge.

Strosahl began firing from a kneeling position. As he squeezed off each carefully aimed round, his shoulder rocked back as it absorbed the impact. Jonas took a lingering look at the man knowing it was probably his last – and ran full out.

7

SETTING A BRUTAL pace, Lt. Chen led the troops around what had been the enemy's western flank. He meant to capture as many as possible. These were the first Americans they had encountered, and as such, they could be made to yield valuable intelligence.

Rounding a knoll, he saw rows of medical cots, many filled, under canvas awnings. But there were even more Americans thrashing about on the ground, their wounds still fresh. Five or six soldiers from another North Korean platoon were running berserk, bayoneting the wounded.

Chen blew a cease and desist command on his whistle and began shoving his troops forward with "Stop those fools!" He strode in behind them, shouting to the other platoon leader, "Get your men under control."

The North Korean soldiers moved back, clearing a space around the cots. Chen surveyed the scene. There were men unconscious on cots, some moaning deliriously, and others who had toppled onto the ground, crawling about. About a dozen men had been bayoneted.

Chen was looking for American officers. An American medic, by the looks of his arm band, lay dead on the ground, several bayonet wounds in his chest and abdomen and throat. A loss. He could have been used to tend to his wounded, thus saving time for their own medics.

Distractedly, he told the lieutenant of the other platoon, "Take your men and hunt for stragglers. This was not an orderly withdrawal, and there are certain to be stragglers. And lieutenant, try to bring some of them back alive."

He dismissed the man without realizing he was giving orders as though he were still a major in China. But his fellow officer obeyed without question, rallying his men, pointing them down the road, shouting at them to hurry after the fleeing Americans.

For by now all the North Korean troops realized these were Americans. They jabbered in wonderment. Most of them had never seen a Caucasian before. The officers, when they'd learned they were facing foreign troops, had not told their men in case any of them held the foreign devils in awe. Now they saw for themselves. These were just men, and men beaten almost as easily as the South Korean enemy.

As Chen looked over the captives, he finally found what he was looking for: an officer. Just a lieutenant, to be sure, but an officer none the less. He would be able to give the interrogation team in the rear some idea of what units the Americans had in Korea.

Chen stepped toward the man, a big man with curly chestnut colored hair and a thin blond mustache, clutching a grenade, finger set to pull the pin. Around Chen a gasp went up and his men pulled back or dropped down low. Three or four trained their rifles on the American.

"Don't shoot," Chen ordered. He saw fear contort the American's features. The man's eyes were now on him. Chen stared back stone-faced. He watched the American's eyes sweep his face, fixing on Chen's blind, milky-white eye and jagged scar, which seemed to unsettle him even further.

Chen shook his head slowly and put out his hand. In English he said, "That would be foolish. There is no need for you to die."

Chen watched confusion flood the young officer's face.

"Do you want to take your fellow soldiers with you?"

The officer glanced right and left, eyeing wounded men stretched out on cots. Chen saw his body seem to fold in on itself, his eyes frozen in indecision. Chen walked forward with measured steps and closed his hand around the grenade and its spoon. He felt the American relax his grip, and Chen took the grenade.

Two of his men rushed forward and yanked the American to his feet. As they roughly searched him for more weapons, Chen turned away and began to examine the grenade more carefully. He had never seen one of this type before. It seemed a good design. Its pin was still properly secured. He put the grenade into his pocket and turned back to the wounded Americans. 'Know your enemy' was the first rule of combat. What kinds of useful intelligence could he find here?

Jonas jogged back down the road to the point where Capt. Dasher had struck off for the railroad tracks to the east. Injured Americans struggled, trying to catch up to the main body.

Jonas found Cpl. Holzer, his eyes bandaged, alone on the bank of a rice paddy. He stood with his arms stretched out. Jonas grabbed him at the bicep. "I'll get you out of here, Corporal."

"Is that you, Lieu?" His voice cracked. "Thank God."

Jonas didn't respond. His mind was still on the men he'd left behind. Men he'd already given up for dead. Imagining Strosahl riddled with bullets, he swallowed hard. He tightened his grip on Holzer with his right hand, his carbine in his left, and began to run with the blind man clumping along beside him, slowing him down.

Holzer stumbled, but Jonas kept a grip on him. They made it across the paddies to the railroad tracks and down the embankment where Capt. Dasher was barking orders to the thirty-some men who'd followed him. Several soldiers were fashioning litters from ponchos.

The captain struck out south, picking up stragglers along the way.

They trudged throughout the evening into the night through rice paddies and around small villages. Every two hours, the captain stopped to rest. He made the rounds, checking on who was in his group, what shape they were in, what kind of wounds the men had, how much water was available, and who had weapons.

He sent out troops to serve as point, and others as flankers and rear guard. They stayed off the roads and worked their way south, first toward Pyongtaek and then, when they learned from a friendly South Korean that the tanks had gone that way, they turned toward Ansong, hoping to find their backup, the 34th Regiment.

By the time they made it to Ansong, they were 65 strong. They arrived to the cheers of the men of their own artillery battery, who had been led to safety by Col. Smith.

More stragglers found their way into camp throughout the day.

Five hours after Jonas had delivered Holzer to safety, Strosahl and the dozen men who'd stayed behind limped in, exhausted, wet, muddy and out of ammunition. Two of the men were bandaged, though to Jonas' grateful eyes, the wounds looked like they were minor.

He made his way through the men thronging around the rear guard and grabbed Strosahl's hand, clapping him on the shoulder.

"Damn, Sergeant, it's good to see you."

Strosahl grunted, barely acknowledging him or anyone. "Just point me to a cot."

He wasn't alone. Most of the men needed sleep. They'd been up for 48 hours. Medics from the 34th Regiment tended wounds, and their cooks fed them.

Capt. Gibson, the transportation officer, was on hand bustling about, organizing vehicles sent up from Taejon. The wounded went out first by ambulance. Later in the day, he got everyone else loaded into trucks.

As Jonas waited to be transported south to Taejon, he eyed those preparing to defend Ansong. The green troops of the 34th stared back at him, mute, with frightened eyes.

Two days later in Taejon, Jonas sat next to Paul Girard on a narrow wooden bench outside Capt. Dasher's office. The captain had temporary use of a small room in the yellow schoolhouse that had been turned into the headquarters of the 24th Division. Jonas rolled his shoulders, trying to work the kinks out of his shoulder and neck muscles, nervous about why he and Girard had been summoned.

The division's support personnel had poured into the town, a thousand men handling supply, transportation, and communication. The 8055th M.A.S.H. (Mobile Army Surgical Hospital) had taken over another schoolhouse in the northeast quadrant of the town. They'd arrived just in time to start dealing with all the casualties pouring in from the 34th Regiment. Jonas was hearing ugly rumors about what had happened to them.

Girard, like Jonas, had placed his steel helmet next to him on the bench. He fiddled with a cigar. "Have you heard what the current count is?"

Jonas clenched his jaws and shook his head. When the task force was routed at Osan, the troops had scattered east, west and south. At first it seemed they'd lost about half their men, but stragglers continued to trickle in, each one a bit of good news. But there was no news good enough to erase the guilt of having left so many of their wounded behind. Or the humiliation of having been routed.

Girard put the cigar in his mouth but didn't light it. "The numbers I got are, of the 406 of us that went up on that hill, a hundred and eighty are missing, wounded or dead. So far. A few more might still show up."

Jonas pulled out his own cigarettes and shook one out of the pack. "You think Buzz is dead?" he said without looking at Girard. It was the closest he could come to broaching the subject no one wanted to talk about.

"If he's lucky," he said, turning his face farther away.

Capt. Dasher's voice rang out, "Girard, Stuyvesant."

Jonas fumbled to put his cigarettes away, grab his helmet, and get into the office. The C.O. didn't sound like he was in a good mood.

Both officers saluted. The captain, sitting behind a desk, saluted back. He was thinner, having lost weight like they all had, and Jonas thought he could see a sadness in the man's bleary eyes that hadn't been there before Osan. At the same time, he noted a tightness in his jaw muscles. Determination?

"Stand at ease."

They relaxed, holding their helmets in their left hands, each resting his right hand in the small of his back.

"How are the men doing? Getting fed and refitted?"

"Yessir," they said in unison. Headquarters' Service Battalion had arrived in Taejon and provided hot meals, portable showers, new clothes and, as needed, new weapons.

"Good, good," said the captain. "I want to commend both of you for the leadership you demonstrated at Osan."

Girard heard this and stood a little taller, but Jonas flinched inside. Yes, he'd done okay. Not bad for someone who'd never been in combat. But when it'd come to making the tough decision, that of picking the rear guard, he'd faltered. The captain hadn't seen that. Only Strosahl knew.

"I've called you here to give you a heads up. I don't know when it will be. Probably two or three days from now, but we're going back on the line. This Korea thing has turned into something much bigger than anyone expected. MacArthur is sending over two more divisions, but until they relieve us, we do the fighting.

"I just got word that the North Koreans trapped the 3/34 in the town of Chonan. There were six hundred men in that battalion. A hundred and seventy-five got out alive. The report is that the C.O. and most of his staff were killed defending the CP."

"Sonofabitch," Girard growled.

Jonas felt like he'd just been plunged into ice water.

"This *police action*," the captain said, the sarcasm in his tone unmistakable, "has turned into a fucking full-blown war." He picked up a transcribed radio message off his desk. "We will be getting two hundred replacements in the next couple of days. Understandably, our men who fought at Osan are—" he looked for the words, "—still recovering."

Jonas cautiously nodded in agreement. Out of the corner of his eye, he saw Girard doing the same.

The captain got to his feet and leaned forward, his hands resting on the desktop.

"You need to do whatever it takes to shape these men up, to get their morale up. The replacements coming in are going to be plenty scared. We need our men who've been under fire to steady them. Understood?"

"Yessir," they chimed.

"Dismissed."

Sgt. Strosahl was in a surly mood, and it wasn't just because his lieutenant was too much of a Boy Scout to be leading a combat platoon. It was because the morale of his men fucking sucked. They needed to buck up and do it quick.

Yes, it was good that they'd been trucked south and were getting a couple of days to rest up in Taejon. It was good that they hadn't had to sleep in foxholes for the last two nights, but instead were billeted in mud huts. There was even a vegetable garden out back with pigs running free. A couple of those had ended up on spits.

They lounged around chatting, tossing a ball, playing cards, or cleaning rifles, but they did everything listlessly. Part of that was because they'd gotten their asses kicked at Osan. But another part was that a numbness always took over men after combat. It usually lasted a couple of days, but it could last longer, especially if they were coddled.

Holzer sat eating a can of fruit cocktail. He hadn't been permanently blinded after all, but he still had to wear gauze bandages to screen out direct sunlight. Word was the bandages might come off today. Guelzo and Fleming, each of whom had gotten nicked, sat around with hangdog looks.

Yes, the men were getting rested, but they were sullen. Of the whole platoon, only Turco still cracked jokes.

Pvt. Damasio threw down a hand of cards with a snort of disgust and shook his head at his partner, Pvt. Boyd. "I can't even think straight. I can't get that shit out of my mind."

Damasio had panicked at Osan, but just because he did so in his first firefight didn't mean he would in the next. He couldn't be allowed to wallow in the memory.

Strosahl strode over to him and dropped down on one knee, eye-to-eye with Damasio. The private hadn't shaved that morning. "What's your gripe, soldier?"

His tone was plaintive. "What the fuck are we doing in this hole, Sarge?"

"You wanna cry, I ain't your momma."

"I had a girl back in Japan." His voice was wistful.

"So you let a little Nip get her hooks into you?"

"Ah, come on, Sarge. It wasn't like that."

"So that's what the U.S. government is paying you for, to get cheap pussy?"

"No, no, what I mean is—"

"I know what you mean, Damasio." He raised his voice. "Now all of you, gather round and listen up." As they stirred themselves, Strosahl packed his cheek with a fresh chaw of tobacco.

The sergeant felt a little guilty calling Damasio's girlfriend a Nip. He'd left his own girlfriend behind.

Mika. She'd found a little house for them on a crowded street. It was weather stained to a blackish grey, had a sliding paper door, a tile roof and a vegetable garden in the back. She'd haggled with the owner until she'd gotten good terms. Once they moved in, she planted oleanders in front.

Thereafter, when he finished his day on the base, he came home to find Mika in a kimono and a house that was spotless. A hot succulent meal was in the pot, waiting for him as soon as he finished his steaming hot bath. It took him a few weeks to get used to the idea that she would be scrubbing him, but he adjusted. She got him to take off his shoes before walking on their tatami mats. Last April she'd taken him to see the cherry blossoms, to come to a full stop and really see them.

Since moving in together, his nightmares had grown less frequent. On those nights when he did wake up thrashing and screaming, she held him until his tremors subsided and he could fall back to sleep.

When he told her he had orders for Korea, she cried. She took her Buddhist prayer beads, placed them about his neck, and made him promise to come back safe.

He looked over the men as they pulled into a tight circle around him. They'd been beaten badly their first time out in combat. Seen men killed on the hill, and wounded friends left behind. The message was clear. None of them was invincible, that the difference between living or dying was a crap shoot. It made sense they'd be longing for the safety of occupation duty and the arms of young Japanese girls.

He scowled. "I know most of you, when you signed up, thought the big war was over. Some recruiter sold you the idea that you could be a soldier and never have to fight." He let his gaze fall on each man successively. "But Uncle Sam spent good money teaching you how to fire your rifle, not how to shoot your wad."

"Yeah, Sarge, but—" the baby-faced Boyd started to say. He hadn't shaved that morning either, but the truth was his peach fuzz was still too thin to need shaving. Here was a kid who was a paradox. He was shy, sort of the platoon's mascot, yet on the line at Osan, he'd been cool under fire.

"—There's no 'buts' to it," Strosahl barked. "You drawing government pay?"

Moans.

"Boyd, did you draw pay first of the month?"

With big and sorrowful eyes, he said, "Yeah, it all went to pay off markers."

There were some chuckles over this, and Boyd, hearing them, looked up and smiled shyly.

"I don't care how you spent it. You took the pay. You take the pay, you do the job. End of story."

"Sergeant." The call was crisp, clear and commanding.

Strosahl turned his head. His bigger problem, Lt. Stuyvesant, stood just inside the entrance to the courtyard.

"Sir?"

"Could I see you outside?" The lieutenant nodded toward the passageway.

"Right away, sir." He turned back to the men. "All of you, turn to and clean your weapons. When I come back, I don't want to see a speck of dust in a single barrel. And Damasio, shave."

He turned his back on them and left them grumbling.

"Holzer," the lieutenant shouted, "don't you have sick call today?"

"At thirteen hundred, sir."

"I'm going with you, Corporal. I'll be here at twelve forty-five."

Strosahl could hardly miss the lieutenant's not even giving him a look as he turned on heel and led the way down the dirt street past mud and wattle buildings. Several doors away, he circled around a building and into a little courtyard, till they were out of sight of any troops.

The lieutenant wheeled on him, his jaw muscle rippling as he clenched and unclenched his teeth. "Mind telling me what you thought you were doing back there?"

"My job. Putting my boot up some butts."

"They just got trounced in their first battle. You think a browbeating is the best way to motivate them?"

"It's no good their feeling sorry for themselves, and I ain't going to mollycoddle them."

He weathered Stuyvesant's attempt to stare him down. He'd withstood the hard, military gaze of lots of officers. This kid just out of college wasn't going to make him sweat.

Stuyvesant said, "You've got a problem with me, don't you?"

"Not my place to have a problem."

"Let's drop the bullshit. You haven't had proper respect for me since you decked me."

He shrugged and tried to look confused.

"Come off it," Stuyvesant snapped, "we both know what happened in that bar."

Strosahl jutted his chin out. "You think something happened, you should bring me up on charges."

Stuyvesant shook his head and rolled his shoulders, loosening them up. "I'd prefer a re-match."

Strosahl tried to conceal a smile. He'd never known an officer to take this tack, but in the old Army, this is what a sergeant did. When he had an insubordinate platoon member, he took him out back and beat his ass. Of course, you had to know you could take any man in the platoon. And Strosahl had never lost this kind of fight, especially not when he was up against a Boy Scout.

But did he want to do this? To beat Stuyvesant was to be rid of the kid. The shame would be so great that the lieutenant would have to find a way to transfer out of the unit, and Strosahl would end up as acting platoon leader until the brass could scrounge up another lieutenant. By then they might all be back in Japan. Not that he wanted to play officer, but he trusted himself more than he trusted this guy. The lieutenant could be offering him a perfect solution. But there was one tiny hitch.

"You've got bars on; and I'm not looking to get court martialed."

"There're no bars and no stripes here. Just two men in the ring."

Strosahl shrugged assent, feigning indifference as he sized up his smaller opponent. Stuyvesant obviously didn't know the difference between back alley fighting and the ring.

"But Sergeant, this time, get rid of your chaw first. You're going to have to take me without blinding me."

A thin smile escaped him, partly as he remembered playing the trick and partly a grudging respect for a smaller man standing up to a larger.

As he turned his head away to spit, Stuyvesant became a blur. He felt the lieutenant's fist drive into his solar plexus, and he bent over double. His mouthful of tobacco juice went spraying out. After taking two more quick punches, Strosahl found himself sitting on his ass.

He looked up rubbing his jaw, eyeing the lieutenant as he caught his breath. The younger man had retreated a couple of steps and was bouncing on his feet and loosening up his shoulders, affecting a relaxed air while his blue eyes blazed away with a fierce intensity.

Okay, so the kid could hit. That still didn't mean he knew how to street fight. Behind the lieutenant's constantly shifting figure was a wall. Strosahl figured he could use that to his own advantage. He got to one knee and pushed himself slowly upright, slow enough to throw his opponent off guard. He rushed him, head tucked down, arms outstretched. He grabbed Stuyvesant in a bear hug, drove him back, and slammed him into the wall.

Not giving the kid time to recover, Strosahl backed up a step and threw a quick punch to the ribs, putting his whole shoulder behind it. But the lieutenant was already moving, and his fist barely grazed the lieutenant's side before his knuckles scraped the wall.

He grunted as he reflexively jerked his fist back, protectively rubbing the bruised knuckles. The lieutenant had circled to his left. Strosahl turned so he'd be facing him – and felt a fist crash into his cheek.

The kid was fast, Strosahl had to give him that. And he was still circling. Strosahl turned again, but now he had to find the lieutenant through vision that was becoming blurred. The next punch was to his ribs, then one to his cheek.

"Ahhgh!" he shouted and charged Stuyvesant, pushing him back two, then three yards before the lieutenant again slipped away to his left and out of his grasp.

Okay, so the kid moved too fast to be pinned. As he turned to face Stuyvesant again, he breathed loud enough to be heard and dropped his arms a bit as though he was already tiring. And it worked. The lieutenant moved in fast, but not fast enough.

Strosahl let loose with a combination, two jarring jabs to the jaw and a right hook that should have sent his opponent reeling backwards. But instead of the punch connecting, he was swinging at air as Stuyvesant ducked beneath his fist and came in close.

The sergeant took two sledgehammer blows to his ribs and then a third punch, an uppercut that sat him back down on his ass.

He shook his head trying to clear it. His vision was swimming. He tried to push himself to his feet, but his legs went all wobbly. The lieutenant, who was bouncing around on the balls of his feet, showed no signs of fatigue. It wasn't just that the kid was fast. He packed one hell of a punch.

Strosahl raised a hand, waving it weakly to signal defeat. "They teach you," he gasped, "to fight like that at Harvard?"

"Yale, Sergeant. I was captain of the boxing team at Yale. And we stomped Harvard's ass. Have the men assemble in the courtyard at fourteen hundred. I want to talk to them."

"Yessir," he said, continuing rubbing his cheek.

Lt. Donna Campbell stripped off her bloody gloves, along with the apron covering her dungarees, and left the operating room. She was exhausted from being on her feet while assisting at surgery for ten straight hours. Although the city of Taejon stank of fish and shit, the air outdoors was still better than that of an operating room that reeked of the smell of seared flesh. She needed to clear her mind of the sights from the night. A young soldier missing half his jaw, another with an arm hanging by strings of flesh, and still another trying to hold his guts in.

She dragged herself through the corridor. Wounded soldiers lay on cots against the walls. They moaned and cried out despite injections of morphine. Pinned on the walls above them were pictures painted by the kids who had recently attended school here. The Army had commandeered a schoolhouse and converted it into a surgical hospital. Outside, medics unloaded ambulances packed tight with the wounded from battle lines fifty miles away.

After so long on her feet, she had sore muscles all over her body. She stretched and shrugged and tried to get above the suffering by lifting her eyes and scanning the horizon. To the north stood a line of hills. A bulwark, she'd been told, against the advance of the North Korean troops. But nothing she'd experienced so far in Korea had convinced her she should believe what she'd been told.

The voice came from off to her left. "What a surprise. You're the last person I ever expected to see here."

She knew she'd heard that voice before but couldn't place it. Turning, she saw a smiling Jonas Stuyvesant making his way toward her. Walking with him was a soldier whose eyes were covered with gauze. He was gripping Stuyvesant's arm, as the two worked their way across the uneven ground.

She heard a rustle behind her as a haggard looking medic detached himself from the medical crews bustling about. He moved past her. "I'll take him from here, Lieutenant."

Stuyvesant smiled and nodded, relinquishing his charge. "Thanks, Sergeant."

She hadn't thought much about him since that night in the officers' club, but it all came back to her in a rush. His gracefulness on the dance floor, the solidity he projected, and the safety she'd felt in his presence. Maybe it wasn't the hills to the north that would be the bulwark that would protect her. Maybe it was soldiers like this one.

When he turned back to her, she smiled for the first time in days.

"You know," he said, "that night when we met in Kokura, I did go looking for you after I finished talking to the general."

"That was sweet of you. But… I just needed to be alone."

"Understandable." He glanced around. His eyes twinkled. "So how do you like your new quarters?"

She looked over her shoulder, up at the second floor of the schoolhouse. A dozen nurses were quartered in one small room, sleeping in shifts on cots, sharing a couple of hand mirrors and taking sponge baths.

She looked back. "They're a little short on amenities."

Suddenly she was self-conscious. Her dungarees were not exactly the most feminine of apparel. She brushed a strand of hair away from her forehead, back over her ear. He looked so handsome. Feeling the telltale shiver race up her spine, she blushed.

"Yes," he said, "this wouldn't be my first choice for a summer vacation. But you have to admit, whatever else is lacking, the cuisine makes up for it." He screwed up his face.

She laughed. "Yes, clearly prepared by chefs from the best part of town. You just have to be careful to take your malaria pills with the dessert."

"Ah yes, the malaria pills." His smile disappeared. "I need to check on that when I get back to my unit. Make sure all the men have taken theirs."

Hearing the shift in his tone, she mentally kicked herself for mentioning the pills. The air of lightness had evaporated, along with the memories of dancing together. The bantering, in an almost flirtatious spirit, was gone.

"The man you brought in, one of yours?"

He nodded. "Flash burns at Osan. We were afraid he was blinded for life. But it looks like he'll be okay. As the saying goes, 'He'll live to fight another day.'"

She felt a tightening in her stomach and realized it was because she was seeing this man back in battle. Officers were hardly exempt from getting wounded or killed. But he obviously wasn't thinking about that. He was focused on his men. But she was focused on him.

Here he was in the prime of his life, a fit sexy male about to go back into a meat grinder.

She pushed those thoughts from her mind. "Will he have to fight another day?"

He pressed his lips together in a thin line for a moment, then said, "There're rumors that we're going to be pulled back to Japan. Because we've taken so many losses. But no, those are just rumors. We're going back on the line any day now. And it's my job to get my men ready."

"How are you going to do that?"

"I don't know. I need to boost their morale, but I'm still trying to figure out what I can say to them."

"Okay… What would *you* want to hear?"

"Me? I always go back to history for my lessons. Those times when a few men held the line and made the difference. But that's me. My men, though, most of them are boys, most of whom barely finished high school."

"Could be you're selling them short."

"How?"

"I grew up in the South listening to folks talking history. Mostly about the war between the states. Not many of them were educated, but their history meant a lot to them."

She looked into his eyes to see how he was taking this. When he cocked his head and turned his face away from her, she became afraid she'd crossed the line. A nurse telling a fighting man how to talk to his troops. She held her breath and waited.

"…Maybe you've got something there. Let me think about it."

She let out her breath and smiled – and was delighted when he grinned back.

The men sat in a semi-circle in a courtyard. Their weapons rested on their laps or lay next to them, close at hand. Jonas faced them, with Sgt. Strosahl standing a little behind him. The sergeant had bandages on the knuckles of his right hand and stood somewhat stiffly, as though his ribs hurt. A bruise was starting to show on his cheek.

"Light 'em," Jonas said. He looked them over as they fired up their cigarettes. The place to start, he decided, was just to say what everyone knew only too well. "We got our asses kicked at Osan."

That got a lot of nods and murmurs of "You got that right." The mood was somber.

"It's easy to forget that this isn't the first time we Americans have taken a beating. Most of you remember the end of World War II when we were going from victory to victory. It's easy to forget we weren't prepared for that war. The Japs surprised us at Pearl Harbor and took out most of our fleet. And then they overran Wake Island and the Philippines. In our first battles in North Africa, German Panzers blasted our tanks away because ours were tin cans.

"This wasn't anything new either. We Americans have a long history of getting our asses kicked in the first round or two of a fight." He looked around at the upraised faces. He'd been working out what he wanted to say. He'd thought of examples from the first year or so of the Civil War, when the North lost so many battles, but a lot of his boys were from the South, and, as he was coming to understand, for them the Civil War wasn't really over yet, so he skipped those references.

"Losing the first round goes all the way back to George Washington and the Continental Army. After he took command of the troops in New York, the British beat him in the battle for Brooklyn Heights. Washington barely managed to escape across the East River in fishing boats to Manhattan under the cover of night and fog. After that he lost every battle in a retreat up the island of Manhattan and, again barely escaped his army being demolished by having them ferried across the Hudson into New Jersey. He retreated all the way down New Jersey until he had to cross over into Pennsylvania."

One private shouted out, "But then he beat the Hessians at Trenton."

Jonas nodded. "Very good, Yergin. You're from New Jersey, aren't you?"

"Yessir. From Trenton. My ole man used to take me as a kid to see the spot where Washington crossed the Delaware."

"So you know. It was Christmas night. Figuring the enemy would be drinking it up, he crossed back over from Valley Forge into New Jersey and caught the Hessians sleeping off hangovers. But do you know what Washington had to do before that?"

Jonas looked slowly around the semi-circle. "He had to turn a *rag-tag, undisciplined, untrained, motley crew...*," he said, giving them a piercing stare that made it clear he was now talking about them, "...into *real* soldiers. And that's what I'm going to do with you men. Starting as of this minute.

"Sgt. Strosahl and I are going to drill you and run you through infantry tactics every damn minute we've got until we go back onto the line. Because we are going back." He heard scattered groans from the group. "And we are going to fight. But this time you will act as a combat unit, as a team.

"You're going to practice squad maneuvers to attack an entrenched enemy. You're going to learn how to support each other and communicate with me when you're dug in, and how to set up listening posts in front of our line, and how to do reconnaissance patrols."

Cpl. Holzer called out, "And if we have to retreat?" A Holzer without bandages on his eyes.

In the sternest tone he could manage, Jonas said, "This platoon does not retreat, Corporal." Then he smiled. "We might sometimes make tactical withdrawals..."

"You mean, advance to the rear, sir?" A laugh went up from the group.

"Exactly. If we have to advance to the rear, we're going to do it the military way. One squad or platoon stays on the line and provides cover while the other units withdraw to a predetermined defensive position. Then the unit on the line withdraws to the new perimeter.

"You're going to practice these maneuvers over and over. And you are going to start paying attention to what the enemy's tactics and weaknesses are. We know now that the North Koreans start with a frontal assault, and when that fails, they try to envelope their enemy. They are good at that, but we saw one major weakness at Osan."

He paused. His troops looked at him blank-faced. "Remember when we first hit the convoy with a mortar barrage? They were totally disorganized until the officers took control. They don't have sergeants and corporals, like we do, who know how to lead. So I want those of you who are sharpshooters to look for the officers. Can you do that, shoot officers?"

The men grinned back at Jonas. He said, "And I mean theirs, not ours." He heard a few "Aw shucks" mixed in with the laughter.

"Sgt. Strosahl," he barked.

"Sir?"

"Take charge of the platoon."

"Yes sir." Strosahl stepped up. "Cigarettes out. On your feet. Fall-in at attention."

As the men climbed to their feet, Strosahl cocked his head, looking at him with a quizzical expression. To Jonas it was as though the sergeant was seeing him in a new light. And when the sergeant then nodded, it had the feel of a grudging acknowledgment.

Jonas, stone-faced, gave him an almost imperceptible nod back, pivoted away and smiled to himself.

8

TWO DAYS LATER, Jonas sat in a classroom in the yellow school-house with twenty other dungaree-clad officers. Morning light filtered into the room through dirty windows. The officers sat and talked in low tones while blue flies maneuvered around the grey streams of their cigarette smoke. Here and there was a new face. New officers who'd arrived along with the much-needed replacements, two hundred of them.

Maj. Martin, the battalion's executive officer, stood at the front of the room, keeping an eye on the back door. Suddenly he stood much straighter and barked, "Attention."

The officers sprang out of their chairs, quickly crushing their cigarettes under foot, as Lt. Col. Brad Smith walked up the middle of the room.

He turned to face them. "As you were."

Chairs scraped the floor as the men took their seats again.

The colonel stood ramrod straight in front of a map pinned to the wall. Jonas searched the colonel's features for signs of the struggles that must have raged within him after the defeat at Osan. He saw no such signs. Hints of tiredness, yes, but mainly he saw the steady glint of determination in the man's eyes.

The colonel picked up a pointer and held it in both hands, waist high, parallel to the floor. "Gentlemen, tonight we are moving back north and joining up with our own Able and Dog Companies at a town called Chochiwon. The regiment's 3rd Battalion is already dug in there ahead of us. This is the situation on the ground."

He turned to the map and pointed to a black circle. "This is the city of Chonan." He traced a line on the map. "South of Chonan the Seoul-Pusan Highway splits, one road going straight south to Kongju, while the other runs east and south to Chochiwon 30 miles north of us." The colonel faced his men. "Gen. Dean has given the 34th Regiment the job of holding Kongju, while we are to defend Chochiwon."

The colonel paused and looked over the room. Jonas saw the man's eyes narrow. His own stomach tightened in apprehension.

"This morning, a few miles north of Chochiwon, our Able and Dog Companies fought a three-hour battle with advance elements of the Communists.... Able Company was... overrun."

Jonas' breath caught in his throat, and he heard a muffled collective gasp go up in the room. Chairs, suddenly shifting, scraped the floor.

The picture flashed through his mind, his fellow American soldiers in their foxholes as the North Koreans swarmed over them. He turned to see how the others were taking the news, his gaze darting around the room. All the officers sat grim-faced. Many clenched their jaws and leaned forward.

"Dog Company... and those of Able who managed to get out... fell back to Chochiwon. There, Col. Stephens ordered his 3rd Battalion to counterattack. They did. And retook those positions." The colonel's face took on an even harder cast. "They found six of our men with their hands bound behind them, in the mud, with bullet holes in the back of their heads."

Jonas clenched his fists and could barely keep in his chair as the officers around him growled obscenities.

"Thirty more men are missing, presumably captured or dead. By last count, we've got an additional twenty-seven wounded."

The colonel paused until the room became stone cold quiet. "Gentlemen, the larger picture is this." He tapped the map with his pointer. "ROK forces, the South Koreans, are defending the western coast of the peninsula. Other ROK forces are making a stand in the mountains on our right flank and on the east coast. We in the 24th Division have the job of holding the central corridor of South Korea.

"Our immediate assignment is to delay the enemy at Chochiwon," he said, each word crisp and clipped. "The town is strategically important because the railroad terminal is the primary re-supply point for the ROK forces. After that there is the Kum River. Taejon is just ten miles south of the Kum. North of Taejon, they will have captured half of the country; but if we have to retreat from Taejon, there are no geographical obstacles to stop the Communists until they reach Taegu and the Naktong River. If we are pushed back that far, we will have lost *ninety percent of the country*."

He paused. It was as though no one in the room was even breathing.

"We must delay the enemy at Chochiwon and stop their advance at the Kum." He tapped his left palm with the pointer, one beat per syllable as he said, "*We cannot let the Communists take Taejon*."

He turned, considered the map for a moment. "You've all studied strategy." He turned back. "The Communists are driving blitzkrieg-fashion down the peninsula. At some point, their momentum slows. Their supply lines become overstretched and vulnerable. Our job is to stop their drive, counterattack and drive them back north." His eyes, hard and focused, swept the room slowly, methodically.

"Any questions?" A hand went up. He nodded.

A platoon leader from Baker Company said, "What about their tanks? Do we get any air cover this time? Or at least bazookas that can stop them?"

Col. Smith gave a curt nod, acknowledging the question. "All our aircraft, except for some scout planes, are stationed in Japan, too far away to know when there is going to be a battle on the ground in time to get to us. We don't have the airfields here in Korea that support fighters or bombers – although the engineers are working on that. So for now, all of our aircraft are assigned to attacking the Communists' supply lines to the north."

Girard raised his hand. "Colonel, what about radios? At Osan they didn't work. We lost contact with our artillery."

Smith nodded. "We just got replacements, and communications tells me they work. This time we will have artillery." He looked around the room. "Any more questions." He waited. "If not, assemble your men. They get a hot meal tonight; tomorrow it's C-rations."

Strosahl stood next to the lieutenant atop the embankment, the thick putrid air teasing his nostrils. All the members of the platoon were alert in their foxholes left and right of them. The whole battalion was dug in on the embankment, stretched out along a mile-and-a-half line.

Here and there he heard the clink of bullets against bullets as a machine gun crew nervously readjusted a belt of ammo, along with the steady murmur of voices from men sharing foxholes. Men wondering if they would get out of those holes alive.

The lieutenant handed the field glasses back to him. "I don't see anything," Stuyvesant said. "The firing's died down considerably. Do you think 3rd Battalion's holding?"

Strosahl took the glasses and spat a stream of tobacco juice over the lip of the embankment. In Korea, spitting was never off-limits. That was the one thing he liked about the country.

"Me, I think they got overrun." He spat again, this time just a small glob of brown-stained saliva. "Poor bastards."

The sun, low above the eastern horizon, was a brilliant orange-red. Overhead to the north, buzzards circled.

The sergeant checked the lieutenant's response from the corner of his eye. He saw the man's jaw muscles tighten. Nothing more.

From the north, occasional bursts of automatic fire punctuated the silence. Shoulder to shoulder they stared across the empty brown fields dotted by rice paddies, those large irregular rectangles of yellow-green water. A mile to the north stood a line of spindly beech trees. All eyes were on that line of trees.

Everyone waited.

And waited.

Movement.

A man broke through the tree line, a G.I. staggering forward, holding his side. Then a few more lone soldiers. Followed by groups of three, or five, or ten. Men in baggy green dungarees, mostly without rifles, canteens or helmets. They limped or ran down the road, or struggled through the mud of the rice paddies that sucked at their boots, many of them supporting fellow G.I.s.

The men of the 3rd battalion.

Faces along the line looked up out of their foxholes, looking to their lieutenant and sergeant, wanting the signal to climb out of their holes to run and help.

"Hold your positions," Stuyvesant shouted.

Good, thought Strosahl, as he turned right and left making sure the men checked their impulses and obeyed the order. Up and down the line, the other officers responded with the same caution, making sure their men did not charge out recklessly and get caught in the open. This could be a trap.

They watched the remnants of the 3rd Battalion struggle forward. There was no sign of pursuit. Strosahl looked to the lieutenant.

"Second squad, hold your position," the lieutenant shouted. "Machine gun teams, stay put. First and third squads, go help." He waved them forward.

"You heard the lieutenant, move it," Strosahl shouted. "Get out and get back. Make it quick."

With a tightly controlled sense of satisfaction, Strosahl watched as nineteen men took off on the double. Even the replacements were performing professionally. So far. The real test would come when the bullets started flying, which wouldn't be long.

The first men to reach the survivors pulled out their canteens, offering water to men who drank in long gulps, and then giving them a shoulder for support.

Behind him Strosahl heard the ambulances rushing up from the rear and parking behind the embankment as the medics prepared to receive casualties.

The lieutenant said, "Get our line reorganized as quickly as possible. I'm going to find out what I can."

"Yessir."

Since the men were bringing the wounded in by the road to get them more easily to the rear, he followed the lieutenant down. As his men handed over the wounded to the medical teams, he grabbed them and sent them back up to their foxholes.

The men were shook. And not just the new ones. Those who'd been at Osan were reliving that rout. Up and down the line the men kept casting worried eyes back on the wounded.

"Eyes front," he shouted. "Watch for gooks. You want to get caught jerking off? The enemy is in front of you, not back there."

He turned to see Col. Smith arriving and jumping out of a jeep. The colonel moved at a brisk pace, weaving in and out of the clusters of men, stooping to check on the wounded and pulling 3rd battalion officers aside to fire questions at them. Stuyvesant and the other officers of the 1st battalion followed closely behind, leaning in to glean whatever intelligence there was to be had.

Finally the lieutenant, his face with a grimmer set now, climbed back up the embankment and joined Strosahl.

He dropped down to one knee. The sergeant followed, moving his head in close. Stuyvesant spoke in hushed tones that would not carry as far as the next hole.

"As best I'm able to get the story, 3rd Battalion got hit around midnight. Artillery knocked out their command post and most of their senior officers. The North Koreans moved quickly to envelop both their flanks and set up a roadblock behind them to keep them from being reinforced."

The lieutenant looked away, his jaw muscles tightening. Strosahl waited, giving him time.

"Six hundred men in that battalion.... So far maybe two hundred and fifty got out.... Eight officers and a hundred and forty or so men are fit to fight. Col. Smith is reinforcing our line with them."

"We can use them," he said. And waited some more.

The lieutenant looked northward. "We'll probably get hit this afternoon." He looked up at the sun. Sweat trickled down his face. "A lot of the men gave their water to those coming in. Get a man to bring up a water can and make sure every man has a full canteen."

"Yessir."

"We're supposed to hold as long as we can, delay them, and withdraw."

Engage but don't let the enemy pin you, Strosahl thought. It's what you had to do when faced with a superior force.

"I'll see to the water, Lieu."

Stuyvesant nodded and stared northward, off toward the tree line – and then up at the sky. Strosahl followed his gaze and saw the buzzards still circling.

The line waited the whole long hot afternoon. Here and there Strosahl heard the steady murmur of voices from men sharing fox-holes. Grey cigarette smoke floated over the line.

The lieutenant said little. Mainly he propped his elbows on the edge of their hole and peered through the field glasses at the distant tree line. His wedding ring glistened in the sunlight.

"Your wife's back in the States, isn't she, Lieu?"

"New York."

"You find any time to write since we landed in this hole?"

Stuyvesant let out a little sigh but did not lower the glasses. "A quick few lines, enough to let the family know I'm alive. Hardly had time to catch any sleep let alone write." He lowered the glasses and turned his head. "You had time to get a letter off?"

Mika, his girlfriend, didn't read English. "No, I've got no one to write to."

Stuyvesant raised his brows. "No family at all?"

"…No." He looked away. "Time I go check the line. Make sure no one's grabbing an afternoon snooze."

Stuyvesant regarded him for a moment. "Right." He turned his attention back north.

Strosahl slipped over the back of the embankment and walked up and down the line, calling to each squad.

By dusk the attack still had not come. The field phone buzzed. The lieutenant answered, listened and replaced the receiver.

"The colonel says to go ahead and eat."

Strosahl nodded and slipped down behind the wall, stopping at each hole. "Chow time. Break out the C-rats. One man eats while the other stays on watch."

At midnight the attack still hadn't come. The colonel ordered the companies to send out listening posts. Turco, who'd had plenty of experience of this kind in WWII, went forward with another man and a radio. The posts reported in every half-hour. They were hearing nothing.

A couple of hours before dawn, fog rolled in, enveloping everything. Strosahl couldn't see more than three feet in any direction. The damp air muffled all sound.

The lieutenant's voice was shot through with coiled tension. "Perfect weather for tanks. They'd roll up on us before we even heard them coming."

"Turco's out there. Nothing will get by him."

A half-hour before dawn, the listening posts pulled back to the line. The sun came up and burned off the fog. They stared across the yellow-green rice paddies toward the line of beech trees a mile north.

Other officers from the battalion's four line companies also stood, peering at the long stand of grey timber. Everyone waited.

Strosahl saw them first. "We've got company."

More than thirty North Koreans slipped through the tree line, fanning out on both sides of the road in two wide V-formations.

The field phone buzzed. The lieutenant grabbed it up. "…Yessir, holding fire." He turned his head. "Pass the word. Hold your fire."

Strosahl called out to the squads left and right, "Hold your fire. Pass it on."

The order rippled down the line, growing fainter as it traveled.

The lieutenant peered through the field glasses with an intensity that to Strosahl seemed almost as if he were reaching out to grab the intruders by their throats.

"…They've spotted us."

A whistle blew to the left of the road and another to the right. The North Korean troops broke into six four-man teams and fanned out farther left and right.

Field glasses clapped to his eyes, the lieutenant rolled his shoulders a couple of times, loosening up the muscles. "Most of them are working their way forward. There're four hanging back. Looks like two officers, each with a radio man." He turned and handed the field glasses to Strosahl. "It's a probe."

Strosahl took them. "Yeah. Question is, how's the old man going to play this?"

The field phone snarled. Stuyvesant snatched it to his ear. "Yessir." Holding the headset at the ready, he said, a quizzical note in his voice, "Riflemen only, get ready. No automatic weapons."

Strosahl chuckled and relayed the order. "All squads, riflemen only! Standby to fire! All B.A.R.s and machine guns, hold your fire! Repeat: All B.A.R.s and machine guns, hold your fire!"

The enemy, hunching in their yellow-brown uniforms as they slogged through the rice paddies, advanced to within two hundred yards. One hundred fifty. One hundred.

Strosahl could hear the crackle in the headset when the order came.

"Fire!" The lieutenant's voice, sharp and clear, sliced through the air.

Up and down the line it sounded like a string of firecrackers going off as the platoon's riflemen fired.

Across the field the enemy soldiers dropped down into the muck of the rice paddies. Here and there one lifted a burp gun and fired back – a useless gesture given the limited range of the weapon.

Only a few of them got hit. A whistle blew, then another, and they began to withdraw, carrying and dragging off four wounded.

Stuyvesant still held the receiver to his ear. "Cease fire! Cease fire!" He waved to his troops in both directions, and the firing sputtered out.

Strosahl laughed. When Stuyvesant turned to him looking puzzled, he said, "That scouting party's going to report they met with weak resistance."

"Okay. I see. Make them think we've got practically no firepower. Not bad."

It was another half-hour before they spotted about six hundred infantry breaking through the tree line. They moved at the double, a formidable looking force.

At the same time, the first tank rolled into view, kicking up a cloud of chalky dust. The low-slung green monster clanked forward along the road. Another and another rolled on behind, the line of tanks barely visible in the dust cloud. The barrel of the lead tank belched fire, and a shell whistled over the embankment. Machine guns on each side of the turret erupted.

They ducked down in their foxhole as the lieutenant let out, "Fuck! Just like Osan."

American mortars arced into the sky and dropped among the advancing troops. Moments later artillery shells roared overhead, the first dropping into the rice paddies alongside the road.

Then a direct hit, with a burst of red flame and the sound of wrenching metal. The lead T-34 lurched to a halt, a smoldering heap of steel.

Jonas let out a whoop.

The rest of the column of tanks ground to a halt. The smoking heap of metal blocked those following from advancing. They couldn't go around the lead tank because they would sink into the muck of the rice paddies. They couldn't back up as more and more of the column pulled up behind and ground to a halt, unable to move forward or backward.

Yes, Jonas grinned, this was how a battle should go.

For the next hour the North Korean commanders forced wave after wave of their troops into a withering line of fire.

The enemy bugles sounded retreat. The firing sputtered out.

Jonas climbed atop the embankment and watched as the Communists withdrew, carrying off as many of their dead and wounded as they could. He took some grim satisfaction in the toll the 1/21 had inflicted on them.

Then came the cries. "Medic! We need a medic!"

He ran up and down the line. There weren't many casualties, but he made sure the wounded were attended to. And that his men got the ammo and water they needed.

Another enemy artillery barrage erupted.

He dropped down into his foxhole across from Strosahl. After fifteen minutes, sitting knee to knee with the sergeant, he heard the pop of an enemy signal flare and looked up to see it bloom green in the sky. He heard the shrill sound of whistles and saw, in his mind's eye, the squads of men, red stars affixed to their caps, charge forward.

To Jonas' ear, the whistling of the first American artillery shells sounded like the opening notes of a symphony. Kettledrums made the ground quake as the now familiar grey-white clouds floated above the battlefield, suffusing the air with the acrid scent of burnt cordite.

The enemy barrage lifted, and the American infantry popped

up from their holes. The sound of gun fire drowned everything else out. Jonas watched the enemy intently, amazed once again that wave after wave of men would rush forward into the hot fusillade. And did so again and again as their officers pushed them forward. And when they fell, wounded or dead, replacements were rushed forward to fill in the gaps in the lines. A never-ending stream of replacements.

During the next lull in the battle, Jonas again walked the line, behind the embankment, checking on his men. Strosahl followed. Halfway down he shouted up to one of the foxholes, "How're you guys doing?"

Pvt. Boyd poked his helmeted head over the rim of his hole. The peach fuzz over his lip showed through the dirt on his face. His smile was taut as he said, almost in wonderment, "Just like a turkey shoot. Want to join us, Lieu?"

"Naw, I wouldn't want to deprive you of your fun."

Boyd grinned. "Plenty to go around."

An explosion shook the ground. He heard a scream from above. Damasio, arms flailing, leaped down between them. The whole front of his body was blackened. He ran two steps and collapsed.

Jonas called "Medic!" but he could see it was useless.

He pivoted back to the embankment. "Boyd!"

There was no answer. He sucked in a lungful of air, screamed in rage, and scrambled up. Strosahl was shouting something, but it was just background noise that made no sense. Where were those fuckers who'd killed two of his men?

A hundred and fifty yards to his front, he saw them. It had to be them. A four-man team with a recoilless rifle. He looked at the carbine in his hand, and, instantly calculating that it wasn't accurate enough at that range, threw it away and grabbed up Damasio's M1. He dropped flat on the ground next to Boyd's foxhole. He sensed rather than saw Boyd's headless torso in the hole next to him, but he blocked that out. He pressed the stock of the rifle to his cheek. Quickly he zeroed in on the team and picked off the first two.

The other two men on the recoilless rifle high-tailed it. A North Korean officer shot one of the fleeing deserters with his pistol. The other kept running.

Blood pumping and jaws clenched tight, Jonas kept shooting. He winged the officer. The man went down clutching his shoulder.

"Goddamn it, Lieu," Strosahl shouted from behind, "you ain't a fucking rifleman. You're supposed to be directing fire." He felt Strosahl grabbing his ankles and dragging him down the back of the ridge to level ground. Jonas slid down the wall and hit the ground belly first. He scrambled to his feet. He was red-faced furious.

"Sergeant, don't you ever—"

An artillery shell exploded above, atop the embankment, right where he'd been lying. The blast knocked them both to the ground.

Jonas got up on hands and knees, rocked up and sat back on his rear. Stunned, he stared around vacantly. Strosahl stared back.

"Lieu?"

Jonas shook his head, and then a shudder went through his body. He looked up at the crater, still smoking. Two G.I.s trudged up, dropped a litter and grabbed hold of Damasio.

"Sergeant…"

"Yes?"

"Nothing." He clamped his mouth shut, stood up and walked away without looking back.

Just after noon, a runner came with the word that the North Koreans were maneuvering to set up a roadblock behind their lines. The battalion was to prepare to withdraw. B and C Companies were to stay on line to provide screening.

"Okay," Jonas shouted, "just like we practiced. Everyone hold your positions until the word comes down to pull out."

There was no panic among the troops. The withdrawal was orderly. In the rear, trucks were waiting. Jonas checked all his men as they climbed aboard and then got into the cab of the lead truck.

Less than an hour later, they crossed a bridge near a town called

Taepyong-ni to the south bank of the Kum River. Engineers were placing charges on the bridges, and later Jonas heard them blow, one after the other.

The 21st Regiment dug in above the banks of the twisting Kum River. Jonas surveyed the tactical situation. Although there was too much river front to cover, the North Koreans would have to cross several hundred feet of water to reach the American line. It would be slow going, and they would make good targets.

He and his men were exhausted. So when the 19th Infantry Regiment, with their clean uniforms and shaven faces, came up from the rear and relieved the 21st, he and all the men on the line gladly surrendered their foxholes. The 21st climbed back into trucks which rolled down through and past Taejon, until they were fifteen miles southeast of the city. The regiment was put into reserve to rest and be resupplied.

9

A LITTLE AFTER DAWN, Capt. Chen, formerly Lt. Chen, rested comfortably atop a knoll five hundred yards from the Kum River, telescope in hand and field telephone by his side. Capt. Hyon had been killed three days earlier and Chen promoted and given his company, a company preparing to cross the river.

The rain had finally stopped. There were few clouds in the sky; and the sun, as it rose, was a brilliant orange-red ball. Flocks of birds swirled overhead in intricate patterns, while those perched in trees filled the air with song. The yellow Kum River, over three hundred yards wide at this point, meandered slowly west and south.

At six a.m. Chen's peace was shattered by the screams of the first artillery shells raining down on the American positions on the far bank. The birds fled the sky and fell silent. Tank cannons and mortar tubes thumped out additional fusillades in a barrage scheduled to last four hours.

There was no return fire from the Americans curled up in the bottom of their foxholes. Chen didn't envy them. His patrols had pinpointed their defenses the night before, while turning back the Americans' own attempts to reconnoiter, leaving them blind, with less than five hundred men on line to cover over ten miles of river-front. Behind Chen was the North Korean 4th Division, which while it was greatly reduced from its original eleven thousand men, could still field twenty tanks, forty artillery pieces and six thousand men, a thousand of whom lay concealed, waiting to cross.

Chen looked to the rear, past his men, to the rocky terrain that rose up behind their line. The rugged hills were dotted with scrub brush and crisscrossed by ridges and ravines. On the peak of one hill, he noticed some movement, movement where there should be none. With his naked eye he could almost make out several small bodies, hunched small, watching. He raised his telescope. Buzzards. Squat, bald-headed carrion.

At eight a.m. the signal flares popped overhead and whistles sounded. A thousand yards downstream of the American lines, the first assault teams, carrying boats, ran for the river. Boatmen began ferrying troops. A half-hour later, an American spotter plane appeared overhead, and Chen waited anxiously for the sound of the American artillery. It didn't come. A North Korean YAK arrived and drove off the American plane.

Chen rose up and led his men at a run down the long sloping ground to the water's edge. Ominously, over the thud of feet and clanking of equipment, both muffled by the ongoing barrage, he felt, more than heard, the faint sound of motors growling far off in the sky, setting up a disturbing hum in his body. His men climbed into their boats as the next company behind him began its run. The boatmen shoved off and paddled against the slow insistent current. The drone of aircraft engines grew louder, and the paddlers heaved against the current, bending into their work. Then the black jets broke into view in the blue sky above.

One, two, three, four American fighters came in on a strafing run. The boatmen paddled harder while Chen's troops huddled low in the boats. The fighters sprayed the churning convoy with .50 caliber bullets, ripping to shreds large chunks of wood and pieces of flesh, sending whole bodies and parts careening into the river until its waters ran red and bodies bobbed everywhere in the lazy current.

Men jumped from boats and pushed through the breast high water, the silt on the bottom sucking at their boots, until they managed to crawl up the bank and scramble for cover. A fighter zoomed down, four machine guns rattling, spitting fire as it sliced everything in its path, cutting Chen's boat in half. Chen found himself swimming, gulping river water and then climbing out to fall sprawled out on the bank, but then having to struggle to his feet and stumble up the long sloping bank to get clear of the action.

Turning back, he saw that the company following his had been hit harder. Some of those last in the boats had been able to jump out and wade back, but over a hundred men had been caught in the open. Surviving boatmen were frantically trying to drag their boats up onto shore, but the enemy planes were making more strafing runs, going after them.

In minutes, there were no men alive anywhere on the river or visible on its banks. Then the fighters went after the tanks and artillery. The North Korean troops hunkered down and waited it out. Chen had been through this once before at the Han River just south of Seoul. That strafing had been even more devastating; but because the American planes were based in Japan, they quickly ran low on fuel, having to return to base.

Chen found a hideaway beneath a ledge of gravel-like rock, crumbly, but secure for the moment. It shielded him from the view of the aircraft. He fumbled in his pockets for his cigarette makings, but they were soaked. He tossed them away disgustedly. He'd been able to keep his tobacco dry through three weeks of drenching rain, but the river had finally managed to do what the rain hadn't.

When the skies were clear again, the North Korean resumed shelling the American lines. And since no more boats were available, the Communist troops still on the other side began wading across.

Chen collected his men, a head count showing he'd lost maybe a third. That would make his mission harder, but not impossible. Most of the troops who had already crossed were circling to attack the Americans from behind. Another company had been assigned to find and set up roadblocks behind the American line to prevent their withdrawal. Chen's mission, however, was to capture an enemy position two-and-a-half miles inland.

He pushed his force of a little over ninety men rapidly along secondary trails. In less than an hour, his lead squad reported sighting an American machine gun emplacement, an outpost on the perimeter protecting an artillery battery.

Pvt. Park apologized. "I think they spotted us."

Chen nodded. "Can I get a look at them?"

"Yes, Comrade." The soldier led Chen off the path into the dense thicket a hundred yards forward. The two squirmed on their bellies until they were peeking out from under scrub brush, the emplacement in clear view.

Curious, thought Chen. Four soldiers stood around a machine gun looking toward the path where they had first spotted Chen's men. They weren't squatting protectively down behind their sandbags, but were standing there making easy targets of themselves, talking animatedly with one another, maybe even arguing. Behind the machine gun crew were a handful of riflemen, cradling their rifles in the crooks of their arms, three of them with cigarettes dangling from their mouths. Could it be these men were not sure whether Chen's men were the enemy or not? Maybe they didn't know how to tell their allies, the South Koreans, from North Korean troops, how to tell friend from foe.

Chen squirmed backwards for a bit, then turned and got up and trotted back to his men, who were catching a second wind, drinking from canteens and checking weapons, all in silence but with the air of men prepared to move into action at a moment's notice.

He had his men squat in a half-circle around him as he laid out his plan. If it didn't work, and he died, the mortar teams were to fire on the emplacement and his second-in-command, Lt. Lee, was to complete the mission.

Capt. Chen walked alone out of the thicket in plain view of the American troops eighty or ninety yards away. Acting surprised to see them, he first stopped and then waved. He turned back to the thicket and gave a scooping 'come on' arm motion. A squad of men followed him out into the open, the red stars cut from their caps, those with rifles trailing their arms and those with burp guns slinging them behind. Dragging their feet, feigning exhaustion but smiling and jabbering, Chen and his men trudged across the open rocky stretch of ground, the black barrel of the enemy machine gun centered on them the whole long way. Approaching to within ten yards, Chen took off his cap and, mopping his brow on his sleeve, said in rapid Korean, "We are sure glad to see you American allies."

The blond American lieutenant, his hand on the butt of his holstered pistol, said, "What's that? Any of you guys speak English?"

Chen dropped the hand with his hat to his side and shrugged, the signal to his men, who whipped up their burp guns and rifles and fired, cutting down the Americans before they could react. Chen stood just where he was as his men rushed forward, jumping over the sandbag barrier, and bayoneting any body still moving. Without looking to his rear, he gave another arm signal, and the rest of his company broke from the dense thicket and ran to take command of the rocky ridge.

The squad turned the machine gun around so that it now faced the American position three hundred yards down the slope. They hauled and stacked the American corpses to form a semi-circle barrier in front of the machine gun, the bodies serving like sandbags to protect against return fire. Behind them the mortar team set up their tube, adjusting its angle to get the right trajectory, while the three platoons of infantry took up prone firing positions atop the ridge. Chen sat down on a stack of sandbags and pulled out fresh cigarette makings he had borrowed from Lt. Lee. He tried to roll a cigarette. His hands shook, and he spilled the tobacco. Walking right up to the machine gun had been one risk too many.

He tried to calm himself by taking slow breaths and observing the scene below. There were several large brown tents that could hold maybe twenty standing men, field operations centers, and a medical station, along with rows of smaller tents for sleeping. The camp was ringed with vehicles: jeeps, trucks, "tractors" to haul the artillery pieces, ammunition carriers, a chow truck, and another with several antennas stretching upwards: a radio truck. Ten artillery pieces, the prized howitzers, the object of this raid, were lined up near the radio truck alongside a large tent, probably the fire command center.

Clusters of American soldiers jabbered excitedly, pointing up toward his position. Other men poked their heads out of the doors of the large tents, looking to see what all the shooting was about. Here and there a lone soldier, realizing what was happening, dove into a foxhole.

As his men fired their first mortar rounds, Chen began rolling another cigarette, this time successfully. American troops ran about in disarray as machine gun and small arms fire ripped through their ranks. Some jumped into trenches, others found cover behind vehicles and returned fire, while more than a few hightailed it south.

His men lobbed mortars at the tents and radio truck, leaving the tents shredded and burning and the truck smoldering. They continued to lay down a solid field of fire while taking only sporadic fire in return. When even that died out, Chen took a whistle and blew the signal to attack. Eighty soldiers jumped to their feet and charged down the hill, burp guns firing staccato bursts.

Chen dawdled with another cigarette, slowly following his men down, preferring to drink in the scent of fresh grass and earth while he could, before reaching the rank smell of smoldering canvas, the coppery odor of fresh blood, and the stench of men who had soiled themselves.

Americans knelt on the ground, hands clasped behind their heads, their eyes bleak. His men dragged out those who were still cowering in holes. Scattered about the camp were bodies. Some lay still while others writhed and moaned. One of his men found a roll of communications wire, and his men used it to bind the prisoners' hands. Once bound, a prisoner was made to sit.

When he did his count, Chen had eighty-six prisoners sitting on the ground. His men dragged off an even larger number of corpses. They had captured over seventy vehicles and ten operational howitzers.

Chen had his men dig in and watch. Today the 4th Division had crossed the Kum. Tomorrow the 3rd Division would cross and rout another American battalion dug in farther east.

Mid-morning, while the barrage was going on upstream, a truck arrived to pick up and transport Chen and his best squad back to regimental headquarters in Konju on the Kum. As Chen entered the town, he could see a blown steel-truss bridge sitting astride the river, gaping holes in its spans, but its supports still intact. Soldiers, directed by officers from the engineering battalion, swarmed over it.

Its repair was crucial because a bridge was needed if the 4th Division's tanks and artillery were to cross the Kum for the assault on Taejon. Then there were the thousands upon thousands of tons of supplies that were needed: ammunition, food, medical supplies, repair parts for vehicles, and fuel, all of which were in short supply, all of which had to be transported down from the harbors outside Pyongyang and Seoul.

Chen found the two-story schoolhouse that served as both division and regimental headquarters. He didn't have to ask. Headquarters was always in the schoolhouse. Whatever the town or village, it was the best-built structure, the one that could accommodate a field command post.

Chen had grown up in a family where learning was valued, but even in China only the largest villages had schoolhouses, and only children of families with means could attend. Chen had been impressed that the Koreans were so invested in education, but then he learned that the schoolhouses had been built by the Japanese during their decades-long occupation of Korea. It was not that they wanted to spread universal education, but that they wanted to eradicate the Korean language and force all Korean children to learn the conqueror's tongue.

A guard directed Chen to a room where Col. Chu sat reading dispatches at a small table next to a radio operator. The operator had a hand cupped around the single earphone while he transcribed an incoming message. A major and two captains hovered near their commander, seemingly with nothing to do but wait for him to finish reading. Kerosene lamps supplemented the mid-morning light that seeped in through oiled paper panes.

An orderly took the colonel the news of Chen's arrival. Col. Chu, a portly man with a pug nose and a thin mustache of silken hair, looked up at the orderly, at first irritated at being interrupted. But seeing Chen, the colonel smiled. He set the dispatches aside and crossed the room, his aides trailing him.

"Comrade Captain, we've all heard of your stunning victory – capturing an entire American field battery." The aides milled around Chen, adding their congratulations.

Chen bowed. "A victory due entirely to the bravery of the Koreans I am honored to lead." "Your commitment to the Revolution is commendable, Comrade," said the colonel. He pursed his lips and said more slowly, "Our Gen. Lee has told me that you have experience infiltrating enemy lines."

Chen nodded while keeping his face immobile so as not to betray his surprise. Lee Kwon Mu was the commander of the 4th Division. And what was this about infiltrating enemy lines?

"Yes, Comrade Colonel. Gen. Lee once accompanied me on such an operation in China." It would, of course, be impolitic to mention that Lee was serving under him at the time.

The colonel put his arm across Chen's shoulder and walked side-by-side with him down the hall to another inevitably dimly lighted room, a room wallpapered with maps. In the center was a large table. "We did not expect to be facing the Americans."

Chen nodded. "It is surprising they were able to get troops to the front so quickly."

The colonel chuckled, "But so far the vaunted American Army has proven to be a paper tiger, easily cut to shreds." He made a scissors-like motion with his fingers.

His aides laughed in appreciation of his wit. But suddenly Chu's mood changed. He frowned, and they abruptly choked off their laughter.

Walking to the map table in the center of the room, he said, "Nevertheless, they are slowing down our advance." He drew a line with his finger from Seoul to Taejon. "Covering this ground has taken us ten days. From here to Pusan is more than one hundred and fifty miles, and Premier Kim wants us to take Pusan in the next four weeks. You see the problem?"

"If the Americans hold us here, we will not advance quickly enough to meet his deadline."

"Exactly. There is little to slow us between Taejon and Taegu, where they can make another stand behind the Naktong River. So it is in the Americans' interest to hold Taejon as long as possible, while they reinforce their defenses around Taegu." The colonel stabbed Taejon with his index finger, the finger thick and blunt. "We must defeat these imperialist forces here and do it quickly and decisively."

Chen stared at the map and nodded. "You need intelligence as to the disposition of the American forces."

"Exactly," said the colonel. Turning to the major he said, "He is just as you said he would be, Maj. Chae, quick." The other aides murmured in agreement.

"Do you have a map of the city?" Chen said.

The colonel waved his hand, and a captain scurried to take one down from the wall, revealing a blackboard, and spread it before them.

"Taejon," the colonel said, "is a market town, about a mile

square, laid out in grid fashion, its population in peacetime, perhaps a hundred and thirty thousand."

"Ummm," said Chen. "Both the railroad and highway run down through the city. The Americans will want to use engineers to blow the tunnels *here* and *here* south of Taejon. We need to secure the tunnels before they can. I'd also place a significant blocking force here at this small airport northwest of the city and blocking forces at all the major roads."

"Exactly," said the colonel, "but to do all that, we need the precise coordinates of their troop placements. Also coordinates for their batteries – we think they have four left – as well as those for their command-and-control center. We will bring an artillery barrage to bear on them like they have never experienced."

Chen examined the map more closely. In a hesitant tone he said, "Are these the only maps we have, Japanese survey maps?"

The major cleared his throat. "We believe this one to be more accurate than some we have had to rely on."

Chen nodded. He had seen several instances in which the North Koreans had shelled their own troops because they'd had to use these old survey maps. "To be truly effective, you need spotters with radios in the city."

"Could you infiltrate the city with a squad of men?"

Chen scratched the side of his throat. "The problem would be getting past American patrols."

"The major has some ideas about that," said Chu, turning to his subordinate.

It was mid-morning. Sgt. Strosahl, walking on his way to the medical station in the northwest quadrant of Taejon, heard a woman screaming behind him down the street. He turned around and saw three ROK soldiers dragging a scrawny man from a house. The woman in a brownish-orange skirt and white blouse followed them, shrieking and waving her arms. The man twisted and turned, struggling to break free. One soldier raised his rifle and struck him with the butt. The man went limp, and the other two soldiers dragged him off into a side street.

The woman wailed. The soldier who had clubbed the man turned on her. Two children clung to her skirts. He held up one hand and shouted at her. He thrust the barrel of his rifle at the house, and when she didn't retreat, moved on her threateningly. She ran back inside, her black bun of hair bobbing as she swept her children before her.

Strosahl spit out a stream of tobacco juice, and then spit out the chaw itself. All Americans had been given strict orders not to interfere with either civilian or the military police. He had no idea why the MPs were dragging this man off. Was he a resident of Taejon who was staying behind because he was a Communist sympathizer? Most of the 100,000 residents had fled, but up to 10,000 hadn't. Maybe the man was a refugee from a nearby village who had a parent too sick to walk, and he had not been able to get space for his family on a train. Maybe they were squatting in an abandoned building, and he had stolen food for them. All Strosahl knew for sure was he had orders not to interfere.

He turned back and headed for the stone bridge where the street narrowed, and a South Korean MP stood guard. From behind came the sound of a truck's motor. He stepped to the side of the road to let it pass. A line of vehicles followed. The MP, ignoring Strosahl, waved an ambulance on across the bridge, his attention fixed on the oncoming convoy of American ambulances and litter-bearing jeeps.

Ducks paddled in the stream. Down on the edge of the waters, among some rocks, an old woman knelt washing clothes. Strosahl remembered Taejon from when he was stationed in the city in 1947. Three streams flowed through the town. In those days he would've seen hundreds of women washing clothes. Children too small to be in school would be playing nearby. Now there was only this solitary old woman.

He waited until the last of the ambulances passed and made his way toward the two-story schoolhouse that had been converted into a hospital. The division's medical battalion and the M.A.S.H. unit shared the hospital facilities. Both medical units were swamped with casualties from the 19th and 34th Regiments who'd been defending the Kum River line.

In WWII there hadn't been anything like a M.A.S.H. unit, a mobile army surgical hospital. If you were wounded and needed surgery, you had to be transported a hundred miles or more to reach a hospital. He saw the large tents pitched around the hospital to receive the wounded. Those needing surgery were prepped and, when a surgical team was ready, carried into the schoolhouse.

He stopped just inside the courtyard surrounding the schoolyard. He could see Lt. Stuyvesant standing outside the front door of the hospital, a different side of him on display. He was laughing in a relaxed, carefree way as he talked to a dark-haired nurse. Smiling, she pushed back strands of loose hair and cast a look into the building. He nodded and took a step back. Strosahl couldn't hear the exchange, but he imagined Stuyvesant saying, "I've got to go."

When the lieutenant saw him, he lifted his chin in acknowledgement and headed Strosahl's way. There was spring in his step. The sergeant couldn't help comparing the grace with which Stuyvesant moved to his own heavy-footedness. He bet the lieutenant had had dancing lessons as a kid. A lot different than his own education, growing up on the farm, making his way over furrows and sidestepping cow patties.

Strosahl grinned as his platoon leader approached. "Looks like you found an old friend there, Lieu. Either that or you are one helluva fast worker."

"What? No. That's Lt. Campbell. I met her once in Kokura. Quite a surprise, seeing her here."

"I'll bet. Pretty lady."

"One tired lady. With the casualties pouring in from the Kum River, all the medical staff are working round the clock. And probably having to pack up soon and move farther back to the rear."

The two men turned back toward the bridge. A jeep carrying four litters raced by. They stared silently after it, then turned and crossed the bridge. A narrow street ran parallel to the stream. The lieutenant looked down it and then turned his head to Strosahl, pointing tentatively that way.

Stuyvesant shrugged. It was okay with him if the lieutenant wasn't ready to go back to the unit. If he wanted to see a bit of the city, it made for a nice break. They turned onto the street, their footfalls sending up little clouds of chalky dust.

Twenty feet of grass and rocks and reeds separated the street from the stream. On their left were one- and two-story buildings that had shuttered up stalls on the first floor. The buildings were brick or stucco-finished and painted brown or muddy green.

They'd walked a dozen paces when Strosahl said, "It was me and a pretty lady smiled like that, I'd be following up. I'd be figuring how to make some time with her."

"Yeah, but it's not like that. It was a surprise for both of us to run into each other again under… under these circumstances."

Strosahl grinned. "Looked to me like there was real electricity there."

The lieutenant looked straight ahead, but a hint of a smile twitched at the corners of his mouth. "No, you're reading too much into this."

"I don't know. I think you're passing up a real opportunity here."

"If I wasn't married, maybe. She is a pretty lady."

"You're a long way from New York."

"I'm still married."

Strosahl stopped in his tracks. Stuyvesant took another two steps, and then turned and faced him, cocking his head.

The sergeant said, "War can change a man's thinking about a lot of things."

A dog poked its head around a corner, spotted them and

retreated. The lieutenant opened his mouth to reply, but a voice from behind interrupted.

"Lieutenant! Lt. Stuyvesant!"

Both men turned. The runner came pounding up to them, right hand on his helmet and left carrying his rifle.

"Lakoff?" Stuyvesant said.

"The captain wants you, sir," the private said. "We're moving out."

10

AT DUSK, CHEN, with three of his men, four women and nine children, approached the first American roadblock three miles outside Taejon. Both the men and women wore the pajamas and straw hats of peasants. One of the younger women was obviously pregnant.

His men had traded their rubber-soled shoes for straw sandals and carried A-frames on their backs. The A-frames were loaded with baskets heaped high with meager household possessions. In their deeper recesses were concealed burp guns, explosives, and a radio. Leading them was a wizened Korean with a thin white beard and a cane. His hands were twisted and crippled.

Chen pretended to look after the children, trying to keep them in line. He carried a sleepy two-year-old girl on his left hip. She dozed with a thumb stuck in her mouth. With his right hand, he kept hold of her four-year-old brother who was cranky because he had to walk, who kept trying to pull his chubby hand away. Chen held tight but was ever ready to let go to get at the pistol hidden in his waistband beneath his peasant's blouse.

The old man spoke in rapid Korean to guards who clearly didn't understand a word. He beseeched them piteously to let him and this band of refugees pass.

Four Americans stood on the road, a sergeant and three soldiers cradling rifles. Chen surreptitiously eyed both them and their backup squad dug in along a ridge a dozen yards from the highway. The Americans, squinting at them as they did, looked a little nervous, but not overly so. They seemed more tired. They hadn't shaved in several days and maybe hadn't slept much.

A bleary-eyed lieutenant with the squad on the ridge suddenly stood up straighter and walked down toward them, eyes darting over Chen's group. He brushed past his soldiers. "You're holding up traffic." He waved them through. "Just keep moving, keep moving."

All the adults made several deferential bows as they shuffled past. Treading the winding road through mountainous terrain, and passing through two more patrols, they reached the outskirts of Taejon well after dark. Just inside the city they halted, resting until two more groups containing the rest of Chen's men joined them.

The houses at the edge of town were mud and stick huts with thatched roofs. As they moved closer to the center of the city, the huts became two- and three-room houses, and then the two-story homes of the affluent. Here and there was a shaded light in a window, but most were black and silent. A mangy spotted dog emerged from the shadows of an alley, bared its teeth and growled. One of Chen's men drew his pistol, but Chen clamped his hand over the man's wrist, giving him a hard look. Shots might give them away to the Americans. Another of his men threw a well-aimed rock, and the dog scurried away yelping.

The old man led them up to the wall of a compound and knocked on the wooden gate. After a few moments, the gate was opened by a smiling, middle-aged man with a goatee and a mouth of crooked teeth.

The man bowed. "I am Pak Waeng-son, and I am honored to have you stay in my humble home."

He ushered them into a rectangular courtyard. Two sides of the rectangle were made up of the L-shaped house, and the other sides by the ten-foot high walls. The house was two stories high. It had a white stucco exterior and a brown tile roof.

Pak clapped his hands. A thin young man, who was standing next to a well, ran forward. He hurried the women and children out a smaller side gate.

Pak said, "They are being taken to other quarters for the night. Tomorrow a Party member will take them to the depot and try to get them on a train, if there are any. Failing that, they will be given food for three days and added to a party traveling south. Not many people want to remain in the city."

Pak turned and walked to the veranda. A young woman with a plain face slid the door open from inside the house and quickly ushered the disguised soldiers into the main room. It was suffused with the smell of cooking fish, rice, and vegetables.

The soldiers sat cross legged on the floor around a long wooden table. The young woman, Pak's daughter Son-a, moved quickly and quietly to serve the dozen hungry men a feast of bok choy, kim-chee, steaming rice with chicken, and mung-bean pancakes. The soldiers gulped down every bit of food they could, smacking their lips appreciatively and belching loudly. The young woman, her hair trailing halfway down her back, smiled modestly and pretended not to notice that these young warriors kept sneaking glances at her in her blue silk dress.

She filled and refilled their cups with hot tea, and when the meal was done, she passed around a crock of rice wine. Chen found himself distracted by the young woman and then realized it was because she had about her the scent of jasmine, just as his own Lu Ling so often did. For a moment he longed to be with Lu Ling back in China, and then shook off the feeling. His duty was here. He smiled at this girl, turning his full face to her with his blind eye and scar, but when she shuddered, he drew back and averted his face. He mentally shrugged his shoulders and turned his attention back to his hosts. He had long known he was not attractive to women.

Pak and the old man who had been their guide tried to engage Chen in conversation. Both were proud of their credentials as Party members. The old man's name was Han. He had been imprisoned by the Japanese for his political activities, his crippled hands the result of torture. Pak, who had become a Communist Party member when he was still a teenager, remained one now that he was a master, an owner of his own business. Both had been beaten by the police of Syngman Rhee's pro-American government.

Pak tamped tobacco into his pipe as Han searched his pockets for his own pipe. "We have been waiting to be liberated for many years now," said Pak, puffing at his pipe, rhythmically drawing down the flame as he lit it, and then passing the burning taper to Han.

Capt. Chen nodded. He reached into his pocket for cigarette makings. "Are there many Party members staying in the city now?" The other soldiers sat around the table listening intently, but not daring to interject themselves into a conversation between their hosts and commanding officer. They sipped wine and began rummaging for tobacco. Soon the blue haze of cigarette smoke mixed with the grey smoke from the charcoal in the cooking brazier.

Pak said, "Not so many; most fled south soon after Premier Kim's troops took Seoul."

"I had heard," Chen said, "that the Party was strong here in the South, that there are over three hundred thousand members."

"That's true," said Han.

Chen was genuinely puzzled. "Then why haven't they risen up and taken over all the towns. That would hasten the unification of Korea and the defeat of the imperialists and reactionaries."

Han looked sad. "It is to be deplored. In our meetings, we talked many times of how, when Premier Kim finally invaded, we would do just that. But no one was really prepared. Suddenly everyone was afraid his family might be killed by one side or the other. It is one thing to talk about how a man will act in a civil war, and another to have it arrive suddenly howling outside one's door."

Chen nodded. Still, he thought, it was strange there were not more signs of an uprising here in the south.

Pak took a deep drag from his pipe. "When Rhee came into power, he had many thousands of leftist sympathizers arrested. Many died in prison. Many were tortured." He nodded at Han. "The younger revolutionaries escaped into the mountains. For the last two years these bands have attacked the smaller towns, burning police stations and public buildings. There are not many true revolutionaries left in the towns."

Chen pursed his lips. Perhaps the revolutionaries in the mountains were even now attacking the ROK troops from the rear as the North Korean troops pressed from the front.

Pak said, "After the invasion, the police here in Taejon began rounding up anyone they suspected of leftist sympathies. Many hundreds have been trucked out of the city. I have heard rumors of mass executions."

Chen nodded. This was not unexpected. "How have you managed to avoid arrest?"

"I have a friend on the police force, Capt. Chae. We went to school together. When my wife was alive, she was kind to his wife once when she was gravely ill. He has shielded me."

When several of the soldiers yawned, Pak instructed his daughter to show them to rooms where sleeping mats had been laid out. Han, Pak, and Capt. Chen continued to talk. Son-a returned and sat on her stool, knees pressed together, hands clasped in her lap and eyes downcast, but Chen noticed that she occasionally stole glances at him, probably fascinated by his disfigurement.

"What progress," Chen asked, "have you made organizing the peasants?" This was an obvious question.

Pak and Han looked at each other, confusion written in their lined faces. "The peasants are not the proletariat. Marx, Lenin, and Comrade Stalin have made it clear that the revolution begins with workers joining other workers in solidarity. The peasant is too much an individualist. He does not understand collective organizing."

Chen nodded. This was a discussion that had gone on in China twenty years ago. "When the Communist Party was driven out of the cities in China, we were forced into the countryside. There we found that, properly educated, these peasants could be the backbone of the revolution."

Pak and Han shifted uncomfortably in their chairs. Han opened his mouth and then shut it, sucking on his pipe instead. Pak cleared his throat. "You've had a long day, Captain, and must be tired."

Chen had to agree. Pak led him upstairs to his own small private writing room. Moonlight streamed in through a single window, lighting the four ink paintings that adorned the walls. A sleeping mat lay on the floor and, suspended above it, a mosquito net. Chen couldn't remember the last night when he had experienced the luxury of a net.

Almost immediately he dropped into a deep sleep. This house was that rare safe haven, a shelter however temporary from the rigors of field living and the dangers of combat. He let his guard down – but not so much that some part of his mind didn't hear the almost silent slide of the door and the ever so quiet pad of footsteps. As he heard cloth dropping to the floor and sensed the mosquito net being raised, his mind sprang to alert.

Even before his eyes could open, his hand whipped out, catching the intruder's neck in an iron grip. He rolled, pulling his assailant flat to the mat while rising up himself, ready to strike.

Son-a lay beneath him, naked, eyes wide. He froze, fist hovering, raised for a lethal strike, now checked. He expelled his breath. She did too.

Trembling, almost crying, she blurted out "I'm sorry."

"Shhh," he whispered, putting a finger to her lips. He smiled at her in the dim moonlight and rolled off her to the side. He stroked her face until she stopped trembling. She stared at the scars on his face and hesitantly traced their patterns with her fingertip.

He made love to her, drinking in the scent of jasmine while remembering his own Lu Ling, the woman who had trudged up mountains with him, stooped next to him while they planted rice together with peasants in the paddies, and who once, when his unit was surrounded by Nationalist troops, reloaded his weapons for him. She had borne him two sons for the Revolution.

Chen awoke alone on his mat, the pale morning sun streaming in on him and the smells of a hot breakfast rising from below. He and his men gathered around the table while Son-a served up dishes of jook, a porridge with meat. Her father eyed her, glancing from her to the men and back to her, but she kept her eyes downcast and her face devoid of emotion. Chen thought he detected a slight glow on her cheeks, but he couldn't be sure.

After breakfast, Chen spread his yellowed copies of Japanese survey maps on the table. Although Pak had never seen a topographical map, once Chen explained how to read it, the older man smiled in delight as he began to recognize features of Taejon's terrain in the squiggly lines.

Pak traced the ridgeline north of the city. The Americans were fortifying four miles of it, he said. Ah, the small airport northwest of the city – the Americans had hauled their artillery up there. Within the city, they had turned several schoolhouses into command centers and a hospital.

As Pak pointed these out, he added, "The Americans are hiring porters to carry supplies up to the ridgeline."

Chen grinned. "I'm sure they could use more help."

Pak sat smoking his long pipe while Chen prepped his men to volunteer as civilian workers. They would make detailed maps of the American positions. In the evening, he could transmit the information back to headquarters via radio.

The soldiers bustled about and left. Chen remained. Son-a served tea and left them alone. Pak continued to draw on his pipe.

Chen cradled his cup appreciatively in his palm. "This is exquisite work."

He rotated the glazed white cup before his one good eye, noting the delicate design with its black inlaid figure of a crane.

Pak withdrew his pipe and bowed. "You honor my humble work."

Chen felt an unaccustomed wave of nostalgia sweep over him. "This piece takes me back to my youth when I was apprenticed to a potter. It was said that I was talented, but I never produced any work as beautiful this cup."

"The design was created by my great grandfather. We Koreans, you know, were the first to master the use of white clay. Would you like to see my workshop? It is just outside."

Chen bowed. "Might I?"

Pak led the way across the courtyard, past the well and through the side gate to a long, rectangular single-story building. The workshop was empty, his apprentices and employees having fled the city.

As Chen walked through the room, Pak said, "You were not born into the craft?"

"No," said Chen, stopping in front of a potter's wheel, one of ten. "My family, as far back as I know, were farmers. A wealthy landlord cheated my father out of our small parcel of land, and we had to move to the city."

He turned and looked at Pak. "To Nanking on the Yangtse River. My father apprenticed my younger brother and me to a potter there." He moved on to the kilns, stooping down to examine the inside of the ovens. "You use ash?"

"It produces the best glaze, don't you think?"

Chen stood and eyed the shelves filled with pottery. He reached up and ran his fingers lightly over brown pitchers, orange bowls and a pale blue vase. "Absolutely."

"May I ask how a potter's apprentice became an officer in the Red Army?"

Chen, his back to his host, continued to inspect the wares. After a long moment of silence, almost with a sigh, he said, "After the Japanese Imperial Army captured Shanghai in 1937, they marched upriver on Nanking. I was 17. My 14-year-old brother and I were conscripted by the Chinese defense forces, given two days of training, and sent into the teeth of the Japanese Army. Most of my company, including my brother, were slaughtered. I was captured.

"When the Japanese breached the city's defenses, they massacred the civilians. They went house to house, dragging residents out into the street and shooting them. They raped the women. If a woman resisted, they bayoneted her. Often, afterwards, even if the woman hadn't resisted, they bayoneted her."

Chen felt his throat tighten up and his eyes water. He reached up and took a vase the color of jade down from the shelf, pretending to be engrossed examining the craftsmanship. He was amazed that after all these years, and all the tragedy he had seen, these memories still evoked such pain. He carefully replaced the vase.

"I learned from a neighbor that this is what the soldiers did to my mother and sister – after they shot my father." He turned to Pak, his face now an expressionless mask; but he could see the soft look of compassion in the older man's eyes.

"I was one of thousands of captured soldiers marched into city squares to be executed. Two men near me tried to escape. While the guards chased them, I slipped into a side street and ran. The executions and rapes and looting went on for six weeks. All that time I hid in back alleys and ate garbage – and rats when I could trap them. Eventually, when order was finally restored, the Japanese caught me and threw me into jail. They beat and tortured me.

"When they released me six months later, I wanted to kill Japanese soldiers. The Chinese government's army was not fighting. Chiang Kai Shek and the cowering Nationalists had withdrawn inland, afraid to fight. I found my way to Mao's Sixth Route Army. There I became a soldier."

"But why are you, a Chinese soldier, fighting for us Koreans?"

Chen paused. There were several answers he could give. He chose one. "China has thrown off the yoke of its Western imperialist oppressors. Now all of Asia cries out for liberation. Mao is even now sending advisors to Ho Chi Minh in Vietnam. Perhaps, after we have driven the Americans and their puppet Syngman Rhee from Korea, I will be sent to join our comrades in Vietnam, and…"

Chen stopped mid-sentence as he caught sight of a pitcher standing alone on a shelf in the corner. It had been easy to miss, because the corner was dark. Fashioned of burnished Korean white clay, it gleamed in the dim light. Walking past Pak, Chen approached it reverently, not daring to take it in his hands to inspect it.

"I am in awe," he whispered.

Pak came up beside him, his hands tucked into his sleeves. "This design belongs to my house."

Chen tried to fathom how the artist had, against this white background, created the illusion of a marsh, with its green shoots and blue water. In the foreground stood a raised figure, a red crane, symbol of luck and longevity. The snow-white bird had a black neck and black wingtips. Its crown was scarlet. Though its head was in profile, Chen had the eerie sense that its dark eye was peering into him, penetrating his inner being.

"At the time my great grandfather created this, the Japanese were forcibly relocating whole clans of master potters to Japan. My family had to pretend to be crude craftsmen to avoid being
caught up in the sweeps."

The word "sweeps" jolted Chen and brought him back to more immediate concerns. He reverted to his official tone. "There is something I need to discuss with you."

Pak knitted his brow, creating a series of creases in his smooth forehead, and waited attentively.

"Our North Korean comrades are about to liberate this city."

"I have long awaited that glorious day."

"Yes, but you need to be cautious when our troops arrive."

"I don't understand."

"War is chaos. Mistakes happen. I would not like to see anything unfortunate happen to your family."

Pak looked frightened. "My daughter…"

"When we took Seoul, there was no looting or raping. That is not what you need to be concerned about."

"Then what?"

"After the army secures the town, they will round up any reactionaries who have not fled. The trials will be quick. Anyone found guilty will, in most cases, be executed on the spot."

Pak's lip trembled. "But I am not a reactionary. I am a loyal Party member."

"True, but you are not of the working class. You own a business. That would normally be sufficient to get you executed. Any political officeholder, wealthy landowner, member of the police, or newspaperman who wrote for a reactionary paper – these also will be purged."

Pak wrung his hands. "What am I to do?"

"Col. Chu gave me a letter for you. It asserts that you are a loyal Party member in good standing, and that you provided essential aid in the capture of Taejon. It is your protection. You must safeguard it carefully while the city is being put under martial law."

Pak pulled at his beard.

"Stay inside. Soldiers will come and escort you to an Internal Affairs office or a City Political Security Bureau to establish your credentials. Just cooperate politely, and all should be well."

He moved away from Chen. When he turned back, he said, "My friend in the police, Capt. Chae…"

"He will probably flee the city before our troops arrive."

"I do not think so. He is brave and stubborn. He will stay at his post until the last possible moment."

Chen took Pak by the shoulders and looked him in the eyes. "Then you need to be clear about this, Comrade. *Do not* try to assist him. Col. Chu's letter will not help you if you do."

Pak looked down at the floor.

"For Son-a's sake, do not be foolish. As a family member, she would also be arrested."

Pak let out a sigh and looked up. "You have given me wise counsel. I thank you."

"Good. Now, let us return to your house. We still have much to do."

At the door, Chen turned to take a last look at the workshop and the pottery on the shelves. He said, more to himself than his host, "I think I would have made a good potter."

He stepped out into the light and Pak followed, closing the door behind them.

Jonas' company was being held in reserve a few miles west of regimental headquarters in Okchon, a town fifteen miles southeast of Taejon. It was oh-seven-thirty. His men were up, had eaten, and were about to be assigned to work details. Sgt. Strosahl was preparing for a run back into Taejon. Col. Stephens wanted him to find his friend Sgt. Collins and see if he could "unofficially requisition" some needed items.

Jonas had just finished inspecting his men – Pvt. Perkins needed to be transported to the aid station because he had a fever – when to the west he heard explosions. He turned and saw two small propeller driven planes, North Korean Yaks, heading his way. He and his men ran for their foxholes. A few minutes later the Yaks flew overhead, but instead of strafing or bombing, they dropped leaflets. They continued on towards Okchon, and Jonas heard bombs exploding a minute later.

Capt. Dasher summoned him. "Get a driver and take these damn things to Col. Stephens on the double." The captain's face was red.

"Yessir," he said and scanned one of the leaflets. It called on American troops to cease fighting an unfair, aggressive, imperialistic war against the peaceful people of Korea. It was a straightforward piece of propaganda written in stilted English. In itself, it looked harmless enough. Any American soldier running low on toilet paper would know what to do with it. But it wasn't hard to guess what had the captain angry. The leaflet was signed by three American officers and three NCOs, men captured at Osan.

Buzz Parker's signature jumped out at Jonas. Alleged signature anyway, because the names were typed. Jonas was filled with conflicting feelings. He was relieved Buzz might still be alive, but an officer wouldn't willingly sign a piece of propaganda unless... Jonas didn't want to think of it. He shivered. If he himself were taken prisoner, how would he stand up under torture?

With a wan looking Pvt. Perkins in the back of the jeep, Cpl. Turco drove Jonas to the regimental CP. The highway ran through the middle of the village of Okchon, and the regimental CP, a schoolhouse, stood just off the highway. Two farmhouses near the CP were flattened, and several bomb craters dotted both sides of the road.

As their jeep drew closer, Jonas made out the regimental motor pool, aid station, walk-in tents, along with the water and fuel trucks. He saw lots of bullet holes from the strafing, but there wasn't as much damage as he'd first feared. Good thing the North Korean pilots weren't better shots.

Turco pulled the jeep in between two others parked outside the CP. As Jonas climbed out, he saw the two stars emblazoned on the next jeep.

"Take Perkins to the aid station and report back here," he said to Turco.

An MP outside the schoolhouse gave him directions to Operations. Jonas recognized Gen. Dean's voice even before he reached the door. "How much damage did those Yaks do to the railroad bridges and tunnels?"

Jonas glimpsed Col. Stephens standing by a map pinned to the wall. "I've got the engineers on it, but no report yet, sir."

Jonas was a little shocked at the general's appearance. He had lost weight, and while he still stood ramrod straight, he seemed to have shrunk an inch or so. The haggard face and bloodshot eyes made Jonas think the man was sleep deprived. Instead of regular

Army fatigues, he was dressed in a pair of green coveralls, but Jonas doubted anyone was going to tell the general he was out of uniform.

Gen. Dean caught sight of Jonas. The seams of fatigue creasing the general's face worked their way into an expression that was a mixture of recognition and puzzlement.

"Lieutenant…?"

Jonas shifted nervously, not sure if he should be barging in. "Stuyvesant, sir."

Gen. Dean smiled. "Right, you're David's brother." He turned to Col. Stephens. "I knew this man's brother in Europe. Hell of an officer. Then this one, the first day he's on the base at Kokura, comes up to me during a party and says he wants to be assigned to a line company, didn't want to be a desk jockey." He laughed. "Of course, we didn't know a war was going to break out the next day."

Smiling, he turned back to Jonas. "So, son, does being on the line still suit you?"

The general's relaxed tone set him at ease. "Yessir," he said, looking from Dean to Stephens. And then, remembering his mission, he blurted out, "Capt. Dasher sent me with these handbills the Yaks dropped on our lines."

Col. Stephens scanned the leaflets. "The same as they dropped on us."

Jonas was a little disappointed his trip had turned out to be unnecessary. He hesitated, not sure whether to leave the room or stay.

Col. Stephens said, "Hold on a bit, will you, Lieutenant? When the general is done here, I may want you to take a message back to Capt. Dasher."

Dean turned to the map. He traced a curving line a little north and northwest of Taejon. "This ridgeline is five hundred feet high – and steep – a good defensive position."

"I agree, sir, but you've only got two half-strength battalions to cover what? Three to four miles? That's not enough. We should withdraw back to Yongdong."

Dean nodded his head without turning from the map. Almost to himself he said, "I'm bringing up another battalion. That will give me three."

"Half-strength battalions," Stephens said, his voice strained.

"Hmm," said Dean and looked at Stephens. His face now seemed younger, as though he'd tapped into some new source of energy. "Taejon reminds me of Gettysburg," he said.

Col. Stephens cocked his head.

"Look." Dean turned back to the map and began pointing. "Gettysburg was a market town with a series of roads converging on it from all directions – just like Taejon. Gen. Buford led his Yankee cavalry to a blocking position west of Gettysburg ahead of the arrival of any other Union troops. He was outnumbered, without enough troops to hold more than a day, just like our situation. He was relying on being reinforced with another division of infantry."

Dean turned back to Stephens. "This is what I'm counting on. Gen. Walker needs me to hold Taejon for the two days it will take to move another division up to relieve us." He smiled. "I would like to see the faces of the generals on the other side when, instead of facing one worn-out division, suddenly they're up against an intact, fresh division."

Col. Stephens returned a much weaker smile. "That's if they get here in time."

Dean nodded, but with energy. "It's a gamble. That's why I need you here, holding the highway open. If we have to withdraw, it's going to be through your lines."

Stephens stepped up to the map. "We're dug in on both sides of the highway," he said, marking the positions. "And we've got a company of light tanks for support. But I wish I had some artillery, sir."

"Sorry, Dick. I need all my artillery in Taejon." Dean turned back to the map. The confidence he'd just shown began to fade from his face. "We can hold if... I should go back to Taejon and take another look at our positions."

"Respectfully, sir, that's Col. Beauchamp's job. Your place is back at division headquarters."

"Yes, it is." Dean chewed at his lip. "But this war is nothing like Europe." He started to pace. "I feel like I need to get right up close to these North Koreans and get a sense of what kind of fighters they are. And communications. We can get messages from the rear to the front, but we can't get them from the front to the rear. The field radios keep going out and the telephone lines, well, lines get cut. There's nothing useful I can do at the rear. My staff back there can handle anything." He stopped in front of Stephens. "I've got to go back to Taejon."

The colonel shrugged in defeat. "Yessir."

"I can't count on the radios working or the telephone lines staying open. So I need a runner, a good man to get a message back to you if the situation goes south."

Stephens furrowed his brow for a second. "How about Stuyvesant?"

"Hmm, yes, he should do." The general turned and nodded at Jonas. "You're with me, Lieutenant." He was already walking toward the door.

Jonas, taken aback, hesitated just a second. Col. Stephens took his arm and pulled him aside.

"Sgt. Strosahl was slated to make a run into the city?"

"Yessir?"

"Take him with you."

"Colonel, that leaves my platoon without me or its sergeant."

"I'll take care of it. Catch up to the general."

Outside, Jonas climbed into the waiting jeep. "Well Turco, let's go pick up Strosahl. We've just been assigned new duties."

"We moving out of the line of fire or into it, sir?"

"What do you think?"

"Just what I was afraid of." He put the jeep in gear.

11

J ONAS ROLLED OVER in his bedroll, feeling the hard, wooden floor beneath him, coming to slowly, and then starting awake, sitting up, knowing something was wrong. The hairs on the back of his neck tingled.

Yellow pre-dawn light filtered through the windowpanes and spread over dark green lumps in bedrolls, soldiers, helmets, and rifles at hand, scattered about the floor of the cool, bare room. No one else was moving. No one else seemed alarmed.

What was wrong? Jonas strained to hear the clue. Muffled voices from down below, men from Headquarters Company working through the night. Birds chirped and sang outside the window. No, it wasn't a sound he could hear that had disturbed him. It was a sound that was missing. There was no artillery booming in the distance.

He let out a sigh of relief and smiled at himself, shook his head in amazement that his life had been so turned upside down that the absence of gun fire was what was unusual. He checked again. Of course, no cannon fire could mean a barrage had lifted and the three battalions outside the city were now being assaulted by North Korean infantry. But if that were the case, there should be a hubbub below, a flurry of voices and activity, with status reports flying back and forth from the line units to headquarters. However, everything below sounded calm, even orderly.

He'd accompanied Gen. Dean into the city the day before, only to learn at headquarters that L Company, holding a blocking position west of the city, was under attack. Dean had rushed with his entourage to the battle. They'd held against an enemy force four or five times their numbers; and just when the Reds started to flank them, and things were looking grim again, a battalion from the 19th Regiment, that third battalion Dean had called up from Division Headquarters, arrived and covered the flank, driving back the Red attack. Then that battalion, a crucial bit of reinforcement, moved north of the city to plug a hole between the two battalions of the 34th Regiment.

Even though he'd gone to sleep to the sound of artillery, he was starting to feel a little better. These North Koreans could be beaten. It took a certain amount of manpower, heavy firepower, and tactics, but it could be done. The 24th Division was holding Taejon. Rumor had it reinforcements, the First Cavalry Division, were on their way.

Jonas stretched, scratched the stubble on his face, and found his way downstairs, carrying his carbine with him, out back to the latrine.

There was water for shaving. A group of young officers in brown t-shirts stood around a wooden bench, hot water in their upturned helmets, white soap on their faces, and makeshift towels thrown over their shoulders.

"Anyone have a spare razor?" He'd left Okchon so quickly he hadn't thought to retrieve his pack, so he was without a razor. Another lieutenant, blond-haired with a fresh nick on his chin, shrugged, grinned, and loaned him his.

"Any chance," he asked as he scraped his cheek, "of a hot meal?"

Dabbing at his nick, his benefactor said, "There's chow wagons set up by motor pool, ten blocks south. Big compound just over the bridge. You can't miss it."

"Thanks," said Jonas and headed off for breakfast. The field kitchen would have some extra mess kits. That was another thing he hadn't had time to retrieve.

The bridge, fifty feet long, straddled a canal and could handle two jeeps passing each other. He strode across it rapidly. The motor compound, about a half-block square, was an open grassy area surrounded by two story buildings. There were at least a hundred and fifty vehicles parked in various groupings: jeeps, trucks of various sizes, ammo carriers and wagons. But it was food Jonas was interested in. He could smell breakfast even before he sighted the chow trucks: steaming coffee and hot biscuits.

Easily a hundred enlisted men and about twenty officers stood on separate lines. A cook gave Jonas a mess kit and ladled out the hot food, powdered scrambled eggs and potatoes, along with fruit cocktail in its thick syrup. He took a sip of his coffee while looking for a place to sit. It was bitter and scalding.

He saw Sgt. Strosahl nearby engaged in talk with Sgt. Collins from supply. They were speaking in low tones, their heads close together. Fifty feet away, Turco and another soldier sat next to each other on ammo boxes, their rifles leaning against the jeep behind them. Jonas decided to join them.

He picked his way through the men and vehicles. "This a private party, or can anybody join?"

Turco looked up and broke into a large grin. "Hey, Lieu, I was just telling my friend Joe about our being assigned to this here duty, you being requested, specially by the general and all."

"Joe Prados, Lieutenant," said the other soldier.

Jonas looked around, found a five-gallon gasoline can, and pulled it around to make a triangle with Turco and Prados. He looked Prados over. A little older than many of the kids here, maybe twenty or twenty-one, with a compact body. He had sleek eyebrows, small ears, and a prominent razor-line jaw.

"What unit you with, Corporal?"

"Recon," he said. Nothing more.

Jonas nodded again. Intelligence & Reconnaissance Company. Tough work, driving out in scout jeeps ahead of the lines to get a fix on the enemy. Easy way to get killed quick, no foxhole around when the shooting starts. Prados looked like he'd already seen a bit of action. He had the far-off stare of a veteran, on the alert.

"You two know each other from before?" Jonas said, biting down into a biscuit that had soaked up some of his fruit cocktail juice. Sweet.

"Oh yeah," nodded Turco, his words rolling over the top of a mouthful of scrambled eggs, a bit of yellow clinging to the side of his mouth. "We're long-time buddies from the ole 1/7."

Strosahl's outfit, the First Battalion, Seventh Regiment, First Cavalry Division.

"How do you like recon compared to regular infantry?" Jonas said.

Prados screwed up his mouth. "Right now it kinda sucks."

"The action a little hot?"

"Don't mind the heat. But like yesterday, we're a good forty miles south of the city, and we make contact.

Jonas stopped chewing. "South of us?"

"South. Advance elements of the North Koreans, no tanks, but definitely Reds. So our lieutenant calls for an air strike. Do we get it? No, the brass back here sitting on their butts decide we got shit for eyes and can't tell friendlies from the enemy."

"You're sure they weren't ROK forces?"

Prados stared back with disdain and didn't answer.

This didn't sound good. Jonas sipped some coffee, now tasting even more bitter, and looked off into the distance. If the North Koreans had already circled that far south, they were enveloping the city. He shook his head, not wanting to think of the implications.

His eyes roamed over the motor pool and surrounding buildings, seeing and not seeing. The compound had probably been a market square with a large grassy area in the center, all torn up and rutted now, clumps of green grass buried in the dirt. The square was bordered with grey and brown two-story buildings, some with tile roofs and more with thatch atop them, the roofs sloping and upturning at the corners, even the ones made of thatch. Most of the buildings had wood shutters for windows, but here and there was some glass. A few of the buildings were stone, but most seemed to be either Japanese-style wood-frame or traditional Korean clay-wattle construction. Here, unlike in the outlying villages, heavy wooden beams allowed for thicker walls and two-story construction. There were walkways separating most of the buildings. Streets found their way into the compound from odd angles.

A muffled sound caught his ear. Both Turco and Prados were also cocking their ears and reflexively reaching for their rifles. They were immediately on the alert, but the clerks, cooks, and mechanics, those soldiers with no combat experience, were going about their tasks. Few of them even had weapons at hand. Most weren't wearing a helmet. This was the rear. Why bother?

Jonas hadn't even identified the sound; but as his gut tightened, he automatically jumped to his feet. Then the clanking grew more distinct, and he and maybe thirty men scurried for cover. The clerks, cooks and mechanics, curious, watched on in frozen poses.

Jonas didn't see the cannon. He was already behind the heaviest vehicle he could find, a halftrack being repaired, when the first shell ripped through the compound. More clanking and screeching. He peeked out to see, on the far side of the compound on each of three feeder-streets, a T-34 tank, with soldiers in mustard colored suits jumping off and scattering, heading into the buildings.

The tanks let loose with a barrage of cannon and machine gun fire, shells exploding in orange flames and flipping jeeps and trucks into the air, bullets tearing through metal doors, smashing windows, men screaming as they were hit. A loaded ammo truck exploded. The concussion smashed windows and shook even heavy trucks, rocked them back and forth on their wheels. The ground shook. White-hot shrapnel tore up men who, although they'd taken cover, got hit from behind when an ammo truck exploded.

The firing went on for a steady ten minutes; and just as suddenly, it stopped. Jonas stuck his head out from behind the halftrack and was mystified to see the tanks roll forward and turn south along the western border of the compound and just drive away. Just like that, it was over.

Screams of "Medic!" rang out.

Someone shouted, "The tanks – they're headed for the hospital."

In the middle of the compound, a large soldier stood up and raised his arm into the air, the three chevrons on his sleeve clearly visible. "Recon, form up on me." About fifteen men, mostly armed with rifles, a couple with heavier B.A.R.s, sprinted to him. Prados was one of the first men to reach the sergeant's side. The group took off after the tanks.

These men hadn't even disappeared from sight before the first shots rang out from the buildings on the far side of the compound. An American soldier wearing a brown t-shirt and a soft covered hat, a wrench clutched in his hand, fell as though he'd been hit with a sledgehammer.

"Everyone down!"

This time there were no laggards. Every soldier scrambled for cover.

Jonas looked from his end of the halftrack to the other end. Turco was checking his ammo. He looked to his left. Twenty feet away, Strosahl was crouched behind a jeep.

An unfamiliar husky voice called out, "I need infantry on the double." The voice came from the direction of the chow truck. Jonas looked Turco's way. Turco shrugged and the two of them ran at a crouch. Strosahl was three steps behind them.

A major, a thin reedy man who looked to be in his late forties, was jabbing a captain in the chest and cursing him out.

"Lt. Stuyvesant reporting, sir."

"Maj. Ellison." The major looked him up and down. Four privates had all come in at a run from the other side of the truck. "Combat experience, Lieutenant?"

"Osan and Chochiwon, sir. I'm from the 1/21."

"Good. You, Sergeant?"

"Plenty."

"The rest of you soldiers?"

"Yes sir," they said, nodding, eyes upturned toward the major. He was the only one standing upright. Everyone around him stood in a crouch.

"Lieutenant, see that building at the end of this street?" He pointed toward an ivy-covered, brown brick building at the southeast corner of the square. Jonas nodded.

"That's a storehouse," the major said. "Take the corporal and these four men. Go get yourself whatever you need. Then get to the rear of those buildings across the compound and clean out those enemy positions."

"Yes sir," Jonas said.

"Sergeant, you're going to help the captain and me organize covering fire to keep those snipers busy. Questions?"

There were none. "Everyone get moving."

Jonas took off at a run, keeping his head down. He burst into the brick building with Turco and the four infantrymen right behind him.

The four privates tore through crates, one of them yelling, "I got grenades here." He raised two high, one in each hand. Turco dug through other boxes as Jonas walked over and began helping himself, stuffing his pockets with the grenades, trying to remember house-to-house combat at Fort Benning, all two hours of it three years ago.

"Alright! Baby come to Poppa!" shouted Turco.

Jonas turned to see the corporal pull an M-3 submachine gun from another crate. Turco held it up. "Got me a grease gun, but it's the only one here." He started stuffing his pockets with magazines.

"We ready?" Jonas said. The four privates, all looked unbearably young and eager, all having cold eyes and clenched jaws, even the one with pimples. "Locked and loaded?"

"Yes, sir!" they said in unison.

The North Koreans occupied three of the buildings on the west side of the compound, the three with the thickest walls. Jonas led his team behind the buildings along the south, circling until he reached the west side and found the rear of the first building held by the enemy. It was a two- story building with thick clay-wattle walls and wooden shutters over holes for windows. He flattened himself against the wall next to the back door. Corporal Turco crossed quickly and stood on the other side, tensed, ready to go. The other four soldiers took up flanking positions, two on each side.

"You four hold tight until Turco and I are inside and clear this first room." They nodded, faces taut, weapons at port.

Sweat ran down Jonas' face. He nodded. Turco tossed a grenade inside. The blast shook the door frame and the ground beneath him. Turco rushed inside. Jonas was right on his heels as Turco sprayed the room. The racket was horrendous. Everywhere Jonas looked there was pottery, much of it now shattered. The air was saturated with orange dust.

Up front, near a shuttered window, stood one large vase, its blue glaze shimmering in the dim light. Unaccountably, the vase was untouched.

Three objects sailed down from above. Thunk, thunk, thunk.

"Grenades" shouted the corporal, and the two of them were a tangle of arms and legs as they tripped over each other trying to get back out the door. Jonas sprawled face down on the ground, while Turco landed on top of him, knocking his breath out.

The first two grenades went off a fraction of a second apart, and then a long second later, as Jonas was still gasping for breath, the third blast hit. This one tore a chunk out of the door frame and showered them with splinters.

Turco scrambled on all fours to one side of the door, as Jonas did the same, to get to the opposite side. The two soldiers there pulled him to his feet.

Turco grinned. "I guess they don't want us crashing their party."

Jonas wasn't feeling the bravado Turco exuded, but he felt he had to try to match it. "Strikes me as downright inhospitable of them, don't you think, Corporal?"

Simultaneously both poked their heads around the door frame, and Jonas caught sight of movement at the top of a stairway off to the right. A soldier, red star affixed to his cap, raised his rifle. Turco let loose with a burst; and the soldier, hit in the shoulder, twirled and fell backward.

Jonas, the first inside, bounded up the steps. He caught sight of the fallen soldier dragging himself deeper into a room at the top. Turco passed by and headed down the hallway toward the next room. Jonas could hear the other four members of his team clambering up the stairs behind him.

He flattened himself against one side of the first door and pulled the pin from a grenade. He could hear three voices inside, one groaning. A grenade had a four-second fuse. He let the spoon flip away, counting one-thousand-one, one-thousand-two – didn't want to give anyone inside the chance to throw the grenade back – and threw it hard so that it would bounce around. One-thousand-three – yells from inside and a scrambling of feet – and then a deafening explosion.

Orange fire, grey smoke – the wall and floor shuddering with the blast. Jonas was through the doorway, carbine held at hip level, sweeping the room as he scanned for any movement. None. Three crumpled bodies, one with its face torn half off, lots of blood-splatter.

From outside he heard the sounds of a grenade blast in the next room – Turco clearing it. The blast was followed by the rattle of Turco's grease gun.

Then Jonas heard a scream, "I'm hit. I'm hit." A jolt went through his body. One of his men was down. He ran out into the hallway.

Turco was there ahead of him, down on one knee, grease gun to his shoulder. Behind the corporal was a G.I. on the ground, two hands pressed against a spreading stain on his abdomen. Another G.I.

pulled the wounded man's battle dressing from the pouch on his web belt, prying the man's hands free to get the dressing on the wound. Ten feet in front of Turco, a North Korean soldier lay face-down, a rifle in his right hand, blood pooling around him. The other two men from their team were nowhere to be seen.

Jonas ran up to the wounded G.I., knelt down and checked him quickly. The man's pale face, strands of sweat-drenched hair straggling down his cheek, told him shock was setting in. He'd need a medic quick.

"Report, Corporal."

Without turning his head or moving from his position, Turco said, "Got one room cleared. Looks like there's more gooks at the end of the hall. The one on the floor shot our man here, and I got him."

Down the hallway, from the doorway of the last room, an object flew in a slow upward arc. It looked like a slender, dimpled can with a short wooden handle attached.

"Grenade," Turco shouted as he dove for the room on his left. Jonas sprang right, rolling into the room Turco had just cleared. The blast rocked the walls, and more plaster rained down. Jonas raised his head from the floor. By the window was a tangled mass of three bodies in red-stained, shredded NK uniforms, men Turco had already taken out. One of them peered back at Jonas from floor level, staring lifelessly from his one remaining eye.

Turning his head, Jonas checked behind him. The two missing members of his team lay nearby, hands clapped over their helmets. They lifted their white plaster-covered faces from the floor.

Jonas leapt to the doorway, hesitated a fraction of a second, and then poked his head around the frame. Turco was again in the corridor, his back against the wall, inching his way to the last room, grease gun in his left hand and grenade in his right. He let the spoon go and flipped a grenade inside. Another blast, and he charged around the corner, firing as he went, disappearing from Jonas' view.

Jonas stepped into the hallway. His wounded soldier was still lying alive on the floor, the white battle-dressing now soaked red, pressed to his abdomen. The enemy grenade had barely grazed him. It had landed near him and exploded, the shrapnel thrown up and outward in a cone fashion, leaving the wounded G.I. safe beneath its trajectory. But the soldier who had been attending him had taken the full blast of the grenade. His face was shredded, unrecognizable, and the rest of his trunk was now smashed up against the wall with his guts hanging out.

Jonas tasted a surge of bile. One man wounded and another dead. Behind him, he heard one of his other two men retching. Jonas turned to them. The man, his back to the scene, was stooped over vomiting. The other private stood staring white-faced at the wounded man and the corpse. He started to shake from head to foot.

"You two," Jonas said, "get this guy back to the medics. Report that we've got a KIA still up here." He stepped over, knelt by the dead G.I., and pulled out the man's dog tags. "His name is Dalton."

The white-faced soldier tore his eyes away from the bodies and looked helplessly into Jonas' eyes. "Who do we report to, sir?"

The corporal walked out of the far room, his machine gun hanging at his side.

"Report to whoever the hell you can find, Private," Jonas said. Turning to Turco, he said, "What've we got?"

"All clear, sir. There's no one left."

"Right. I'd better take a look." He strode down the hall past Turco.

Turco said, "You heard the lieutenant. Get this man down to the medics." He turned on his heel and followed Jonas back into the room.

Jonas stepped over the four bodies, two riflemen and two with burp guns. Cautiously, not wanting to make a target of himself, he stepped to the side of the window. He could hear the stuttering of a light machine gun coming from nearby. Probably from the building next door.

He took a careful look outside at the courtyard. It wouldn't do to get shot by an American sharpshooter. A couple dozen of the vehicles in the courtyard were overturned, burning, some now just scrap heaps of metal. Dead and seriously wounded soldiers, unable to crawl, lay where they fell. No medics could get to them. The North Koreans had everyone pinned down, men scattered all over the compound behind any cover they could get, a couple dozen returning fire.

Then he saw, from the far side of the compound, a head and shoulders pop up from behind a jeep, a tube on the right shoulder. Recoilless rifle. An orange blast shot out its rear and a rocket roared in Jonas' direction. He dropped to the floor, covering his helmet with his hands.

The explosion set his ears ringing. Everything shook. Clay plaster rained down from the walls and ceiling. Rattled, Jonas gulped air and looked around. No damage here. The rocket must have hit the building next door, or maybe the one two buildings down.

Still shaking, he leapt to his feet. Turco was down on his knees looking stunned. He hadn't had any warning.

"Rocket," Jonas said. "Our guys taking out the machine guns next door. Hope Strosahl gets word to those guys that there are friendlies in here." He ran past Turco, who got up and followed.

Outside Jonas approached the next building, the one that had just been hit by the rocket. Its roof was burning, clumps of fiery thatch falling down around them, smoke spiraling upward. More black smoke billowed out of the back door. He poked his head in the doorway and saw that the inside of the building was ablaze. No one could be alive and hiding there. The rocket had already killed any enemy combatants. That was a relief. A building he and Turco didn't have to take.

The wind carried the thick acrid smoke their way. Two of the buildings were now fully ablaze. Maybe, he thought, they should just wait. The wind was shifting; the fire would spread farther. They didn't have to risk themselves taking this last building.

But the building was brick, wouldn't burn easily, and even from the back Jonas could hear sniper fire pouring out of the second floor. And not just rifle fire – a machine gun, a heavy one.

But what if the Americans in the compound found another rocket? Someone had to be scouting one up. Turco and he could be caught in the blast. What is it Strosahl would say? We're not getting paid to fuck around. We've got a job to do; let's do it.

Jonas shook the tension from his shoulders. "You ready to take on this last building? There's just you and me."

Turco adjusted his helmet. "Wouldn't want to miss the fun."

Jonas ran at a crouch to one side of the back door. Turco took the other side. Taking a deep breath and exhaling slowly, Jonas pulled the door open. He tossed the grenade in a smooth, coordinated move. Another explosion, the concussion vibrating the wall he was leaning on, chunks of plaster raining down on him.

Looking in, Jonas glimpsed three bodies collapsed in a far corner and heard noises, pounding feet, coming from the floor above. The bodies didn't look like any soldiers he'd seen. He peered through the settling dust and saw that it was a woman and two children who lay in the corner. She was faceless, the grenade blast having ripped it off. Hair and flesh and blood were splattered on the wall behind her. The two children were crushed to her breast, one in each lacerated arm. Both were missing the backs of their heads. Pulpy clumps of grey matter oozed down their necks.

Jonas' throat and chest tightened into knots, and he squinted to blink back the automatic tears. He shook his head. I did this. I threw the grenade.

He heard the sound of rifle fire and the plunk of the round hitting the wall next to him. He jerked back away from the doorway. He'd just had time to glimpse a soldier standing at the head of the stairs on the second floor. He signaled to Turco who stepped into the doorway and fired a full magazine at the stairway.

Turco jumped back to his side of the door a half second before the return fire blasted the door frame. This time it wasn't a single rifle shot, but automatic fire. It sounded like they now had two burp guns up there covering the doorway.

"I'm all for forcing our way in," Turco said, "but as long as they've got the door covered from above, I don't see us making it."

"Watch the door," Jonas said. He stepped back from the building. There was a balcony up there off the second floor. If the two of them could scale the wall, they might be able to get at the shooters from behind. Rummaging behind the building, he found several lengths of rice rope. Jonas cut and tied the pieces together with square knots to make a seven-foot long stretch.

"Okay, Corporal, here's the plan."

"Always did favor having a plan."

"You do one grease gun sweep so they don't come down checking on us anytime soon."

"Got it. What then?"

Jonas held up the rope. "Then we're going up the side of this building. You boost me up and I lower the rope for you."

Turco shook his head. "Climbing a damn rope, that's one thing I'm not so good at."

"You don't have to climb. I'll pull you up."

"With all this gear on, I probably weigh two hundred pounds."

"I bench press more than that."

"That's your plan?"

"That's it." Jonas looped the rope across his upper torso and slung his carbine over his left shoulder.

Turco took a breath. "Okay, here goes." He stepped into the doorway and fired a long burst across the room. Then he hopped over to Jonas' side while slinging his weapon. He bent his knees and interlocked his fingers. Jonas stepped gingerly into his hands and, as Turco boosted him, thrust himself up.

Jonas' fingers clamped over the protruding floor of the balcony. With Turco continuing to lift, he pulled his chin up over the floor and then thrust his right hand straight up, his fingertips gaining a precarious hold on the top of the balcony wall, inching them over the ledge until he had a secure handhold, and then swinging his left hand and arm up, he secured his hold. Simple. *Now all I've got to do is chin myself.*

He pulled himself up as smoothly as a gymnast working the horizontal bar, then raising his leg until he got one foot on the bit of shelf, he was up and over the ledge.

He grinned tight-lipped down at Turco. The corporal saluted back. Jonas dropped the rope and in short order hauled him up, his feet scraping against the wall all the way as he tried to get a toehold.

"Nothing to it," Jonas grunted.

Turco adjusted his helmet, which had slipped back on his head. "Yeah, when we get back to the States, we can try out together as a circus team."

Crouching, the two made their way along the balcony and under an open window. Jonas knelt beside a door, while Turco peeked over the bottom of the window into the room. All clear. Jonas caught his signal and slipped inside. The next moment, Turco joined him.

Taut-faced, Turco whispered. "Was there another part to this plan, sir?"

"You're the one with all the house-to-house combat experience. I thought I'd let you make it up."

Turco grimaced. "Grenades would be a start. Have you got any left? I'm fresh out."

Jonas checked. "Two."

"Gettin' low. Might be enough." Turco slipped a fresh clip into his gun and checked to make sure he had another clip ready. He exhaled heavily. "My plan" he said, gesturing toward the door, "would be to first clear that hallway."

They both moved to the door. Jonas listened for voices in the hallway – there seemed to be two – estimated their direction and distance, pulled the pin, let the spoon flip away, counted off two seconds, praying that the manufacturers had perfected the timing on these fuses, and tossed it.

The two voices squealed, and then the explosion rocked the walls. Cpl. Turco darted into the hallway. Jonas followed. Turco had gone straight across the hall into the room on the other side through the open doorway. A burst from his machine gun told Jonas everything he needed to know. The two voices he'd heard in the hallway were now silent.

Turco joined him. "One room to go, he said, pointing back to the last room with his grease gun. "The machine gun must be there."

Jonas put his back to the wall and inched his way forward. His stomach churned figuring these guys would now have their weapon turned on the doorway. He didn't know how he was going to get the grenade into that room without being cut to shreds himself.

As if the enemy was reading his mind, a burst of machine gun fire, large caliber ammunition, tore through the doorway, shredding the frame and the wall about the door. Grey light streamed through the jagged holes, some of them big, holes placed right about where he'd have to stand to toss the grenade inside.

This would be a good time for an assist from the troops in the compound. Maybe this machine gun crew, their backs to the window now, were showing a bit of helmet and a sharpshooter out there could nail them. Maybe the Red gunners would figure they were in an impossible situation and find a white flag. Did they know what a white flag meant? Maybe one of our guys has got himself a rocket launcher and is taking aim right now.

"Corporal, how'd you like me to put you in for a medal?"

"Whatever it is you have in mind, I'd rather you put yourself in for one, sir."

"See that big hole nearest to me?"

"Got it."

"Put a burst through there; I'll follow up with a grenade."

Turco crawled along the bottom of the wall. The hole was about two feet off the floor. He reached up without raising his head and put a long burst into the room, emptying his clip, the port of the gun pointed skyward and the empty brass shells kicking up into the air like a geyser, raining back down on Turco's helmet.

Jonas was up, pulling the pin, and throwing the grenade into the room as he crossed from one side of the open door to the other. As quick as he was, the machine gunner inside got off a burst, two shells whipping by his head, the hair on the back of his neck going electric. He heard the grenade bouncing around on the floor, voices, scrambling feet and the explosion and hot white flash followed by the concussion wave and screaming shrapnel.

Nothing. Silence. Jonas looked at Turco who still lay on the ground. The corporal eyed him and shrugged his shoulders. Jonas stuck his head around the corner and saw a soldier with a red star on his cap pushing another soldier's body off him and reaching for the machine gun. Jonas flung himself back away from the door as the machine gun ripped holes in the wall next to him.

Turco sat up, his face now level with the hole he'd fired through, and emptied another clip, this time held steady on his target until there was no firing coming from either gun.

Jonas crept back for a look. Five bodies were scattered about, twisted, one missing an arm, lots of flesh, blood, and grey matter splattered about.

Jonas let his legs collapse under him as he slid down the wall with a sigh. "Done." He turned and, looking around the door frame, surveyed the carnage. He shook his head and reached for a cigarette. "Better get that machine gun – in case more gooks come calling."

"Oh yeah," said Turco.

Jonas nodded. "Just don't show your face at that window or one of those clerks might get in a lucky shot and take your head off." He pulled out a cigarette and lit up.

"Right." Turco got down on all fours.

As he crawled forward, Jonas drew deeply on his cigarette and started to climb to his feet. He had one foot under him when he heard a 'whoosh' of a rocket and dove to the floor. The rocket exploded, the heat of the fireball washing over him. Those damn clerks had found a rocket!

He scrambled back. The door frame was aflame. The wooden beams in the stuccoed walls were burning. He ran into the room, red-orange flames dripping from the ceiling. The North Korean bodies were masses of blackened meat. Jonas let his carbine fall. His stomach roiled and went queasy from the smell of burnt flesh.

Turco lay belly-down, his helmet smoking and all the clothing on his back scorched away, his body charred. The skin on his back from neck to foot was a smoking, black crust. His skin was cracked, broken open, pink ribbons of muscle showing.

His body began to quiver furiously. He turned a blistered, contorted face to Jonas and let out a high-pitched scream.

"Turco!" Jonas ran over and dropped to his knees.

The corporal howled. "Aaeiiighh!"

"Turco!"

Gurgling and choking, Turco forced out unintelligible syllables. "Sht seee!"

"What?"

A rasping sound. "Shoot meeeeee!" Blood and white froth bubbled out of his mouth.

Jonas rocked back on his heels.

Turco screamed, "Jesus, do it! Do it now!"

Jonas jumped back stunned. Turco let loose a scream that seemed never to end.

Tears streaming down his cheeks, Jonas dropped back down next to Turco, pulled his .45 out of his holster, pushed the safety off with his thumb and put the barrel to Turco's temple. His hand trembled. He tried to pull the trigger – but couldn't. His chest felt like it would explode, and his whole body went cold like he had just plunged into freezing waters. "God help me, I can't do it."

Turco wailed and screamed.

Jonas turned his head away, shaking it no, no, no. And then, as though his finger had a will of its own, as though it was moved by its own brand of compassion, he felt it pull the trigger. He jerked the pistol away from Turco's head. It kicked back in his hand and the bullet splattered stucco on the far wall. The single casing ejected and spun out, bouncing across the floor.

Jonas heard the tromp of footsteps behind him, running into the room. He looked up as Strosahl dropped down next to him.

"Shooot me," Turco pleaded.

"Goddamn, Lieu," Strosahl said, and took his .45 from him. "I'll do it, good buddy," he said – not to Jonas, but to Turco.

He put the .45 to Turco's temple and squeezed the trigger.

The shot echoed throughout the room. Turco's body jerked and lay still. Fire continue to drip from the ceiling.

"Come on, Lieu, we've got to get you out of here."

12

Jonas felt Strosahl take his arm and ease him to his feet. "You go downstairs. I'll stay here with him."

He did as he was told. Maj. Ellison was there, inspecting the grisly tableau of the dead civilian family. A squad of riflemen and four litter bearers milled about just inside the doorway.

The major's face lit up. "Damn, Lieutenant. You did it. By God, you cleaned out the whole nest." He walked over, grabbed Jonas' hand and shook it. "You saved a lot of lives today."

Jonas stared at him, not hearing. "I was supposed to take care of him – and I couldn't."

"Who?"

"My man, Cpl. Turco."

"Where is he? Hurt? I'll get a medic to him."

"Dead. He's dead."

Maj. Ellison shook his head. He signaled to the litter bearers.

Jonas turned and looked up the stairs. "North corner, facing the compound. The room's burning."

Ellison turned to the litter bearers. "Be quick about it. The roof might go." Two soldiers ran up.

Ellison turned back to Jonas. "Follow me, Lieutenant," and led the way out the back door and through the gap between the buildings.

Jonas was numb all the way to the compound. Behind them the whole row of buildings crackled in flames. Thick black smoke swirled out and over the compound, mixing with the smoke from a half-dozen burning vehicles. Medics, soldiers, and litter bearers scurried about.

"We've still got a job to do, son," Maj. Ellison said. "You up to it?"

Jonas wanted to laugh at the absurdity. We still have a job to do? But immediately he realized his thinking was crazy. He did have a job to do. He had to put what had just happened out of his mind. He had to try.

"I'm up to it."

"Good. Take charge and see that all the wounded get to the regimental aid station."

"Yessir."

"I've got to report to Gen. Dean."

Jonas saluted, and the major returned it, pivoted, and strode off through the open square of burning vehicles and soldiers running in all directions.

Jonas followed a few steps but veered off to the right when he heard moans. He found a casualty sitting behind a jeep, rocking and holding his head, blood streaming through his dirt-smeared fingers. Jonas called, "Medic," and within seconds one appeared.

His numbness continued to dissipate. He was acting, making decisions, giving orders, even if he felt a bit like an automaton. As the last of the litter bearers trudged off, Jonas followed behind. The two-story wood-and-masonry school building had a large hole blasted through one wall, right at the corner. The hallway and landings were filled with wounded men, some lying on litters on the floor, others sitting, being patched up by medics. The smell of disinfectant saturated the air.

Jonas helped teams load the wounded into trucks and ambulances for transport to the train station. No one knew how long the trains would continue to run. Another detail was putting corpses into body bags and stacking them in a truck. He saw Turco's body laid out, one body in a row. Jonas watched the soldier from graves registration close the zipper over the blistered, burnt face with a bullet hole in the temple.

A team of soldiers packed up the medical station even as the medics continued their work. The M.A.S.H. unit and the 24th Medical Battalion had evacuated a day earlier, leaving only this one medical company behind. Whatever wounded they couldn't get to the train would have to travel the whole thirty bumpy miles to Yong-dong by ambulance.

Jonas helped out until he'd done all he could. He made his way back to Gen. Dean's headquarters where he found mass confusion. Men were piling equipment into trucks, while others were using thermite grenades to destroy the documents and equipment that they didn't have time to pack.

He gleaned scraps of information from this and that man scurrying about. Col. Beauchamp, the C.O. of the 34th Regiment, had taken off in a jeep two hours earlier. Nobody knew where he had gone, and nobody had heard from him since. Orders to withdraw had been sent to the three battalions on the ridgeline, but only one had confirmed. There'd been no radio contact with the other two for hours, and the runners sent from headquarters hadn't returned. Five American tanks had arrived from Yongdong to support the evacuation, but that was all the help the force in Taejon was going to get from the rear.

"Where's Gen. Dean?" he said.

A sergeant pointed along the front of the building to an open tent next to the corner, housing an array of communications equipment. "There, at Tactical Air Control. He's calling in air strikes."

Jonas trotted down to the tent and saw the general, mike to his mouth, looking drawn and haggard, his voice a little hoarse, but still firm, as he directed several bombing and strafing runs. Jonas couldn't help but wonder: where was the officer who was supposed to be doing this job? It certainly wasn't the general's job.

Catching sight of Jonas, Dean waved for him. "Stuyvesant, I want you in a jeep near the head of the column, behind the first or second tank. As soon as that tank gets clear of the city, you and your driver take off ahead.

"Get to your regiment and let Col. Stephens know we are coming through his lines. Make sure they know back there these tanks are ours. We don't want them turning those new bazookas on *us*, now do we?" The general gave the slightest hint of a smile.

"No sir," Jonas said, but Dean had already turned away and was giving more orders.

Jonas trotted off, his carbine on his shoulder and his .45 bouncing against his hip. He saw a familiar face.

"Capt. Gibson."

"Stuyvesant." Gibson cocked his head and smiled a tired smile. "Isn't your unit in Okchon?"

"I'm on special assignment for Gen. Dean. He wants me in a fast jeep," he said, and explained.

Gibson thumbed through the sheets on his clipboard. "I've got the man for you." He turned his head and shouted, "Someone find Reynolds for me." To Jonas he said, "He's the best I've got, but don't tell him I said that."

He took Jonas aside. "Since you're going ahead of the column, maybe I could ask you to do something for me?"

"Sure."

Gibson pulled a folded envelope out of his breast pocket. His voice went husky. "I'm bringing up the rear, and you never know — if I don't make it out, would you see this gets mailed to my wife?"

Jonas took the envelope and put it in his pocket over his heart, tapping it lightly. "When we meet down the road, I'll give this back."

"Thanks.... Your jeep is that one right over there. I'll send your driver as soon as he reports."

The captain turned away, barking out a series of orders. Jonas found his jeep. He scanned the column of vehicles forming up for any sign of Strosahl but didn't see him anywhere. He took a seat in the jeep. About five minutes later a skinny, freckled soldier climbed in beside him.

"Pvt. Reynolds, sir," the gap-toothed kid grinned.

"You going to get me to Okchon ahead of this column, Reynolds?"

"Those are my orders, and I reckon I know more about burnin' rubber than any other driver in this here outfit."

Reynolds put his jeep in gear, drove along the column, and found a place behind a truck a few vehicles behind the second tank. He turned off the ignition and settled back. They were on Army time: hurry-up-and-wait.

"You regular infantry, sir?"

Jonas nodded, distracted, just wanting to be moving.

Reynolds slapped out a snappy drum beat on the wheel. "I got me a taste of that today."

"Oh yeah?" A lot of Headquarters and Service Company had.

"The general, he formed a squad and took us tank huntin' with that new three point five rocket launcher? A load just come in today, and he wanted to try it out first hand 'cause he said those tanks been givin' our boys a hell of a time. So about eight of us are makin' our way thru these streets, takin' some sniper fire, and we come round this corner and there is the biggest-for-to-jesus tank I ever seen. And it's takin' aim right at us. I'll tell you, Lieutenant, I thought my ass was fried."

Jonas nodded. "I've been there."

"You know what I'm talkin' 'bout then. Well, the general, he's no fool. He gets us out of there and takes us behind and into the buildings, so we come up to this window overlookin' the street, and if that damn tank ain't already takin' a bead on us. But the general, he quick pops a rocket in the tube, and the shooter fires this sucker right down that tank's throat."

Jonas raised his brows. He thought, I guess when the general said he wanted to see the enemy up close, he wasn't kidding.

"Whoooeee! The back blast from that launcher nearly blew this room apart. Fire shoots out – that's how my eyebrows got burnt," he said, pointing to the dark lines. "Plaster is fallin' all over us, and by this time I'm on the floor. But the general, he pops in another rocket and whoosh! Number two goes right home to mama and makes a baby. I get on my feet and I tell you, that was one hell of a sight, that damn tank just sitting there smokin'!"

Jonas smiled a tired smile. "So, are you ready to transfer out of the motor pool to a line outfit?"

The private took a deep breath and shook his head slowly. "I'm thinkin' not. That action today, that'll hold me for a while. It's a good story, but I'd like to live long enough to tell it to my children, you know what I mean?"

"All too well." Images of Turco flooded him.

He turned his head away, so Reynolds wouldn't see his eyes watering. He looked up and down the column of tanks, jeeps, trucks, ammo carriers, a half-track rigged up with anti-aircraft guns, and artillery tractors with their drivers ready to go. The 3rd Battalion came in from the ridgeline, and their trucks joined the column; but as soon as they arrived, rumors began to fly. The 3rd Battalion had lost all contact with the other two. Nobody knew what had happened to them.

3rd Battalion's L Company was assigned as rear guard. The sound of small arms fire to the rear had been steadily increasing, more than just sniper fire. Jonas could picture it clearly: lead units of the North Korean Army were already at the edge of the city, and L Company was alone back there, protecting their rear, trying to give the rest of the column time to escape.

Jonas could feel the unspoken dark reality settle in on the troops: the other two companies were not coming down from the ridgeline. Diesel engines began firing up, and Jonas heard the lead tank open throttle and saw it lurch forward. He drummed the floor with his foot, anxious to be gone.

"Room for me?"

He turned his head and saw Strosahl standing a couple feet behind him, his carbine on one shoulder and a green canvas pouch hanging from the other.

"Hop aboard."

Strosahl nodded and climbed into the back, settling in, a clinking sound coming from his pouch as he carefully positioned it on the floor.

Reynolds put the jeep in gear and pulled into the column, eight vehicles behind the lead tank.

"Lieu,..." Strosahl said.

Jonas, lips pressed tightly together, looked at him.

"There was nothing else to do for him."

"Let's not talk about it."

Reynolds inched ahead.

Wanting to change the subject, Jonas nodded at the pouch. "What's in there?"

The sergeant pulled the flap back and showed the six bottles of booze and two metal flasks inside.

"What the..."

"The staff officers at regiment ponied up and sent me to see if I could convince my friend Sgt. Collins to part with some of his precious stock. Having tried some," he screwed up his face, "I'd say he's mixed good American whiskey with Korean booze. It's got quite a kick."

The air was hazy with smoke and, in the distance, cannons thumped. The traffic ahead had come to a stop. Reynolds turned around and eyed the bag. He licked his lips. "Any chance of getting a taste?"

"You get us to Okchon alive, and you'll get more than a taste. Deal?"

"Deal." Reynolds smiled broadly. He tapped the accelerator like a drag racer waiting for the light to change. Jonas rolled his eyes.

"What?" said Strosahl.

"We'll talk about it all when we get out of this."

The jeep crept forward. Jonas' body was taut with tension. It was all too slow. Why couldn't the column just move? The city was feeling more and more like a trap.

There were only a few streets wide enough for motor vehicles. The column began to wind its way through these, searching for the Seoul-Pusan Highway. MPs waved the vehicles forward. There was an urgency to their signals. Move it. Move it along. It was time to stop crawling and open throttle. The street opened up and straightened out for four blocks, with businesses and residences crowding in on both sides, a line of telephone poles on the right.

Machine gun fire burst from a second story window, and then the whole street erupted. Mortar shells and rockets exploded up and down the line. Hand grenades rained down from above. Machine guns chattered away, orange tracer rounds sweeping up and down the convoy.

In front and behind them, trucks burst into flames and riflemen leaped out, scrambling to find cover. Jeeps careened and slammed into buildings. The turrets of the two lead tanks began rotating as they sought targets.

Jonas saw immediately that it was suicide to stay and fight it out. He leaned over and yelled in Reynolds' ear, "Get us out of here."

Reynolds gave a curt nod, threw a glance over his shoulder and jockeyed the stick shift into reverse. The jeep jumped back five feet, brought to an abrupt halt as Reynolds hit the brake. He yanked the wheel to the left and whipped around the troop truck with its soldiers crouched behind and crawling under it, trying to find targets in second-story windows.

Reynolds wove in and out of vehicles, squeezing through where Jonas was sure there wasn't enough room, as machine gun fire cracked overhead and mortar rounds exploded in red bursts before and behind. A jeep ahead of them, hit by a rocket, flipped over on its side. Reynolds, trapped behind it, reversed again and pulled around.

The thatched roof of one building roared into red and blue flames, the fire jumping roof-to-roof with alarming speed, moving up and down the street and finally gaining such intensity that flames leaped across the street and set ablaze the thatched roofs on the other side.

But not all the roofs were thatched. Buildings with tile roofs were scattered throughout, temporarily exempt from destruction, the snipers concentrated in these buildings. This was a quick impression that Jonas got as they raced up the block, around two tanks, just before Reynolds cut left into a narrow hole between two buildings, a darkened side street or alley that swallowed them up in its protective gloom. Suddenly they were alone. The fighting, it was all behind them.

Chen stood at the center window and surveyed the unfolding carnage in the street below. Machine gunners at the two end windows fired down on the Americans, while assistant gunners fed them ammo and poured water on the barrels to keep them from overheating. Beside Chen a soldier with a recoilless rifle had just taken the tread off a tank, leaving it dead and smoking in the middle of the street, blocking other vehicles from escaping the ambush.

A lone jeep wove in and out of the stalled traffic. The recoilless rifleman tracked it and Chen noted both the jeep and his man with satisfaction. But out of the corner of his eye he saw a half-track farther back down the street. Its twin fifty-caliber machine guns swiveled up and locked on his position.

Chen threw himself against his shooter and the soldier's assistant, and the three of them went down in a heap as fifty-caliber bullets ripped through the window above them, knocking out whole chunks of wall. Whole portions of the wall and ceiling exploded, raining down on them.

From beneath the rubble, Chen saw that one of his machine gun teams had been wiped out. The other was cowering in a corner. He scrambled on all fours to the window and poked his head over the lower edge. The half-track's guns had rotated away from Chen's building and were taking aim at teams positioned across the street.

Hauling the rifleman and assistant to their knees, he grabbed the recoilless rifle, intending to thrust it into the shooter's hands; but the man was trembling so badly, Chen mounted the tube on his own shoulder.

"Load now," he ordered, and the assistant shoved a rocket into the rear. Chen quickly took aim on the dark profiles of the half-track's gunners. He pulled the trigger, and the rocket roared off, the back-blast shaking the room. He saw the red explosion of a direct hit – and the smoldering wreckage as the smoke cleared.

"Load now." He drew down on another target, and then another. When he ran out of rockets, he dragged away the bodies from the machine gun position, found the gun still worked, and fired that until the last belt was exhausted – long after he could find any target showing a sign of life.

Chen stood up, his face blackened with cordite, blew his whistle, and waved to squad leaders in other windows. Up and down the line, the firing began to sputter out. Although he could hear the battle still raging in nearby areas, here it was over.

He scanned the narrow street. Many of the buildings were on fire, the ones with thatched roofs having gone up first, black hulking forms burning red in the night. He had positioned his men in the safest buildings, but even these were threatened now, and he would have to withdraw soon.

The crackling red-and-yellow flames lit up the night, the light filtering through the fog of gunpowder and smoke. The haze hovered over the scene of burning trucks and overturned jeeps, many slewed across the street, jamming up the road for the vehicles behind that had been trying to escape. Drivers were slumped over their wheels.

American soldiers were down everywhere, some sprawled besides the transport trucks, others in doorways where they had taken cover.

What was the American phrase? Like shooting fish in a barrel? Well, not quite. His men had taken out only one tank with mortar fire; and, although the Americans on the ground had been able to shoot back, he had taken few casualties.

He was satisfied. Some vehicles had gotten through, but not many. Those Americans who had escaped the trap were mainly on foot and would have to make their way through the hills back to their now retreating lines. He could leave the rest of the mop up to his lieutenants while he took a well-deserved rest.

The jeep tore through deserted narrow backstreets. Reynolds, bent over the wheel, peered through the stench-laden black smoke rolling in on them from all directions. Jonas heard explosions going off to the northeast. He estimated them to be in the railroad yards. Twice he heard shots, one hitting the tail of the jeep.

A right-hand turn and the jeep sped under train track trestles. A few minutes later, they broke out of Taejon onto the highway. The terrain turned hilly, and the dirt road wound through the contours of the landscape, scrub brush and shrunken trees dotting the rocky, grey-brown hillsides that stretched up and out, merging into mountain ranges on the north and south.

Reynolds reached forward and flipped off the headlights. Jonas grunted in agreement. No use giving a homing beacon to any wandering enemy patrols. The roar of the motor in the quiet of the night was enough of an announcement. Jonas rested the butt of his carbine on his thigh, finger at the trigger, ready to snap off a shot. He looked back. Strosahl was scanning both sides of the road, his rifle too at the ready.

It was only ten miles until they would reach the tunnels for the railroad and highway, then a mile or two beyond that to American lines and another three miles to regimental headquarters. Jonas clenched his teeth and focused his mind on his report for Col. Stephens. The cool air whipped around his head.

Rice paddies and bean patches dotted the landscape along the road. The jeep bounced past a silent village, mud farmhouses that gleamed darkly in the silvery moonlight.

The miles fell behind them, carrying them almost halfway home. The jeep rounded a bend and Jonas' gut suddenly tightened as he heard that now familiar but dreaded whistling sound. The rounds exploded one, two, three, four ahead of the jeep, rocking its chassis and spraying the front of the jeep with metal fragments, shattering their window. The vehicle careened from one side of the road to the other as Reynolds fought the wheel.

Jonas snatched a quick glance at the boy. He had gashes all over his face, and his hands were lacerated. Shards of glass covered them both, but Reynolds was still in control of the jeep. Behind, Strosahl hung on, grim-faced but untouched by the spray of glass.

Rounding the next bend, Jonas glimpsed the road stretching straight out for a mile. They had either broken through the roadblock – or were about to run a gauntlet. He prayed they were past the danger.

The first machine gun opened up, a stream of bullets cracking overhead, followed immediately by sporadic rifle fire, and then the next machine gun, orange tracer bullets streaking at them from paddies and ridges, swarming around and chewing up the jeep.

The rocket hit. Their engine exploded as the jeep lifted off the ground, spun and flipped. Jonas felt himself whirling head-over-heels into the inky blackness.

He came to slowly, stunned and numb, not knowing where he was – or even remembering what had happened. Bits and pieces started to come together. He looked at the ground rising on each side and guessed he was sprawled in a ditch. The more conscious he got, the more pain he felt. His vision was blurry, and the right side of his body was on fire from his shoulder all the way down to his thigh, as though he'd been jabbed repeatedly with a hot poker. He was afraid to turn his head in case his neck was broken.

He heard Reynolds moaning, maybe a dozen yards away, but not calling out for help. The kid, he guessed, was barely conscious. He didn't hear anything from Strosahl. That worried him more. He could smell alcohol. The sergeant's pouch must be nearby, the bottles now broken.

There were other sounds that sent a shiver down Jonas' spine: the muffled pad of many feet running over hard, rocky ground and high-pitched voices chattering in gook-talk. This was not good. He had to get out of here.

Jonas cautiously moved his head. No broken neck. Then he tried to roll over and get to his hands and knees, but the pain almost made him cry out. He bit down on his lip and choked down the groans. He scanned the ditch for better concealment. Maybe he could drag himself into some bushes. Nothing. If they checked this ditch, he was going to be captured or killed.

Jonas heard Reynolds groaning. Shut up, kid. They're almost on you. Jonas could hear them, the pad of feet converging on Reynolds. Everything was quiet for a moment; then there was a staccato burst of gunfire. Nothing more from Reynolds. More silence, then one voice sounding like it was giving orders.

The rapid patter of footsteps fanning out to scour the area. They wouldn't miss the ditch. And somewhere nearby, Strosahl had to be sprawled out. This was going to be bad for both of them. Jonas' body strained itself taut with desperation. The white moon hung in the sky, a merciless spotlight fixed on him.

He knew now that he wouldn't make it out alive, and his mind was flooded with memories of his wife. Even before they were boyfriend and girlfriend, he remembered her as a Bobbysoxer screaming and swooning at a Frank Sinatra concert. He saw her lithe body as she dove off his sailboat, her slenderness cutting the blue waters. And now lying here in this black ditch, he was dazzled by the memory of her in her white wedding dress.

He desperately didn't want to die, to have his life cut this short. There had to be something he could do.

13

H<small>E GRITTED HIS</small> teeth and began arranging his body as best he could, with his bloody side up, pulling his head back at an unnatural angle, his mouth hanging open and slack. Open-eyed, he stared at a scrawny shrub a dozen feet away, his eyes as blank as he could make them. Dirt and blood caked his face. He barely breathed.

More gibberish, then from almost right above him on the edge of the ditch a jubilant cry. They've found me, he thought, every cell in his body wanting to deny it.

Eight men. He could hear eight gathered around him. Then he saw the pants legs and rubber-soled, canvas boots as two soldiers moved into the field of his fixed stare. He waited for the bullet to the brain. Not the bayonet, he prayed, not the bayonet. Warm piss dribbled down his leg. Would they see his wet pants?

More gibberish from one of the soldiers behind him. Jonas heard footsteps and tensed. Pain! His kidney exploded in pain. The kick lifted his body, his frame lurched up and fell back just like - he hoped - a dead man's would. He felt his eyes widen in shock and pain. Did any of the soldiers notice?

Laughter. Were they laughing because they knew? Then one man bent over him and yanked his .45 from his holster. Another stepped forward, babbling to his comrades, as he leaned down to Jonas' face. Jonas smelt garlic and fish on the man's breath and the rank stench of weeks in the field without a bath. A sour liquid rose from Jonas' stomach up his throat into his mouth. The man stripped him of his watch. Another tugged his canteen free. Insanely, Jonas hoped they wouldn't go after his wedding ring trapped beneath him. Another soldier picked up his carbine.

Excited laughter broke out nearby, and the soldiers standing around him scrambled to join the fun – whatever that was. A couple of minutes later, one of Strosahl's flasks bounced by his face. There was nothing left in it to spill out. The soldiers had drunk it all.

A bugle sounded from the far side of the highway, and all the North Koreans headed back toward their lines. When he was sure they were well away, he let out a deep breath, and then gulped several more, mixed with sobs of unbelievable relief. A feeling of lightness swept through his body, and he could feel his blood pounding out a pulsating exaltation: alive, alive, alive.

He rolled over on his back, groaning over the sharp pain in his kidney. The white moon bathed him in its now beneficent light. He began to breathe in and out at a normal rate. What was next? He had to take some action. He was bleeding. He had to find a way to take care of that.

Strosahl had no idea where he was. He opened his eyes and found himself staring at a sky with stars that were slowly swirling in a wide circle. He turned his head and saw a white spotlight and realized it was the moon. He raised his head an inch and groaned as his whole body came alive as a single mass of pain. He reached out to his right and felt shrubbery. He rocked a little left and right, the dry bed of shrubbery beneath him crackling as branches broke.

His head hurt. His back hurt. Everything hurt.

"Shit."

He tried to roll over to get to his hands and knees, failed, tried again and got there. He hurt too much to stand up, so he pushed his way through the brush.

"Sarge, over here." The voice weak and hoarse, but he recognized it as Stuyvesant's. It came from his right, maybe eight yards away. With that he remembered where he was – a combat zone –and froze out of caution. What had happened? Yes, the jeep. There was an explosion. That's all he remembered.

He fingered the string of prayer beads hanging around his neck. He was tempted now to say a prayer of thanks – but didn't. That kind of superstition was foreign to him. When Mika had pleaded with him to take them, he had – not because he thought they'd keep him safe, but because taking them made her feel better. And he'd felt better knowing she cared for him.

He began to crawl in the lieutenant's direction. His own helmet was gone, his face all scratched up. He reached the ditch and saw the sprawled form.

"Damn, Lieu, what the fuck happened?"

"We took a rocket."

He did a quick scan of the surrounding area. "Where's the kid?"

"Didn't you hear? The gooks got him."

"I guess I was out cold." He looked back in the direction he'd come from. "Landed in the middle of a clump of bushes." He turned back. "Gooks were here?"

"A whole squad. Went over all this ground."

"And missed me. Damn." One more time he was a damn lucky sonofabitch. He shook his head and slid down into the ditch. "Let me take a look at you."

A quick inspection showed him that Stuyvesant had taken a lot of shrapnel along his right arm, side, and leg. He was bleeding. His face was okay. He might or might not have some broken bones, but the bleeding had to be stopped, and fast.

"Wait here."

Stuyvesant grinned. "Like I'm going anywhere."

"Right."

Strosahl scrambled out of the ditch, his whole body protesting as he forced his muscles into action. He found the jeep, and in the back a first aid kit. He looked around for his rifle but couldn't find it. On his way back, he found his canvas pouch and scooped it up, but it was filled with broken glass. Broken glass, but no metal flasks.

He heard Stuyvesant call from the ditch, "They got it."

"What?"

"The flask."

"Shit. Both of them?"

"Just one I think."

He did a quick sweep of the area and spotted the missing flask beneath a small bush. He grabbed it and dropped down into the ditch. Pulling his Ka-Bar from its sheath, he slit Stuyvesant's sleeve, the side of his shirt, and his pants leg and saw a couple dozen wounds, all bleeding profusely. It didn't look like any arteries had been hit. That was good.

"Grit your teeth," he said.

"Why?"

He uncapped the flask and began pouring the alcohol over the wounds.

"Goddamn it!"

"I said 'Grit your teeth.' It's not like they stock these kits with morphine." He pulled out his canteen and put it in Stuyvesant's hand. "Drink."

He started bandaging his platoon leader. The lieutenant took a pull from the canteen and choked. "I thought you had water here."

"Why would I have water?"

Stuyvesant shook the canteen. It was only half full. He handed it back. "Here, you're running low."

"Drink up. You need all the fluids you can get."

Stuyvesant hesitated, then drank to the last drop.

Strosahl heard the first faint rumblings far to the west. The lieutenant, his ear cocked, said, "What do you think?"

He listened some more. The sounds gradually intensified. Diesel motors and then clanking. He continued with the bandaging.

"A tank. More than one." He strained to hear.

"American?"

"Can't tell."

He tried to focus on the job at hand and not on the possibilities. If they were American, then maybe part of the column had broken through the ambush in Taejon; and the tanks were leading the way. But if they were North Korean… God, he hoped they were American.

He finished the leg. "Do you think, if I help, you can get to higher ground? We can get a better view."

Stuyvesant began to push himself to his feet, and Strosahl got his arm around him to help. "There's a small rise behind us."

Atop it, even with the extra five feet or so of elevation, he still couldn't see the tanks. If the tanks were American, the North Koreans would start lobbing mortars. He didn't hear any explosions. The tanks had to be North Korean. He shot Stuyvesant a glance and saw from his expression he was thinking the same thing. Not the whole column. The Commies couldn't have destroyed their whole column. At least some other American troops had to have broken through.

He raised his head, only able to vaguely discern the grey silhouette of the tank as it rolled into sight around the bend. No, that did not look like a Russian-made T-34.

The first rattling of machine gun fire was punctuated by the explosions of mortar shells. The North Koreans were firing. These had to be American tanks! Three tanks, not just one. And coming around the bend a longer string of vehicles, maybe fifteen. There was a column. These few, at least, had broken out of the ambush in Taejon.

Strosahl wanted to get to his feet and wave, wanted the tanks to stop and open up on the North Korean positions, to take out the whole line. Then he could get the two of them down to the road. There were jeeps and trucks down there, maybe a medic. They were still three hundred yards away; but if the column stopped and engaged the Communists, he would find the strength to get both of them down there.

The explosion was unlike any he had yet heard. The lead tank stopped dead, smoking. Its hatch popped open and a charred figure wearing a tanker's helmet tried to climb out but collapsed.

A landmine. The North Koreans had landmines. The tank now blocked half the highway. A jeep tried to race around it – exploded and flipped up and over. Another landmine. The column lurched to a halt, soldiers leaping from trucks and scrambling for cover that didn't exist.

The tanks, trucks, jeeps, and an artillery tractor, all the vehicles were under fire, red explosions and orange tracers everywhere. Another tank pushed its way forward past stalled vehicles, seeking to find or force the path through the wreckage so that the others could follow. It hit a pair of landmines, and miraculously kept wobbling forward a dozen feet, then creaked to a dead stop, just off the side of the road.

Strosahl saw a big burly man running behind trucks and jeeps, gathering men. He climbed into the cab of the artillery tractor. Soldiers scrambled aboard the back. He fired up the engine and pulled out. A troop truck and a jeep got on his tail and followed close behind, while the tractor raced through the hole the two tanks and jeep had opened in the landmine field.

Those three vehicles got through, while the rest were left behind exploding, burning, or gutted. G.I.s crouched behind the remaining hulks, strung along in a thin line. Some returned fire sporadically.

"Poor sons-of-bitches," Strosahl said. He wiped his hands up and down his thighs, discharging nervous energy.

"...Nothing we can do for them," Stuyvesant said.

"No, look, off the road behind them. That shallow ravine."

"Okay. I see it. Running parallel to the road, but it doesn't provide any more cover than where they are now."

"But look how it curves and runs away from the road. If some of those men could get to it, they might slip away unseen."

The North Koreans continued to pour machine gun fire and mortars down on the ragged American line.

"I don't know, Sarge, that's a long shot."

"Our guys can't see it from where they are. It's behind them, but it's screened."

Strosahl turned and looked Stuyvesant up and down. His first duty was to his wounded platoon leader.

The lieutenant said, "You think there's a chance you can get any of them out?"

"I don't know. I don't want to leave you alone."

"You don't even have a rifle."

"As many dead as there are, finding a spare rifle won't be hard." There was no disguising the bitterness in his tone.

"You take the pay, you do the job. Right, Sergeant?"

Three mortars exploded one after the other. A G.I. screamed.

The lieutenant said, "Go – do what you can."

The firing from the North Korean line was slowing down. Soon they would be sending troops down to finish the job.

"Okay. But, Lieu, you get moving as soon as you can. You don't want to get caught up in a sweep. Can you walk at all?"

"Don't worry about me. I've taken worse beatings than this in the ring. I once fought five rounds with a broken rib." Stuyvesant grimaced as he smiled.

"Keep traveling parallel to the highway. If I can get some of those guys out, we'll try to pick you up on the way. But we might be forced back into the hills – In which case you're on your own."

"You talk too much. Get out of here."

Strosahl gave Stuyvesant's good shoulder a squeeze and scuttled away, head tucked down.

Jonas watched as his sergeant slipped down the rise behind them, and made his way concealed by the brush, until he reached a point right behind the American scrimmage line. The North Koreans had ceased firing altogether. The silence was ominous.

Strosahl was behind a burning truck now. He had his hands on two G.I.s shoulders. He pointed behind him. They looked back, looked at him and headed for the ravine. Strosahl ran to the next vehicle. He was saying something to the soldier crouched behind the rear tire. The soldier shook his head. Strosahl ran to the next vehicle.

Jonas glanced across the road. Up along the ridgeline the North Koreans were massing. They began to move down the hill, walking fast at first, then trotting. A bugle blared. They broke into a run, yelling as they charged.

He had lost sight of Strosahl. There was chaos among those G.I.s still taking cover behind their vehicles. No one was in charge. There was no organized resistance. The North Korean infantry raced forward shooting. As they started bayoneting the wounded, Jonas turned his head away, sickened.

Jonas, who had been kneeling to watch, dropped down prone. A sense of dread spread through his veins. He was truly alone now, too wounded to walk, stranded in enemy-held territory.

The sound of gunshots faded. All he could hear was high pitched shouts and laughter.

He tried to get to his feet unaided, but the pain in his kidney caused his head to swirl, and he collapsed. Trying again, he forced himself onto his knees and left arm, and began to crawl.

His right arm was useless. It just hung down, and although he could kneel on his right knee, his whole right side and thigh were lacerated, so that every foot he tried to crawl forward caused waves of pain to shoot up and down his side.

He remembered those stories he'd read as a kid about a wounded mountain man crawling a hundred miles through Indian country to the safety of the nearest trading post. It could be done. Suck it up. Put that hand out there. Grit your teeth and pull your damn carcass another few feet.

Down this ditch... but can't stay on this track too long... it's too damn close to the road... too easy to be spotted... just got to keep moving.

He squirmed and dragged himself along the rugged ground until he found a gully that led away from the highway and made his way foot-by-foot along it. Pain. He'd known lots of pain in school, playing football, boxing, on the rowing teams, with coaches screaming at him the whole time to push harder, harder. No matter what he'd said to Strosahl, this was way beyond anything he'd ever experienced. But he couldn't let himself think about that. He had to keep moving, to get to help.

After an hour, Jonas managed to drag himself into the cover of a bean field. The eerie grey light of the moon settled over the terraced rice paddies and fields surrounding him. Those few times when he looked up from the ground, he caught glimpses of the sky overhead, dazzling with its stretches of stars.

He rested and crawled on. He got to his feet and managed to drag himself a few steps before it got too painful. He sat down heavily, wanting to cry. The tunnels couldn't be that far away. He could walk there in twenty minutes. At this rate, it would take him hours.

He knew he had to make it to the American lines if he was going to stay alive. Maybe Strosahl would find him. Maybe the sergeant was dead. Jonas pushed the idea from his mind.

He struggled on.

The house of Pak was not burning. Chen entered the enclosed court-yard by the side door and called out for the old man. Pak slid open the door to the house and stood there wide-eyed and trembling, his daughter a mere shadow behind him.

"Is it over?" Pak said. Son-a, moving almost up to her father's side, stared boldly at Chen.

Chen nodded. He glanced around at the bundles of household

goods strewn inside the doorway. Pak was ready to flee. "You won't need those," Chen said.

"But the fires." His voice quavered.

"The wind is blowing to the southwest. The buildings in this area aren't in danger."

Pak led him back to the kitchen and dropped into his seat on the floor, shaking his head. Son-a trailed behind the two, and immediately began blowing on the coals in the brazier and putting water into the tea kettle.

Pak said, "The city, it's…" He left off, unable to find the words.

"What did you expect?" said Chen.

"Not this, not so much destruction."

Chen stared for a while at the shrunken figure in front of him. "This is the Revolution. Revolution tears down in order to rebuild."

Pak looked up, tears streaming down his lined face. "Yes, the imperialists and capitalists have to be purged, but where are the workers to live? What is there left for the people who fled to return to?'

"Beware, Comrade," Chen said, a little more harshly than he intended. After all, this man had been of inestimable help over the past few days. But life here in Taejon would be chaos for a while, and Pak's services to the Revolution could easily be overlooked by the new administrators with more pressing problems on their minds. "Voicing such bourgeois sentiments could lead to your being purged."

When Pak started and looked up, fear etched in his features, Chen became annoyed. Was it his job now to protect fools? How could a man who had spent so many years studying Marxist-Leninist doctrine be so naïve?

Chen stood up. "I would like to wash." He was acutely conscious that his clothes reeked of gunpowder. He rubbed his face, brought away his hand and looked at the grime.

"Of course," said Pak, sounding a little flustered as he too quickly got to his feet. "Son-a, get our honored guest a robe and attend to him."

Chen did not wait for Son-a to find a washing bowl but strode out into the sheltered courtyard, moonlight streaming over its walls. He stripped in front of the well, tossing his uniform to one side, and poured a whole bucket of water over his now naked body. It was deliciously shocking, cold against his skin. He shook himself, stretched his muscles, and turned his head side-to-side as he twisted the kinks out of his neck. Only now was he becoming aware of all the tension bound up in his body.

He looked over at Son-a, who was staring at him unabashedly, but who immediately dropped her eyes. He said. "Can you have my uniform cleaned by morning?"

"It will be ready." She handed him a brush and soap.

He scrubbed himself thoroughly while Son-a drew another bucket of water. Again he poured the whole bucket over himself, and then one more. She handed him a towel and he dried himself, smiling all the while as the memories of the ambush flashed through his mind. He flushed with pride. It had been one of the finest victories he had ever experienced.

He looked at Son-a. "I will eat in my room. Bring me whatever you have." He glanced toward the doorway. Pak stood there watching the two of them. Chen met his gaze. The old man quivered, then scampered away. Chen shrugged his shoulders. There was no helping another man's weakness. He had done what he could for Pak.

Son-a's head was bent, and she smiled demurely. She said, "I will bring you whatever this poor house has to offer."

Chen lifted her chin and kissed her, tenderly at first, then with a fierceness, biting at her lips. She threw her arms around his neck, pulling him to her, and pressed her lips and breasts against him harder. He picked her up and carried her into the house and up to his room where he found his sleeping mat spread out on the floor.

He stripped her and fell upon her; but she, the quiet, gentle Son-a, came back at him so that, even though he was atop her, he hardly knew who was attacking whom. He pulled her head back, exposing her throat, her eyes rolling up until he could see only white orbs, and entered her. She wrapped her legs around his back and gripped him, while he thrust and thrust and she tore up his back with her long fingernails.

He expected to come quickly, but he didn't. After he finally did, Son-a lay back, languorous and smiling. She nestled her head on his shoulder, traced patterns on his chest, and spoke hesitantly about how angry her father was going to be.

He listened as she prattled softly. She was so young. He couldn't remember ever being that young. Briefly he wondered if he had missed out on something, but he concluded that he had not. He was growing hard again. Interrupting her eager talk, he took her hand and put it on his cock. She looked down in surprise and then smiled into his eyes.

He began to kiss her, firmly, but with no biting this time, and glided his hand down over a breast and then between her legs, stroking her inner thigh with his fingertips. She inhaled sharply and purred. She was wet. He pushed her flat on her back and mounted her again, this time achieving a slow, steady rhythm. He took his time, savoring every sensation, knowing with each thrust that within days he would be in battle again, that this might be the last sex he ever had.

14

A T THE TUNNELS, Jonas rested for an hour. He had to. His thirst was mounting, his breath ragged and his right side on fire. He checked the bandages Strosahl had applied. They'd slowed the bleeding, but not stopped it. His shirt and trouser leg were damp with blood. As he rested, he tried to apply pressure to the worst of the wounds, hoping that would help.

There were two tunnels: one for the railroad and one for the highway. There had been no American vehicles traveling the road in either direction. He gave up on anyone arriving to help him.

The pain put his brain in a fog. He forced himself to think. Using a tunnel would save him time, but the tunnels were probably rigged with explosives to delay the enemy. The engineers would have orders to blow them. The question was when. He could be buried inside. He shuddered at the thought.

His only alternative was to crawl over the hill. But if he took that long detour, he might die of his wounds. He'd lost a lot of blood. How long could he go on? And if he took too long, the regiment might be ordered to withdraw. The Communists would be advancing behind him, sending out patrols, scouring the countryside. He'd take the risk and use the tunnel.

The moon disappeared as he crept into the dank hollow. Cold

steel rails ran straight through the passageway over a bed of crushed rock. The cinders and rock bit sharply into his knees, so he got up on his feet. He put as much of his weight as he could on his left side, bracing his hand against the moist wall, shuffling his left foot forward in small hops, and then dragging his right from behind. Decades of smoke caked the walls. The thick acrid air burned his lungs. He kept scanning the walls for signs of wires and explosives. There weren't any. That might mean his regiment had pulled out so quickly, the engineers hadn't had time to rig the tunnels, but he didn't want to think about that.

He got to the other side, but the exertion left him exhausted, and he passed out with the moon once again shining down on him. Waking before dawn, damp with dew, he struggled to begin again. As the red sun rose, he crawled painfully through bean fields and around patches of green bamboo.

It was several hundred feet to the ridge where he'd left his men on guard. He called out all the way in his weak voice, "Don't shoot. It's Stuyvesant."

No one answered. No sentry challenged him.

At the top he found only empty foxholes. Scattered about were the remains of some C-rations and crushed cigarette butts. He pushed himself up to a standing position and scanned the road as far east and south as he could see. Deserted. Not a soul, American or Korean. Just barren, rocky hills.

He sank to the ground and cried. Then he crawled to each of the foxholes, gathering whatever meager remains of C-rations he could, and licked the tins clean.

It was two miles to Okchon, and another fifteen to Yongdong. He knew he couldn't make it to Yongdong, but he might be able to drag himself to Okchon. The Division would have recon patrols out. If he could get to Okchon before the North Koreans, a patrol might get him to his lines.

Two miles. Less than an hour's walk – if he'd been able to walk, but he wasn't on his feet. He was on his knees, when he could. Much of the time he was on his belly. He was crawling foot-by-foot, and he had over ten thousand feet to crawl. The sun had risen high. His uniform was drenched with sweat. Blue flies buzzed about his dried scabby clots, while mosquitoes drilled him for fresh blood. He struggled down the hard, rocky back of the ridgeline, then across more dikes that cut through paddies, where the air seemed even hotter because of the humidity. His tongue was swollen with thirst. The yellow-brown water in the paddies looked inviting, but he knew it was contaminated.

Working his way through a small cluster of deserted mud and wattle huts, he found a melon growing in a garden in a dooryard. He broke it open and scooped out all the sweet pink pulp. In the house he found a forgotten rice ball. Best meal he'd ever had.

Outside, he rested and checked his bandages again. The blood was dried and caked.

So far there was no sign of Communist patrols, but he knew the American lines could be pulled back faster than he could advance. He tried not to calculate his chances of making it out alive.

As he again scanned the bleak brown hills that seemed to go on forever, his mind slipped away to Ellen. He could almost see her standing mirage-like in front of him. She shimmered in her evening dress, her thick brunette hair flowing down her back. He loved to run his fingers through it. He heard the soft purr of her voice. She tilted her head up toward him, closing her eyes. She had the most kissable lips he had ever known. His breath caught as he remembered how they'd lost their virginity to each other in the back seat of his Packard. He reached out for her.

Empty air. She was gone. Instead of being able to take her into his arms, he was stuck in this damn hell hole, surrounded by brown hills and rice paddies.

He took a deep breath and started out again.

Jonas crawled through the deserted streets of Okchon to the

schoolhouse which had served as regimental headquarters. Its court-yard, once crowded with vehicles, was completely empty. There were no Americans to be seen anywhere.

He dragged himself up onto the step of the front door, a door he'd confidently walked through just two days earlier – just after the bombing and strafing attack. Sitting on the stoop, he stared at the flattened houses and shops scattered around the handful of criss-crossing dirt streets. There wasn't so much as a dog sniffing in the rubble. He could make out, a couple hundred feet away, the small railroad station, the only stone structure in the town. Still standing, it'd escaped the bombing; but there were no peasants lined up hoping for one more train to take them south.

He'd been sitting there feeling faint for twenty minutes, trying to figure out what more he could do, when he heard the voices. Definitely Korean voices. Men. No – there was a woman's voice mixed in with the men's. A small group moving through a nearby street. He could hear the creaking of a cart, and then a baby's bawl.

The group of a dozen Koreans in white peasant garb, surprised by his presence as they emerged from a side street, initially shrank away, and then gathered around him. Four men, two women, and six children. Three men had A-frames on their backs, while the oldest was pulling a cart piled high with what looked like bedding. The men chattered excitedly among themselves, while the women huddled behind them, the younger of the two trying to hush the baby.

Jonas tapped his blistered lips, begging for water. One of the younger men, a teenager, immediately reached for a gourd hanging at his side, but another pushed him and started pointing at Jonas and then gesturing at the road that ran back to Taejon. An argument broke out. Jonas could well imagine their fear. To offer him help could get them executed by the Communists, and who knew how far away the North Korean Army was? Or maybe the angry young man was a Communist sympathizer and Jonas was the enemy.

Finally the oldest of the group, a wiry man who looked to be in his fifties, spoke sharply to the two younger men and took the gourd. He squatted in front of Jonas and offered him a drink.

After Jonas had taken several long pulls, the man tried to communicate with hand signals. Jonas pointed down the road toward Yongdong and then pointed to himself and the cart. The man stroked his chin. The other three men murmured in strained tones. One of the women called after a child as he wandered up to take a closer look at the strange white man.

When the old man looked down the road and then back to his cart, Jonas began to frantically feel in his pockets for something to offer in exchange for the ride. He'd been stripped of his watch. What else did he have? He took off his cartridge belt with its empty holster and held it out. The man examined it and shook his head. Jonas took American dollars out of his billfold and offered them. The man took the money and turned the bills over in his hand examining them, then gave them back, pointing instead to the leather billfold. Jonas hesitated, took out the pictures of his wife and his I.D. and handed it over. The man smiled, stood and, bowing his head repeatedly, pointed to his cart. The young men helped Jonas get up and climb atop the bundles. When he was settled, the old man began pulling. The other three men with their A-frames, and women with loads on their heads and children at their sides, fell in behind.

By the time they reached the American lines outside Yongdong, Jonas was semi-delirious. Drifting in and out of consciousness the whole time, his world disintegrated into a series of disconnected images. Time was a blur. At the regimental aid station, medics pumped him full of blood plasma, picked some of the shrapnel out of him and, short of surgery, patched him as best they could. An aide emptied his pockets, put the contents in a little bag, and tied it to his wrist. He was packed into a boxcar with other wounded soldiers for a night-ride south. Doped up with morphine, he didn't care. It was all just a series of events, none of which had much to do with him.

When the train reached the massive stone railroad station in

Taegu, the door of the car was rolled aside and light flooded in. Attendants handed his litter down to a pair of Korean bearers. He lay for an hour on the platform, in the sun, on one of a long line of stretchers. Other bearers carried him to an ambulance, where he was loaded with three more wounded men. The ambulance tore off as though their lives depended on the driver saving every second he could.

Unloaded at the hospital, he lay in a dim hallway for another hour. The last shot of morphine wore off. His right side felt like it had been worked over with a tire iron. As his eyes watered, he clenched his teeth against the pain.

A male attendant inspected the tag on his chest, made a check on his clipboard and called for stretcher bearers. They deposited him on a table with a bright light shining down in his eyes. The room reeked of alcohol. A team of gowned figures wearing cotton masks gathered round him. Two of them cut away what was left of his clothes, while another fitted an ether mask over his face. After a couple of breaths of gas, the whole affair struck Jonas as unimportant.

When she saw his eyelids flutter, Donna Campbell quickly wiped the traces of tears from her eyes and leaned in closer. His eyes opened. They were blue, just as she remembered them. A little bleary, but still a dazzling blue.

He blinked and turned his head left and right, then focused those eyes on her.

She wondered if he recognized her. She hoped he did, but why should he? She fought to keep her tone just caringly professional. "We thought we were going to lose you to the fever."

"Fever?" His voice was hoarse and broke on that single word.

"After the second operation on your shoulder and hip. You've had a bad time of it, Jonas." It felt like a risk to use his familiar name. She knew she should be just addressing him as Lieutenant.

"I…" His voice cracked. "I know you, don't I?"

Yes, he recognizes me. She smiled and said more warmly, "We once danced together at an officers' ball in Japan. You were dressed as a pirate."

"Scarlett O'Hara."

She nodded, peering intently into his eyes.

"Donna Campbell. Taejon," he croaked.

She smiled again.

He shifted a bit and made to move his right arm but looked confused when he couldn't.

She laid her hand gently on his shoulder. "Your whole right side is bandaged up tight. You're not going to be able to use that arm for a while."

His eyes went wide. Fear.

"It's okay," she said. "No broken bones and no permanent damage. You took a lot of shrapnel, but the surgeons got most of it out. You'll heal."

She kept quiet, watching as he tried to take that in.

Then in an instant, his look changed, and his words came out raspy and anxious. "Strosahl. Did he make it?"

She didn't know. But she did know he shouldn't excite himself. "Lay still. Don't try to talk. Here, try this."

She put a bottle of water with a straw to his blistered lips, holding it there for him. He sucked the cool liquid down as fast as he could. She didn't try to stop him.

She put a hand to his forehead – and held it there a little longer than she needed to. Embarrassed, she pulled it away. "Your fever is coming down."

His eyes began to lose their focus, and he slurred his words. "I'm tired."

"Sleep. You'll be hungry when you wake up."

When he awoke again, he was stunned by all the white. The walls were whitewashed. All the sheets, bandages and casts were white.

Everything was white, except for the blue pajamas on twenty gaunt patients. Gone were the olive-drab uniforms and brown landscapes of the field. He was in a hospital ward.

A wave of excitement coursed through him. He was alive! He hadn't lost any limbs. He wasn't in a foxhole with artillery and mortar shells exploding around him. He wasn't in a jeep weaving in and out of burning vehicles as machine gun bullets whipped by. Yes, he felt drug-dulled pain all along his right side; but he'd made it to the rear alive. Lying in a bleak room on a hard mattress, he found himself growing exceedingly happy.

The gravelly voice came from his right. "Feels good, doesn't it?"

He looked over. The patient next to him stared with intense grey eyes. He had thick black hair and high cheek bones that looked like they'd been planed down.

"What?"

"It feels great to be safe. Look around. Can you imagine a hospital ward back in the States with patients as torn up as these guys are, and everyone is this happy?"

Jonas scanned the room. It was true. Most of the men had smiles – or at least looks of contentment – on their faces. He turned back. "Jonas Stuyvesant, lieutenant, with the 1/21."

"Jack Carlton, lieutenant, 3/34. And I'll bet you're pretty hungry right about now."

"Ravenous."

"So was I when I first came to. I'll get an aide."

He looked to the far end of the ward and waved at a soldier standing at a cart checking meds. Carlton pointed at his neighbor. The aide nodded and left the ward.

"Any way of finding out if one of my men is here in another ward?"

Carlton shifted in his bed, and Jonas blinked and swallowed hard when he saw the man's left leg had been amputated above the knee.

Carlton said, "Mortar shell got me at Chonan. My million-dollar wound." He sat up and swung both legs, the left leg of his pajamas pinned up. "Ask one of the aides about your man. They can get hold of the list of who's here."

Carlton rummaged in his shirt pocket, pulling out a pack of Lucky Strikes and matches. He shook out a butt and offered it. While Jonas lit up, he said, "They've got me slated to go back to the States for rehab and discharge."

Jonas sucked in a long stream of warm, soothing smoke.

Carlton said, "What about you? Think they'll send you back to the line?"

Jonas started. He hadn't even considered the possibility. The cigarette dangled from his lip, limp.

Carlton's voice sounded far away. "That's what they do here, get you back into the fight as soon as possible. But you're banged up some. It's probably too early to tell where you'll end up."

"Too early to tell," Jonas mumbled.

Carlton bent forward and pulled a crutch from underneath his cot. "They want me to get up and about when I can. These days I eat in the mess hall rather than in bed." He hopped up on one foot and adjusted the crutch under his armpit. "I'll let the aide know you need smokes."

"Thanks," he said. Carlton hobbled off.

The aide brought him food. Four trays of hot food. Chicken, potatoes, salad with tomatoes, and oranges. He ate it all, awkwardly, with his left hand. When he finished, he lay back stuffed and dreamed of the next meal.

He woke up. Carlton was off somewhere. The air was warm on the ward, the light a little hazy, and his pain manageable. He drifted in and out, dozing for a while. Another aide came by, this one with blond hair and a breezy manner. He brought meds and cigarettes and said he'd check to see if there was a Sgt. Strosahl in the hospital.

Carlton returned, crowing about winning at a poker game on another ward. He went to sleep.

Dinner came. Jonas was surprised he was hungry again. An hour later, the aide reported that the sergeant hadn't been admitted. Jonas thanked him. He was relieved just for a moment, but then realized the news didn't mean Strosahl was alive. He might have been killed back at the site of the ambush.

Another aide came around with meds. He woke up Carlton, who took his and rolled over and went back to sleep. Jonas downed his and found himself soon drifting off.

He woke up to find it was night on the ward. Two incandescent bulbs, hanging from the ceiling by wires, burned a dull yellow. There was just enough light for an aide or a nurse to find their way up and down the aisle. He stared at the ceiling until he drifted off again, memories swirling in his mind, memories that seemed like dreams.

He was sitting by a doorway with his back to a wall. Cpl. Turco said "Right," and began to crawl into the room on all fours. Jonas' gut grew taut. He wanted to yell, "No, get back," but before he could, he heard a "whooosh" – and the deafening explosion.

He scrambled to his feet. The doorframe was afire. The wooden beams in the walls were burning, and red-orange flames dripped from the ceiling. Six of the bodies on the floor, North Korean soldiers, were masses of charred meat. His stomach roiled and went queasy from the smell of burnt flesh.

Turco was screaming. He lay belly down, all the clothing on his back scorched away showing a blackened crust of outer skin broken open, exposing the pinker bloody flesh beneath.

"Shoot meee!" he shrieked. Blood and white froth bubbled out of his mouth. "Jesus, do it! Do it now!"

"No," Jonas cried. Warm piss dribbled down his leg.

He felt a hand gripping his.

"You're okay. You're safe. You're here."

It was a woman's voice.

He felt the mattress beneath him and opened his eyes. Sitting next to him, on his left, was Donna. She held his hand.

"You're going to be okay," she said.

His pajama pants were wet against his leg. He hoped she didn't see it. He sniffed the air and couldn't smell his urine. The ward was dark, so maybe she didn't know.

Both her hands were wrapped around his. "You're safe now."

His voice cracked. "Right."

Another patient across the aisle and down the row began to moan. Donna looked that way in concern.

"You okay now?"

The other patient began thrashing.

He really didn't want her to leave. But he wasn't sure, either, that she was actually at his side. Maybe she was the dream. He hesitated.

The other patient screamed.

"I'm okay," he said. "Go on."

She gave his hand a last squeeze, got up, picked up the little stool she'd been sitting on, and quickly made her way toward the screams.

He was glad she hadn't seemed to notice that he'd pissed on himself. He'd ask the aide for clean linen.

When the early morning light began to filter through the windows, an aide pushed a cart down the center aisle, distributed meds and recorded vital signs. Breakfast came. Carlton complained that his missing foot itched.

"Sorry about last night," Jonas said.

"Hey, I've had those nights myself. Everyone here does." There was an awkward moment of silence, then Carlton grinned and said, "What's up between you and Nurse Campbell?"

Jonas frowned and looked closely at the amputee for signs he was joking. Seeing none, he said, "What do you mean?"

"The way when she passes your bed, she takes a little longer looking at you than she does, say, me."

"No, you're just imagining that. We don't even know each other. Well, I mean, we have met before. Briefly."

Carlton raised his brows. "Oh?"

"When I first arrived in Japan, there was a party." He shrugged. "We danced one dance."

"Okay, so first it's you don't know one another; and now the two of you have danced together." Carlton rolled his hand. "So give with the rest."

Jonas squirmed inside. He wasn't about to tell him about the two meetings in Taejon. "If she's looking out after me, it's probably just because she recognizes me. That's all."

Carlton shrugged. "Maybe. She does seem to be paying particular attention to another guy on the ward, and he was from division headquarters staff. She probably knew him in Japan too."

"Who's that?"

"Capt. Gibson. Down at the far end of the ward."

"Gibson? The transportation officer?"

"That's the one. Know him?"

"He was assigned to the advisory group here before hostilities broke out. I met his wife in Japan."

"He got shot up bad getting out of Taejon."

"Damn. But at least he got out alive; he was afraid he wouldn't. Even gave me a letter for his wife." Jonas suddenly brightened. "When I get on my feet, I can give it back to him." Then he frowned.

"What's the matter?"

Jonas looked down the length of his body. The only personal effects he had were his dog tags. "I don't know where my things are. I had the letter in my shirt pocket."

"At the first aid station, didn't they take your things, put them in a bag and tie it to your wrist?"

Jonas thought back. Everything was a blur. "I sort of remember something like that."

"Whatever you come in with, they store."

"Good to know," he said. "It looks like I won't be walking for a few days yet. If you get down Capt. Gibson's way on one of your rambles, would you say 'Hi' to him for me?"

"You've got it."

Hours later, Donna Campbell brought him several envelopes. "Your mail is starting to catch up with you."

She stood there as he inspected the return address.

"From my wife."

She nodded. "Ah."

She didn't say anything about his nightmares, so he didn't either. Curious because of Carlton's comments, he checked her face for any sign of more than just professional interest. He found nothing.

She moved on down the line, distributing more mail. He looked after her, then eagerly turned to his letter. The earliest was post-marked June 24th. Before the war had broken out.

He still couldn't use his right hand, but he managed to get his left index finger under the flap.

> *Dearest Jonas,*
>
> *I know you weren't expecting a letter from me until you got settled in your duty station and could send me your new address. But your brother David said you were almost certainly going to be assigned to General Dean's staff with the 24th Division, and that I could post a letter care of headquarters and count on it getting to you. David says that the Army can be slow delivering your mail when you are first assigned to a unit. I didn't want you to have to wait.*
>
> *I am anxiously awaiting your news about life on an Army base. Especially the quality of the medical care. No matter what your brother says about Army hospitals, I'm a little frightened of giving up the family doctors here. It's just hard for me to believe that, when I get pregnant, some Army doctor will give me the care that Dr. Lieberman would.*
>
> *I'm also a little afraid of whether I would fit in with the other*

wives. David drove me to the Post Exchange in Ft. Hamilton in Brooklyn. Not exactly like shopping at Saks or Bergdorf's.

David and Caroline took me to Broadway to see "Come Back, Little Sheba." It was such a powerful show, and Shirley Booth was just marvelous. But it brought it home to me that to join you in Japan, I would have to give up several seasons of Broadway, the symphony, and the opera. I would, mind you, because being with you means so much more to me than anything New York has to offer.

I really am loving New York more than I ever have, but I would throw it all away tomorrow to be with you again. I miss you. Please send me all the news about what the base is like, so that, if I'm coming, I can start packing.

With all my heart,

Ellen

Jonas stared at the letter. He shook his head and laid it down. He heard Carlton's voice. "Bad news?"

Jonas tried to smile but grimaced. "No… it's just I got this letter." "Yeah?"

"My wife… back in the States, she's living such a different life. She has no idea…"

"How long since you've seen her?"

"Two months."

Two months? Only two months? Wrangling a line officer's post from Gen. Dean at the masquerade ball in Japan, deployment to Korea, the battles at Osan, Chochiwon and Taejon, and being ambushed on the road escaping from Taejon.

Carlton looked around the ward reflectively. "Over here, that can be a lifetime. War changes you."

Jonas knit his brows. Now that he thought about it, he'd seen signs of that in his own men. After Osan, of course, they'd been dispirited, but there was something else. A quiet somberness had settled on each of them. They'd stopped looking like high school kids, and a little more like Turco – men with fewer illusions.

He put his wife's letter aside. He'd have to think about how to answer it later. "Have you heard anything about what's happening up north?"

Carlton pulled a copy of the paper "Stars and Stripes" from under his pillow. "Got the official version right here."

"Which is?"

"The 24th Division put up a spirited defense of Taejon, before being forced to withdraw."

"What about getting our asses kicked during the retreat? What does it say about that?"

"What you would expect. Not much. Here, read it for yourself." Carlton got up and handed over the paper, saying, "I'll go see if your Capt. Gibson's awake."

"Thanks." He sat up so he could spread the newspaper on his lap. Two new divisions, the 25th and the 1st Cavalry, had replaced the 24th and were trying to hold the central corridor. Reading between the lines, they seemed to be getting their asses kicked too.

Jonas looked up from the paper. He felt profound relief that his men had been pulled out of the action, but he didn't imagine they would be out for long. The North Koreans were moving too fast. What was it going to take to stop them? Then there was the thought he didn't want to think: What if they couldn't be stopped?

He looked down the aisle.

Carlton was hobbling back. When he reached the foot of Jonas' bed, he said, "The captain doesn't look too good. He says to hang onto that letter awhile yet."

"Right." He wasn't sure it had survived.

Jonas awoke for no apparent reason. The ward was silent. No one was screaming or even moaning. The two light bulbs dangling beneath the ceiling gave off their dull yellow light. He turned his head, searching out the far end of the ward.

In the dim light, he could see Donna sitting on the other side of Capt. Gibson's bed. She sat still, holding his hand. Jonas stared, transfixed by the tableau. Time seemed to halt. Suddenly Gibson stiffened. His jaw jutted up, and then his body went slack as his head rolled to one side.

The nurse didn't move at first, then her tiny frame shook briefly. She fixed her stethoscope's tips in her ears and its diaphragm on his chest. Settling the tips back around her neck, she pulled the sheet up over the man's head, rose, and walked back up the aisle. Her head was bowed and her lips pursed in a thin tight line. Jonas felt a hollowness in his chest. He lay there thinking about how Cecilia Gibson flirted with him his first night in Kokura, and then saw the captain handing him the letter to her as he organized the convoy escaping Taejon.

When Jonas woke in the morning, Capt. Gibson's bed was empty – only to be filled an hour later.

15

W HEN HE HEARD the machine gun fire and mortars exploding ahead, Capt. Chen told his driver to halt. A runner trotted back to his jeep.

"Heavy resistance a mile ahead, sir."

Chen nodded and waited for the soldier to catch his breath.

"Lt. Kim estimates five hundred American soldiers dug in on a ridge."

"Americans?" Chen frowned. There shouldn't be any Americans along the route to Kochang. He pulled out his map. The rugged hills on each side of him, about a half-mile distant on each flank, began to converge from this point forward. If the column stayed on this road, it would be forced into a draw. The enemy could fire down on the North Korean column from both sides of the road. Chen grunted. The enemy commander had chosen his defensive position well. There was no readily accessible means of flanking him, no roads through these hills. Men on foot could do it, but it would be a long march, and Chen guessed the enemy's orders were to delay this column as long as possible.

Chen continued forward and joined Lt. Kim in an observation post in a peasant's hut. Kim had sent three scouting patrols forward to probe the enemy's line. The crackle of gunfire told Chen they were doing their job aggressively.

Another jeep pulled up outside the farmhouse. Two men climbed out. The regimental commander, the portly Col. Chu, ducked his head to get through the door. An attentive but rigid appearing aide trailed behind, both entering the dwelling with its mud-covered walls and thatched roof. Chu took in the room in a single glance and joined Chen and Kim at the window.

"What do we have here, Comrade?"

As Chen described the situation succinctly, the colonel pulled out his binoculars and slowly scanned the ridge from left to right. He lowered the field glasses and continued to stare at the ridge, chewing on his lip. He asked to see Chen's map. Lt. Kim found the family's kitchen table, with its short stubby legs, and put it in the center of the room. The four officers seated themselves around it on the hard-packed floor. Chu traced various routes on the map, then shaking his head, said, "It would take two days to get troops behind them. I don't see any way to flank them. They are spread out a little thin, but there are no obvious gaps in their line. I think we're going to have to do a full assault, and it's going to have to be at night."

"A night assault, sir?" said Lt. Kim. His troops had been pushing hard all day with no rest.

The colonel nodded. "Kim Il Sung himself has ordered us to keep this column moving at all costs. It's overcast again today, so we haven't had attacks from the American Air Force, but we can't count on that tomorrow. Air strikes in support of that line could hold us here for days."

A few days out of Taejon, Chen's company was leading the North Korean 4th Division's thrust down the western coast for a strike on what was supposed to be the American's exposed flank.

Chen said, "If I may make a suggestion, Comrade Colonel?"

The colonel nodded.

"I would wager that the enemy commander has placed a command post on this hill on his far-left flank." Chen tapped the position on the map. "It's higher than the rest of the ridgeline. He would have a clear view of the whole field from there."

"Hmm, that could be. But it's a guess."

"I have scouting patrols out. They should tell us whether I'm right."

"If you are right, Captain, what then?"

"Have our artillery lay down a barrage all along the ridgeline but put an extra concentration on this high point. With that covering fire, I will infiltrate my company up the hillside where it is steepest, and when the barrage lifts, my men will take the command post. From there we can fire our mortars on the rest of the ridge. That will create confusion across the ridgeline, allowing your troops to overwhelm the other positions."

Col. Chu shook his head, and his aide, seeing this, frowned at Chen. Chen turned his scarred cheek and fixed his milky white eye on the aide, who immediately dropped his eyes.

The colonel said, "There are two problems with that. One, that slope is too steep to climb; and second, there is so little cover up there that, when you are detected, you will lose half your command. Then I've got one less company, significantly weakening the assault."

Chen bowed respectfully. "I have considered those points. First, bring up another battalion. It will take my men time to get into position, giving you the time to move those additional troops forward."

"True enough, but you cannot get your men up that hill."

"Sir, these men fought with me in China. I know what they can do." Chen pointed at the map. "There is a long defile just southeast of that hill. I can move my men through it and have them in position before the artillery barrage begins."

The colonel nodded. "It could work." Then he shook his head. "But not all your men are veterans. You've just received green replacements, conscripts whose loyalty has not been tested. They could give your position away before you are halfway up."

"I will put the new men at the rear. They will not come up the hill until I have secured it."

The colonel pondered the map, then got up and went to the window. He scanned the ridgeline again.

"Your timing will have to be perfect, Comrade. If you are not almost to the top of the hill at the moment the barrage lifts, you will be exposed. There is no cover up there. One well-placed machine gun could wipe out your entire unit."

Chen said nothing. He could only guess at the pressures his superior was under. The colonel paced in the small room and returned to the window to scan the ridgeline.

"Those hills are terraced with rice paddies."

He lowered the field glasses and turned to Chen, who said what he thought the colonel must be thinking. "If you do not use my plan and send all our forces against the center of their line, the rice paddies will slow our assault and increase our losses, making it highly probable that we will have to attack repeatedly."

Chen waited silently as Chu looked through him, finally grunting. "If your scouts confirm the hill holds a command post, we'll proceed with your plan."

Suddenly the troops outside began shouting catcalls and whooping victoriously. Chu looked at Chen quizzically, while Chen could only shrug. The door opened and one of Chen's scouts entered and saluted.

"We have captured four Americans, sir."

Chu smiled. "This is good. We will send them back to division headquarters for interrogation."

"Might I suggest, sir," said Chen, "since we need whatever information these soldiers have, I could conduct a preliminary interrogation here, right now. I speak their language."

Chu stared expressionlessly at Chen for a moment before saying, "Yes, you speak English, but to extract information quickly, you would have to…"

"Interrogating them now might save the lives of hundreds of our men, not to speak of crucial hours if not days."

"Do what you have to do. I will step outside to smoke."

A moment after he left, Chen's men dragged four Americans into the hut and threw them on the floor. His men began kicking the soldiers who tried to draw themselves into protective balls, covering their heads and faces with their arms.

In English, Chen barked, "Get on your feet," and when they didn't, he ordered his men to get them up. They forced the Americans up and into a line with their backs pressed against the wall. On both sides of Chen his men stood with rifles aimed at the enemy.

The first in line was a broad-shouldered man, about five-foot-eleven, dirty, needing a shave and looking haggard, but trying to hold himself erect. He had a gash above his swollen right eye, but otherwise wasn't wounded. He had three chevrons on each sleeve.

Chen, a contemptuous look on his face, placed himself immediately in front of the man. "What is your name, soldier, and what is your unit?"

The American stared straight forward, and said, "Rossey, Sergeant, U.S. Army." He rattled off his serial number.

Chen looked at the other three soldiers, none of whom had even one chevron. Privates. They would know little. The first was a thin, willowy boy who was trembling. He held up a shorter, stockier soldier who pressed his left hand to a bullet wound in his side. The last private held himself with his arms wrapped around his middle, his eyes darting about the room.

Chen turned back to the first man. "You are a prisoner of the North Korean People's Army. You have no rank. All rank is abolished. You have no serial number. Now tell me, what is your name and what was your unit?"

"Rossey, Sergeant, U.S. Army." Again he gave his serial number.

Chen took out his pistol and put it under the sergeant's chin. "One last time. What is your unit?"

The prisoner hesitated, then said, "The Geneva Conventions for prisoners of war…"

Chen sidestepped down the line to the boy with the darting eyes. He shoved his pistol under this soldier's chin and pulled the trigger. The sound of the gunshot was deafening. A flash of light momentarily blinded him, and he felt blood, brain, and flesh splatter across his face. The boy's body slammed against the wall, crumpled and fell to the floor, pushing against Chen's shins.

Turning back, Chen pushed his own bloody face and disfigured eye in the sergeant's face. "I will ask you again, and if you do not tell me what I what to know, I will execute another of your men. Now, what is your unit?"

Chen did not have to shoot another prisoner, and twenty minutes later he left the house and joined Col. Chu, who flinched slightly at the sight of Chen. Wordlessly, the colonel offered Chen a cigarette, while the soldiers who had been clustered near the farmhouse now gave the two commanders room to confer.

Chen exhaled a stream of smoke slowly. "These men are from the American 21st Regiment."

"…Are you sure?"

"Yes."

"Our intelligence says we rendered the whole 24th Division, including the 21st Regiment, combat-ineffective."

Chen spit out a couple flakes of tobacco. "These troops are exhausted and low on materiel, men who have already seen much combat. No, they are from the 21st Regiment."

"The command post?"

"Is where I thought it would be."

"Very good, Chen. You may get your men ready for the infiltration."

"Yes, sir."

"And Chen…"

"Sir?"

Chu averted his face. "Wash that blood off your face."

Chen's men crawled up the steep hillside in the inky blackness. Even though the artillery barrage was intense, it wasn't continuous, and in the intervals when shells were not raining down on the hilltop, the enemy shot illumination flares into the sky. Whenever one popped, his men froze instantly, even those whose footholds and handholds were precarious. One soldier, losing his grip, fell two hundred feet without screaming. Only the slightest muffled thump signaled he'd hit bottom.

It had taken longer to get through the defile than Chen had expected, and now halting for the flares had further slowed his progress. He estimated they were fifteen minutes behind schedule. The barrage should lift any time now, and his men were not far enough up the hill.

Fortunately, there had been no rounds falling short of the target and hitting his own men. Everything was going according to plan. Except that they were late.

Another illumination flare popped overhead. Then he heard what sounded like a rock bouncing down the side of the hill from the top, only it wasn't a rock. Grenade. Some nervous soldier on watch up there had seen some movement or heard something or just imagined it, but now the grenade was bouncing toward his men.

As it landed in the middle of the lead platoon, Chen watched one of his soldiers throw himself on it. The explosion was still loud, but there was no bright flash or smoke. Chen gritted his teeth, then he was on his feet. All of his men were up and running, leaving the dead man where he lay.

A gentle slope rose for the last hundred yards, giving the enemy clear fields of fire; and the Americans opened up with rifles and machine guns spitting out streams of orange tracer bullets. The first of Chen's men fell.

Armed with burp guns, his men cut loose, firing green tracers in return, orange and green streams of fire whipping past each other in a cacophony of overlapping bursts. His second platoon, behind the first and not able to fire because the first platoon blocked them, swung to the right and charged, firing as they went, every third man falling as they ran forward.

Too many casualties. Chen could see he was taking too many casualties. He ran back to his mortar platoon.

"Shell the ridge."

His mortar men stood frozen. They couldn't lob mortars up there and not hit their own men. This wasn't the plan. They were supposed to set up only after the defensive position had been overrun, to fire on other ridges.

"Now. Fire now," he shouted.

In seconds his three mortar teams had found the most level spots available, dropped their plates, rammed pins in the ground to hold them in place, and adjusted for trajectory. The first round thunked in the tube and blasted off. It arced high and a little long, landing behind the defensive perimeter. One soldier adjusted the aim, and a second dropped a mortar down the tube. This time Chen could see the flash atop the ridge. Just bring the next one in a little closer, he thought. His team did. The blast blew an enemy soldier out of his foxhole.

The three mortar teams began rapid firing, walking the mortars left and right, feeling out the perimeter, suppressing much of the defenders' fire.

Chen ran back up the slope, getting those men who were not wounded or dead back on their feet. They rushed the remaining distance with burp guns firing. The mortars quit firing at the last possible moment, and Chen's men made the crest, firing down into foxholes. Chen raced past the perimeter toward the command post. Too late he saw an American captain taking aim at him with a .45 pistol. Chen tried to drop to his knee while raising his own pistol, but saw the American officer's barrel following him down, centered on him. As though in slow motion, he watched the man squeeze his trigger. Chen flinched. Nothing happened. Wide-eyed and helpless, Chen watched as the American tried again, and again, but his pistol had jammed. Chen raised his own gun as the captain stared. Chen fired three times, grouping the rounds in the middle of the captain's chest.

On the rim, his men methodically dispatched all the Americans making a stand, those that weren't running down the backside of the hill, while his mortar teams lugged their equipment to the crest and began setting up. Chen blew several whistle blasts, and his reserves and replacements began hauling ammunition and mortar shells up from the defile. The replacements also served as litter teams to get his wounded and dead down from the hill. They dragged American bodies over the far rim of the hill and dumped them.

Chen let out a deep sigh. The rest of the night would be much easier. His infantrymen set up a perimeter to defend against any attack from down the ridgeline. He didn't expect a counterattack — and there wasn't one. The enemy was too busy defending first against another artillery barrage, and then the follow-up infantry assault. His men were doing their jobs. Chen walked back down the slope to check on his dead and wounded, letting his gaze sweep the field, resting here and there on the bodies as the medics and litter bearers moved among them. Those who could get to their feet with help and hobble down the hill, would survive. But most of those with chest and gut wounds, and those needing amputations, would die. If not from the wounds themselves, then within weeks from infections. There was no penicillin. The most that could be done for them was to give them morphine, but with the Americans bombing the supply routes, morphine supplies were running low.

Chen exulted that the North Korean Army was in control of three quarters of the South. But the Americans now had airfields on the peninsula. They had been able to keep up a more intense bombing and strafing program, at least during daylight hours, slowing the North Korean advance. Ahead was the Nam River. The Americans would blow the bridges. That would slow down his troops, but not by much.

The road ahead led directly to the port of Pusan. Chen thought the strategy brilliant. By circling behind the two American Divisions now engaged in the central corridor and eastern coast, the North Korean Army would capture the port of Pusan. And when Pusan was taken, the Americans and ROK forces would be trapped between a hammer and an anvil. They could not be supplied or reinforced, and they could not escape. The North Korean Army would grind them to powder.

16

Jonas had been anxiously waiting for Carlton to return from the mess hall, hoping to get news. He and the rest of the men on the ward had been living on frayed nerves for days. First the casualties started pouring in from all the units of the 24th Division. Word was two of his men were in the enlisted ward. He had no idea how many others might be dead. Then came the rumors the North Koreans were driving toward Pusan.

It was like the German blitzkrieg rolling toward Paris. There seemed to be no stopping them, and the entire hospital staff was on edge. Everyone was talking Dunkirk. But Jonas knew that if the Communist forces took Pusan, the only South Korean port of any significance, there would be no escape by sea. The American and South Korean forces would find themselves in a meat grinder – the worst defeat in American history.

"Well?" he said as the other man dropped down on his cot. It was maddening the way Carlton was taking his time, settling in, leaning his crutch against the wall, making sure it was resting properly, and frowning like he was trying to frame a thought.

He patted both empty breast pockets on his pajamas. "Got a cigarette? I'm out."

"Sonofabitch." Jonas pulled out his pack, shook a butt loose.

Carlton took the cigarette, then tapped his pockets again. "Got a light?"

"Oh come on." He threw him his book of matches. Carlton fired up a cigarette, took a couple of quick puffs and then a long drag. He exhaled a stream of blue-grey smoke.

"Gen. Walker plugged the hole in our perimeter." Carlton's face lit up. "He fucking stopped the Reds cold on their push to Pusan."

Jonas let out his breath. "Who did it? Which units?"

"The 1st Marines and the Army's 27th Regiment."

"Damn. Someone was finally able to hold the line." He felt lighter.

"And listen to this." Carlton leaned forward and tapped Jonas on his knee. "You might be going back to Japan with me, old buddy."

Jonas furrowed his brow. "How's that?"

"Word is the whole 24th Division is being pulled out. We've taken so many losses, the Army no longer considers us *combat-effective*. They're shipping in the 7th Division to replace us."

Jonas' whole body wanted to sing out. "Damn, that'd be fucking great!"

A cacophony of wolf whistles interrupted them. Jonas turned to see which of the nurses it was. He guessed it was the perky, red-haired Lt. Mary Coburn. But it wasn't. Donna, nonplussed by the greeting, grinned and waved her clipboard at the men. She quipped, "Glad to see so many of you boys on the mend," and turned to the aide who was checking the meds on the cart.

"Here comes your girlfriend," Carlton said.

"She's not my girlfriend."

"What do you say? We get back to the Land of the Rising Sun, and we double date. Mary and me, Donna and you?"

"I think you've got an infection that's gone to your brain, and you'd better get a shot of penicillin – via a large-bore needle in your ass."

Jonas closed his eyes and waited as she made her way through the ward. His impulse was to watch her every movement, but he wasn't going to let that happen. He was married. He had rules. Besides, he knew male patients often developed crushes on their nurses. That's all this was, a passing infatuation. And if the rumor was true, and the 24th was being shipped back to Japan, then he could look forward to his wife joining him there. He tried to imagine that, to recall Ellen in the same vivid way that he had when he was crawling back to American lines. But he couldn't.

As he heard Donna finishing up with Carlton, Jonas opened his eyes.

She flashed him a smile but looked exhausted. "I see the doctor has removed the restraint from your arm."

Even tired, hers was a particularly warm smile. Despite himself, he wondered whether he should read anything special into it. He thought he heard certain undertones, slight signals that she might be feeling some attraction too, but he wasn't sure. He glanced at Carlton, who winked.

Jonas shot him a frown and turned back to Donna. He was going to keep this on a strictly medical basis. He rotated his right shoulder and lifted his arm – and winced at the pain. But the pain was not nearly as bad as it had been just days before. "The Doc says I'm healing fine, but not to go throwing any baseballs around soon."

With quick flicks of her wrist, she began to shake a thermometer down.

"I knew you were a dancer. Are you a baseball player too?" she said, her eyes twinkling. Before he had a chance to think of a witty comeback, she said, "Open up."

She stuck the thermometer in his mouth, fastened the cuff around his bicep, pumped it up, and inserted the stethoscope under the edge of the cuff. She cast her eyes down and was quiet as she released the pressure and listened.

She looked at the other entries on the clipboard before scribbling hers. "Hmm, a little high." Jonas, feeling the first stirrings of a hard-on, felt himself flush.

She took his wrist and put her thumb on the pulsing vein. "And your heart is racing a bit." She took out the thermometer.

"No fever," she said. "That's good. The doctor wants you to start getting out of bed and moving around, as long as you don't overdo it."

"I've heard a couple of my men might be on the enlisted men's ward. I'd like to go visit them."

"That depends on how they're doing. What are their names?"

"Privates Harris and Speirs?"

Donna flipped through pages on her clipboard. "Right." She lifted her head. She had such soft brown eyes. "It looks like that would be okay, but don't stay too long. They're just a few days out of surgery."

"I'll need a crutch."

She frowned. "We're a little short right now." She looked at the crutch leaning against the wall. "Maybe the two of you can share. Lt. Carlton will be flying back to Japan in a day or two."

"What?" Carlton said, "So this bum gets my crutch?"

Jonas smiled in relief. All this talk was distracting him, and his hard-on had shrunk.

Jonas hobbled into the enlisted men's ward. He scanned the cots and, seeing his men at the far end, worked his way to them.

"Hey, Lieu." A blue-eyed Harris looked up at him in surprise from his cot, his voice weak. Even though he was brown from his weeks in the sun, he looked pale. His right hand and arm were in a cast, with only three fingers protruding, his thumb and forefinger gone. "Lookee here, Speirs, and you were saying you thought the lieutenant bought it. What did I tell you? No gook was going to kill Lt. Stuyvesant. Ain't that what I said?"

Speirs was unable to reply because his jaw was wired together, but he grunted agreement.

"They treating you two okay?" Jonas asked, sitting himself down on the edge of Harris' cot so that he could see Speirs at the same time.

He laid the crutch on the floor. He wanted to ask them upfront about Strosahl, but they might think he wasn't really there to see them.

"Okay?" Harris said, forcing a smile on his haggard face. "You hear that, Speirs, he wants to know whether they're treating us okay. I tell you what, Lieu, this doctor comes by this morning and tells us we both got million-dollar wounds, and we're being shipped stateside as soon as we're in shape. Together. The doctor says we're being flown out together on account I got to look after my good buddy here. Ain't that right, Speirs?"

Speirs grunted and nodded.

"And Sgt. Strosahl, he kept telling us you were going to make it."

Jonas felt the tightness in his chest release. Strosahl was alive. "The sergeant's doing okay?"

"Last I saw. But we were in a middle of a fire fight." Harris' eyes clouded over. "Guys going down all around me. Most of them didn't end up here, so I think a lot of them bought it. The sergeant's not on another ward?"

Jonas shook his head. Now he was back to not knowing whether Strosahl was alive or dead.

To change the subject, Jonas pulled a pack of Luckies and matches from his breast pocket and shook several cigarettes loose. "Smokes?"

"L.S.M.F.T. – sure," smirked Harris.

Jonas cocked his head. He knew the slogan, 'Lucky Strike Means Fine Tobacco,' but Harris seemed to be referring to something else. He fired up Harris' cigarette and reached over, fitting another into Speirs' lips.

"Lord Save Me From Truman," Harris crowed. "Ain't you heard that one yet, Lieu? Where you been?"

Jonas smiled. "Off the line too long, obviously."

"Yeah, we could have used you those last couple of firefights." His face clouded up. "The platoon's got a new lieutenant, we're all hoping he's temporary like, 'cause you know, he's still green. But the Sarge, he watched over us good."

Strosahl. The tightness was back in his chest.

He forced himself to grin. "Tell the truth guys, don't you prefer these pretty nurses to having Strosahl watching over you?" They grinned back at him. Jonas handed Harris the pack of cigarettes and said, "I'll double-check with the doctor just to make sure there are no snafus with your flight out of here."

"You comin' with us?"

"No, it looks like I'll be fit to return to duty in a couple of weeks."

"From what I hear," said Harris, "the whole division might be pulled out by then and sent back to Jap Land."

"There is that rumor going around."

"Ain't just a rumor, Lieu. I got this from a buddy who knows a clerk at division headquarters, and he says this clerk is typing up transfer orders like crazy. They already got the ships on the way to evacuate the whole mother-fucking division. What's left of it." He took a drag off his cigarette and expelled the smoke in a long stream. "You can take this one to the bank."

Jonas stood up, thinking he wished he could do that. He forced a smile. "There's nothing I like better than going to the bank."

He turned to Speirs. "The Army's got great doctors back in the States. They're going to take good care of you."

Speirs grunted something with his wired-up jaw that could have been taken for a "Yessir," and tried to smile, but winced.

Looking at Harris, he said, "You take good care of him."

"I will, sir," he said, as though this were a new order, and something he wasn't already dedicated to doing.

Jonas reached out and squeezed his shoulder, looking him straight in the eyes for effect. "And you take good care of yourself."

"Yessir," Harris beamed.

As Jonas hobbled back up the aisle, he heard Harris saying, his voice hoarse now from the exertion, "See, what did I tell you? Didn't I tell you no gook was going to kill the lieutenant? But no, you were sure he was a goner. See, what you need to understand, my man, is…"

Jonas sat down heavily on his cot. "It's a fucking mess."

Carlton, stretched out, turned his head toward Jonas. "Been to see your men?"

"…You know what really burns me?"

"What?"

"When we landed in this shithole," Jonas said, "riding the train north to the first battle, we all thought we were going to be fighting peasants armed with pitchforks. They sent us up to the front, and G-2 didn't even know the North Koreans had fucking tanks! The Russians had to be building and training this army for years. Did the Pentagon know? Did fucking MacArthur's staff know? What were they doing?"

"Our intelligence was shitty. That's a fact."

"So these kids get shot up, and when they get back home, nobody's going to care what happened to them, except maybe their families. They'll just be forgotten. What they've sacrificed will be forgotten."

"Don't kid yourself. We'll all be forgotten. Forgotten Americans."

"Probably right. First we get screwed, then we get forgotten. Do the fucking brass have any idea what's going on?"

Carlton said, "You want to be the one to ask?" He grinned wickedly.

"What do you mean?"

"Listen."

"I don't hear anything."

"Exactly. Not now, but before, didn't you hear someone next door yell "As you were?""

Jonas shrugged his shoulders.

"If you go outside right now, you'll see a jeep with three stars on it."

"Like in three-star general?"

"Like in Johnnie Walker, commanding general of the whole Eighth Army, making hospital rounds."

An expectant silence fell over the ward. Twenty minutes later a lieutenant with chiseled features and a brisk step walked in and began inspecting the charts hung on the end of the cots, glancing back and forth from the charts to his clipboard.

Carlton whispered, "Walker's aide."

A few minutes later the officer stood at the foot of Jonas' bed. "Lt. Stuyvesant?"

"That's me."

"The general is going to stop and talk with you. He's going to look like he has all the time in the world."

Jonas cocked his head.

"He doesn't." The aide glanced at his wristwatch. "The general is on a tight schedule. Don't slow him down."

The aide didn't wait for an answer but pivoted and walked to the door just as Gen. Walker entered, accompanied by a doctor, Capt. Mitchell – and Donna Campbell.

Jonas started to stand to attention, but before he or any of the patients had a chance to stir, the general said, "As you were, men."

Jonas had heard others described as bulldogs, but none fit the bill so well as Gen. Walton "Johnnie" Walker. He was short, had a massive chest, beady eyes, and if not jowls, cheeks that certainly gave that impression. Every step he took in his polished cavalry boots said, "Don't get in my way." Yet he moved from bed to bed, smiling, inquiring, patting this and that patient on the shoulder. Between beds, Dr. Mitchell said a few words about the next patient. Sometimes the doctor turned to Nurse Campbell for an additional comment.

The aide stood at the foot of his bed. "This is 2nd Lieutenant Stuyvesant."

Gen. Walker smiled. "How are you doing today, Lieutenant? The doctor tells me you're healing well."

All of Jonas' bluster disappeared. Out of the corner of his eye, he saw Carlton suppressing a grin.

"I'm doing fine, sir."

"Good, good. Maj. Ellison has written up a fine report on how you cleaned out those sniper nests in Taejon. You saved a lot of lives, son."

Jonas squirmed as the memory of Turco flashed through his mind.

"You've earned yourself a promotion." His aide handed him three small boxes. Walker opened one. "These are your 1st Lieutenant's bars. Congratulations."

Jonas, his mouth dry, said, "Thank you, sir."

"And this is your purple heart for wounds sustained in service to your country. And this," Walker paused, "is your award of the bronze star for gallantry in action."

Jonas was at a loss for words. So many conflicting thoughts and feelings rushed up. He saw images of men, many of them dead, whom he thought deserved the medal more. He saw the rout at Osan. And he remembered Cpl. Turco, a man who'd fought in Africa, and Europe, and Okinawa, dying here in Korea. Those men deserved the medals.

Behind the general, the doctor wore a neutral look, but Donna was beaming. He glanced over at Carlton, who nodded back with a smile.

The general's face and voice grew a little tense. "Son, how would you like a staff position here in Taegu? With my G-2 section analyzing intelligence."

"Sir,… I've heard that the whole 24th Division is being rotated back to Japan, given the bad shape it's in."

The aide looked at his watch and fidgeted, but Gen. Walker slowed down. "That rumor's false, though God knows any division that has taken the kind of losses yours has deserves to be pulled off the line entirely." He shook his head. "But I don't have any choice. The North Koreans are massing ten divisions along our perimeter. We are stretched thin. I've had to order the 24th back on line."

The news chilled Jonas. But if the situation was so desperate, why wasn't the general talking to him about rejoining his unit? And why had he been tense when he offered Jonas a staff position? The suspicion crept in that his family had meddled, using their political influence to get him pulled out of combat.

Walker stood there waiting, his face a stiff mask. When Jonas didn't immediately respond, he added, in a slightly softer tone, "Think about it, Lieutenant. When the doctors have finished with you here, you can return to your unit, or you can join my headquarters staff. It's your choice."

He turned to his aide, "Don't we have a schedule to keep?"

"Yessir."

"Well, let's get a move on."

"Yessir."

The aide turned away, but Walker paused and then turned back, forcing the doctor and nurse to pull up abruptly. "You were with Gen. Dean in Taejon?"

"Yessir?" Jonas said. The aide, who had already walked off a couple of steps, hurried back to the general's side.

"Did you ever hear him say that I had ordered him to hold for another two days?"

"'Asked,' sir. He said you asked him to hold. Till the twentieth."

"He said that, till the twentieth? Not the nineteenth?" And then, more to himself, Walker said, "How could he have thought I meant the twentieth?"

Jonas shifted uncomfortably on his cot. "Why don't you ask Gen. Dean, sir?"

Walker jerked his head up and looked at Jonas as though he'd just realized he was there. His face clouded over. "Because Gen. Dean is missing in action. Dead, captured, or wandering somewhere out there in the hills, we don't know."

Shaking his head, as though chewing over an unsolvable problem, Walker turned away. Jonas watched silently as the general moved quickly, but distractedly, his little party stopping at each of the remaining beds on their way out.

He turned to Carlton. "I don't begin to know what to make of that."

"About Gen. Dean being missing?"

"More than that. He's saying there was some kind of mix up, some misunderstanding on Dean's part. The whole thing is a goddamn mess. Lousy intelligence, botched orders, a general missing-in-action. What kind of war is this?"

No longer needing a crutch, Jonas limped out of the enlisted men's ward into the press of medical personnel. He squeezed through a narrow hallway and out a back door into the courtyard. He didn't want to return to his own ward yet. Carlton had been shipped back to Japan. The officer who now occupied the cot next to him was in a coma. There was no one he'd found that he wanted to confide in.

Shortly after Gen. Walker's visit, the North Koreans launched a new offensive just as the general had predicted. Casualties were beginning to pour in from the 24th Division. The 34th and 19th Regiments were hit harder than his own, but two of the men who'd been with him at Osan and Chochiwon now lay unconscious in the enlisted ward, likely to die of their wounds.

Outside, he thought he would get a chance to clear his head, but the courtyard too was bustling with personnel. Across the yard a chow truck was parked. Men passed down a line with metal trays, carrying their food into a tent where they sat at long tables. Jonas wasn't hungry.

There didn't seem to be any place where he could be by himself. Then he saw a far corner with its eight-foot high walls, an area screened by flowering bushes. He wouldn't have even noticed it except for the path of small grey flagstones that wandered in that direction. He headed off, curious. A yellow butterfly with black markings on its wings raced ahead of him.

The bushes concealed a stone bench. An area for meditation. Donna sat there, her head sunk on her breast, her small hands gripping the edge of the bench. She was trembling.

He stood for a moment, feeling awkward, then stepped backward, but scraped his foot against the flagstone. Startled, she looked up, her face pale and drawn.

"I'm sorry," he said. It was stifling hot. Yellow bees buzzed and darted over the purple flowers.

She forced a smile. "No, it's okay."

"I'm intruding."

"You don't have to go."

He pointed to the bench. "May I?"

She made space for him, and he sat down next to her on the cool stone. She didn't move away from him at all, and he turned so that their knees almost touched.

He cleared his throat. "You know, we've really got to stop meeting like this." And immediately he wanted to kick himself. She had been crying, and all he could do was crack a lame joke.

She laughed, and he felt relieved.

She said, "You mean at dances and in hospital wards?"

"People will talk."

"Oh good. Life is so boring in a war zone, it'll spice things up a bit."

He smiled and looked around. They were sitting on the edge of a rock garden. Three craggy reddish-brown rocks sat in the middle of a circle of sand that had been raked into smooth, swirling patterns.

He said, "Finding a spot like this… in the middle of a war." He looked at her.

"You should do it."

"What?"

"Take the position."

He furrowed his brow.

"With the general's staff." When he didn't answer, she said, "I know I shouldn't be saying this. It was part of my nursing training, how to talk to men to get them back to the front. Get them talking about the men in their unit. That's what I was taught. Soldiers don't go back because they believe in a cause, or for patriotism, or duty. They do it because of loyalty to their buddies."

He nodded.

"I don't want to be part of your going back."

He tried to deflect what she was saying with a touch of dark humor. "If this war keeps going like it is, it'll come to us. We'll be fighting them right here in the streets."

She grimaced. "That's not what will happen – and you know it."

He looked at her, hearing the anguish in her voice, but didn't know what to say.

"If the North Koreans start to break through," she said, "the general's headquarters staff and all the brass will be evacuated. Then comes the hospital and rear-echelon service staff. The infantry at the front will be ordered to 'delay the enemy at all costs.' Which means most likely they end up dead or captured. Isn't that right?"

"…Yes."

"If you're up there, you'll be sacrificing yourself for nothing. It won't make a difference. Not to the Army."

She touched his knee with hers and put her hand on his. A pair of butterflies flitted over her head. One landed for a moment on her shoulder, then rejoined its companion, and the two disappeared over the wall.

She blushed, looked down, then got up. She walked away quickly.

He wanted to run after her, but with his limp he knew he could not catch up.

17

IT WAS ALMOST dawn. Chen stood ankle-deep midway across the three-hundred-yard-wide river. Normally, if he'd waded and breasted his way out to this spot, the stream would have risen to his chin. But he was standing on a submerged bridge of logs and rocks. It was a clever engineering coup designed to conceal the structure from the air.

The Americans had blown all the bridges across the Naktong, and they would bomb any beginnings of new ones – as soon as their planes spotted them. This novel solution required having conscripted peasants work on underwater bridges all night, when the American Air Force could not fly reconnaissance missions.

American scout planes would soon start their morning flyovers. Chen waved his weary workers back off the 'bridge' and out of the water. As they climbed out of the stream, a jeep arrived at the shoreline. Lt. Koh, a bright young engineer, strode over to the driver, engaged him in a short conversation, and turned, signaling the captain to join him.

Soon Chen was in the jeep, bouncing alongside a morose driver who knew nothing except he was to transport the captain to regimental headquarters as quickly as possible. He handed Chen a ball wrapped in brown leaves. It was the size of a small cabbage.

Chen peeled back the leaves and found a fresh, sticky rice ball. On occasion Col. Chu could be quite thoughtful. Chen munched as the jeep ground its way over rutted, twisting, narrow backroads, and he was delighted when he found a plum concealed at the ball's center. A delicacy. He washed down the meal with Korean rice beer. Even more of a treat.

Two hours later, the jeep pulled up before a large farmhouse in a small village. A guard passed him through the courtyard gate, while another soldier slid the inside door open. A portly Chu turned from his aide to see who was entering, and his drawn tired face broke into a relieved smile.

Chen saluted.

The colonel returned it. "Ah, Comrade Chen, my friend."

Under the scrutiny of the pinched-face aide, Chen became acutely conscious that, in contrast to the clean uniforms of these two officers, his was filthy.

"I wanted to clean up before reporting, sir, but the driver said—"

Chu brushed his words aside with, "We've received new orders from Gen. Lee."

Gen. Lee Kwon Mu, although trained by the Russians and raised up to command the now illustrious 4th Division, had previously served with distinction in China, fighting the Japanese. Chen had known him there and respected the man.

Chen smiled and stood straighter. "Is he giving our regiment the honor of leading the attack across the Naktong?"

Chu pulled at his chin whiskers and pursed his lips. "Yes,… but you and I will not be on the line. We have been ordered to provide logistical support for the campaign."

Chen's mouth fell open. "But, sir, my place is with my company. I've already been detached from them too long."

"Your place, Capt. Chen, is where the general sends you."

Chu abruptly rotated his face away. When he turned back, his tone was softer. "I am as disappointed as you, but Gen. Lee personally summoned me, saying that he specifically wanted the two of us to ensure that a steady stream of supplies reach our men after they have crossed the river."

Chen stood silently.

"Gen. Lee remembers the work you did as a regimental logistics officer in China. He ascribes much of the success of a particularly difficult campaign to your work."

Chen replied, turning the conventional response into an ironical reply, "The general does me too great an honor."

Chu regarded him a second, turned away, and walked to a wall map. "Join me, Captain."

Chen did. He saw outlined on the map a rough semi-circle, much of it following the Naktong River, stretching 140 miles around the port city of Pusan and the tip of the peninsula.

"Premier Kim is still pressing us to rout the imperialists by August 1st. The plan devised by the high command is to launch four separate lines of attack to penetrate this perimeter."

Chen smiled and said, "An excellent plan. I think I grasp the general's intent. The enemy, because it must defend the whole perimeter, will not be able to shift its forces to reinforce any one area that's under attack. And when one stretch of the perimeter begins to cave in…"

Chu nodded. "The whole perimeter will collapse. The Americans will not have time to evacuate all their troops – probably only their headquarters staff. They have only the port of Pusan and perhaps two smaller ports available to them. None of them adequate to handle a large-scale evacuation.

"We will overrun them from several directions, cutting up their units. The South Koreans, who know the Americans will not evacuate them before their own troops, will throw down their weapons and try to hide among the civilians."

"It will be utter chaos."

"For them. For us, a well-organized, victorious sweep. But for that to happen, our troops must not run short of food, water, ammu-nition, and medical supplies.

"Across the river from us are our old enemies, the American 24th Division, whom we have defeated repeatedly. Our spies in Pusan tell us the 24th has been given this stretch because their intelligence tells them we are unlikely to attack here. The 24th is barely operational. Another division, the 2nd, has already been assigned to relieve them. We need to attack before that can happen."

"When do we attack?"

"In three days."

"Then, Comrade Colonel, I had better get the bridges completed."

Jonas was resting on his cot with his eyes closed. He knew Donna was somewhere on the ward. He didn't want to torment himself by watching her every move, but he often found himself following her out of the corner of his eye.

Letters from Ellen and his brother, replies to his own, lay next to him. Ellen, in her letter, was trying to be loving and supportive, but no matter what she wrote, it showed she had no idea what the war in Korea was like. And David wrote mainly to urge him to join Walker's headquarters staff. His brother didn't say it, but it was clear the family was behind the general's offer.

He couldn't get Donna out of his mind. In the days since their meeting in the meditation garden, she'd spent as little time on the ward as she could. When she was making rounds, she avoided eye contact with him, dropping her head while taking his vitals. She blushed. He got frequent hard-ons.

It all seemed impossible. There was practically no privacy in the hospital. Besides, he was a married man. An affair was out of the question. But he found himself fantasizing what could happen if he took that position on Walker's staff. There had to be somewhere in Taegu where they could be alone, even in the middle of a war. He couldn't get them out of his mind, the images of taking Donna into his arms, the slow deep kisses, unbuttoning the top button of...

Lying there, he was vaguely aware of the sound of heavy footsteps in the aisle. Definitely not a woman's. They stopped at the bottom of his bed. Curious, he opened his eyes and found himself in the shadow of a large man. He sat up.

"Figures," Sgt. Strosahl said.

"What's that?" Jonas said, feigning nonchalance.

"You living the life of Riley. Some guys get all the breaks."

Jonas nodded and gestured open-handedly toward the rest of the ward. "Yeah, what more could a man want? Three hots and a cot." As he gestured, he saw Donna looking at him and his visitor, and smiling as though she was glad to see him with company.

Then he let himself break into a full grin of elation. "How are you doing, Sarge?"

Strosahl smiled broadly and gripped the outstretched hand. Jonas winced slightly.

"Other'n there's a war on, I can't complain."

"So what are you doing here?"

Strosahl shifted about uncomfortably. Jonas could see the lump in his cheek, his chaw, and knew he was looking for someplace to spit.

Not finding even a bedpan available, he said, "Saw some of our men, they say you've been looking out for them." He reached down to the pocket on the leg of his fatigues and pulled up the top of a metal flask for Jonas to see. "Is there some place we could be by ourselves?"

Jonas glanced up and down the ward. Donna was changing one patient's dressing, and an orderly was giving another an injection.

"Let's go outside." He led the way limping.

The courtyard in front of the hospital was crowded with empty ambulances, jeeps, and trucks. The drivers and medics were mostly in the back courtyard having lunch. Jonas wove through the deserted rows of vehicles until he reached a sycamore tree.

He grabbed a couple of empty five-gallon gas cans from beside a fuel truck, and the two of them perched astride them facing each other. Strosahl let loose with a stream of brown juice and pulled the flask from his pocket, uncapped it and passed it over.

"Bourbon."

"Good man," Jonas said and took a sip. He offered it back.

Strosahl shook his head. "That's for you. I got a couple of fifths to take back."

"How are the men?"

"Last push by the gooks, we lost Decker, Kosinski, and Brill."

Jonas winced.

The sergeant eyed the flask. "Maybe I will have some of that."

Jonas passed it. Strosahl took a swallow, handed it back, and said, "The captain asked me to see when you'd be coming back."

Jonas slowly stood up and took the two paces that put him at the sycamore. He tapped the trunk lightly, reflectively, with his fist. "Not going back." He turned to face Strosahl.

The sergeant cocked his head. "You don't look hurt that bad."

"…I'm healing fine." He massaged his right bicep and rotated his shoulder a bit. "I just don't want to go back. I've been offered a job in Gen. Walker's G-2 Section."

Strosahl shook his head and looked at the ground between his knees. "I didn't expect this of you, Lieu." He looked up. "Your replacement – well, I don't think he's going to cut it. I mean, he'll stick till he gets himself and others killed, and then I've got to break in another new man."

"I'm sorry, I really am, but I'm out of it now."

"The men are going to be disappointed to hear that." He shook his head. "Look, I know how it can be. I've been shot up a couple of times, and there were times when I didn't think I could go back. But my men were counting on me, and I knew how to do the job that had to be done. And you know how to do the job. You don't know everything yet, but you've got the right instincts. You're careful when it counts, and aggressive when it's time."

"It's not being wounded. If it were that, I'd be on the line tomorrow."

Strosahl got to his feet. "Well, what the fuck is it then, Lieu? Because I never took you for yellow, not even when you were pissing in your pants, because I was there pissing beside you, and that's just what we do when we're being shot at. It don't mean nuthin'. You just go on doing your job."

Jonas felt his face flush.

Strosahl pushed on. "You know what I think? I think you sat through all those goddam ROTC lectures so focused on the ones about taking care of your men, you didn't get what a line officer actually does, which is send 'em into the line of fire."

Jonas dropped his head. "It's just like I'm putting a .45 to their heads and pulling the trigger myself."

"That's what's eating you?"

He raised his eyes and stared bleakly. "That's it."

Strosahl got right up into Jonas' face. "Goddamn, what the fuck did you think it meant, being an officer?"

"I'm supposed to lead men, take care of them. I promise them I'll get them home safe to their families, and that's a lie."

"You think they don't know that? Yeah, each one of those kids wants it to be true, prays it's true, but every swinging dick in the outfit knows the mission comes first. You lie and they know you're lying. And they want you to lie."

"Well then I've stopped lying to myself."

"That's it?"

Jonas turned his head away.

Strosahl spit out a stream of tobacco juice. "I'm wasting my time here."

Jonas looked at the flask in his hand and held it out.

The muscles along Strosahl's jaw rippled. "Keep it. You'll be needing that more'n me." He turned on heel and stalked off.

For the next week, Jonas was in a foul mood. The bourbon Strosahl left him was gone the first evening. He barely slept at night, didn't shave in the morning, and avoided conversation with his fellow patients. He chain-smoked while limping up and down the center aisle of the ward, until the complaints of other patients forced him outside. He circled the hospital, occasionally stopping at the meditation garden where he'd smoke three or four cigarettes, tossing the butts into the cleanly raked sand. When Dr. Mitchell suggested he might want to see the psychiatrist, Jonas barked at him.

In the hall outside the ward, he almost collided with Donna pushing a cart loaded with the evening medications.

As he pulled back from her, a little wobbly on his feet, she said, "You don't look well."

He scowled. "I'm well enough."

She waved for an aide. "Give out these meds will you, Carl?" To Jonas she said, "You're coming with me."

"I don't need looking after."

"That wasn't a request; that's an order. On this unit, I'm the general."

She took Jonas by the arm, propelling him into a small windowless room. It was furnished with a table, a few chairs, and the cot that staff used for breaks. A yellow light bulb hung overhead from twisted strands of wire. She pulled out a chair.

"Sit."

He grumbled but sat. She got two cups of coffee from an urn on a little battered stand by the wall.

"Milk? Sugar?"

"Black." His tone was clipped. He stared at the floor.

"You got anything left in that flask you've been hiding?"

Jonas looked up, surprised. Although he'd finished what Strosahl had given him, he'd quickly found another source. He reached inside the shirt of his pajamas and pulled the flask loose from where he had taped it, atop his liver. He unscrewed the cap. Donna held out her cup. He poured her a stiff one, and then one for himself.

They sipped in silence.

She rested the cup on the table, clasping it in both hands. "Dr. Mitchell says you can be discharged in a week."

He nodded, staring into his drink. "G-2. Intelligence. Whole other ballgame, trying to see the big picture."

"Is that what you want?"

"Yes.… No. It's what you want me to do, isn't it?"

"This… this can't be about what I want. I should never have said what I said in the garden. It was selfish."

He reached across, placed his hand on hers and squeezed gently. "Not wanting me to get killed, that's not entirely selfish."

She smiled weakly, then dropped her eyes and pulled her hand away. "Everything's changed since that sergeant visited you."

"Strosahl."

"Yes."

"He's out there. My men are out there somewhere." He pushed his hands up and down his thighs as his muscles bunched up. "I've got to get out of here."

"Whoa, hold on. Your wounds aren't that healed."

"Anything that can't be handled at battalion aid?"

"…No."

"Well, are you going to help me or not?"

"Just leave? Go back to your unit without orders?"

"What're they going to do? Court martial me?"

She shook her head and blinked back tears.

He looked at his pajamas. "Can you get me a set of fatigues?"

Her lips quivered. "Yes."

She brought him clean clothes and a .45 the operating team had taken off a captain earlier that day, an officer who wouldn't be needing it again, along with a pair of field glasses in their case. He picked up the pistol, examined it, and then the field glasses. He set them back on the table and smiled at her. She sat down and didn't smile back.

He stripped down to his shorts and dog tags and dressed as she watched. He strapped on the pistol. When he was done lacing his boots, he saw the small blue bag on the table.

"Your personal possessions," she said and pushed it toward him. "Everything you came in with."

Standing over her, he loosened the drawstrings and pulled out a crumpled envelope, his picture of Ellen, Army ID, and some cash. He stuck everything in his breast pocket but the envelope. The ink was a little smudged, but the name was clear: Cecilia Gibson.

"Will you make sure this gets mailed to the captain's wife?"

"Of course," she said. She stood and took the letter. "So this is it?"

He shifted his weight from one foot to the other. "I guess so."

She ran the fingers of one hand through her hair, pulling loose strands into place. "It seems I always get to be the girl who's left behind."

"I'm sorry." He didn't know what to do for a moment, and then he reached for her to pull her to him, to kiss her.

"No," she said. "...I can't."

He stared a moment and slowly pivoted.

"No, wait," she said.

He turned back, and she rushed to him. He kissed her, holding her close, a long deep kiss. And then gently took hold of her shoulders and stepped away.

He turned and walked out of the room. He passed through the ward, stopping at his cot to retrieve his 1st lieutenant bars from underneath his pillow. He started to leave the purple heart and bronze star behind on the bed. Other men, like Turco, deserved them just as much or more. But maybe, in leaving them behind, he dishonored them as well. He scooped up the medals, put them in his breast pocket and strode out of the hospital.

Jonas hitched rides in jeeps, and supply and troop trucks. About one in the morning, a driver dropped him off in a small village in front of the two-story schoolhouse, now 1st Battalion headquarters. Nearby, a battery of howitzers fired continuously into the smoke-filled skies.

Greeted inside with smiles, handshakes, and slaps on the back, he made his way to the crowded operations center next to the radio room. Against the wall, a phone operator was busy taking messages. In the background, a generator purred away, powering the radio and the yellow light bulbs hanging from thin wires strung along the ceiling.

The three officers standing at a map table, Lt. Col. Smith, Capt. Dasher and Dasher's XO, Capt. Kirby, all turned as he entered. Smith smiled, but Dasher looked surprised, probably, Jonas thought, because Strosahl had told him he wasn't coming back. All three officers looked a lot more worn than when he'd last seen them.

He saluted. "Lt. Stuyvesant reporting for duty, sir."

Col. Smith, still his lean, leathery self, returned the salute. His eyes, though bleary, were still piercing. "Glad to have you back, Lieutenant."

"Hoping to be reassigned to my platoon, sir."

Smith grimaced and nodded to Dasher. The captain removed his glasses and squeezed the bridge of his nose. "That poses a problem."

Jonas' first thought was I screwed up; they know I'm AWOL. But he also was aware of the background noise of cannon thumping steadily. And not just a single battery firing from one location. Many batteries, scattered miles apart, pounded away in the night, creating a sound like waves of thunder overhead.

On second thought, they could care less how I got here. Something a lot more important is wrong.

Dasher turned to the map and passed his hand over it. "The 24th Division is defending this whole sector, about ten square miles. We call it the Naktong Bulge because it's just that, a bulge of land that the river has to circle around. The river itself is three to four hundred feet wide, a natural moat."

Jonas took in the strategic situation at a glance. On this side of the Naktong there were no more natural defensive barriers all the way to the sea, a mere fifty miles away. There was no place else to retreat to – except Japan.

"The night of August 5th & 6th, elements of the North Korean 4th Division began crossing the river. We managed to repel them in our sector, but they did cross south of here and engage the 34th. Over the next four days, the rest of the North Korean's 4th Division crossed the Naktong, pushing us back. We counterattacked, but the enemy has secured a bridgehead here." Dasher used his finger to trace a set of wavy lines on the map. "This is Cloverleaf Hill and the Oblong-ni Ridge." He turned his head back to Jonas. "This is critical terrain. It controls the main roads to Taegu and Pusan."

Then the captain averted his eyes and put his finger on a hill overlooking the river four miles northeast of Cloverleaf. "On the 10th, your platoon went out on a reconnaissance mission." The captain kept his eyes averted. "They got caught in an ambush. They've been surrounded and cut off for the last five days."

Jonas pushed up to the table and bent over the map. The hill overlooked a road and a possible river crossing point. "Are we in radio contact?"

"We were the first night," Smith said. "After that we couldn't raise them. Could be they were overrun, or just could be their damn batteries failed."

That wasn't good. Without radio contact, his platoon couldn't call in artillery support. "Can we get a fly-over?"

Smith said, "All aircraft are engaged. The whole damn sector is under attack." He turned to the map.

Jonas couldn't focus on the plight of the whole division when his men were cut off. "Who's leading the platoon?"

Dasher said, "Lt. Edwards, your replacement, took them out. But we got a report he was killed the first day. Strosahl's in command."

Jonas thought he heard a note of hope in his tone when Dasher said Strosahl was in command. Capt. Kirby, standing a little behind Dasher, his owl-like eyes bloodshot, looked sympathetic.

A runner trotted in with a message for the colonel. While he read the dispatch, Smith said, "I don't have a force available large enough to get your platoon out, Lieutenant. I'm sorry."

Jonas felt like he'd been punched in the gut. "We can't just leave them there."

Dasher shook his head. "Division loaned us a patrol from Intelligence and Reconnaissance Company, that's all we've got. They tried to bring them out but got stopped by a roadblock five miles from the hill. They couldn't break it, not enough men or fire power."

The colonel busily scrawled out a dispatch for the waiting runner, while the field telephone continued to ring in the background.

"Maybe if I took that patrol back, I could get through."

Smith shook his head. "I know how you feel, Lieutenant, they're my men too, but I debriefed I & R myself. They were up against too much firepower. Tanks could get through, but all our tanks are committed."

"I'd like to talk to that patrol."

The irritation in Smith's voice was marked. "Lieutenant—"

Dasher cut in. "Sir, Lt. Stuyvesant is the man who took out those machine gun nests in Taejon. It won't hurt to have him talk to recon."

Smith paused, looking off into space for a moment while he considered the idea, then said, "Okay, go ahead and talk to them."

"And if I come up with a plan?"

"Clear it with Capt. Dasher." He turned back to the map.

"Thank you, sir," Jonas said, but Smith was already engrossed in more pressing concerns. Jonas backed away quietly. As he turned to leave, he found Capt. Kirby falling in beside him. He looked questioningly to the XO, who shook his head and pointed to the door.

Outside Kirby turned to him, shifted his weight onto one leg and stuck his thumbs in his web belt. "I can assign you an eight-man rifle squad. Just arrived from Japan yesterday, no combat experience."

That there were any men available at all was encouraging. "And trucks. I'll need trucks."

"I'll see what's available." Kirby clapped him on his upper arm, right where the doctors had cut out shrapnel. Jonas gritted his teeth.

The captain started to turn away but hesitated. "There could be another reason we lost contact with Strosahl."

"Sir?"

"The Reds might have been jamming his frequency. Stop by the radio section and get yourself a new frequency and an alternate, just in case."

"Thanks," said Jonas, nodding, and watched the captain go back inside.

18

I N A TEN-BY-TEN field tent, Jonas found the reconnaissance patrol leader, one of several men there, asleep on a cot. He made the mistake of giving the man's shoulder a shake, and the soldier came out of his bed in a single bound, bayonet in one hand and Jonas' collar gripped in the other.

"Whoa, stand down, soldier," Jonas shouted.

The man, about Jonas' height, shook his head and looked about him. "For Crissake, don't you know better than to—"

"—Don't you know better, SIR!"

Almost no light shone in the tent, but with their faces pressed up almost against each other, Jonas could see sleek eyebrows, small ears and a prominent razor-line jaw.

"Prados? Is that you? It's Jonas Stuyvesant. Turco, you, me, Taejon?" He watched Prados' face light up in recognition.

By this time several men were shouting, "Hey, knock it off," and "Take it outside you two, we're trying to sleep in here."

Jonas took him by the arm and led him out of the tent. "We've got to talk."

"At this hour? Lieu, I ain't had but four hours sleep in the last two days."

But a few minutes later, Jonas had Prados in the operations center looking over a map and pointing out the bend in the road where the North Koreans had opened up on the nine-man patrol with mortar fire and burp guns.

Jonas stared at the map. "The Reds have any heavy-caliber machine guns?"

"Don't think so, sir. Just burp guns, so they were up close, I'd say no more than fifty yards off the road. The mortars, they were back a lot farther. I'd put them at a thousand yards. There was a little village back there." Prados tapped a spot on the map.

Jonas measured the distance from the point where Prados was attacked to the hill where Strosahl and his men were surrounded. Five miles of winding road. Lots of places where the North Koreans could lay more ambushes.

Jonas could see why the hill was important. It commanded the road and what had been a ferry crossing; and although the ferry had been destroyed, North Korean engineers could get one running for resupply. Or more likely, the river could be forded nearby. But whether the Reds had a ferry or were moving supplies by fording the river, Americans holding the high ground could call in artillery strikes on them.

The idea that the North Koreans needed to get supplies across the Naktong set off a train of associations for Jonas. On his trip from the hospital, he had been struck by just how many trucks it took to haul all the ammunition and other supplies to the front. One supply officer had told him it took five thousand tons of materiel a day to keep the U.S. and ROK forces supplied. If intelligence estimates were correct, and as many as eight to ten thousand North Korean soldiers were now operating on this side of the river, they would need constant resupply too. But the bridges were all out, and they couldn't get materiel across during the daytime because of American airpower. Jonas had a hard time believing they weren't hurting for ammunition.

"When they hit you, how was their fire discipline?"

Prados thought for a moment. "Good. Very good. They weren't wasting their ammo, used just enough to drive us back.

Hmm, maybe conserving because they are low on rounds. "If we went back, and I was to send you around that bend, was there any place you could take cover?"

"I saw a stand of poplars that might do, if they didn't pick us off before we got there. But the mortars from the village would make short work of us once we got set."

"What if I could take out their mortars?"

"You do that, Lieu, I've got a .30-caliber machine gun that will tear the shit out of their burp guns."

Jonas stared at the map, calculating distances. "I think I see a way."

Capt. Dasher wasn't happy about being roused after only two hours of sleep, but he threw some water on his face, adjusted his steel rimmed glasses on the bridge of his nose, and sat himself down to listen in a canvas camp chair. Jonas had cobbled together a crew: three recon jeeps with mounted .30-caliber machine guns, their crews, and the eight-man rifle squad. He had a plan for how to use them.

Dasher listened attentively. "You should have a radioman and a medic as well." He turned to Kirby, who had gone ahead into Dasher's tent to wake him.

"Olsen," Kirby said. He scratched his head. "…and Jaynes."

Dasher nodded and turned to Jonas. "Let's be clear about what I'm authorizing. You take this patrol out, but if you find you can't break the roadblock, you get those men back here. That rifle squad goes on the line tomorrow, and Division wants their recon patrol back."

"Understood, sir. But about the trucks—"

"Two is all we can free up."

"But—"

Kirby gave him a warning shake of the head.

"Two it is," Jonas said, his chest sinking as he acceded. "Thank you, sir. I'll get everyone back by nightfall."

Jonas ordered the men to assemble right after an early breakfast at 1st Battalion's motor pool, or rather, outside the tent that served as the motor pool's company office. The jeeps and trucks were scattered in and around the village, both because there was no one open space large enough to hold them and to protect against an artillery barrage wiping out most of their vehicles.

The thing that worried him most was having only two trucks. A two-and-a-half-ton truck carried twelve combat-equipped soldiers – put another man in the cab with the driver, and that made thirteen. His rifle squad, plus a medic and a radioman, was already eight men, and Lt. Edwards and Strosahl had taken twenty-eight men into the field. Presuming most of his men were still alive, how the hell was he to get them all back?

While extra water, C-rations, and ammo were being loaded into one canvass covered truck, his green rifle squad climbed into the back of the second. The motor pool's duty sergeant circled the trucks while checking off boxes on a form on his clipboard.

Jonas, carbine slung over his left shoulder, walked over to the two parked recon jeeps. He had some mild pain in his right side where he'd been wounded. He felt a little stiff, not yet accustomed to moving about this much.

Prados and his second team leader, Cpl. Clemens, were talking together.

"Prados, where's Gaddis?"

"Should be here any moment, sir. Just had a little errand to attend to."

Clemens lounged against his jeep with arms folded. He was a tall blond-haired kid, with a smooth untroubled countenance. He might have been standing outside the drug store in his home town in North Dakota, watching chattering high school girls stream in after classes to get a soda and play the juke box.

Prados suddenly lifted his head and looked past Jonas. "There he is now."

Jonas turned and saw a jeep followed by a two-and-a-half-ton truck with a canvass covered bed. He stood waiting, his weight more on his left leg, his right hand on the butt of his .45.

Gaddis' jeep pulled to a stop a few feet from him. The black-haired corporal sat grinning in the passenger seat, his fatigue shirt open on a bare chest, with his dog tags dangling. His sleeves were rolled up over his biceps, revealing a tattoo of a rose. The truck braked to a stop behind him.

Gaddis, waving a piece of paper, stepped out of his jeep and sauntered over. He handed it to Jonas, who quickly scanned it – a standard requisition form for a truck, but with an illegible authorizing signature scrawled at the bottom.

Prados stepped up and leaned his head near Jonas' ear. "I wouldn't examine it too closely, Lieu."

Jonas eyed Prados, raising his brows.

Prados shrugged. "The corporal here did a little trading. These rear-echelon types like to have some war trophies to take home and show the folks, prove they saw real action."

"What kind of trophies?"

"You don't want to know, sir. Just hand the paperwork over, and let's get moving."

The staff sergeant finished looking the new truck over and walked over to Jonas, a completely neutral look on his face. Jonas handed him the authorization. He scrawled something at the bottom, nodded to Gaddis, and walked away. Now Jonas had his three trucks, instead of just two.

The convoy, with dew still fresh on the hoods of the vehicles, pulled out of the village and wound its way north on a dirt road more often used by oxcarts. Diesel trucks ground their gears up over brown, denuded hills and down through humid, yellow-green rice paddies, then up again hill after endless hill in the shimmering heat, and down through small, claustrophobic village after deserted village, crawling on toward the Naktong. The sun rose higher, the temperature climbed above a hundred. Sweat poured off Jonas' chest and back, soaking his fatigues. Blackbirds, sheltered in the occasional tree, kept watch on them, their caws the only sounds beside the motors to interrupt the silence.

By mid-morning, Prados had led them within a half-mile of the bend in the road where he'd been ambushed. Jeeps and trucks pulled over to the side of the road. The corporal had his driver park beneath the meager shade of a lone sycamore. The ground stretched out east and west flat and barren for half-a-mile in either direction, until it began to rise up into low rolling hills.

As his men off-loaded, Jonas pulled his map out of a protective rubber pouch and spread it across the hood of the jeep. He felt invigorated to be up and around, back in the field, leading men again. His right shoulder, side and hip, the sites of his wounds, were feeling a little stiff after riding so many hours the night before and this morning.

The recon team leaders, Prados, Clemens, and Gaddis, as well as his new squad leader, Cpl. Grey, gathered around him. Jonas put his finger on a spot in the lower right-hand quadrant.

"This village is our first objective." He went over his plan until he was sure the team leaders were clear. Then he had Cpl. Grey collect the other seven men of his squad, and the radioman and medic. He went over their specific duties – and his contingency plan in case everything went to hell.

"Leave your packs in the trucks. Make sure each of you is carrying grenades." He looked at the taut faces in the little circle. "I know this is your first time out. Just remember your training and you'll do fine."

He knew he was giving them false assurances. Training was some preparation, but the only thing that prepared a man for combat was combat. They were about to get their first taste, and if his plan was any good, most of them might even get through the next couple of hours alive.

Images flitted through his mind of being ambushed in Taejon, then wounded on the road outside. He clenched his jaw. He was tired of defensive fighting. It hadn't been his style as a boxer, and he didn't want to be fighting that way now.

"Check your weapons. Lock and load."

He checked his carbine first and then removed the magazine from his .45, re-inserted it, and chambered a round. All around him he heard bolts slamming home.

Leaving Prados on the road in charge of the recon teams and trucks, he led his rifle squad on a wide circle that took two hours. Using a stand of trees here and a defilade there, and crawling on their bellies without any cover, he brought them up on the village from the far side. A dense stand of bamboo screened the last leg of their approach.

The cane stood an easy nine feet high. The soldiers moved through it, parting the way ahead with rifle barrels and stepping slowly so as to create as little movement of the cane as possible.

Halting a foot before the end, Jonas spread the green bamboo stalks just enough to get a look at his goal. Thirty L-shaped, mud-and-wattle farmhouses with thatched roofs were spread helter-skelter over a kidney-shaped, flat level surface. Paths wound between the farmhouses. Between the bamboo stand and the village lay a bean field.

He could see a few troops at the end of a long path that looked like it opened up into a large flat area surrounding a well, but other farmhouses blocked any more of his view. He couldn't get a count of how many enemy there were, but if he led his men forward from this point, they were sure to be seen.

Backing away, he moved east, looking for an exit point that would be shielded by the random arrangement of the farmhouses. He had to try three more spots in the brake before he found the position that allowed him and his men to emerge without being seen.

He led them running at a crouch in single file across the bean field. Once safely clustered behind a farmhouse, he signaled one four-man team to go left and the other right. He and his radioman, Olsen, darted up a path in the middle, scrambling from the cover of one building to the next.

Jonas took a quick peek from behind an animal stall and sighted a dozen North Korean soldiers lounging just beyond the village, about fifty feet from where he stood. The area the enemy troops had chosen for their mortar tubes was a level, hard-packed clay surface. Their three tubes stood angled away from the village, pointed toward the road.

The soldiers lounged near their mortars. Four were squatting, engaged in what looked like a game of dice. Two more men chatted, while passing a canteen back and forth. While another five seemed to be napping, one soldier stood watch with a pair of field glasses, his back to Jonas as he scanned the road almost a thousand yards away across the intervening rice paddy. None of the soldiers had his rifle near at hand. There were three stacks of four rifles, butts on the ground and muzzles pointing skyward like tepee poles.

Jonas took his pistol from its holster, inched around the stall, and took aim at a sleeping soldier sitting with legs spread, his back against a scrub pine tree and his cap pulled down over his face. Jonas sighted first on the red star on the cap and then lowered his gun until he lined up on the center of the man's chest. He squeezed off the round just a little too quickly. The gun bucked in his hand. The shot went high, splintering wood two inches above the soldier's head. The man jerked up straight, his hat falling into his lap, shock on his face.

With Jonas' shot, his men, concealed around houses to his left and right, opened fire. The two automatic rifles caught the whole crew in crossfire, mowing down the dice players and finishing off the man Jonas had missed. Soldiers trying to get to their feet were knocked back to the ground. Those near the stacked rifles were shot down as they rushed for their guns. His green-clad men ran forward, firing at any sign of life in a brown uniform.

They were still mopping up when Jonas turned to sight his next objective, and quickly spotted the North Koreans guarding the road half a mile away. They'd climbed out of their trench and were standing on the ridge. While craning their necks to see what was happening in the village, a recon jeep roared around the bend behind them, Prados spraying rounds in their direction. The driver whipped the jeep around in the stand of poplars; and once stationary, Prados was able to concentrate his fire more effectively.

Jonas watched as the North Koreans, now caught between Prados on the road and his team behind them, panicked. Some dove into their trench, while a few tried to get off shots at Prados, the closer target. Another handful fired their burp guns in the opposite direction, toward Jonas and his men, but they were out of range.

Pausing only to make sure he'd left no enemy alive behind him, Jonas raced his squad across the dikes of the intervening rice paddies to a low flat dike three hundred yards from the North Koreans' position, still out of their range, but well within that of his own riflemen. While Prados pinned the Koreans from his side with sweeps of .30-caliber fire, Jonas' men, hitting the ground and firing from prone positions, picked them off. He called "Cease Fire." By his count only three enemy soldiers in the trench were unaccounted for.

Jonas and his men crept forward. One enemy head popped up with a burp gun, but both American automatic rifles let loose before the soldier got off a single shot. Silence. Jonas looked left and right, his men kneeling all in a line, rifle butts jammed into their shoulders. Jonas holstered his pistol, laid his carbine on the ground, and pulled out a grenade. Two more of his men did the same. He pulled the pin; so did they. Almost simultaneously, the three of them let their spoons fly. Jonas held back a second while his men let theirs fly.

The two grenades arced high. One fell on the soft bank of dirt piled up on the lip of the trench and began a slow slide downwards. Two hands reached up frantically for it, but it slid through them. The grenade that had dropped cleanly into the trench came flying back out. Jonas' dropped in from above. Jonas and his men dove to the ground. The ground underneath rocked from the explosion in the trench.

He was on his feet charging. Only one of the North Koreans was moving. He crawled on his hands and knees trying to get away. Jonas held his .45 up, barrel pointed to the sky. An image flashed through his mind, that of Reynolds, his driver in their escape from Taejon. He saw Reynolds lying wounded in the ditch, surrounded by North Koreans, and being summarily shot. He blinked and refocused on this North Korean. He squeezed off the round with deliberation, putting the bullet in the center of the man's forehead.

"Check 'em," he said, and two of his men jumped down.

"And you two…" Two more of his men stepped forward. "…go back and collect those mortars and any weapons and get rid of them." He didn't want to leave weapons around that the enemy could retrieve.

The men looked confused. The private said, "How do we do that?"

"Throw it all down the well."

He waved to Prados, who stood in his jeep behind the mounted .30 caliber. Prados gave a shout, and the other two recon jeeps sped around the bend to join him by the stand of poplars, followed moments later by the trucks.

As Jonas headed toward the road, he heard the squad behind him begin chattering excitedly, congratulating each other. They were now combat veterans. Taking down this enemy had been easy.

Right, Jonas thought. This part had been easy, but he'd had good intel from Prados about the disposition of the forces making up the blockade. He didn't know what lay ahead.

"Mount up," he shouted without looking back. They hurried to the road and climbed into their truck, laughing like they were horsing around in a high school locker room.

Jonas walked out ahead of the lead jeep and looked down the road that twisted and turned and rose and fell for about five miles through the narrow, mile-long valley. The jagged row of hills on each side jutted up at steep fifty-degree angles.

Going forward, the valley was too rocky and dry for rice paddies. Here and there lumps of scrub pine sat side by side with masses of grey rock, but mainly the sides of the hills were brown and barren. That was good. There wasn't a lot of cover for the North Koreans to set up an ambush.

It got trickier, though, as he surveyed the road farther on. There were stands of elms and larger pines, and plenty of boulders. Beyond that, closer to the river, rice paddies again flanked both sides of the road.

He guessed there'd be at least two more ambush sites, because the North Koreans didn't just set up a roadblock at one juncture of a road; they created a gauntlet.

It would take time to clear the road. How much, he didn't know. A jeep would have to go ahead until the North Koreans fired on the crew, and then he'd have to assess the situation.

While he stood making his calculations, the drivers, infantry-men, and the recon crews lit cigarettes. They talked in quiet, strained tones or stared silently at one another's dust-and-gunpowder-streaked faces. They uncapped canteens and took long swigs as they chatted and smoked.

The infantrymen in their dirt-covered dungarees trickled back to the second truck and re-supplied themselves with ammo. Prados and his two machine gunners climbed into their jeeps and fitted fresh belts into their guns.

In the distance, Jonas could see the crest of the hill, his objective. There was no fighting going on up there that he could hear. If he did get up there, what would he find? He looked at his squad. If the North Koreans had already taken the hill, neither he nor any of his men was likely to get back down alive. He had two decisions to make now. First, whether to even go on, given the risks. Was it fair to risk the lives of these men? He looked at the cluster of determined faces waiting for his command, and he thought of the men who'd fought with him at Osan and Chochiwon.

"Prepare to move out," he shouted; and, as his infantry squad climbed into their truck, he walked back to Prados' jeep.

The second decision, who would take the lead, was harder. Those men were the most likely to get killed. It would be a recon team, because scouting ahead was what they were trained to do. But which one?

As if reading his mind, Prados jerked his thumb over his shoulder and pointed to the next jeep. "Except for me, Clemens has the most experience. Gaddis hotdogs a bit."

"Right," Jonas said, looking at the tall lanky kid who leaned back against the front of his jeep, arms crossed, cigarette still dangling from his lower lip. The kid looked him straight in the eye.

"Clemens, take point."

19

CLEMENS NODDED, FLICKED his cigarette away, and turned to his men.

"Let's get a move on."

The lead jeep peeled out. Jonas took the passenger seat in Prados' jeep. Prados manned the machine gun behind Jonas, the assistant gunner kneeling next to him. Crammed in the back with them was their radio, crackling with static.

While the trucks followed Jonas at fifty-yard intervals, the third recon jeep acted as their rear guard. The jeep ahead kicked up a swirl of dust, concealing the vehicle within the cloud.

Three tense miles later, the cloud disappeared around a bend, and Jonas heard the rapid fire of burp guns. They clattered away, and then he heard the punctuated bursts of .30-caliber machine gun fire, the recon team returning fire.

"Step on it," he told the driver. He could hear the machine gun belt clink behind him as Prados adjusted his grip.

By the time they reached the bend, all firing had stopped. Jonas felt his gut tighten. It'd all happened too quickly. He squinted and peered forward, as though trying to see around the bend, and then had his driver pull to a stop just before he was able to get a glimpse. His jeep sat idling.

Had Clemens and his crew found cover, or were there three slumped, bullet riddled bodies in that jeep? His whole body strained forward as he listened for a clue.

A squawk from behind him, the radio, made him jump.

"Red Rover One, this is Red Rover Two." It was Clemens.

Jonas grabbed the mike from Prados: "This is Red Rover One. Report."

"All clear, Red Rover One. Come take a look."

Jonas looked up at Prados, who shrugged. Jonas handed the mike back to Prados. "Let's go." The driver shifted into gear.

Red Rover Two idled seventy-five yards around the bend. Leaving the muzzle of his machine gun pointed skyward, Clemens had turned toward the oncoming jeep and stood with one foot resting casually on the tail his vehicle.

As Jonas pulled up alongside, Clemens pointed to a clump of rocks and scrub pine fifty yards off the side of the road. "Two full squads armed with burp guns and a mortar crew, they all took off like rabbits with a pack of hounds nipping at their behinds."

Jonas stood up in his jeep to get a better view. "Where are they?"

Clemens pointed to a stretch of full-grown pine a hundred yards northeast of the ambush site. Over a dozen men were breaking from cover into the open.

"They're making for that apple grove." He pointed east to a cluster of trees that lay closer to a rice paddy north of them.

Jonas pulled out his field glasses and sighted in on the fleeing soldiers. Indeed, the last of the North Koreans were running as though in a panic into the grove, none of them stopping to look back.

Jonas lowered the binoculars. "Why would they do that?" he asked Prados.

The corporal shook his head. "Dunno, new one on me. Haven't seen North Koreans bug-out before; seen them pushed back, but never run full-out like that."

Jonas ran his tongue over his teeth and scanned both sides of the road. "I don't like it. You think it's some new tactic?"

Prados chewed on the question. He looked up the road and back towards the bend. "Could be they are going to wait 'til we pass, and when we come on the next roadblock, close up behind and catch us in the middle."

"Could be," Jonas mused. "But I haven't heard of a roadblock like that. Those troops didn't even wait to see what they were up against."

Prados looked at Jonas as though to say, It's your call.

Jonas looked again toward his objective, the hill, now just two miles away, and listened again for any gunfire from the top. Still nothing. He could be leading these men into a trap.

If he was going to creep farther into enemy territory, he needed to make sure the road behind was held open in case he needed to make a quick retreat.

He took the mike again to call Gaddis. "Red Rover Three, this is Red Rover One."

His third jeep came on the air. "This is Red Rover Three. Over."

"Red Rover Three, you are to stay behind and cover the rear as the rest of the patrol goes on to the objective. Over."

"Will do, Red Rover One. We'll be waiting here for you. Out."

Jonas gave the mike to Prados and nodded to Clemens. "You've still got point. Move out."

As Clemens and his crew pulled away, Jonas felt his shoulder muscles bunch up. Something wasn't right. The North Koreans just didn't run like this. Images from the night he was ambushed burst in his brain like mortar shells. He saw the red tracer-bullets streaking through the night, the explosion ahead and his jeep lifting up and flipping over with him flying through the air. He was on the ground again, in shock.

"Lieutenant? Lieutenant?" The voice came from far away. And then he was looking at the trail of dust that hid Clemens' jeep from sight. Why was he so far down the road?

"Shouldn't we be following, Lieu?" Prados was saying.

"Let's go." Jonas let out his pent-up breath as he barked the order. He undid the chinstrap on his helmet, took it off, and wiped the sweat off his forehead with his sleeve. It had to be over a hundred degrees, but that wasn't why he was sweating. He replaced his helmet and refastened the strap while scanning the terrain for possible ambush sites. He kept expecting fire to erupt from the hills off to his right, just like it had that night outside Taejon.

He forced himself to stop drumming the floor of the jeep with his foot and instead gripped the side of his seat. His shoulder, side, and hip all began to burn.

Clemens' jeep, or rather the dust trail, disappeared from sight over a rise. Jonas heard two "coughs." Gunshots? Small explosions? No, he decided. Just a motor backfiring. Everything was silent again, except for the sound of motors and crows cawing.

But Jonas could see no crows. Maybe this was some new signaling system. Instead of using whistles, the North Koreans were imitating bird sounds.

Three crows took flight from a stand of poplars, and he relaxed a bit.

No sound of mortars or burp guns. The silence began to wear on him. He started when Prados adjusted his position on the gun behind him. Jumpy. Too jumpy. It's not good for a team leader to be this jumpy. Maybe it had been a mistake to leave the hospital. Maybe he should have taken that desk job in G-2.

Then there was no sound or sign of the lead jeep. It had disappeared around another bend. His driver slowed and crept around the curve in the road, and then eased his way up over a crest, all with no signal from the jeep ahead.

Jonas stood up to get a peek over the crest before his crew became too exposed. The road rolled down in a straight line, three-quarters of a mile to the base of the hill that was his objective. Halfway there stood his lead jeep, motor idling, with Clemens perched behind his gun. Here the rice paddies edged up next to the road, the road a brown strip running through the middle of glistening green waters.

Jonas signaled the two trucks behind to hold up as his jeep rolled cautiously forward.

His driver pulled up next to Clemens. "Watchya got?"

"There's a bunker ahead."

Jonas didn't see anything suspicious himself, so he pulled out his field glasses and scanned the road. It ran up almost to the base of the hill, and then circled around to the right. Just where the road began to curve to the east stood a blackened, leafless tree, a skeleton sentinel, scorched by some fire years past. Behind it was the beginning of a footpath that snaked up the back of the hill.

Clemens said, "The bunker's at one o'clock."

Jonas shifted his view to the right and found what at first appeared to be just a mound of dirt, but which, on closer inspection, was a bunker of sandbags screened by clumps of bamboo.

"Got it." The position lay about fifty yards east of the beginning of the trail that led to the top of the hill. Jonas guessed that it was not a concrete structure, because the North Koreans had been in the area only a few weeks, and concrete was not a crucial supply need. There would be a hole in the ground, dug to chest level, with wooden posts holding up a roof, the whole structure covered with several layers of sandbags. Openings, one-foot high and two-feet wide, gave the shooters inside wide fields of fire. Jonas couldn't see a doorway to the bunker, but he guessed it would be on the opposite side from him, the north side, because the road was right there.

Prados and Clemens both had their machine guns trained on the mound of sandbags. Prados said, "They've got all the key terrain covered. We don't have mortars, and without mortars it'll be a bitch to dislodge them."

Jonas climbed out of the jeep and walked around front. He stood, hands on hips, assessing his options. There was no way to get behind the enemy. To take that position, they'd have to drive right up to it or else his squad would have to cross open rice paddies taking automatic fire all the way. They'd never make it.

Then a movement caught his eye. Up in the sky, a large dark form, too big to be a crow, swooped down and landed awkwardly on the mound, running hunched like an infantryman on short stubby legs along the rim of sandbags, its bald head tucked between its shoulders.

"A vulture." Jonas laughed disgustedly and shook his head. "There's nothing alive in that bunker. Hell, whoever was on guard there probably ran when they saw the other team scooting through the trees. Clemens, check it out."

The engine roared and the jeep jumped forward as the crew raced ahead. They took no fire from the site and soon Clemens was standing atop it, waving the rest of the patrol forward.

The vulture, though, had taken flight and come to rest in the blackened tree. Another bird joined it, and then another. Jonas glanced skyward. At least ten vultures circled over the crest of the hill, itself looking like the back of a bald skull.

Clemens' driver got on his radio. "All clear. No one here."

When Jonas and his trucks arrived at the base of the hill, the vultures in the tree flew off and joined those circling overhead endlessly, patiently. His squad jumped to the ground and began unloading emergency supplies: ammo, boxes of C-rations, two five-gallon cans of water, and medical supplies. The men on the hill, if any of them were still alive, had been up there six days now. They'd gone on patrol with only two canteens of water apiece, and two days of rations.

Maybe he was just putting the men with him in danger. There had been no sign anyone on the hill was alive.

What bothered Jonas most, as he surveyed the rim of the hilltop, was that no one had gotten up and signaled. Anyone standing guard up there had a clear view of the road for miles. The jeeps and trucks were unmistakably American. There should be at least one G.I. standing up and waving or climbing down to meet them.

Prados climbed down from behind his gun and walked over. "What do you think?"

Jonas stood assessing the situation. A switchback path ran up the side of the hill. He'd climbed a lot of hills since coming to Korea. This was the first time he'd seen a path carved into the side of one. But it was what was in the sky that commanded his attention.

"Those vultures, they're circling but not landing. So someone's still alive up there."

"Could be the gooks."

"Maybe," Jonas said, staring up at the seemingly vacant rim. "Let's see if I can raise someone." Jonas signaled for his radioman. Olsen trotted over and Jonas took the handset. "Stakeout, this is Red Rover One."

Jonas released the button on the mike and waited. The radio hissed static. He pressed the button again. "Stakeout, this is Red Rover One en-route from Stationhouse. Come in, Stakeout."

Again, he and Prados and the radioman stood together and waited. "Once more," Jonas said. "Stakeout, this is Red Rover One. Can you hear me, Stakeout?"

Again there was no reply.

Time to throw the dice.

Jonas turned to Prados. "Clemens can stay down here, guard the trucks and keep our back door open; but I want you and your machine gun with me. If there are North Koreans up there, we'll need the extra firepower."

Prados nodded. He climbed back up into his jeep and unbolted his .30-caliber machine gun. He took the tripod base from the bed of the jeep and attached it. His assistant gunner hauled belts of ammo out of the vehicle, while his driver picked up additional boxes of ammo.

Jonas brought the handset back to his mouth. He had to check on Gaddis' team. "Red Rover Three, this is Red Rover One. Over."

For a few seconds Jonas heard only static. Then, "Red Rover One, this is Red Rover Three. Receiving you loud and clear."

"Roger, Red Rover Three. Any sign of hostiles?"

"That's a negative."

Jonas pushed the button on the mike. "We are at the jump-off-point for phase two. Hold your position and wait for orders. Report immediately if you spot any sign of enemy activity."

"Roger that, Red Rover One."

"Red Rover One. Out." Jonas handed the mike back to the radioman.

"Load up with food, water, and medical supplies," Jonas ordered. The men groaned but began pulling more supplies out of the truck. Jonas lashed on a five-gallon can of water to the frame of a backpack. He carried his carbine in his left hand but kept his right free to get at his pistol and to use the radio.

The hill was a steep climb, three hundred feet high, with the switchback carved into its side. Jonas estimated the winding path to the top to run at least fifteen hundred feet. The wall at the start of each incline was about seven feet high, and so his men, by hugging the wall, had some cover. But the walls tapered down until, at the turns a man could be seen from up above, seen and fired upon.

Clemens, his assistant gunner, his driver, and the three truck drivers would cover their rear. Jonas spaced each of his thirteen men ten yards apart and started them up with their loads. He and his radioman took a position halfway up the column.

The early afternoon sun beat down on them. The upward slope of the path put a strain on Jonas' thigh muscles. He peered at the men ahead of and behind him. Each soldier was bent forward, each alert, casting glances upward and out over the immediate landscape, watching for the first hint of danger, each with his finger on the trigger. The only sounds were those of their boots shuffling through the thick dust.

An eerie silence settled over the hill as the vultures circled high overhead, ever watchful, seemingly hopeful.

Fifteen minutes later, halfway up the hill, the point man for the column came to a sudden halt. Jonas crept forward to find out why.

He'd only gone a dozen feet when he wrinkled his nose in disgust. A slight breeze carried an unmistakable odor down from above, the smell of decaying flesh.

A queasiness gripped his stomach. He leaned back against the wall of dirt and let the wave of nausea pass. He didn't want to go forward. He didn't want to see what was left of his platoon, corpses. But he had come this far. Even if they were all dead, there were families who would want to know what had happened to them.

For a moment he forgot that North Koreans might be waiting above, and he pushed ahead of his troops, quickly rounding the next two turns of the switchback, the water can on his back thumping away as he strode forward.

He felt a hand grab his arm and turned to see the concerned look on his point man's face. "Sir," the young soldier said, chiding him for his recklessness.

Before Jonas could respond, a croaking, garbled sound came from high above him. Jonas looked up and strained to hear what had to be words. Were they English? Was that a North Korean who spoke English, but not well? Finally, when the croaking sound repeated itself, he made out the sense: "Who goes there?"

Hope and disbelief mingled together, and he shouted, "Strosahl! Is that you?"

"Give... the... damn... password,... shavetail." Each word sounded like the last gasp of a dying man, but a man determined to go out with a wisecrack.

Calling him a shavetail even now. It had to be Strosahl. A grin spread across Jonas' face. "Babe Ruth," he shouted back. He thought he heard a croaking sound in reply that could have been "Yankees," the countersign.

Jonas shouted, "Sarge, have your men hold their fire. I've got a relief party coming up."

20

THE WATER CAN on his back made it impossible to run up the grade, but he sped up as fast as he could. His thighs and back strained under the load.

As he came around the last switchback, he found himself staring into the muzzle of an automatic rifle. He froze. Eight feet from him, just below the rim of the hill, knelt Strosahl, his finger hovering about the trigger. Grothe and Connery flanked him. Jonas let out a sigh of relief. At least these three, bearded and filthy as they were, their lips blistered and cracked, were alive.

Strosahl's face was so blackened with gunpowder that his tobacco-juice-stained teeth looked white by comparison. "Took you long enough to get here."

Jonas shrugged off the water can and ran to Strosahl. He went down on one knee, pulled out his canteen and put it to Strosahl's lips. Men coming behind him ran to the aid of Grothe and Connery.

The sergeant grabbed the canteen with both hands and downed a long pull. Then another, water trickling down both sides of his mouth.

The rest of the rescue party passed them and climbed up over the lip of the hill. Jonas helped Strosahl to his feet and supported him

262 | Richard Thomas Lane

as they trudged the remaining few feet together. Once over the rim, Strosahl slumped to the ground. Jonas surveyed the hilltop.

The ground was flat with sod-covered humps jutting up from its surface. Many of the mounds, each about two feet high, were ringed with carved stonework. It took Jonas some seconds to understand where he was. The hilltop was a Korean graveyard.

Men who barely resembled men, the remnants of his platoon, began to crawl out of foxholes, hands outstretched for canteens. Right away he picked out Holzer, LaBatt, Helton, Cavetti, and Shore. With each face he recognized, he felt more elated. There were others, men who had joined the platoon as replacements right before Chochiwon. Bankart, Fulton, and Petosa followed. Several men he didn't know also crept out of their holes. Replacements he hadn't met yet. Maybe even green troops on their first patrol.

Then there were the others, the figures in foxholes who didn't move, who, Jonas quickly grasped, were never going to move. He counted seven silent bloated sentinels, holding their positions as flies swarmed about their helmeted heads.

Jonas turned in a full circle, taking it all in. "Jesus, what the hell happened here?"

Strosahl leaned back against a grassy mound. "Started to think we weren't getting out of this one." He upended the canteen again.

"Go easy. You'll get cramps." He said this automatically as he tried to get a count. How many were still alive? With seven dead, there should be twenty-one more walking around.

"Sweeter than bourbon." Strosahl licked his lips. "We ran out of food three days ago, and then our water. It would be a hundred degrees in the shade, if we had any. Don't suppose you brought along any chewing tobacco? I'm out of that too."

"Couldn't find any." Jonas squatted down next to him. "Tell me what happened."

"We were doing a recon on the ford down below, mid-afternoon. There wasn't any sign the Reds were moving supplies, but Lt. Edwards decides to check out the village across the river. He took first squad into the water, and bam, halfway across the gooks let loose."

Strosahl paused for a moment, his eyes clouding. "The lieutenant took one in the chest and floated away. I don't know why no one else got killed, but the squad high-tailed it back. Then we started taking fire from this side of the river, so I led the platoon up here. Next thing I know, we're surrounded. We hadn't brought a lot of supplies. The plan back at battalion was, if we needed them, they could be trucked in. But the Reds threw up roadblocks, and we were cut off."

"Jesus, Strosahl, you've got a perimeter made up of corpses."

Strosahl went into his breast pocket and pulled out a piece of paper. Jonas scanned the names. McCarthy, Goshgarian, Moore, Kenner, Lederer, Slote, and Hess.

"Couldn't you have covered them over?"

Strosahl stared back at him. "I needed the gooks to think there were enough of us alive up here to put up a fight. The first two days, they tried to overrun us, and I lost too many. So when a man died, I filled in the foxhole up to his chest, and left him with his rifle, made them waste rounds on dead men."

Jonas stood up and shook his head. All around him the survivors were upending canteens of water and scooping C-rations out of cans. It'd been over a month since he'd left them to go into Taejon. The differences he saw shocked him. Not just the dirt and the beards. The faces of these 18- and 19-year-olds were seamed and creased. They looked so much older. And harder. They were gaunt, without fat, and they had less muscle. After two months of fighting and retreating, sleeping in foxholes but never getting a whole night's sleep, with barely a chance to bathe, and going days without hot chow, yes, they were thin, exhausted shells of the boys he'd brought with him out of Japan.

They laughed and cried as they were cared for by the relief squad, clean-shaven boys who were barely tanned. The medic, PFC Jaynes, scurried about from one wounded man to another, bandaging, sprinkling powder on sores, giving shots of morphine. The vultures still circled overhead.

"Time to get you guys out of here." Jonas called Olsen over, and taking the handset, he clicked the mike so he could contact Clemens waiting below with the trucks. "Red Rover Two, this is Red Rover One. Do you read me?"

"That's a Roger, Red Rover One."

"Standby to receive evacuees."

"Okay, listen up. We've got to get everyone down to the trucks. Prados, you've got point. Any of you guys from the hill who can walk alone, do it. Leave the water cans but take all the weapons and ammo."

The seven corpses would have to be left behind. They couldn't be helped, and he had men who needed medical attention. If the Reds ever got pushed back across the Naktong, then a graves registration detail could be sent for them.

The men converged into a line and began trudging down the switchback, several needing assistance. There were two improvised stretchers for men too wounded to get on their feet. Jonas walked up and down the column, checking on them, clapping this one and that on the shoulder. More than one said, "Sure glad to see you, Lieu."

Halfway down the hill, the static on the radio abruptly cut out, and Clemens' voice came on, his tone urgent. "Red Rover One, this is Red Rover Two. We've got company."

Jonas heard the mortar shell whistling – whisshh-shh-shh – through the air. He and everyone on the switchback dropped to the ground. It exploded east of their position.

"Shit," he blurted out. He cursed, both because he had to fight another battle to get his men out, and because he'd landed with too much of his weight on his right side, and it hurt like hell.

Ignoring the fire in his side, he scrambled to his feet and pushed past his men to get to the turn of the switchback. A cloud of white phosphorus rose in a plume fifty yards east of where his vehicles were parked, near the empty bunker. It was a spotter round, a shot made just to register range.

Half a mile to the east, on the dusty ribbon of road, about sixty North Koreans were double timing it in his direction, their weapons at port. They were still beyond the effective range of their burp guns; but at the rate they were advancing, they would soon close with his men. They had to be stopped.

Jonas pulled out his field glasses. The flat brown ground was almost barren even of scrub. Behind the advancing infantry, almost three quarters of a mile away, was the three-man mortar team that had lobbed the round. There was little cover for them. They were so exposed that, if Jonas had had a mortar or a rocket launcher, he could have taken them out on the spot. But he didn't.

He scanned the ground below, his eyes seizing on the deserted bunker. If the enemy set up there, they would slaughter his men as he tried to load them into the jeeps and trucks.

Jonas grabbed the mike from his radioman. "Red Rover Two, secure that bunker. And put that fucking mortar out of action."

Clemens came back with a quick, "Roger that. We're on it." His team sprinted forward.

From the east came the whistling of mortar rounds, increasing in volume each fraction of a second. Below Jonas a handful of his men had reached the bottom of the hill and were taking cover behind jeeps and trucks. One driver wormed his way beneath his truck and was crouched behind a wheel. As the three mortars streaked their way, everyone dove for the ground, Jonas and Strosahl landing side by side.

The explosions came in rapid succession, shrapnel clanging on metal. Jonas lifted his head to see a jeep tilting, tires shredded, its frame riddled.

Clemens fired his machine gun. His first bursts were aimed at the infantrymen to slow their advance. Then he quickly shifted his aim, going for the mortar team, but the mortars were just out of range. His bullets kicked up the dirt a dozen feet in front of them.

His fire, seemingly ineffective, still worked. The mortar team began trying to find the range of the bunker. Good, Jonas thought. Better the bunker than his trucks. The trucks were the way out of this hell hole.

Jonas leaped to his feet. He grabbed Strosahl's arm. "Send Prados to back up Clemens," he shouted. He ran down the hill with his radioman, and they took cover behind the burnt skeleton of a tree.

Prados and his team raced forward to the bunker. Clemens and his men had set up on one side. Prados set up on the other. His assistant gunner pulled out belts of ammo as his driver built them a protective wall of sandbags.

The enemy infantry, taking advantage of Clemens' shift in targets, began leapfrogging forward along the sides of the road. Prados opened fire, catching three men in a single burst. Even as their bodies were falling in sprawled, mangled heaps, he began a sweeping fire from left to right. The squads dove to the ground, many crawling, fanning out, looking for cover.

The mortar team peppered the area around the bunker with showers of burning shrapnel that repeatedly sent Clemens, Prados, and their teams diving. Grey smoke enveloped the bunker, making it impossible for Jonas to see his men.

He grabbed the mike to call the battalion CP. "Stationhouse, this is Red Rover One. Come in, Stationhouse."

"Red Rover One, this is Stationhouse."

"Stationhouse, I've reached the objective but am pinned down by mortar fire. Enemy infantry advancing on my position. Are there any aircraft in the area available to assist?"

"Stand by, Red Rover." There was a pause broken only by radio static. Then, "That's a negative, Red Rover. All aircraft are currently assigned."

"How about artillery?"

"All artillery engaged in support of Cloverleaf. Best estimate, we can get you artillery fire in thirty minutes. Can you hold?"

Two mortar rounds came whistling through the air. Jonas' practiced ear immediately knew they were coming his way. The enemy was shifting fire back towards his vehicles. He and his radioman squeezed as tightly as they could behind the tree. Two almost simultaneous explosions rocked them, and one of his trucks exploded, sending more jagged hot metal spraying in all directions.

Behind him Jonas heard a cry of "Medic!"

"Stationhouse, we're taking casualties."

Black smoke billowed up from an orange mass of flames engulfing the twisted metal wreck.

His men were spread out. Strosahl had gotten most of them away from the trucks. Some had found shallow depressions which offered minimum cover. Others had grabbed their entrenching tools and were trying to scrape out holes beneath them even as they hugged the ground.

He realized now, despite the screening fire provided by Clemens and Prados, it would be too dangerous to try to get his men into the remaining trucks. Before they were half loaded, the mortars would have their range.

"We can't hold. We need an assist."

"Roger, Red Rover, we're working on it."

At that moment, as the billowing smoke from the vehicles moved his way, he sighted a mile to the east a mass of sixty or more mustard-colored uniforms, emerging from around a hill, running at the double. Their officer halted them while he took in the situation, and then instead of joining the squads who were already pinned down, he started his troops south across the dikes of a rice paddy. Jonas could see that he meant to cut off their escape route and attack their flank.

The black smoke rolled over him and erased the scene. He grabbed the soldier nearest him, a short compact man with freckles and buck teeth, one of the clean-shaven ones. "Ross, run to the bunker. Tell Prados and Clemens keep up covering fire, but to get ready to fall back. You stay with them and watch me for the signal."

He could only hope the smoke would clear enough that Ross could see him.

Ross took off, running bent over, rifle in one hand, his other hand atop his helmet. Jonas, his eyes burning, squinted and scanned the smoke-filled area for Strosahl. He found him. The sergeant had pulled a man away from the burning transport truck and was turning him over to the medic. Jonas waved, and the sergeant sprinted back to him in his heavy-footed way. They huddled together by the tree, while the radio operator crouched a few steps away.

"We've got to get back up the hill," Jonas said.

Strosahl jerked his head back. "Lieu—"

Jonas pointed south. "There's a company of infantry moving into a blocking position. Do you really want to try to break through that?"

Strosahl looked down the road and back at Jonas.

Jonas said, "They'll line up in the road, spray the cabs, shoot the drivers, and then

cut down our men as they try to get out. Just like Taejon."

Strosahl gave a sharp nod, his jaw clenched tight.

"Set up a relay. Get every man who can walk to pack supplies up the hill. Water and ammo are the priorities. Food if we've got time."

Strosahl whirled and barked the orders. Men scrambled up from wherever they'd taken shelter and raced to the supply truck.

He divided the men up into parties – a man in the truck sliding supplies along the bed to the tailgate, another handing them to a succession of G.I.s who ran with whatever they could carry to the foot of the hill. Other G.I.s ran the supplies up to the first bend in the switchback. They dropped their loads there while others grabbed what they could and ran them up the incline to the next bend.

The medic was supporting one man, wounded in the leg, up the switchback, followed by another whose left arm dangled uselessly.

Jonas hoped Prados and Clemens could keep up the pressure, and that there was enough smoke to screen the movements of his men. He couldn't see his machine gun crews at all. They had to be firing blind themselves.

He took the mike and called Gaddis and his recon team still two miles back up the road. "Red Rover Three, this is Red Rover One. Come in, Red Rover Three."

"This is Red Rover Three."

"Red Rover Three, do you see that party crossing the rice paddies at your two o'clock?"

"Roger, Red Rover One. I have them in sight approximately a mile northeast of us."

Jonas paused for a second, running different scenarios through his mind, and pressed the button to talk. "Red Rover Three, advance along the road and lay down harassing fire on those troops. Pin them down. We are going back up the hill. You are to delay the enemy until we have withdrawn, and then you are to return to Stationhouse. Do you understand?"

"I copy, Red Rover One, but we could try to break through and join you."

It was tempting. Three men and an extra .30 caliber machine gun could make a real difference. "That's a negative, Red Rover Three. The enemy will deploy to envelop you. You are to delay only and return to base when it gets too hot. Do you copy?"

"Roger, Red Rover One. I copy. We will engage, delay, and withdraw. Over."

"Red Rover One, out." Jonas turned back to the hill to see how the relay teams were doing. The five-gallon water cans were already halfway up the hill. Boxes of ammo were stacked at the bottom of the hill and at several junctures on the path.

The smoke screen he had been counting on began to dissipate. More mortars began their soft whsshing through the air. It took only a split second for Jonas to calculate that these were aimed at the base of the hill. As his men scrambled and dove for cover, he frantically tried to figure out which side of the tree he should hide behind, shifting to the east side. The first, second and third mortars descended.

The quick succession of explosions rocked him. And even as the blasts shook the ground, more mortars whined overhead. He heard Prados and Clemens open up again with machine gun fire.

"Get up the hill," he shouted, waving his directions with his rifle.

21

A BLAST RIPPED A second truck and then the third. Black smoke rose into the air and began to envelop everything again.

All his men, except for the machine gun teams, were running. Ross, at his post with the machine gunners, his eyes fixed on Jonas, was barely visible now, almost disappearing in the darkening cloud. Jonas waved frantically for him to withdraw, then turned and began running for the hill, churning up the ground as he sprinted up the incline of the first leg of the switchback, and the next, and the next.

As Jonas mounted the rim, he saw Strosahl already deploying the men. He'd sent four-man teams to keep watch against surprise attacks from the north or west. He also sent the medic and the two wounded men to that half of the hilltop where they would be farthest from the action. But he concentrated his troops east and south, where the enemy was massed. Three men passed out ammo. Soldiers pulled canisters of hand grenades, two and three at a time, out of boxes and shoved them into pockets.

Down the hill, Clemens and his men, having withdrawn from the bunker, took up a position on the eastern end of a switchback. They laid down covering fire for Prados and his men. Farther east the North Korean infantry, which had been pinned down for most of the fight, jumped to their feet and started closing the distance to the hill. But as they began taking fire from Jonas' men atop the hill, an officer slowed down their advance. He had them spread out and dig in.

Jonas looked south along the road. Time for Red Rover Three to break off and return to base. Instead, the recon team was barreling down the road toward him. Behind them North Korean soldiers poured onto the road, firing at the jeep. Gaddis stood in the back, crouched behind the sights of his gun, firing short bursts at them as the jeep bounced along.

Prados and his two team members reached the first turn of the switchback and relieved Clemens and his men, taking up their positions.

The jeep careened into the parking area at the bottom of the hill, swerving to avoid the burning jeeps and trucks, and spun around to a stop. Immediately Gaddis began unbolting his machine gun from its mount as his team grabbed boxes of ammo, their carbines, and the radio. Prados, on the switchback, provided them with cover as they raced up the first incline.

When Clemens and his two men reached the top, Jonas sent them to the northern end to set up. Gaddis and his men, having passed by Prados, came up next, grinning as they came. Jonas directed him and his team to set up their machine gun to watch the southern approach to the hill. Prados and his men came up the last incline and up over the lip. Some of the troops gave them a "Hurrah!" Jonas directed them to a cluster of rocks that provided some shielding.

Then Strosahl and he trotted along the perimeter, stooped low, checking to make sure all the men had designated overlapping fields of fire, and that everyone had ammunition and grenades. The air reeked of the smell of the seven corpses ringing the hilltop.

"Hold your fire, men. Hold your fire," Jonas said. "They're not advancing on us. Don't waste your ammo. We're going to need every round."

He turned full circle, eyeing the corpses, Strosahl's silent sentinels. The new men, as they started to dig in, were keeping their distance from the bodies.

"Sergeant, have the men throw dirt over our dead. Cover them up. It'll make breathing a little easier.... And when you're done, join me."

Strosahl nodded and walked away. Jonas picked his way around the humps in the ground to the center of the hilltop. To the west, the battle for Cloverleaf was in progress. Artillery thumped steadily.

He knelt on one knee, his glance darting from one sod-covered hump to another, each ringed with stones. How appropriate, he thought, to be trapped in a Korean cemetery. They bury their dead sitting up. When we get overrun, we can be buried like them, sitting in our foxholes.

Strosahl broke in on his thoughts. "The men are almost set."

Cannon thumped in the distance.

"I thought I had a chance to get the platoon out. I lost that bet but good. All I did was get more good men trapped up here."

The shadow of a buzzard swept over them.

"It means something to the men that you came here for them, Lieu."

"Yeah, now at least they get to die with smiles on their faces."

"Worse ways to die."

"...What do you think their next move will be? Night attack?"

Strosahl scratched the growth on his cheek. "They've got better things to do right now than waste men trying to wipe us out."

"Like...?"

"Down river from us, they've built three bridges. You can't see them – they're beneath the waterline. Invisible to reconnaissance from the air." He was without his chaw of tobacco, but gathered some saliva, turned his head and spit. "The gooks ferry their supplies across all night long."

"Damn." Jonas stared down river and said nothing more.

Artillery thumped continuously in the distance, both sides raining shells down on the Cloverleaf.

Strosahl finally said, "Any word on how the battle was going?"

"Not good," said Jonas, "It's not good the Reds have gotten across the Naktong. If we don't drive them back, our whole perimeter's in danger of collapsing." He turned to Strosahl. The sergeant stared back at him intently. Jonas shook his head. "That's where we should be, helping root them out, not stuck helpless on this hill."

Strosahl said nothing.

Jonas went back to staring down river. "Where did you say the bridges are?"

Strosahl turned so that he was kneeling side by side with Jonas. He pointed. "See that sandbar?"

He pulled out his field glasses. "Got it."

"Go fifty yards beyond that, where it looks like there are a couple of logs beached on the bank. That's where the first bridge starts."

He put the field glasses to his eyes, adjusted the focus, stared for a few moments, lowered them and said, "We've got a radio that's working. I could call in an artillery barrage on those bridges – slow down their resupply."

"I thought about that but decided it wouldn't do much good. Gooks are quick at rebuilding – and then they'd hit back."

"We annoy them, and they wipe us out. I see what you mean." Jonas looked around at the perimeter. Taking advantage of the lull in the action, he said, "How've the men been doing?"

"The mail caught up with us a few weeks ago. That's usually good for morale. Except Cavitch, he got a 'Dear John.' He was moping around, saying he hoped the gooks killed him." Strosahl chuckled. "Then Perosa shows him a picture of his girl, and says she's got a sister that he can set Cavitch up with. All of a sudden he's buddy-buddy with Perosa."

Jonas grinned.

Strosahl nodded toward the south. "Connery was due to be rotated back to the States in a month. He's not too happy. Fulton's been beating everyone at cards. I think three of the men owe him a month or more of pay. And Grothe, I've never seen anything like it. I swear he likes C-rats better than he likes mess hall chow."

From the east came the drone of fighter planes. Both turned their gaze skyward. Four fighters passed overhead on their way to Cloverleaf.

"I'll be damned!" Jonas exclaimed.

"What?"

"I just realized where the North Koreans' weakness is."

"Well tell me, 'cause I haven't seen it yet."

Jonas shouted out, "Listen up." He raised his arm, circling with his fingers. "Squad leaders, with me. Prados, you too."

The squad leaders broke off what they were doing and came over and knelt down in a circle. He looked around at the dirty, tired, disappointed faces.

"I'd hoped to get you out and back to base," he said, "but we're stuck up here." He paused and, scraping up some loose dirt, let it trickle through his fingers.

"Prados—"

"Sir?"

"The North Koreans have us hemmed in tight, but what are the chances a recon team could slip through their lines and get across the river undetected?"

Prados chewed on it. "There'll be almost no moon tonight. If we go upstream far enough, we should be able to evade their patrols. It would take a few hours, but yeah, I can get my men to the other side. What do you want us to do there?"

Strosahl looked at him quizzically. "You go poking the hornets' nest for nothing…"

"You're the one who says, "You take the pay…"

22

I T WAS 2 am and so dark that Chen had authorized some of the
parked trucks to leave their headlights on to provide enough
light for the porters to work. Chen paused before climbing
into the jeep. He eyed the supply depot one last time to make sure
he hadn't missed anything. The porters, mostly conscripts, loaded
up their A-frames at the tailgates of fifty trucks. More trucks stood
waiting to pull in off the road to be unloaded. Conscripted soldiers
guarded the area. Chen had only a few experienced officers to supervise the operation.

He was not happy with the assignment. He should be across the
river with his old unit defending the Cloverleaf Hill and Oblong-ni
Ridge sector. But when the division's senior supply officer came
down with malaria, Gen. Lee Kwon Mu himself chose Chen as the
replacement.

Everything was running smoothly, as smoothly as could be
expected when all supplies had to be transported in the middle of the
night to avoid the American fighters and bombers. An hour earlier,
Chen's mouth had gone dry and his stomach knotted up when a stray
artillery shell exploded a hundred yards from his trucks. Fearing it
was a spotter shell, he had immediately ordered the trucks to move

out of the field – but no barrage followed, and soon everyone fell back into their routines.

He climbed into the jeep and ordered the driver to take him back to his command post in the village a mile away. They had just started moving down the center of the road, flanked by lines of porters on each side, when Chen heard the artillery shells flying overhead – not one after another as was usual, but a rain of shells. It was as if dozens of freight trains were hurtling simultaneously through the air, all together, all launched at once, from multiple batteries, crashing down and exploding en masse. The ground rocked. The jeep leaped into the air from the shock and Chen's head slammed into the dashboard.

His hand clasped to his forehead, he shouted, "Turn around! Go back!"

The driver, fumbling, got the vehicle pointed in the opposite direction. On both sides of the road, porters lay cowering. Ahead, stacks of ammo and grenade boxes began to explode, lighting up the dark field in jagged flashes.

Chen stood up even as the jeep came to a halt. It was as he feared. Dozens of shells had hit simultaneously, blanketing the whole area. There had been no place to which the drivers, porters or soldiers could escape. With artillery shells exploding over three hundred square yards, red-hot shards of metal had spun out in all directions. It didn't matter where a man tried to hide - in front of a truck, behind a truck or under a truck. Hundreds of bodies lay inert or thrashed about wounded. Piled up boxes of ammo continued to explode.

Helplessly he fell back into his seat and stared at the red fires and black smoke from the explosions.

These were crucial supplies meant for his men across the Nak-tong. In the morning the Americans would launch an assault. The men of his 4th Division desperately needed ammo for rifles, machine guns, and rocket launchers. They needed the rice and the water. They needed medical supplies. A sense of defeat momentarily swamped him. But he took a deep breath and rallied himself, pushing the feelings away.

He saw a young officer entering the ring of carnage on the far side. The lieutenant had been up the road directing traffic.

Chen sprang out of the jeep. "Chung, over here."

The young man looked up, startled, as though being shook from a nightmare. When he saw his superior officer, relief spread over his face and he sprinted across the field.

"We need to get organized," Chen said.

Lt. Chung looked back around, his attention drawn by the screams and cries of the wounded. A group of women porters who had been outside the kill zone were wailing.

"Listen to me," Chen commanded, "see if you can find another officer – even an NCO. There's an apple orchard and a clearing half-a-mile west of here. Our trucks that are still on the road need to be re-routed. And we've got to get the porters there."

"But the wounded, sir."

"Detail a quarter of the conscripts to collect the wounded and send the rest to unload supplies in the new staging area. I'll go back to the village and send the medics."

And, he thought, I have to get on the radio and report to Col. Chu. Distractedly he returned the lieutenant's salute as the man hurried off. Chen climbed into his jeep.

"Back to the command center." When the driver, who had not had any combat experience, sat frozen, Chen lost his patience.

"Did you hear me, soldier?"

Startled, the driver mumbled an apology and cranked up the engine. The young soldier hit the horn, and the mass of porters, standing in the way, clogging the road as they pressed forward to gawk, moved back out of the way. The jeep had barely gone a hundred yards when Chen heard another barrage of artillery shells on the way, but this time falling far short of the supply depot.

"Hurry," he shouted even before the reverberations of the massive explosions reached them. He didn't have to see the target to know the village, his command post, had been hit.

The road back was littered with loads dropped by fleeing porters. Others who hadn't deserted stood on the side of the road or clustered paralyzed in the middle, pleading to know what was happening. The driver wove in and out, leaning over the steering wheel trying to see the path ahead, not daring to use his headlights because of the blackout orders.

Reaching the village's perimeter, Chen saw that all the mud-and-wattle farmhouses were flattened and burning. The only structure still partially standing was the single-story brick schoolhouse, and even half of it had caved in under the brunt of the explosion.

The pattern was the same. Several batteries of guns had fired simultaneously so that the shells all hit at the same moment, covering every square yard with searing shrapnel. There had been no place to hide.

He got out of the jeep slowly and made his way through the bonfires. Bodies lay strewn about. He passed dead men with limbs missing who had already bled out. A medic lay sprawled, disemboweled. Across the village he saw his other medic who had somehow survived. The man wandered dazedly from body to body, dragging a ridiculously small first aid kit behind him, crying helplessly.

He picked his way through the smoke, and the bonfires, and the bodies until he reached the schoolhouse. The front wall was just a pile of collapsed rubble. His radio operator lay face down, unmoving. He hoped the man was unconscious and not dead. Kneeling, he turned the body over and saw at once the open, blank gaze. He let out a sigh and rolled the corpse back over, face down.

He walked up the two steps and across the hallway through the door into his radio room. The ceiling now littered the floor. But on a table, sheltered in the corner, stood his radio unscratched.

For a moment, he just stood and stared at the green metal box and its dials. This was going to be a hard report to make. The thought filled him with shame.

As he stood collecting his thoughts, trying to compose the message, he heard more shells hurtling through the air. His body turned ice cold when he realized they were headed for the river. The first shell exploded, then another, then another. A standard artillery barrage this time. Aimed at his bridges. Bridges which were impossible to see from the air because they were beneath the water.

The events of the day took on new meaning. It was clear that the Americans, who had been helplessly trapped on the hill, now had an aggressive commander. This officer had sent out a patrol or patrols to locate his depot and had called in artillery strikes.

He leaned back against the wall and let his legs go limp. He sat there shaking his head as shell after shell exploded for half an hour. He waited. There was no reason to send Col. Chu a report until he heard from his men.

Finally a breathless runner arrived. "Sir, the enemy has attacked—"

"The bridges. Yes, I know. What is the extent of the damage? Was Lt. Koh on site?" The lieutenant was his best engineer.

The runner was bent over, catching his breath. "The lieutenant reports two of the bridges are extensively damaged." He stood up, taking in lungfuls of air. Though he looked barely old enough to shave, he had a thin mustache. He picked his words carefully, as though he was trying to recall verbatim the message he was to recite. "They will take days to repair. The third can be ready by tomorrow night – if there are no more barrages."

If there are no more barrages, Chen thought. How was he supposed to prevent that? He waved his hand, dismissing the soldier.

The early morning light poured in through the missing ceiling. The radio hissed in the background. Col. Chu paced back and forth in what was left of the radio room, hands clasped behind him. "I don't understand how you could have let this happen, Captain."

The room, with three of its walls still standing, was empty except for the two men. The radio and the map on the wall were about all that was left of the command post.

Chen expelled his breath. "The artillery strikes were totally unexpected."

"Unexpected? You left an American reconnaissance patrol sitting on a hill overlooking your position. What did you think they would do? Of course they called in their artillery."

"We jammed their radio frequency the first night they were on the hill."

"You should have wiped them out the first day. Why didn't you?"

His shame made it almost impossible to talk. "I..."

"Speak up, Captain."

"Sir, it was a small force without radio communication. I judged them unable to do us damage. But they were well equipped to defend their position. I would have lost valuable men and time trying to overrun them. I calculated their water would run out. My blocking forces could kill them as they tried to escape."

"But they were *reinforced*."

"I put up roadblocks to prevent that, sir. The first was manned by my best men."

"Yes, and your best men were taken by surprise and wiped out. If they were so good, how did that happen? And what about your men at the second roadblock deserting their posts? Then one of your lieutenants loses a whole platoon in a suicidal attack on the hill?"

"New men, in need of seasoning, an overzealous officer who lacked proper training. These conscripts I have to work with, they've barely had a chance to learn to use a rifle."

Chu snorted. "A third of the supplies for the division flow through here. Our men rely on you."

Chen's body stiffened. Through clenched teeth, he said, "The Americans will not be able to slip their reconnaissance team through our lines again. Tonight I will blanket this whole area with patrols. Then I will dislodge these foreign pigs from the hill."

"With what? You will have to use whatever men you have for the patrols."

"I have a plan. I need only a squad to execute it."

Chu regarded him coolly. "A single squad?"

"If you will put concentrated artillery fire on their hill today, I will wipe out the Americans tonight. I will destroy their radio and kill every man on the hill."

"If you fail—"

"I will not fail. You have seen me take a hill at night."

"Yes, that is so.... But reinforcements are arriving from the north later today. I could release a full company to you tomorrow morning."

"I prefer a night attack, using a smaller force. I will take fewer losses that way."

"As you wish. However, you still will need new troops for operations here."

"Yes. And more porters. We have no idea how many are dead, or how many deserted during the night. I also need a new radio operator, one who understands English."

"I will attend to it.... There is one other matter."

"Yes?"

"Pak Waeng-son, your liaison in Taejon..."

Chen felt his heart constrict. He said nothing.

"Apparently he tried to intercede in behalf of a policeman. A people's court executed him as a reactionary."

"...He had a daughter."

"Hmm, jailed, I think. But the point, Captain, is that you wrote a favorable report on a man now deemed to have been an enemy of the Revolution."

"His help probably saved hundreds of lives and allowed us to take the city at least a day early."

Chu's tone softened. "My friend, our Russian advisers have never been happy with you, a former Chinese officer, being assigned to this division. And there are certain senior members of the general's staff who do not trust you."

"But—"

Chu raised his hand. "Your report was not prudent under the circumstances. You have enemies, Chen. They can make a case that the fault for tonight's debacle, the loss of so many trucks, supplies and porters, lies with you. It is crucial that you dislodge the Americans from the hill, not just for the sake of the mission, but for your sake as well."

Jonas, his carbine slung over his left shoulder, knelt on one knee behind Gaddis and his machine gun. He scanned the road behind the hill with his field glasses. Three-quarters of a mile away, he could see about a half-dozen North Korean soldiers. He guessed there were more out of sight somewhere. In any case, the roadblock was still in effect.

Down the switchback, at the bottom of the hill, the burnt-out hulks of his trucks were a grim reminder the trek back was long. A dozen patient vultures sat on the barren limbs of the fire-blackened tree.

Stooping low as he walked, he crossed the hilltop and knelt again to survey the other side of the river. Immediately across from him was an observation post keeping an eye on his defenses. He didn't even need binoculars to see them. They were just watching, as he was, and seemed to pose no imminent threat. He raised his field glasses again and swept the far bank going downstream. Crews of bare-chested Koreans waded waist-deep, salvaging materials from the demolished bridges.

Seeing no immediate signs of a counterattack shaping up, he made his way back to where Strosahl was working on their two-man foxhole. In the center of the hilltop this time, rather than on the line. The command center from which they could see the whole perimeter.

Olsen sat by his hole, "next door" to theirs, monitoring radio traffic as he finished off a tin of peaches. He couldn't seem to get enough peaches. His helmet lay on the ground next to him.

Nearby PFC Jaynes patched up Cpl. Prados' shoulder at the make-shift aid station, a hollowed-out area that already held two severely wounded men. The medic had gotten soldiers to help uproot headstones from the graves scattered across the hilltop and replant them around the hollow to shelter his patients.

Prados and his men had run into a North Korean patrol while making their way back from locating the supply depot. The firefight was brief, but Prados was wounded in the shoulder. He sat on a mound with his shirt off, as the medic swabbed out his wound with iodine. Jonas squatted in front of him. Cannons fired continuously in the distance.

The corporal attempted to grin even as he grimaced from the pain. "It was something to see, sir. I've heard of calling in a 'time-on-target' artillery barrage but seeing all the damage done when those shells arrive at the same time – wow! That was something else again."

Jonas tried, but couldn't conceal his own smile. He too had never seen the tactic used but had only read about it in a training manual. He needed now to radio an after-action report back to base.

Four fighter aircraft streaked by overhead, racing toward Cloverleaf Hill.

"What kind of damage did you see?"

"Had to be forty or fifty trucks parked in that field, and none of them are ever going back into service. That's just one huge junk yard now."

"Casualties?"

"Maybe three hundred. We had to get out quick, so I don't know how many dead and how many wounded. But I tell you, it was grisly."

Jonas turned to the medic. "What do you say, Doc?"

"I think the sooner we get off this damn hill, the sooner I can get these men proper medical attention. In the meantime, I don't have room in this… *aid station*. Prados here is going to have to sit in a foxhole and try to keep from getting dirt in his wound."

"Can you handle that, Prados?" Jonas said.

"I haven't had a wink of sleep since you dragged me out of my cot the night before last. Drop me in a hole, and I'll be asleep before I hit bottom." He yawned. "Don't worry about me, Lieu."

"Good man," Jonas said, clapping him on his good shoulder as he got up.

He walked another half-dozen steps, stooped over low, to where Sgt. Strosahl was putting the final touches on their foxhole.

Jonas did a quick scan of the perimeter. All his men were dug in, their foxholes roughly evenly spaced from one another, although the line was thin. The machine guns and B.A.R.s were well positioned. He wished he had concertina wire, landmines and mortars, but he had what he had. A large enough force could overrun them. But as Jonas figured it, it would take at least a company, and the assault would have to be well executed. His stomach kept clenching and unclenching. He hoped he hadn't left anything to chance.

He stood by his radioman, dug out a message pad from a side pocket, and wrote up his report. Passing it to the operator, he said, "Encode this – send it ASAP." He waited long enough to make sure Olsen had no questions, and then moved on to Strosahl.

More fighters streaked overhead. Artillery fired from both sides of the river, and explosions reverberated steadily from the direction of Cloverleaf.

"The men had breakfast?"

Strosahl rolled his eyes. "We've been over this, Lieu. Yes, they've all eaten. I made sure every swinging dick on the perimeter drank a canteen of water and is carrying a full one. The ammo is distributed; everyone's got grenades." The sergeant snapped his fingers. "Oh, that's it, you forgot to order them to shower and shave."

"Okay, okay."

They lapsed into silence.

Jonas cocked an ear. "Does it sound like the battle is slowing down?"

Strosahl nodded. "Yeah, but is that good news or bad news? Who's winning?"

"Wish I knew. Hitting the enemy's staging area last night should be helping us today." Jonas squatted and began absentmindedly pulling at a brown tuft of grass.

"You know what just might drive the nail into the coffin?"

Jonas cocked his head.

"Send out another recon team tonight, get a fix on their new staging area – they have to be preparing a new one – and flatten it as well."

Jonas shook his head slowly. "I don't know, Sarge. It was one thing to send out Prados last night. He's experienced. I'm sure the North Koreans had patrols out, but nothing like they'll have now. That whole north side of the river is going to be crawling with troops, just to make sure we don't try to pull another surprise."

"Hit them again tonight, and you might be saving dozens of our guys' lives tomorrow. Maybe hundreds. Like you've been saying, the Reds' whole campaign depends on being resupplied."

"It's too dangerous. Who am I going to send out? Prados is wounded. Clemens is good, but he doesn't have the experience. Gaddis takes too many risks."

"Me. I'll take Clemens and his men out."

"You?"

"I ran lots of recon patrols behind Jap lines on Guadalcanal."

Jonas hesitated, then shook his head. "I don't like the odds. They'd be waiting for you."

Jonas sat down and slipped his legs over the edge of the hole. He saw the brown beads hanging around the sergeant's neck. "That a rosary?"

"Buddhist prayer beads."

He was shocked. "You're *Buddhist?*"

"I'm not; the girlfriend is."

"Didn't know you had a girlfriend."

Strosahl glanced away. "I took the beads and promised her I would come back safe."

"I didn't know you had a girlfriend, but I want you to get back safe to her. I'm not sending you out."

The vultures fled even as the first artillery shell screeched through the air across the Naktong and exploded at the foot of the hill. Jonas slipped down into the hole across from Strosahl, clutching his rifle between his knees.

"Spotter round," he said. "I think we're in for it."

"You're the one who was so eager to piss the gooks off."

Jonas grinned and adjusted his helmet.

The second shell hit almost dead center atop the hill, three feet from Jonas' and Strosahl's hole. The deafening explosion shook the ground all around them. Clumps of dirt pelted their helmets.

Silence. Jonas' ears felt clogged, as though he had been underwater. He moved his jaw around, and the eardrums cleared, first one and then the other, with little pops. He brushed dirt off his sleeve.

He inspected the walls uncertainly and looked back at Strosahl. "Anyone ever get buried alive in a foxhole?"

"Sure."

The sergeant started to say more, but the next shell screeched through the air, followed by the next, and the next and the next.

Jonas reflexively tucked his head between his shoulders and stared at the brown earth below. The flashing explosions outside turned the light in the hole red. Every lungful of greasy air he sucked in was filled with dust and burnt powder. Ground tremors shot up his spine, cracking against his skull and setting his teeth on edge. He tried to distract himself with memories of life in the States, but he couldn't.

The pounding grew continuous, blocking out the sound of the whine of incoming shells. Explosion overlapped explosion, thunderclap with thunderclap as the ground reverberated. White-hot steel fragments whirled overhead from all directions. He lost all sense of time.

His ears rang. His body went cold, and sweat dripped down his face, while fire scorched the ground above. A shell had to find their hole. He knew it. Even as he stared at the ground, he could see the lethal bomb arcing down from above, fixed on his exact position. He shuddered. His intestines twisted into knots. The shelling went on and on.

He stole a glance at Strosahl, his gaze traveling from the man's broken nose down to his crotch. The sergeant's dungarees were wet. And then Jonas' own bladder released, and he smelled piss. The sergeant grinned or grimaced. Jonas couldn't tell which. It seemed bizarre that the last thing he might see on this earth was Strosahl with his prayer beads, squashed nose, brown teeth and wet crotch.

He couldn't swallow, not even when sour stomach juice streamed up his throat and filled his mouth. There was nothing to do but sit there, take it and sweat it out. And sweat he did, a cold clammy sweat.

He knew some of his men had to be dead, even though he heard no screams. The constant explosions blocked out any other sounds. But he couldn't bring his mind to focus on them at all, because he was so filled with his own sense of helplessness and terror.

The pounding reverberating din went on and on – until it didn't. Suddenly there was just the ringing in his ears. He felt blood trickling down from his nose. He wiped it off.

Strosahl stared at him with blank, dull eyes.

Jonas said, "Is it over?" He hardly dared hope. His voice sounded strange to him, hollow and detached, like he was in a large dark cavern.

"Dunno. But I'm not going to poke my head out there yet."

Then, scattered about the perimeter, the screams started. And the shouts, "Medic!"

Jonas peered over the rim of his hole. The smoke-filled air was hazy.

He saw no other heads at first. The ground, which had been covered with brown dried grass was now black and smoking, littered with thousands of shards of grey metal. The hilltop was pitted with craters. There were no more mounds marking Korean graves. None of the headstones survived. They were reduced to rubble.

A cry "Medic!" came from his right, and then again, from behind, another "Medic!"

He automatically looked for the 'aid station.' It didn't exist. There was no hollowed-out defile with two wounded soldiers being tended by a medic. They were gone. The doc was gone. The ring of protecting headstones was powdered white dust, coating the blackened ground and twisted shards of metal. Jonas couldn't even make out the outlines of the hollow, because the whole area was pitted with craters.

He crawled out of his hole, leaving his rifle behind, and stood. Other helmeted heads appeared around the perimeter. He walked like a drunk the three steps to Olsen's hole. The radio operator stared up, the whites of his eyes large in his gunpowder-blackened face. He sat on his rear in the hole in a near fetal position, shaking, clutching the radio to him like a teddy bear.

"Medic! We need a medic!" The call came from behind Jonas.

He turned and shouted angrily, "Medic's dead. We've got no medic."

The brief outburst of anger made him feel a slight bit better, less helpless. It cleared his brain of the fog a little.

Strosahl joined him. To the west, artillery began to thump, the firing coming from both sides of the river, the explosions on Cloverleaf. The main battle had resumed. He felt relieved that someone else was now taking the brunt of the battle – and flushed with shame for feeling that.

Men climbed out of their holes and rushed to help those who couldn't. Battle dressings came out of pouches. Jonas struggled to assess the damage. He counted foxholes. Five were missing. There were craters where foxholes should have been. Five artillery shells had made direct hits, obliterating all trace of the men in them.

The wounded moaned and cried as their fellow soldiers tried to treat their wounds. There were no medical supplies except the battle dressings. No sulpha powder, no iodine, no morphine.

His anger flared up anew. He clenched and unclenched his fists. When his voice came, it reverberated with rage.

"Sergeant, you still up for a recon patrol tonight?"

"Yessir."

"I want to hit them, hit them hard." He slammed his fist into his palm. "I want to fucking crush those cocksucking bastards!"

23

CHEN LAY QUIETLY on the side of the hill. It was moonless, and a cloud bank had rolled in, obscuring the starlight. The Americans above clearly didn't have illumination flares, or they would be periodically lighting up the landscape. If he believed in the gods, he would have taken this as an omen they were on his side. But he didn't believe in the gods. He believed in History, yet he had seen too many brave comrades fall in History's service not to be cautious.

Two of his men inched up the hill to his left and two more to his right. Twenty feet below him were nine more. These were the best soldiers he had, stealthy and ruthless. It was, from most points of view, a ridiculously small force. Even so, this would not be the first time he infiltrated a small group through the perimeter of a larger, defending force, overwhelming them.

He was armed, as were each of his squad, with a burp gun, a pistol, a knife, and a half-dozen grenades. Fourteen men armed like this could defeat a force two or three times its size – if they managed to surprise the defenders.

He felt the ground above him for loose material that might start to slide once he moved. Nothing. He pulled himself up another six inches. Slowly. So slowly that anyone watching from above could not detect movement. He stopped and listened. He could hear no movement on either side. His men were as silent as he. That was good. He worked his way up another six inches. He estimated he was only ten feet beneath the foxholes.

Crickets chirped. He and his men moved so carefully and slowly that while the crickets in one area might go silent for a bit, others all over the hill sporadically contributed to the chorus. This was good, because chirping crickets lulled the enemy into thinking there was no danger anywhere nearby.

He strained his ears to hear and interpret any sound from above. The occasional cough or clearing of the throat. The clink as a soldier, having unscrewed the cap for his canteen, let it knock against the side as he lifted the container to his lips. The quiet rattle of an ammo belt as the machine gunner nervously "straightened" it out for the fifth time.

Most of all he was listening for a quick agitated exchange, a man on guard calling in a whisper to a nearby buddy, "Hey, Mac, I think I hear something. You hear anything?" Most soldiers didn't want to be the one who let loose with a cautionary burst of fire only to discover no enemy was near, that it was all in his imagination. Most soldiers, the inexperienced ones anyway, wanted a buddy to confirm the suspicious sound before shooting into the night.

He heard nothing but the sound of a man shifting in his hole, the faintest of sounds; but he got a whiff of tobacco smoke as it drifted down to him. The American, who would soon be dead, was smoking. He wouldn't be stupid enough to have his head exposed. No, he had ducked down into his hole to smoke.

Chen felt ahead and carefully gathered some pebbles and clumps of dirt that might slide and give him away. He put them to the side and inched up another six inches. He clutched his burp gun in his left hand; a pouch of grenades lay on the small of his back. The canister of each stick grenade was wrapped in cloth so as to muffle any sound of rattling as he moved.

The fighting would be close-in, intense, and over quickly. His muscles were coiled, ready for action. He could feel the blood pounding in his temple. Still, he had to move ever so slowly.

He had drilled his men over and over on the plan. The first four men would go over the rim in wedge formation with Chen as the point. While Chen headed for the command center, they would fall prone on the hilltop and begin firing at the American soldiers ringing the perimeter. The Americans, attacked from behind, would turn their backs on his nine men below to return fire – but would probably fire too high while becoming clear targets themselves. His second line of attackers would mount the hilltop and move around the perimeter, clearing the foxholes one by one.

His teeth were clenched tight. He felt more anger and shame than he did fear. The destruction of his supply depot was not the only military setback he had ever experienced, but it was the most humiliating. A small ragged bunch of soldiers trapped on a hilltop with barely enough weaponry to defend their position had found a way to choke off a third of the supplies flowing across the river to the brave 4th Division, the pride of the North Korean Army. It was the 4th that had led the way into Seoul and Taejon. It was the 4th that was destined to lead the way into Pusan. To do that, they had to break out of the Cloverleaf.

His old company, somewhere on a maze of ridges, was counting on him to get supplies through to them. It was over a hundred degrees during the day, and there were no springs or wells on the Cloverleaf. Water was rationed. Food was rationed. Ammo was in short supply.

He inched his way up again. The rim of the hill was a mere three feet above him. He barely breathed. These Americans would all soon be dead – or he would be. But more important than killing any of them, he had to knock out their radio. Even if the attack failed, if he destroyed their radio, they could not call in another artillery strike. The new staging area was almost done. One of his three underwater bridges would be operational by morning.

There. He heard it. Radio static. A few degrees to his left. Somewhere near the center of the hill should be a command post. The radio would be there.

He carefully shifted the pouch from his back to his side. He removed a stick grenade and armed it, unlocked the safety on his burp gun and gathered himself to spring.

Jonas had commandeered a five-gallon water can for a chair. He sat on it midway between his foxhole and Olsen's. The radioman was perched on an empty ammo box. Both leaned forward in the dark, ears attuned to the static on the radio, waiting for Strosahl's recon team to report.

Olsen scooped out pork and beans from a C-rat can. Jonas could hear the soothing sound of crickets chirping and an owl hooting in the distance. It had been a long day. He was having a hard time keeping his eyes open.

The static broke into a squawk: "Stakeout, this is Red Rover Two. Come in, Stakeout."

Jonas came wide awake. Strosahl. He grinned.

The thought had barely flitted through his mind when he heard a soft 'thump' on the ground next to him.

"Grenade!" he shouted.

Shooting broke out along the western perimeter. Olsen dove for the ground. Reflexively, Jonas scooped up the grenade, tossed it into his own empty foxhole and threw himself to the ground.

The grenade exploded. Burp guns clattered. Up and down the perimeter grenades detonated, muzzles flashed, and men shouted and screamed. Red and orange tracer rounds streaked in all directions.

Jonas looked up from the ground to see a compact man with a disfigured face rushing toward him, firing a burp gun, swinging it left-to-right as he charged. Jonas rolled to one side as a spray of bullets snapped, snapped, snapped over his head, one bullet grazing his left shoulder, whistling by his ear. Olsen wailed in pain.

Jonas came out of his roll and up on one knee. A few feet away, breaking through the din, he heard Strosahl on the radio, "Stakeout, this is Red Rover. Come in."

His stomach clenched up as he saw his attacker stop and cock his ear at the sound of the radio. Jonas fumbled to get his pistol out of his holster, catching his assailant's eye. The dark figure turned to face him and pulled his trigger as Jonas threw himself flat on the ground, the burst of rounds snapping overhead. Rolling over and up to one knee, Jonas almost had his pistol out as the man strode forward and drove the butt of his burp gun into Jonas' jaw. A blinding pain ripped through his head and his vision went black. He landed face down on the ground. Groggily he tried to push himself up, but his arms wouldn't work, and he collapsed.

He turned his head up and saw, in what seemed slow motion, his attacker, a dark silhouette, legs spread wide, jamming a curved magazine into his machine gun. The barrel rotated down toward him. Time was so stretched out, he knew that when the bullets left the gun, he would be able to see the line of them floating toward him.

A piercing howl shocked him back into real time as Olsen, one arm dangling, threw himself at the attacker. The two went down in a tangled heap, rolling one over the other.

Olsen screamed. The attacker jumped to his feet, leaving Olsen crumpled on the ground. Jonas forced himself to his feet and rushed to help. He closed with the assailant and, catching him off-balance, landed a punch to his chin. As the man staggered back, Jonas waded forward, ready to throw a combination of blows.

But even as he launched his first punch, his opponent pivoted on one leg and kicked him just below his sternum. The air rushed out of his lungs, and he bent over in gut-wrenching pain. He almost blacked out, staggering back, hands clasped to his stomach. He fell backward onto his ass, panicking that he couldn't get a breath, sure he was suffocating.

Grenades exploded. Bullets were flying, zinging and snapping all around him. He fought for air. As he got his first breath and his sight began to clear, he saw Gaddis and another soldier, Gaddis' driver, tackle the man, one hitting him high and the other low. They went down together.

Jonas struggled to push himself up. A bullet snapped by his ear. Muzzles flashed red, grenades burst white everywhere around him, and the smell of burnt gunpowder stung his nostrils.

The pile of three men turned into a snarling, thrashing, screaming tangle of limbs. The brown-clad enemy, his burp gun lost, fought like a trapped cougar. His fists, knees and feet flew in all directions. Not even in the boxing ring had Jonas seen any human deliver so many blows so quickly. The man sprang to his feet, leaving Gaddis and the other soldier broken and writhing on the ground.

Stunned by the fighter's ferocity, Jonas forgot everything he'd ever learned in the ring. He charged yelling and swinging. But his opponent pivoted like a bull fighter; and as Jonas flew by him, the man hit him in the kidney with a solid blow, his full weight behind it. Jonas went down to his knees and collapsed.

He rolled over on his back only to see his attacker in midair diving at him. Jonas pulled a knee up to protect his stomach. His kidney was on fire. The fighter landed full force on him, his face a twisted, snarling mask. One eye was a white orb with scarring all around. His breath was putrid as he screamed what had to be curses.

Jonas grabbed hold of the epaulettes on the man's shoulders, pulling him forward and simultaneously thrusting up with his knee, throwing his attacker over his head. Jonas rolled over and tried to jump to his feet, but he stumbled. His opponent was having the same problem. Panting, they both struggled to get up.

His enemy staggered back a few steps, losing his footing as he almost tripped over an American body draped over the lip of a foxhole.

Jonas grabbed for his sidearm. So did his attacker. Jonas got his .45 out first and fired. The shot went wild. The enemy brought his pistol up and leveled it. Jonas squeezed off three more shots as fast as he could. At least one shot wasn't wild.

The shadowy figure grabbed his right bicep, the force of the bullet spinning him around. He tottered on the rim of the hill – and then disappeared into blackness.

Jonas stood stunned, not grasping what had happened. The shooting stopped. There were no more explosions. He looked right and left. There were bodies up and down the line, some in foxholes, some on the hill, some American, some North Korean. There were no North Koreans firing.

Jonas raced to the edge of the hill and stared down into the darkness. He could neither see nor hear anything. It was pitch black. If the man down there was alive, he wasn't moving. Jonas waited. Some of his men began to cluster behind him, chattering. He kept listening for some noise that would give him a direction in which to shoot.

"All of you shut up!" he ordered.

He listened. He still heard nothing. His temples throbbed.

"Who's got a grenade?"

Three voices piped up, "Here, sir."

"Give them to me." He grabbed one, pulled the pin and tossed it downhill so that it bounced as it rolled. He threw another to the left and the last to the right, the explosions ripping the air one after the other.

No screams. Nothing to indicate he'd wounded or killed the man. He hoped that meant the animal was dead. He should take three or four men and go down into the dark and make sure – or hunt him down. But the chill that snaked down his spine said he'd lose at least one man, maybe all of them.

Behind him the radio squawked and hissed. "Stakeout, this is Red Rover Two. Come in, Stakeout." Strosahl was still trying to raise him.

He tore himself away from the rim. "Everyone back to your posts. Squad leaders, see to your men."

As they all hurried off in the dark, Jonas limped to the radio, right hand clasped to his kidney. His left shoulder hurt like hell, burning where the bullet had nicked him.

Olsen sat on the ground holding his nose with one hand, blood leaking through his fingers. The other arm, with a bullet lodged in it, dangled uselessly. He couldn't even hand up the mike.

Jonas reached down and grabbed the handset off the ground, relieved the radio hadn't been damaged.

"Red Rover Two, this is Stakeout. What is your status?"

"'Bout time, Stakeout."

His headache was splitting. "We got busy up here, Rover. What've you got for me?"

"The coordinates. Are you ready to copy?" Strosahl's voice sounded faint, muffled.

"Hold one." His whole body felt bruised. He pulled out his message book and pencil from his side pocket. "Go ahead, Rover."

He took down the information and checked the coordinates on his map, squinting through the pain as he did so. There was a small clearing at that location. "Stand by, Rover, while I call for your fire mission."

Sgt. Strosahl pressed the button on the walkie-talkie. He cupped his other hand around the mouthpiece and his lips. "Red Rover standing by. Over."

Clemens, King, and Sutton looked back over their shoulders at him with strained faces. They lay prone, facing the other three corners of the compass. Their faces had mud smeared on them to cut down on any reflection. Not that there was much chance of that on a moonless, overcast night like this.

"Now we wait," he said in a hoarse whisper. His mouth was dry.

He laid the walkie-talkie on the ground next to his carbine and settled into a prone position with his field glasses. It was too dark, and the North Korean staging area was too far away to see clearly in the moment. But he wanted to be ready once the fireworks started. It took a while for a request for a fire mission to work its way up the chain of command and over to the artillery batteries – forever, it seemed.

Strosahl wished he and his men could find a position with more cover, something thick and dense like a bamboo grove. The ground in this area was too dry and hard for growing much anything but scrawny scrub brush. The elevation was good. They lay on a patch of land that was about ten feet higher than the staging area. The ground was uneven, which allowed each of the riflemen to find a small hollow to nestle in; but their best cover was the night itself.

No one talked. The four-man team had slipped by several patrols. It had taken them hours to find the staging area. Now there was less than an hour before it began to grow light. The longer they stayed, the harder it would be to get out alive. No one wanted to try crossing the river in the daylight, wading a hundred yards in cold water with their backs to the enemy.

Suddenly they heard the thundering roar of shells hurtling through the air, and the deafening explosion as they hit. The ground shook and the flashes of the explosions, like floodlights, bathed the field in light. Strosahl swept left-to-right with his field glasses and back again. The cascade of brightness flared, lingered, and died.

It was another American 'time-on-target' artillery strike, that left those in the staging area no time to flee. Then the stockpiles of ammo began to explode. He shut out the screams of the wounded as he concentrated on counting.

"Stakeout, this is Red Rover Two. Come in, Stakeout."

"Go ahead, Red Rover."

"Mission a success, Stakeout. It was a direct hit. I count thirty-plus trucks and ammo carriers destroyed. Stocks of ammunition still exploding. Unknown number of casualties. I see—"

Bullets snapped over his head. His body went cold.

Clemens yelled, "Enemy at eleven o'clock," and started firing.

King and Sutton shifted their positions and fired as the fusillade of incoming increased.

"Red Rover, come in. What's going on? Over."

"We've got company here. Got to go. Red Rover out."

"I'm hit. I'm hit," Pvt. King yelled. He rolled over on his back and pressed his hands to his hip.

Strosahl quickly crawled over to the man. "It's okay. It's okay. Show me where you're hit," he said, reaching for a field bandage from the man's pouch on his cartridge belt, while trying to get King to pull his hands back. Bullets kicked up dirt all around them.

The sergeant took one look at the 'wound' and smacked the soldier in the arm. "Damn it, King. The bullet got your bayonet. You're not hit."

King looked down at his hip wide-eyed. There was no blood, but his scabbard was bent. "I thought—"

"—Get shooting, damn it."

King rolled back over and put his rifle into his shoulder. As he took aim, a round caught him in the forehead and blew out the back of his skull, flipping his helmet up into the air. It bounced on the ground. A grenade exploded simultaneously.

They started taking fire from the southwest. A second patrol had closed in on their position.

He shouted, "Clemens, give us some covering fire. We'll run back fifty yards and lay down cover for you."

"Right."

"Sutton, with me."

Strosahl crawled to the edge of their little rise and slipped over the eastern side. He didn't wait to see if Sutton followed, but using the little mound to block the enemy's view, ran stooped, full-out over a good fifty yards, until he found a little hollow, and dropped into it. He rolled over bringing his carbine up as Sutton, hand on his helmet, jumped down beside him.

He could hear Clemens firing. A grenade exploded on the rise.

Clemens stopped firing. Strosahl waited a half minute. No sign of Clemens. He could hear the gooks chattering excitedly as they topped the rise.

"Come on." He didn't wait for Sutton's answer, but leaped to his feet and ran. He threw a quick look over his shoulder, just long enough to see Sutton thrown forward by a bullet in the back. A cold wave washed over him like ice water surging through his guts. He ran faster than he ever had.

In the still dim light, Jonas strained to see any hint of movement along the far side of the riverbank. The cloud cover overhead was breaking up and moving on. The brightening skyline obscured the stars to the east, while those immediately above still glistened. Kneeling three hundred feet above the river, he scanned it from west to east with his field glasses. Thin white mists hung over the churning yellow-brown waters. A flock of birds skimmed over the surface, flapping rapidly and then gliding, flapping and gliding. High above his own head, broad-winged vultures circled the hilltop.

His shoulder muscles bunched up as he tried to figure out where Strosahl's patrol would try to make its crossing. Close by his side, the radio in its backpack bristled with static. He heard a splash. He swiveled his head to the right – but saw nothing. Then he heard a splash to his left, but again was too late to catch sight of anything.

"Damn, Lieu. Did you see that?" On his left, Pvt. Vorderer sat behind a B.A.R., his mouth agape.

Cpl. Schore on his right exclaimed, "Biggest goddamn fish I ever saw. And I've fished some good holes." He turned his head, "Hey guys, come look at this."

Exasperated, Jonas shouted, "Everyone maintain your positions. You're watching for our recon patrol. And the fucking Reds, damn it. You got that?"

A simultaneous "Yessir" came in from every point on the perimeter.

Pvt. Vorderer rubbed the blond stubble on his chin. "Sure wish

I could get one of those into a frying pan. Hell, just one of those mothers would fill several frying pans."

Schore barked, "Vorderer, you heard the lieutenant. Shut up and keep your eyes peeled for the fucking enemy, or you're the one that'll be in a frying pan."

"Okay, okay. I was just saying—"

"—Well don't."

"Alright, alright, jeeze."

Jonas blocked out the chatter and concentrated on tactical issues. His perimeter was thin, very thin. Between the artillery barrage and the night attack, he'd lost eleven men. That was in addition to the seven men who'd died before he mounted his rescue operation. All eighteen were buried Korean style, sitting upright in their holes, with a mound of dirt piled over their heads. There had been no time or energy to dig regular American-style graves, even shallow ones.

For all he knew, there were four more of his men dead on the other side of the river, the recon patrol. But no, that's what Strosahl did. He'd bring men out alive.

Half the men left had some kind of trauma, ranging from blistering burns to incapacitating wounds. Maybe twenty were fit to fight, a mere five men to cover each quadrant. The others were unconscious or feverish, hunched down in their holes. Those still unscathed had done their best to tend to their comrades, but if the platoon didn't get off this damn hill soon, more would die.

Gaddis had a broken arm that Jonas, drawing on his own experience of being hospitalized, had done his best to immobilize. Nevertheless, the man insisted on staying at his post, on guard at the 'back door'.

Still no sign of the recon team trying to cross upriver or down. The yellow-orange sun would soon be crawling up over the horizon. The battle for Cloverleaf would resume.

"Stakeout, this is Red Rover Two. Come in, Stakeout. Over." The voice was hoarse and strained.

Strosahl. Jonas, a surge of relief flooding through him, grabbed the handset. "Red Rover, this is Stakeout. What's your situation? Over."

There was no answer, just radio static. Then, "Stakeout, I need you to call for some Willie Peter. That's ASAP, Stakeout. Over."

White phosphorus? Why the hell would Strosahl want white phosphorus? Jonas wasn't going to question the request. That would take up precious time. With the day's battle for Cloverleaf about to start, he didn't know whether he could even get an artillery strike approved.

He pressed the button on his mike, his own voice strained now. "Red Rover, where do you want the package delivered? Over."

"Stakeout, I lost my map. Plot the coordinates for the riverbank directly across from your position. I need six rounds."

"Roger that, Red Rover. I'm relaying the request now. Hold tight. Over."

"You got that right, Stakeout. It's tight. Red Rover out."

Jonas quickly found the coordinates, got on 1st Battalion's frequency, and relayed the request, giving the coordinates in encoded form. He hoped the sense of urgency in his own voice would carry weight.

He got an immediate reply. "Stakeout, this is Stationhouse Six."

Jonas' head jerked. Col. Smith himself was answering. The C.O. of a battalion or regiment was "Six," his X.O. was "Five," and on down the line.

"Stationhouse Six, I have you five-by-five." Loud and clear.

"Stakeout, is this a priority? Our artillery is already committed. Over."

Jonas took a deep breath. "This is a Priority One."

"Stakeout, hold on. I'll see what I can do. Over."

Jonas gripped the mike tightly, choking up a bit. One of his officers needed unusual fire-support, and the colonel was trying to get it. No questions asked.

He waited, staring across the river, wondering where Strosahl was and what he was up to. He glanced left and right. His men fell silent and eyed him. They're feeling my tension, he thought.

"Stakeout, this is Stationhouse Six."

Jonas jammed down the button. "Stakeout here."

"Stakeout, that's an affirmative on your fire-mission. I say again, that's an affirmative. Over."

He breathed a sigh of relief. "This is Stakeout. Roger that. And thanks, Six. Over."

"Stakeout, good luck and good hunting. We're pretty busy here, so this is Stationhouse Six, Out."

He quickly switched back to Strosahl's radio frequency. "Red Rover Two, this is Stakeout."

"Red Rover here."

"Red Rover, your fire-mission is coming. What's your situation? Over."

At that moment, artillery fire resumed to the west. The battle for Cloverleaf Hill was on again. American artillery south of the river began thumping, trying to soften up the enemy's fortified positions in advance of the infantry's assault.

"Stakeout, be advised, three dead. I'm alone, trying to make it back. Also be advised that directly across from you there is what looks like a full company of North Koreans, probably a hundred and fifty men, readying for an attack. They're still dispersed, or I would have called for a fire mission to try to break them up. They're heavily armed – machine guns, grenade launchers, rockets, mortars. You name it, they've got it. The shit is about to hit the fan. Over."

"Red Rover, receiving you five-by-five. How long do we have? Over."

At that moment the shells roared up from the south and rushed overhead. The first hit on the north side of the Naktong. Five more followed. Plumes of smoke billowed up and spread out, quickly creating a dense white cloud along a hundred yards of riverbank. The massive white sheet roiled up, blocking Jonas' view of anything beyond.

24

Jonas waited. A long minute went by. Then he discerned a dark shape pushing through, emerging from the cloud. Strosahl. The sergeant was sprinting full-out, rifle in one hand and walkie-talkie in the other. He ran into the water, noticeably slowing once he was in it up to his thighs, the sprint becoming a stride. The brown rushing current was waist-high, and then chest-high. He held his rifle and walkie-talkie above his head, the current slowly pushing him a foot downstream, and then another foot. He struggled to maintain his balance.

The men on both sides of Jonas stood up and began to cheer.

"Get down," he shouted.

Strosahl was midway across. The white cloud cover behind him was thinning. The sergeant pushed on, the water level reaching his arm pits. As more of the cloud dissipated, Jonas started to see the vague shapes of stationary forms across the river, scrub trees.

His chest tightened as he tried to calculate the rest of Strosahl's route. From the water's edge, the land rose gently at first, gradually becoming steeper over the first fifty yards. Then it rose at a sharper incline for another twenty-five, with a web of small ridges or spines erupting from the hillside, the pitch of the incline suddenly rising to forty-five degrees. Halfway up the hill, it got steeper again.

Strosahl emerged from the river, but at the same time a dozen men in mustard-colored uniforms appeared on the opposite bank. They shouted excitedly, pointing at Strosahl. One raised his rifle and fired a shot. Strosahl, bent low, pumped his legs.

Up on the hill, Vorderer didn't wait for an order. He sighted in with his B.A.R. and fired three quick bursts. The dozen North Koreans scattered, finding cover as best they could, and took up firing positions. They began squeezing off rounds. On Jonas' right, Perosa, the machine gunner, quickly joined in, his rounds kicking up dirt around the kneeling and prone enemy, catching one of those kneeling in the chest and hurling him backward, his rifle flying out of his hands.

A North Korean machine gun crew broke into view, raced forward, and set up behind a beached log. With his field glasses, Jonas could see the red stars on their caps, the determined looks on their young faces.

Strosahl was struggling up the uneven, steep, spiny ground, still only a third of the way up to the hilltop, when the machine gun fire forced him to hit the ground and crawl for cover. Immediately a mortar team across the river began hunting the sergeant's range, with two shells exploding twenty feet below him.

Jonas' radio crackled with static. "Stakeout, this is Red Rover."

"Stakeout here."

"Damn it, Stakeout, I need more covering fire. Over."

"Working on it, Red Rover." Jonas turned to Perosa. "Take out that mortar team." Perosa began to fire. The machine gun clattered away, spewing spent brass.

Jonas leaned over to Vorderer. "Nail their fucking machine gun."

The Browning rattled, raking the far shore with a long burst. The acrid scent of burnt powder charged the air. Ejected brass rounds piled up.

A private, one of the convoy's truck drivers, came running up and knelt next to Jonas, holding his rifle awkwardly as though he wasn't familiar with it. "Lieutenant—!"

Jonas turned his head. He could barely hear the man above the din of automatic fire. "What is it, Dodd?"

The private cupped his hands around his mouth. "Cpl. Gaddis wants you to know sixty gooks are double-timing it up the road from the south."

Jonas started to reply but stopped himself and began sweeping the far riverbank. East and west of him, enemy troops were wading across, out of machine gun range. His mouth went dry.

Directly across the river, three more mortar teams disappeared behind a rise. They had to be digging in. Even as he tried to figure out what to do about them, flickers of movement caught his eye. Jonas adjusted his field glasses. There, across the river on the crest of a hill several hundred yards away, stood a small knot of men with maps and a radio. The enemy command post. It was out of B.A.R. and machine gun range.

The six men were talking and gesticulating, all of them except one man in the center. Jonas zeroed in on him. When he saw the scarred face and the white orb of an eye, he recoiled. It gave him little satisfaction that his adversary's left sleeve dangled empty – the arm tucked inside the jacket, in a sling no doubt. If the way this man had fought inside the American perimeter was any indication of how he commanded troops, the impending attack would be brutal. At least, Jonas thought, with the battle for Cloverleaf in progress, the enemy commander wouldn't be able to get artillery fire diverted to this tiny outpost. But that was small comfort.

He looked down the slope. Strosahl lay face down in his wet dungarees, clothes that were more brown than olive-green because of all the dirt on them. He had settled into a prone position, with the stock of his rifle resting against his cheek.

Perosa's fire had temporarily halted the mortar fire. He'd hit two men, while the other two had fled with their mortar behind the rise concealing the other teams. Perosa relaxed his trigger-finger a second before Vorderer did the same. The enemy machine gunners hadn't been dislodged from behind the log, but they were keeping their heads down.

In the comparative silence, Jonas said to Dodd, "Tell Gaddis to focus on taking out their mortars – if he can. If they get dug in where he can't see them, try to get their spotter. They'll want to pin us down with a mortar attack while they work their infantry in close. Got all that?"

"Yessir," sounding like he wished he didn't understand but understood only too well. He ran off at a crouch.

Jonas grabbed for his mike. "Red Rover, this is Stakeout. Over."

He could see Strosahl reach out with his left hand and pick up the walkie-talkie without even shifting his rifle from the firing position.

"What do you want, Stakeout?"

Jonas could almost see the man release his thumb from the button. "I'm going to try to get you back up here. Over."

Strosahl didn't answer. His rifle barked, the recoil slamming into his shoulder. Across the river, a soldier who had poked his head above a log fell back, both hands clutched to his forehead.

Jonas smiled. "Nice shot, Red Rover."

"Thanks, Stakeout. A hundred-and-fifty more to go. Over."

"You're forgetting the sixty-some behind us. Over."

Chen stood perspiring amid the excited babble of his inexperienced aides. The morning air was still cool, but the climb up the hill had drained his limited physical reserves. His shoulder wound had taken more of a toll on him than he wanted to admit. Col. Chu had offered to take charge of directing the battle, but Chen refused. It was shameful enough that the Americans had struck his supply depots two nights in a row, and even more shameful that he had lost his squad in the night attack, without destroying the enemy's radio. He could recover face only by wiping out every last man on that hill. There could be no more mistakes.

From behind him, his new radio operator called out excitedly,

"Captain, I have found the frequency the enemy is using. Do you want me to jam their signal?"

Chen turned and strode back. Two lieutenants, one holding a map outstretched, closed in behind him. "Let me hear."

Chen was the only one at his command post who understood English. His last radioman, who did speak English, was killed in the artillery barrage the first night.

The new man, sitting on an ammo-box across from his radio, handed up his headphones.

Chen didn't take them. "Switch to the speaker so we can all hear."

He did, and Chen listened to the exchange.

"No, no!" Chen checked himself before he called the man an idiot. "That's the command post talking to their man holed up on the side of the hill. Why would we bother to jam that?" He calmed himself. "I need to know the frequency he's using to communicate with his battalion headquarters. I need to know if he is calling in any artillery or air strikes."

The radioman looked confused. To the west, the artillery fire on Cloverleaf grew more intense.

In an even tone Chen said, "I will listen and tell you when their commander says he is switching frequencies. Then you will quickly find the new frequency, and I will tell you whether or not to jam the transmission."

Chen turned and surveyed the far hill. He felt the slump in his posture. It was not good for troop morale to see a tired commander. He forced himself to stand taller.

More to himself than his staff, he said, "If he is not able to get fire support, I will not jam his transmissions. I will let those in the rear at his battalion headquarters hear how he and his men are dying."

Jonas glanced quickly east and west, as four American Mustangs flew overhead on their way to the battle on Cloverleaf, laden with bombs and rockets. Oh, for a little of that fire power – but all of it was being used for the larger battle.

The enemy troops, now marshalled up and down the river, seemed poised to move out. They were waiting for the signal. He had to think of something if he was going to get Strosahl back inside the perimeter.

"Stakeout, this is Red Rover."

"Stakeout here. Over."

"Stakeout, the gooks have got to have their machine gun zeroed in on my position. I can't move. When they start lobbing in mortar shells, I've got no cover. I hope you're working on a plan. Over."

"Red Rover, I'll have to get back to you on that. Over."

He pulled out his map, and quickly noted the coordinates of where the enemy troops were massed. He grabbed the mike and switched frequencies. "Stationhouse, this is Stakeout. Do you read me? Over."

He waited, his guts churning. No answer.

"Stationhouse, this is Stakeout. Come in, Stationhouse. Over."

Static.

"Stakeout, this is Stationhouse Six. Go ahead, Stakeout. Over."

"Stationhouse, enemy at line-of-departure, prepared to move into position to overrun us. Can you get us artillery support? Over."

There was a pause. Holding the mike in one hand, Jonas fixed his field glasses on the enemy command post. Several enemy officers were huddled around their radio.

"Stakeout, this is Stationhouse Six. That's a negative. All our fire-support is committed. You're going to have to try to hold on. Over."

On the far hill, the commander, his back to the Americans, said something, and the men about him broke into smiles. He said something more, and they became more subdued.

The bastards are monitoring my transmissions, Jonas thought. "Stationhouse, this is Stakeout. I understand, Six. Will hold. I have a few surprises waiting for our visitors. Over."

"Stakeout, this is Stationhouse Six. Keep me updated, and we'll get you support when we can. Stationhouse out."

Jonas kept his field glasses glued on the enemy command post. He thought, they didn't look so happy now, but began to jabber excitedly. Trying to figure out what kind of surprise I'm cooking up. I wish to hell I had one. But maybe thinking I have something unexpected waiting will give them pause, slow them down from launching the attack.

Their commander, though, stood silently facing Jonas' position while his aides chattered behind him. He stroked his chin. Jonas thought, he's calculating whether or not I'm bluffing.

The enemy commander motioned with his hand, and a soldier rushed forward with a bugle. Without looking at the man, he said something. The bugler raised his horn and blew a series of rapid, piercing notes.

Immediately the mortars coughed behind the rise, and the first rounds whistled across the river and exploded on the side of the hill. Fragments flew. Clouds of grey smoke rapidly expanded. Vultures scattered.

Jonas lost sight of Strosahl in all the smoke. He looked to his right at the riverbank. The North Korean troops were advancing. He looked left. The second column started to double-time. Behind him, he heard Gaddis' machine gun banging away. North Korean troops were moving up from the south.

The enemy mortar teams 'walked' their fire up the side of the hill, covering the ground step-by-step, a steady drone of explosions. As the shells closed in on him, Jonas crouched deeper in his hole. He sucked in the acrid air, which burned the inside of his nose, throat, and lungs. His eyes watered up, and not just because they stung. He'd been too late to get Strosahl up the hill.

The mortar fire, five shells hitting the side of the hill just below him, set his ears ringing. Dirt fell in from the side of his hole. Runnels of sweat streamed down his forehead and his chest. He couldn't shake from his mind the picture of a round dropping right into his hole. His whole body shook with tremors.

The barrage rolled over his position, hitting in front of him, three feet behind, and then passed on. He let out the breath he didn't realize he was holding.

Tentatively, he poked his head up and stole a look down the hillside. The smoke was thinning. Where was Strosahl?

The hollow where Strosahl lay concealed was now just a gaping crater. There was nothing left of the sergeant, not his limbs – not even the remains of his rifle. The shock hit him in the chest like a pile-driver.

Mortars continued to shower down over the hilltop behind him. He started choking up, but then he stopped, confused by what he was seeing – or not seeing. Something wasn't right. An artillery shell could completely obliterate a man – but not a mortar round. A mortar usually left parts scattered about. Jonas quickly scanned the rest of the area. His eye caught a bit of movement a dozen feet to the right of the crater, and five feet farther down the hill. Strosahl!

The sergeant had made a break for better cover. He'd found it where two small spiny ridges joined together like the prow of a boat. Crouched behind this uncertain bulwark, he was furiously scraping and digging with his Ka-Bar to get deeper into the ground.

In the distance, artillery pounded away, mere background noise as mortars continued to explode all around Jonas and his men. Four more Mustang fighters roared overhead, carrying rockets and bombs to unleash on the North Korean defenders of Cloverleaf.

At the foot of the hill, along the riverbank, the enemy platoons converged. Their officers were organizing them into assault waves. Perosa and Vorderer stuck their heads out of their holes, and seeing the soldiers below, fired a quick burst into their ranks. Immediately machinegun fire erupted from the north side of the river, kicking up dirt all around them.

They ducked back down. More machine gun fire. Two rockets

struck just below the rim. The mortars poured down on the front of the perimeter again. His men were pinned down, unable to return fire. The infantry attack would begin soon.

In his hole, Jonas clutched the mike to him. "Stationhouse, this is Stakeout. Come in Stationhouse. Over."

"Stationhouse Six here. Over."

"Stationhouse, we are about to be overrun. I say again, we are about to be overrun. Over."

"Stakeout, hold one. Over."

Jonas could just imagine the glee of the officers at the enemy command post who were monitoring this.

25

STROSAHL WAS RELIEVED that, for the moment at least, the mortar fire was concentrated on the top of the hill and not on him. He counted his ammo as he eyed the assault lines readying to advance. Three clips for his carbine, half-a-dozen grenades. Oh, and a flare-gun with two rounds. A lot of good they are, he thought bitterly.

He pulled his canteen from its pouch on his hip and shook it. There were only a few swallows left. He figured he had ten minutes more to live – fifteen at the outside, depending upon

how quickly the Reds launched their attack. No reason not to finish off the water. He did and then stuck his Ka-Bar in the ground, right at hand. He wasn't going to be taken prisoner.

The gooks didn't know he was still alive. That's why he was still breathing. If he tried to make a break for the top of the hill, fifty riflemen would be firing at him. He didn't want to die, but he especially didn't want to die with a bullet in his back.

He picked up a grenade and rolled it in his palm. At least he could sow a little havoc.

Maybe, he thought, the recon patrol hadn't been such a good idea after all. But then he remembered the sight of all those wrecked enemy trucks and the exploding stores of ammo. No, it had been a good night's work.

He felt the weight of the grenade: one-and-a-half pounds. He wished he had a launcher; but lacking that, he knew he had a damn good throwing arm. He wished he had a half-dozen arms and a few dozens of these babies. Then he could do real damage.

He stopped. That wasn't such a bad idea. He picked up his walkie-talkie and keyed it. "Stakeout, this is Red Rover. Come in Stakeout."

No answer. Come on, Lieu, where the hell are you? I know you got your head buried deep in a hole trying to keep it from getting blown off but answer your damn radio.

"Stakeout, this is Red Rover. Over."

He peeked over the rim down toward the river. The enemy officers were doing a last weapons check. Stuyvesant was probably on the radio with battalion. No way to raise him.

Strosahl eyed the flare gun. He grabbed it, broke it open, popped in a canister, turned over on his back and aimed it towards the top of the hill. He squeezed the trigger. The round shot up and exploded in a red starburst hundreds of feet above the rim.

He broke open the gun and shoved in another canister, waiting, breathing hard. There was just a few seconds delay before he heard, "Red Rover, this is Stakeout. Over."

"Stakeout, I got an idea. Over."

"Go ahead Rover. I'm open to anything. Over."

"When the next flare pops, everyone up there start throwing as many grenades as far out over the hillside as you can. No one even has to stick their head out of their hole. But wait for my signal. Over."

"Red Rover, I read you. I'll pass the word. Over."

Strosahl rolled back over onto his stomach and saw the first wave stepping off. Even more mortars whistled overhead to pin down the defenders on the rim. He grabbed his rifle and went up on one knee. He fired half a clip straight down the hill into the ranks of the men coming toward him. Then, as they scattered in confusion, he began searching out officers. He put rounds into two, and then shot at several soldiers running a few steps ahead of the line.

He ejected a clip and jammed in another and laid the rifle down. He picked up a grenade, pulled the pin and threw it as high and far as he could at those directly in front of him. He pulled another pin and threw, and another pin. The three grenades were exploding as he pulled the fourth pin.

The assault waves, especially the knots of men directly down the hill from him, started to disintegrate. But four or five North Korean soldiers kept their heads and began firing back. Strosahl dropped down behind cover and grabbed for the flare-gun. He pointed it skyward and fired. Even as the load shot up, he was on his stomach again, grabbing his rifle and firing at the advancing soldiers.

All along the hillside, grenades began to drop from above. They bounced and rolled toward the front line, as their fuses ticked off the seconds: three-four-five-ka-boom! A dozen grenades raining down – and a dozen more.

Enemy mortars dropped furiously along the rim of the hill. Machine gunners blasted away, and rockets hammered the perimeter, trying to stop the hailstorm of grenades. But the initial North Korean attack had already fallen apart. The troops were falling back to the river, milling around. Strosahl threw grenades and fired as they retreated until the hammer fell on an empty chamber and, he was out of grenades.

He collapsed behind cover.

The mortar and rocket shelling died out. No longer under fire, Jonas cautiously peeked over the rim down at the chaos below. A few North Korean soldiers were waving their arms, barking orders, trying to organize the ranks.

Strosahl was on his back, his face black with gunpowder, staring up at him. He waved weakly, and Jonas waved back.

Jonas took his mike. "Red Rover, come in."

"Stakeout, you got a reprieve. But I'm out of ammo now. All I got left is this." He lifted his Ka-Bar. The light glinted off its blade as he turned it back and forth.

"Red Rover, can you make it up the hill? Over."

Strosahl didn't answer but jumped to his feet, ready to sprint. Immediately the machine gunners across the river opened up on his position. He dove to the ground and rapidly crawled back to cover.

At the river, although the North Koreans had lost two of their officers, a young bull was waving his pistol and shouting. From the hill across the river behind them, a bugle blew commands. The lines began to reform.

"Red Rover, another attack is forming up. They are not waiting. I have to get back on with Stationhouse. Maybe they've got something for us. Over."

Strosahl didn't even answer. He waved, and rolled over, peering down the hill. As Jonas switched frequencies, the radio crackled with static.

Chen's arm throbbed. He wished he had a stool so he could sit, but he pushed that thought out of his mind. This battle would soon be over. He could last. He watched as his mortar teams and machine gun crews finished their preparations to support the new attack. To the west, artillery fire thumped steadily. There was no slowdown in the battle for Cloverleaf. If the 4th Division held fast against the Americans, he was sure that he could begin to resupply them tonight.

In the background he recognized the voice on the radio.

His radioman called, "The enemy commander is trying to raise his battalion's headquarters."

Chen allowed himself a slight smile. He was sure the enemy commander was the man who had wounded him the night before. The fact that he carried a pistol marked him as most likely an officer. By now he would realize the end was near. Chen wished he could deliver

318 | RICHARD THOMAS LANE

the death blow himself but had to content himself with directing the assault.

The radioman called out, "Captain, do you want me to jam the signal?"

Chen cocked an ear to monitor the transmission.

"Stationhouse, this is Stakeout. Do you read me? Over."

"Stationhouse Six here. We've been trying to raise you, Stakeout. Over."

"Roger that, Six, but we've been pretty busy. Over."

This was good. The command staff at the headquarters in the rear, those who had authorized the patrol, could now listen as their men died. Chen shouted back to his radioman, "Not yet." He turned to his bugler. "Signal the mortar teams to begin."

The bugler blew with gusto. Immediately, the mortar teams dropped shells into their tubes. The machine gunners raked the enemy's position with continuous fire, sweeping back and forth across the rim of the hill. Mortar shells began bursting all across the crown.

Chen fought through his pain and fatigue to stay focused on his battle plan. He peered through his telescope. The Americans had disappeared into their holes. It was time to sound the assault. It would soon be all over.

One of his lieutenants tapped his shoulder. "Captain, the radio operator has been calling to you."

Irritated, he turned away from the battlefield. "What is it?" he shouted.

"Sir, the enemy commander has switched frequencies."

Exercising patience, he called back to the radioman, "Is he talking to his man on the hill?" That was the most probable explanation, and not a matter of concern.

"No, sir."

Chen felt a slight flutter of apprehension in his stomach. He strode back toward the radio, dragging his bugler by the arm as he growled, "Find the frequency he's on. Now."

The radioman began frantically turning his dial. Chen barked to his bugler, "Sound attack."

The mortar-fire intensified. Jonas was crouched down in his hole pressing his headphones to one ear and clutching his mike to his mouth. Over the ruckus of exploding shells and rattling gun fire, he heard the insistent blare of a bugle.

On the orders of Stationhouse Six, he had switched to his tactical air channel. Two fighter planes were en route. A rocket exploded fifteen feet to his right. He heard one of his men scream.

"Firefox 4, this is Stakeout. Do you read me? Over."

"Stakeout, this is Firefox 4. We are approaching from your southeast. Are you able to mark your location? Over."

"Firefox 4, that's a negative. We are pinned down. You'll have to do a visual on a flyby."

Jonas could not hear the droning planes' engines over the din of exploding mortars. He pushed his back against the north wall of his hole and tipped his head skyward. Two Mustangs were bearing down on his position.

"I see you, Firefox. We are on a hilltop directly on your flight line a hundred yards south of the river. Enemy troops are massed on the north and south sides. On the south side, there are several burnt-out vehicles. Over."

"Stakeout, we have you in sight. We'll do one flyover to fix the enemy's position and then drop our loads on the next run. Over."

"Roger that, Firefox. Over."

Jonas let out a long breath. A bombing-run would help. Help a lot. The North Korean troops would scatter and go to ground, so there was no way the planes were going to take out all the enemy. If the fighters were armed with machine guns, they might take out more on a second pass.

The Mustangs began their descent. Jonas could make out their outlines clearly – single-prop fighters, manned only by their pilots.

From the belly of each hung a large bomb. He hoped they were armed with rockets as well.

The mortars abruptly went quiet. All firing ceased. Jonas lifted his head over the edge of his hole. Down the hill, the North Korean advance halted. As the Mustangs approached, the troops scattered, scrambling for cover. Now as the fighters retreated, sporadic firing broke out. North Koreans knelt or stood firing rifles at planes well out of their range. Their enraged officer yelled and ran among the ranks, knocking barrels groundward, kicking men to get on their feet, trying to get their lines reformed.

Jonas saw Strosahl frantically keying his walkie-talkie, trying to reach him. He switched frequencies and heard a desperate sounding voice, "Stakeout, this is Red Rover. Come in, Stakeout. Come in, Stakeout."

"Red Rover, this is Stakeout. Over."

The sergeant gave up any pretense of maintaining radio discipline. "Shit, Lieu, do you know what those Mustangs are carrying?"

"Red Rover, they're loaded with bombs. Maybe rockets. If you dig down deep, there's a chance we can still get you out. As soon as the bombs have hit, make a break for it up the hill. We'll give you covering fire. Over."

"That's a negative, Lieu. Those babies are hung with *napalm*. Oh shit, if I'd had known this was coming, I would have saved a bullet for myself."

Jonas fell back against the wall of his hole. Napalm? Jellied gasoline that would scorch the whole side of the hill. Strosahl would be burned alive! He didn't know what to do. The Mustangs were circling back for their bombing run, traveling now almost side-by-side, coming in on a straight line.

"Red Rover, I'll call off the attack. I'll have them abort!"

"Negative, Lieu. This run is the only chance you and the men have to get off the hill. Over."

"Sarge, there has to be another way. Over."

"Lieu, you know better. This is what they pay you the big bucks for. Get back on the air and do what you have to do. Red Rover Out."

Jonas pulled in on himself, his shoulder muscles bunched up, his jaws clenched. He switched back to the air tactical frequency and heard "Stakeout, this is Firefox 4. Are you receiving, Stakeout? Over."

"...Firefox 4, this is Stakeout. Over."

"Stakeout, we are making our final approach. Keep your heads down if you don't want your eyebrows singed. Over."

"Firefox,... Make your run. Over."

He had barely lifted his thumb off the button on his mike when his ear was filled with a high-pitched whine. He immediately realized the North Koreans were jamming his signal.

Jonas watched paralyzed as the Mustangs rushed forward, diving, down, down – and leveling off. The huge bomb-like silver canister under its belly released. It waffled and then glided downward, accelerating as it homed in on its target.

Jonas ducked his head beneath the rim of his hole. He waited for the shockwave. It hit. Immediately, he thrust his head up. Below him a massive stream of fire flowed, poured, rushed from west to east over the whole bottom-half of the hill. Flames leapt up a full three hundred feet, brilliant-red scorching flames, followed by billowing black smoke and the roar of rushing wind. Like a giant wave smashing against a cliff, the flames surged up and then fell. And as they receded, he heard the first screams.

Everywhere men were on fire. They ran blindly in all directions. They ran in circles, balls of fire, thrashing wildly with their arms, screaming as they ran.

There, the figure nearest him. A large flaming torch, spinning, his knife held high above his head.

Jonas shouted, "Vorderer, give me your B.A.R.!"

Vorderer stood in his hole, looking down on the conflagration, his face white. "What?"

Jonas ripped the automatic from his hands and centered the sights on the flaming figure of Strosahl. He squeezed the trigger. His shoulder and torso vibrated rapidly as the rounds sped down the hill. The flaming mass spun around and crashed to the ground. Jonas continued to pour rounds into him, even after there was no hint of movement.

Schore, his voice cracking, whispered, "Jesus, Lieu!"

"Shut up," Jonas snapped. "All of you just shut up."

More and more North Koreans collapsed. The bodies pulled in on themselves in a last desperate, reflexive attempt to escape their pain. They curled up and died. Finally there was no one standing on the bank.

The bottom third of the hill was dotted with puddles of red fire and blackened, charred lumps.

Only a handful of flaming men had made it to the river. They thrashed about. Soon inert bodies bobbed in the yellow current.

Far across the river, the men of the command post stood transfixed. No one moved. Even Chen stood stock still. He'd heard of napalm but had never seen it. All the destruction he had seen in over a decade of war had not prepared him for the sight of a whole company of men burned alive. That the Americans even had such a weapon in their arsenal momentarily shattered his will.

The radioman called to him. The rest of his men were already gathering around the radio, stooping as if to hear it better. He plodded back and joined them.

Still shaken, he had difficulty grasping what he was supposed to do. A voice came from the radio. Col. Chu. The colonel was giving him some kind of order. It didn't make sense – or it made all too much sense. He was not sure of much anything. He took the mike and acknowledged the command. His hand with the mike dropped to his side, and he shook his head.

He turned back around and surveyed the smoking remains of the company. His bugler stood to his left, waiting. Chen gave the order. The bugler lifted his horn and sounded a series of plaintive notes.

On the riverbank, machine gunners slowly climbed out from behind logs, and the mortar teams came out from behind the cover of the rise. They stared at each other in bewilderment. Small clusters of men turned their back on the river and began trudging away.

Chen waited until all of his weapons platoon had retreated, and then turned and, without saying another word to his staff, walked to the rear of the hilltop and began his descent.

Jonas and his men waited, perched behind their guns. They waited throughout the afternoon. Artillery thumped to the west of them, halted for an hour or two, and began thumping again with the ebb and flow of battle.

The vultures descended on the charred lumps at the bottom of the hill. They strode among the corpses, pecking here and there, trying to find scraps of edible meat.

Jonas and his men crouched in their foxholes. There was almost no talk. They waited. They waited for the retaliatory counterattack, when there would be no air support and no artillery support, when they would be overrun by a vengeful enemy. With the resignation of doomed men, they waited throughout the burning heat of the afternoon, as the stench of burnt carcasses wafted up and settled over the hilltop.

They waited through the deceptive cool of the evening and into the descending darkness of the night. There was only the slightest hint of a moon. They counted their grenades and last clips of ammo, knowing they didn't have enough to repulse another attack. The crickets chirped, but this night no one was lulled into the belief that this meant they were safe. A cold dew covered everything, rifle barrels, C-ration cans, helmets, until long after the sun had risen in the morning.

"Stakeout, this is Stationhouse Six. Come in, Stakeout. Over."

The voice sounded weak because the radio's batteries were wearing down. Jonas clutched at his mike. "Stationhouse Six, this is Stakeout. Over."

"Stakeout, be advised the North Korean 4th Division has retreated back across the Naktong. Over."

Jonas' hand shook. "Stationhouse, say again. Over."

"Stakeout, you're coming home. A convoy is on its way to pick you up. Prepare your men to leave the hill. Over."

Jonas pressed the button but couldn't speak. He let go, sniffed back the tears and tried again. "Stationhouse, roger that." He choked up. "Thanks, Six. Over."

"Stakeout. You did good, son. Stationhouse Six out."

26

CHEN JINQUAN, TEMPORARY captain in the Korean People's Army, affected a relaxed demeanor as Col. Chu read the order. Chen was wary. Why was this order delivered by hand? And by an officer rather than by a lowly runner? The officer, a lieutenant standing at attention, had a determined look. Contributing to Chen's sense of unease was the way a squat sergeant stood behind him. He wore the uniform of the military police.

The four of them stood alone in the farmhouse, the largest in the village. It had walls made of grey fieldstone, a thatched roof and hardwood floors. It probably had stood for three hundred years.

Underneath Chen's jacket, his left shoulder was still bandaged. His left arm, resting outside, was in a sling. The wound was healing rapidly, but the arm hurt. Chen ran his fingers lightly along the bottom of the sling.

The colonel did not look at Chen but stared at the paper in his hand. Finally, he folded the orders over and creased them with care. He looked sad. When he raised his head, he said, "Capt. Chen, these men are here to put you under arrest."

"…May I know the charges, Comrade Colonel?"

"Gross negligence of your duties." Chu tapped the palm of his hand with the orders. "You allowed the Americans to choke off a vital supply line, and this led to the deaths of many men on Cloverleaf Hill. That's what's here, but you know how these things go. They will add other charges before the actual court martial." There was a hint of distaste in these last words.

"I understand, sir." And he did understand that there were those at division headquarters who wanted someone to blame. Kim Il Sung, the glorious leader, would want someone to blame. And he was to blame. He was to blame for not simply jamming the Americans' radio signal so that they could not have called in the napalm strike. He'd had no way of knowing that the Americans would free up aircraft in the middle of the battle for Cloverleaf, but he had allowed fatigue and his desire for revenge on the man who wounded him to cloud his judgment.

The lieutenant turned to him and said in clipped tones, "You are to surrender your sidearm to me, Comrade, and accompany us to headquarters. I have a jeep waiting outside."

There was no respect in his voice. Chen sensed he was dealing with a bully. He could also feel the sergeant tense up behind him.

Col. Chu stepped back as though wanting to disassociate himself from this unpleasantness.

"...I understand," said Chen. He raised his right hand slowly, displaying his thumb and index finger as though to say, I am just using these two fingers, so you don't have to be nervous. He lowered his hand to the handle of his pistol and lifted it slowly from its holster.

The lieutenant gave the briefest hint of a smile tinged with triumph, snatched the pistol away, and handed it to the sergeant.

At the moment when the sergeant reached for the gun, Chen slid his right hand into his sling and extracted the knife. In a single flowing motion, he brought the seven-inch blade up, slashed the lieutenant's throat from left to right, and continuing to pivot, did the same to the sergeant as the man looked up to see what was happening. Blood gushed from both men's throats as they dropped wide-eyed to the floor.

Chen whirled and faced Chu, but the colonel had taken several steps back and held his own pistol pointing squarely at Chen's chest. They stood in silence for a moment, neither one moving.

Chu said, "I don't believe that knife is authorized issue, Comrade."

"No. I found it still clutched in the American's hand when we removed the bodies after the napalm strike."

"It looks like a good knife."

"I thought it might be useful."

"You put me in a difficult position, Chen Jinquan. I can't be party to your escape."

"I could tie you up."

"That would be an acceptable solution. But how are you going to evade capture? It is a long way back to China. You will have many roadblocks to go through."

Chen slipped his knife back into his sling and unbuttoned his jacket. He pulled out a small rubber packet taped to his left side. Awkwardly, he opened it, and pulled out a piece of paper. He offered it to Chu.

Chu pursed his lips and re-holstered his pistol. He stepped forward and took the paper from Chen.

"This orders all military and civilian personnel to provide you with any and all assistance that you might need. And it is signed by Marshall Choe Yong Gun, Minister of National Defense and Deputy Commander-in-Chief of the Korean People's Army." Chu looked up. "I've never seen Marshall Choe's signature. Is this authentic?"

"It will pass."

"There have always been those who believed you were here spying for Mao Tse Tung."

"Let us say, instead, that I am acting as a liaison, and that this would be an opportune time for me to go north to the Chinese consulate in Pyongyang and make my report."

"Before you can do that, Chen…"

"Yes, sir?"

Chu averted his face. "You need to wash that blood off your face and get a clean jacket. And you'll have to replace that sling."

Twenty minutes later, Maj. Chen of the Chinese People's Army, wearing a clean uniform of the Korean People's Army, stepped out of the farmhouse onto the porch. His white sling was immaculate. The crickets were chirping and the birds singing. He looked up at the blue sky and took in a deep breath.

Turning to the sentry, he said, "The colonel is going to be busy with the lieutenant for some hours. He does not want to be disturbed."

"Yessir."

Chen walked across the courtyard and out the double gate. He surveyed the vehicles parked there. To another sentry, a young Korean man who looked like a week earlier he had been tending his family's rice paddies, Chen said, "You remember the lieutenant and the sergeant who arrived a little while ago?"

"Yessir," the young private responded with enthusiasm. Boots for the new recruits had not yet arrived from the north. He was wearing straw sandals.

"Where is their jeep?"

The young man grasped the sling of his rifle with his left hand, as he swiveled and pointed with his right. "It's the third from the end, sir."

Chen walked over, climbed in, and turned on the ignition. He backed up, eased the jeep onto the road, and drove off without looking back.

SEPTEMBER 17, 1950

Sgt. Davin Patrick Kelly felt jittery as he stared across the Naktong, trying to make out Hill 174. The 1st battalion's orders were to take that hill. It was a little after 4:30 in the morning. He could barely make out its outline by the light of bursting artillery shells and exploding bombs raining down from the B-26s.

In the apple orchard behind him were the men of Lt. Stuyvesant's platoon. Soon, Kelly knew, he would regard this as his platoon as well; but he'd only arrived a few days earlier and was still finding his way as their platoon guide. He grasped the sling of the carbine on his shoulder a little tighter. He was feeling insecure because, although he had six years of Army experience under his belt, and a year as a sergeant, he was the only man in the platoon who had not yet seen combat.

After the North Koreans had finally been driven back across the Naktong on August 19, the 2nd Infantry Division took over the defense of the river line, while the 24th went into reserve to rest and re-outfit. At the beginning of September, the North Koreans launched another attack across the Naktong. That battle lasted a week until the 2nd Division, reinforced by the 1st Marine Brigade, drove them back. The 24th was back on the line at the river, but no longer on the defensive.

A debate had broken out among the men. Pvt. Bankart was firm in his opinion. "I don't think there are any gooks left on that hill."

Kelly pivoted round to join them. The first light of the pre-dawn was still a half-hour away, but there was enough moon and starlight to make out the intense faces. He hoped Bankart was right, but he doubted it.

Holzer jumped in. "What do you mean? The Army wouldn't be shelling them if they weren't still there. The gooks are there, and they are well dug in, you can bet on it."

Bankart shook his head. "See, you got no concept of strategy."

"Ah, come off it," Cavitch threw in. "You wouldn't know strategy from a cow's ass. You think you went to West Point or something?"

"You heard the same thing yesterday as I did. MacArthur landed the Marines at Inchon, right outside of Seoul. They got the fucking Marine Corps behind them cutting off their supply lines – and the whole fucking Eighth Army is about to counterattack them from this direction. If I was them, I'd be making for the hills."

Cpl. Holzer snorted. "I've been fighting gooks since Osan, and gooks making for the hills is nothing I've seen. MacArthur or no MacArthur, they're planning a reception for us over there.... I wish to hell the boats would get here."

Cavitch looked up at Kelly. "Yeah, Sarge, any word on the boats? We were supposed to be crossing already, you know, in the dark so our buddies on the other side of the river can't see us."

Every man had an idea of what it would be like trying to cross the river in broad daylight under enemy fire. He couldn't blame Bankart for hoping for a break.

Masking his own nervousness with a tone of professionalism, Kelly said, "Nothing on the boats yet. Is everyone ready when they do get here? We're going to have to load up and get paddling quick."

The voices rang out: "All set here, Sarge," and "Ready to go."

He looked the group over. There was no one he was going to have to take aside and give a pep talk to. Lots of signs of nerves, but no one breaking down.

Cpl. Holzer, leaning forward, said, "And I'll tell you what. If it's like I think, and the Reds are dug in, I'm sure glad it's Lt. Stuyvesant I'm with. If anyone is going to get me back alive, it's going to be the lieutenant. He practically carried me out of Osan."

Kelly turned away puzzled and kept walking through the orchard. The corporal was just saying what he'd heard others say. The soldiers in this platoon seemed to think the lieutenant was some sort of good luck, that he could get them out of tough scrapes. The unit had been engaged in combat over and over for just under two months. Most of the original platoon were gone – missing, wounded, or dead – as well as a lot of the replacements. That didn't sound particularly lucky to him; but if believing the lieutenant could get them home alive kept the men's spirits up, he sure wasn't going to quote statistics.

Looking up, he saw Stuyvesant, carbine in hand, striding along a narrow path that led from a farmhouse, the battalion's CP. The officers had been meeting. The lieutenant had a grim look on his face. Kelly caught the signal that the lieutenant wanted to meet him off to the side, out of earshot of the men.

Jonas picked a spot facing the river. Kelly joined him, standing side-by-side.

"The men ready, Sarge?"

"Yes, sir. The boats coming?"

"About another twenty minutes. We're going to have to get aboard fast." He looked to the east. "No way we're going to beat the sunrise."

He kept his tone even despite his exasperation. The usual logistical snarls had delayed the arrival of the boats. And the crossing couldn't be put off another day.

He pulled out a pack of gum, took one piece himself and handed another over, saying, "I'd offer you a cigarette, but you know—"

"We're on blackout." Kelly took the stick and began to unwrap it. "You think they're over there waiting for us, sir?"

"Oh, they're waiting alright." The lieutenant looked in the direction of the river, staring but not focusing on anything. The bombardment continued. On top of everything else he had to deal with, his platoon guide was inexperienced. The man looked good on paper, had plenty of training, and his C.O.s had given him glowing fitness reports. But you never knew how a man was going to handle combat until the bullets were zinging and the shells bursting.

The sergeant didn't interrupt his thinking. That was good.

Finally Jonas said, "Col. Smith is steaming. It's the usual foul-up, the boats getting here late. We'll be sitting ducks crossing in daylight. At night we would have taken maybe five to ten percent casualties. Now it's going to be more like twenty-five."

He watched out of the corner of his eye as Kelly jerked his head back an inch.

"Twenty-five percent?" His voice was hoarse.

Jonas watched. The sergeant recovered quickly. He wasn't cocky. That was good. He was nervous, but not shaking. That was good.

"Well, Sarge, you take the money, you do the job. Right?"

"Right," Kelly said without enthusiasm.

Jonas looked back to the river. He chewed his gum. Spearmint. It might be the last thing he ever tasted. He pushed the thought from his mind.

"Okay, so this is the way it's going to be. We get the men onto the river and paddle like hell. On the other side, the beach is only about two feet deep, and then there's a rise. We've got to keep the men moving no matter what's going on. Just like Normandy, our job is to get the men off the beach. Third battalion will be coming across after us. We can't get bogged down. Keep the men moving – that's the main thing."

"Yessir."

"You and I have to keep separated in case one of us gets hit. I want you to brief the squad leaders so they are clear, in case both of us are put out of action."

Jonas said it matter-of-factly, watching to see how Kelly handled the idea. The man pulled himself up a little taller.

"…Right away, sir."

Kelly, he decided, would probably hold up. Behind them, in the direction of the farmhouse, Jonas could hear motor vehicles approaching.

"Let's get the boats ready to go."

At five-thirty they began crossing. Kelly climbed into a boat after half the platoon was already in the river paddling. Halfway across the Naktong, artillery and mortar shells began dropping among the lead boats. Machine gun bullets snapped overhead – and then as the gunners got the range, ripped into the plywood boats. Some men paddled faster. Others gave up paddling and crouched down. Boats began turning in circles, drifting down river.

"Keep moving, everyone keep moving," Lt. Stuyvesant shouted from the lead boat.

"Keep moving," Kelly shouted, head down as he paddled.

He looked up. Stuyvesant was on the shore. The lieutenant turned to the boats and began waving them forward with his carbine, an officer taking his men into fire. Jonas turned, raced up the embankment, and disappeared over the rise.

THE END

DEDICATION

This novel is dedicated to all those who were caught up in the Korean War, military and civilians alike, on both sides of the conflict. I especially want to acknowledge the men and women of the 24th Division, the first American troops who rushed to confront the invading North Koreans. I hope I have done some modicum of justice to the following historical figures: Lt. Gen. Walton (Johnny) Walker, C.O. of the 8th Army, Maj. Gen. William F. Dean, C.O. of the 24th Infantry Division, Col. Richard "Dick" Stephens, C.O. of the 21st Infantry Regiment, Lt. Col. Charles B. "Brad" Smith, C.O. of the 1st Battalion, 21st Infantry Regiment, and Capt. Richard Dasher, C.O. of Company C, 1st Battalion, 21st Infantry Regiment. I created Lieutenants Paul Girard, Buzz Parker and Jonas Stuyvesant. In real life, the platoon leaders of C Company were Lieutenants Harold Dill, William Wyrick and Philip Day. I salute them for their courage and their sacrifices.

ACKNOWLEDGMENTS

For decades I've been reading other authors' acknowledgments of the family, friends and professionals who stood behind them, making their work possible. No writer creates in a vacuum. So, I will continue this long-established tradition by acknowledging the following: My writers group: Ken Kraus, Kelly O'Donnell, Rick Spillman and Stephanie Feuer. All first-rate writers and a great support group. My friend Mark Nachmias deserves credit for the title. Early in my process I got invaluable editorial advice from Lou Aronica of The Fiction Studio, as well as from Jason Brown, a Writers Boot Camp instructor, who drilled me in story structure until I finally got it. I also want to thank my friends Steve Hayes and Pieter Taselaar for their special support. And, of course, my wife Pam. It is safe to say that if she hadn't taken a stand one day, demanding that I either write my novel or shut up about it, this work would never have gotten to page one.

AUTHOR

I was born in Indiana in 1947 and entered the Marine Corps in 1966 where, in 1970, I served a tour as a battalion message center chief in Vietnam. After graduating from San Francisco State University, I moved to New York City and, in 1979, became an alcoholism counselor. I received my MSW from Fordham University in New York, then trained with Harville Hendrix, PhD to become an Imago Relationship Therapist, and from 1990 to the present I have worked as a psychotherapist in private practice, specializing in the areas of addiction, trauma and couples therapy. The great joy in my life is my marriage. I wake up every morning feeling blessed I am married to my amazing wife Pam.

TO LEAVE A REVIEW

Nothing helps a writer get the word out to other potential readers than a review from a reader like you. I would really appreciate your taking the time to leave an honest review at Amazon. If you haven't left a review before and aren't sure how to, go to the listing for this book on Amazon and scroll down the page below the book description. You'll find "Reviews" and clear directions on leaving one. It doesn't have to be long. One, two, or three lines does the trick. Thank you.

WATCH FOR THE NEXT EXCITING
JONAS STUYVESANT NOVELS

Want to be notified when these next books come out?
Sign up for my mailing list at: **richardthomaslane.com**

THE
FORGOTTEN
AMERICANS

He came home an unwanted hero. He thought he'd left the darkness buried in the prisoner of war camp. To save himself, will an ex-POW reveal the secrets of war?

New York City, 1955. Lt. Jonas Stuyvesant's PTSD is a daily reminder of horrors from the Korean War. After spending nearly two-and-a-half years in a Chinese POW camp, he thought his nightmare was over. But when he's recalled to active duty only to be charged with collaboration and murder, the only way to preserve his freedom is by reliving the past.

During his torturous captivity, Jonas maintained his sanity by befriending a black fellow officer named Leon. Staving off non-stop brainwashing, the Chinese jailers resort to more insidious means of breaking them down: exploiting racial tension to pit American against American. To protect his friend from a racist fellow officer, Jonas must do the unthinkable. But is he willing to share what truly happened to avoid being imprisoned anew?

The Forgotten Americans is the captivating second book in the Jonas Stuyvesant action-adventure series. If you like realistic historical drama, complicated heroes, and untold wartime tales, then you'll love Richard Thomas Lane's thrilling novel.

BLUE HAWK, RED DRAGON

He bears the scars of war. She wears the robes of peace. Can one man find love, save a nation, and face down his greatest enemy?

Tibet, 1959. After enduring horrific battles and imprisonment, CIA agent Jonas Stuyvesant's next mission is for peace. Tasked with spiriting the Dalai Lama out of Tibet before Chinese Communists capture him, he never planned on falling for a beautiful local shaman. But when he learns the interrogator who tortured him years earlier is part of the occupation force, the former POW is caught in a web of duty, love, and hate.

With the pacifist Tibetan by his side, Jonas must stave off a ruthless Chinese assault to preserve his mission. As their mutual feelings grow deeper, time begins to run out. To save the Dalai Lama and enact his revenge, will Jonas abandon his one chance for true love?

Blue Hawk, Red Dragon is the gripping third book in the Jonas Stuyvesant action-adventure series. If you like complicated heroes, dramatic historical tales, and thrillers with a touch of romance, then you'll love Richard Thomas Lane's fascinating novel.

Want to be notified when these next books come out?

Sign up for my mailing list at: **richardthomaslane.com**

Made in the USA
Middletown, DE
04 December 2020